FAN MAIL

JOSEPH LEWIS

Black Rose Writing | Texas

ISBN: 978-1-68513-168-5
PUBLISHED BY BLACK ROSE WRITING
www.blackrosewriting.com

Printed in the United States of America
Suggested Retail Price (SRP) $23.95

Fan Mail is printed in Garamond Premier Pro

*As a planet-friendly publisher, Black Rose Writing does its best to eliminate unnecessary waste to reduce paper usage and energy costs, while never compromising the reading experience. As a result, the final word count vs. page count may not meet common expectations.

OTHER BOOKS BY JOSEPH LEWIS

The Lives Trilogy

Taking Lives (Prequel)
Stolen Lives
Shattered Lives
Splintered Lives

Caught in a Web

Spiral Into Darkness

Betrayed

Blaze In, Blaze Out

Fan Mail is like my other books, yet different in many ways. Like my other books, *Fan Mail* has most of the same characters you've come to know and enjoy. Like my other books, *Fan Mail* is written in the thriller-crime genre. However, it is more than a thriller-crime novel. There is a coming-of-age story with an LGBTQ+ theme running in the pages. I am certain you will laugh and weep throughout the book. I found myself doing that when I wrote it and again, when I edited it.

In *Fan Mail*, I wanted to make certain I was correct in areas I am unfamiliar with or where I don't have training. I needed technical advice in order to make the writing true to life. Therefore, I want to thank the following individuals for their help in creating *Fan Mail*: Erik Painter and Brenda Hat, for their help with Navajo culture, language, and vocabulary; Police Chief Jamie Graff, Detective Mindy Warnick, and Sheriff Deputy Earl Coffey, for their help with crime scene techniques, firearms, correct procedure and terminology; James "Skip" Dahlke, for his help with forensic techniques and terminology; Sharon King, for her help with all things related to medical care and hospitals; and Theresa Storke, who has been a support and sounding board throughout my last principalship and now as a writer. I want to thank the many kids I've worked with over my 46 years in education for their stories, struggles, and inspiration. You will find them in the characters and amongst the pages in *Fan Mail* and in all of my writing. I want to thank my wife, Kim, and my daughters, Hannah and Emily, for giving me the time to write and for their encouragement. Last, but not at all least, I want to thank Reagan Rothe and the superb team at Black Rose Writing for giving my writing a home. I appreciate their trust in me as a storyteller.

When you marry someone, you also marry their family. I've been blessed to join and be accepted by Kim's family almost thirty years ago. This book is dedicated to Rolyn and Judy Jorgenson; Brenda and Mark Ganther; Deanne Jorgenson (deceased); and Brian Jorgenson and Jessica Arneson Mederson.

FAN MAIL

"When I get hate mail, I get really down on myself, and I read it to my mom, and my mom is like, 'So what? Who cares? These people don't know you, so you can't take praise or hate to heart.'"
–Nikki Reed

"From the deepest desires often come the deadliest hate."
–Socrates

"Heroes aren't born, but they are created in times of strife and struggle. Everyone is capable of being a hero in their own way; often without even knowing it, they are a hero to those around them."

–Anonymous

CHAPTER ONE

The boys, victorious in the soccer match against their cross-city rivals, walked away from their end-of-game team huddle when the first of the explosions rocked the ground they stood on. No one knew what the explosion was, only that it came from the stadium parking lot. Several explosions, actually. Two at least, maybe a third.

The stadium shook. The press box, not the newest of structures, fell down on one side and those in the box scrambled, pushing and shoving to get out.

Stunned, the crowd was silent.

At first.

Then, in panic and confusion, they ran, sometimes climbing over one another, knocking down whoever was in their way.

"Guys! Stay here! Get down!" Brian yelled as he ran out in front of his team, his arms out like a traffic cop.

The boys listened and hit the ground, huddling with one another.

Brian and Coach Bennett stood facing the crowd.

"Here! Here!" Brian waved his arms, his eyes locking in on his brothers and friends in the first row.

They responded by jumping over the fence and down onto the track separating the field from the bleachers, and ran to join the team laying frightened and confused on the ground.

Most of the parents followed.

Jeremy sent Vicky and others to the field.

Jamie Graff, Pat O'Connor, and Paul Eiselmann- all three detectives-stopped parents and spectators from going into the parking lot, and redirected them to the field.

Fortunately, the stadium had emptied as the press box fell completely into the top rows and rolled half-way down the bleachers until it broke apart and came to a precarious rest.

Graff took charge and shouted, "Stay where you are until we determine what happened. 9-1-1 has been contacted, and the fire department is on the way!"

He and the two other cops, Jeremy, and the assistant principal, Bob Farner, made their way to the parking lot. Eyes blinked back tears caused by the rancid smoke. Coughing expelled as much smoke that had been inhaled.

Three vehicles towards the back and side of the lot were on fire. They sat in a row near the visitor bus and the marching band trailer. Fortunately, they were situated away from other vehicles.

The heat and smoke kept them from venturing too far. Parents were kept away from their cars until the fire department could assess the situation. What they could see, three vehicles were twisted and burned or burning.

"Jesus!" Jeremy uttered.

"Yeah, I know," Farner responded.

"No, I mean, that's Jeff's SUV in the middle."

CHAPTER TWO

APPROXIMATELY ONE MONTH LATER

Brian crumpled up the call slip summoning him to the guidance office. He pushed it to the corner of his desk as far away as possible without tossing it on the floor. His English teacher, Penny Rios, looked at him questioningly, but didn't question him about it.

Brian didn't want to see his father, Jeremy. The ride to school was not only unexpected, but uncomfortable. Normally, Jeremy signed his own slips, not Farner, the assistant principal. That was a twist. Still, he ignored it.

Besides, Rios was one of his favorite teachers, and the discussion they were having on *Lord of the Flies* was a good one. Even though they were only supposed to read up to the fourth chapter, Brian had reread the entire book in three days. Because only a third of the students had read the book, Rios decided to have the entire class read *Lord of the Flies*, or in some cases, reread it.

"Who would you consider a strong, independent character? Perhaps a leader among the boys?" Rios asked.

The answers ranged from Jack to Ralph to Piggy. Brian's friend, Shannon Pritchert, mentioned Simon, which was an unusual answer.

Puzzled, Rios asked, "Why Simon?"

"I don't consider him to be a leader, but he was independent. He wasn't buying into either side. He spent most of the time by himself," she said.

Brian nodded.

"Brian, you're pretty silent today. What are your thoughts?"

He said, "It depends upon what you think strong means. Honestly, I don't think any of them are strong. Being strong means having integrity. Ralph didn't defend Piggy even when he was being picked on. If he had integrity, he would have defended Piggy no matter who was against him. Jack broke rules he felt weren't necessary, even though there needed to be order. A person with integrity doesn't break rules just because he might not like them. Piggy whined and complained, but he tried to establish order. I think because of his size and his whining, no one paid attention to him. A leader has to have followers."

He looked over at Shannon, smiled, and said, "I have to think about Simon. I hadn't thought of him being independent until Shannon mentioned him."

"What is your definition of integrity?" Rios asked.

Brian didn't wait to be called upon. He said, "Someone who speaks the truth and lives it even when others don't. A person who is genuine."

"That can make someone pretty unpopular, don't you think?"

Brian nodded and said, "It's what makes someone strong. Speaking the truth and following the rules, no matter who else does or doesn't. Being willing to take a stand, even if it's unpopular. Standing up for your beliefs. If you don't do those things, you don't have integrity and you aren't strong."

There was a knock on the door and Tommy Harrison, the head basketball coach and one of the physical education teachers, stuck his head in, smiled at Rios and said, "I'm here to get Brian Evans. He's wanted in the office."

Brian first stared at the crumpled call slip and sighed. Then, reluctantly, he stood up.

"Bring all your stuff." Harrison turned to Rios and said, "I don't think he will be back in your class today."

"Okay, thanks," Rios smiled and said, "Brian, your assignment is to read the next two chapters by Friday."

Brian grinned at her. "I finished the book already."

She laughed and said, "I thought so. Just skim over the next two chapters so they're fresh in your mind for Friday."

Brian stuffed the paperback, his notebook, and his pen into his backpack, and left the room with Harrison.

As they walked down the hallway, Harrison asked, "Since when do you ignore call slips from the assistant principal?"

"I thought it was from my dad."

"Since when do you ignore call slips from your dad?"

"We were having a discussion on *Lord of the Flies*. It was a good one."

Harrison smacked him playfully on the shoulder and said, "The book or the discussion?"

Brian laughed and said, "Both!"

They walked into the guidance area. There were three students sitting at a table, and one working on a computer in the corner. All four stopped what they were doing and stared at him.

He also noticed the silence and the lack of a hello from Kristi Johnson, the guidance secretary and his dad's friend. Normally, she was smiling and outgoing. Today, she was quiet. She looked sad as if she had been crying.

"Kristi, are you okay?" Brian whispered as he stood in front of her.

She barely glanced up at him and nodded. She dabbed at her eyes with a tissue.

Brian turned and saw his dad's dark office with the door closed.

"We're in the conference room," Harrison said as he put an arm around his shoulders, guiding him through the guidance area and down the small hallway.

"We?"

Harrison nodded, and then before opening up the conference room door, he hung onto Brian's arm and said, "Bri, I want you to know if you or the guys need anything, and I mean anything, all you have to do is ask."

Brian wanted to ask him what he meant, but before he could, Harrison opened up the door and stood to the side so Brian could enter. Inside were his brothers, minus Two, who was at Butler Middle School. Jeff Limbach was there, along with his son, Danny. Bob Farner, the assistant principal, Chuck Gobel, the principal, and Gloria Beatleman, one of the other counselors, were there.

Detectives Pat O'Connor, Jamie Graff, and Paul Eiselmann stood against the wall behind Randy, Bobby, and Danny. George sat at one end of the table, facing Farner and Gobel. On the other side of the table were Billy and Brett, with an empty chair between them. Brian assumed the empty chair was for him. Harrison stood with his back against the closed door.

Brian's father was not in the room.

Brian and his brothers were puzzled. No one knew why they were called to the office, and he was certain his brothers wondered where their father was, just as he did.

Farner was a big man with a bald head on top and brown hair on the sides, and the guys liked him, especially Danny and Randy, who supplied him with songs after they recorded them.

He cleared his throat. As often as he spoke in front of groups, he was uneasy and less than confident. He said, "Guys, I have some news to share. Please, let me finish before you ask questions, okay?"

The guys nodded. Brian glanced at O'Connor and then at Graff to see if he could read anything from their reactions. He couldn't, though O'Connor's eyes met Brian's.

"This morning, just after the start of first period, your dad fainted. When he woke up, our nurse checked your dad's blood pressure. It was higher than normal. Your father also complained of chest pressure and tingling in his left arm."

"Heart attack," Brett said quietly, not taking his eyes off of Farner.

Ignoring Brett for the moment, Farner plowed on. "As a precaution, we called for an ambulance, and they took your dad to the hospital."

Ignoring the no question request, Brett asked, "Did you call our mom?"

"Yes, we did," Farner nodded. "She requested the ambulance take him to Froedtert Hospital, where she works. She's planning on meeting the ambulance at the hospital."

"Have you heard anything about how Dad is doing?" Brett asked.

Farner shook his head and said, "No. Nothing yet."

Brian glanced around the room. Bobby and Randy wept quietly. Billy cried openly and unashamedly. Brian reached over and held his forearm.

Danny sat with his hands folded on the table. He couldn't read George's or Brett's expressions. Probably they were as stunned as he was.

Brett turned to Brian and asked, "When dad took you to school, was he sick then?"

Brian shook his head and said, "He didn't seem like it."

Gobel said, "Mr. Limbach is going to drive you guys to the hospital so you can be with your mom and dad."

Brian held up a hand like a traffic cop and said, "Does our brother Michael know?"

"Oh shit," Farner muttered. "Sorry, excuse the language. No, I didn't think of it."

Brian half-turned to Jeff and said, "Jeff, would you take Randy, Brett, Bobby, and Danny to the hospital? George, Billy and I will go to Butler and pick up Michael."

Jeff nodded and said, "Yes, I can."

Brian explained to Farner and Gobel, "Brett and Bobby need to be with mom. Their mom. Randy needs to be with dad."

"What about Billy?" Randy asked.

"George and I will be with him. We won't be far behind."

"Brian, I don't think you should drive," Gobel cautioned.

"I'll be fine," Brian said with finality. "Mr. Farner, can you call the middle school and tell them to have Michael ready? But make sure no one tells him about dad. George and I will."

"Brian," Mr. Gobel objected, when O'Connor cut him off.

"I'll escort them to Butler and then lead them to the hospital." To Brian, he said, "Do you know how to get there?"

"I've been there once or twice, but I'll put the address in my nav system just in case." With the amount of construction and his lack of familiarity with that area of Milwaukee, he wasn't so sure. O'Connor knew it.

Brett, who had driven Brian's truck to school, searched his backpack for Brian's keys and placed them on the table in front of Brian.

To Farner, Brian said, "It's important they don't tell Michael. We will. I don't want him freaking out when no one is with him."

There didn't seem to be any further discussion, so Brian stood up and said, "Okay, let's go."

Graff said to Jeff, "We'll bookend you. I'll lead, and Paul will be behind you." To Brian, he said, "Bri, I want you driving carefully."

Brian nodded.

"Are you sure you're okay to drive?" Graff asked.

Brian leveled his gaze at O'Connor and then at Graff. He said, "I'm fine."

"Can you please let us know any news?" Farner asked.

"I have your cell. I'll call or text you and coach," Brian said. He stopped at the doorway and asked, "Is Kristi going to be okay?"

Gobel smiled and said, "We'll take care of her. It was thoughtful of you to ask about her."

The boys, the cops, and Jeff filed out of the conference room, leaving Harrison, the administrators, and the counselor standing there in silence. It was Farner who broke it.

"Brian, wow! I didn't expect him to take charge. Brett, maybe, but not Brian."

Harrison smiled, shook his head and said, "It was crunch time for them. Now you know why, if the game is on the line, the guys look to Brian. If there's one shot left, Brian will take it. You saw the same thing in football with the forty-seven-yard field goal to win the sectional final. Brian is scary calm and most always in control."

"I always thought Brett was the leader. Maybe Randy," Farner said.

Harrison shook his head. "In some ways, maybe. Probably a lot of ways. With something like this, all of them follow Brian."

CHAPTER THREE

They arrived at Butler and parked in the visitor section in the front loop of the school. Brian turned off the ignition, and the truck's engine ticked hotly. O'Connor stood on the school steps with the tips of his fingers in his front pockets, waiting patiently.

The boys sat in silence for a moment. Billy wept, though not as hard as he was in the school conference room.

"Are you okay, Billy?" Brian asked.

Billy nodded.

"Dad will not die. It will not be the same as your other dad."

Billy shrugged, but didn't make eye contact with Brian.

Brian reached over and held onto Billy's forearm and said, "Are you okay with helping tell Michael?"

Billy nodded.

"How do you want to do this?" George asked from the backseat.

"I think you should tell him," Brian said.

George frowned, pursed his lips and then said, "You don't think you should?"

Brian shook his head and said, "Not after last night."

He didn't wait for a response, but pushed open his door, shut it behind him, and started a slow walk to the building. Two truck doors opened and shut with a thunk behind him. He waited on the sidewalk for George and Billy to catch up.

George stepped up on his left, with Billy on his right.

"Okay, let's do this."

Together, they followed O'Connor into the school.

The warm musty air slapped them in the face, along with the stale smell of something old. Butler was certainly old. All three boys graduated from Butler, and despite the old smelly building, the walls held memories. Memories, both good and not so good for each boy, separately and together.

Class was in session, so no one was in the hallway. They spotted Two through the glass partition, sitting in a chair off to the side, but facing the door. Smaller and thinner, he was strikingly similar in appearance to George. In fact, Two could have been George at a younger age. He saw his brothers and stood up. Concern was on his face.

O'Connor stepped up to the receptionist and said, "We're here to sign Two out of school."

The secretary smiled at Brian, George, and Billy, and said, "Hi, boys! It's been a while. You've grown so much."

"Hi Mrs. Fohey," Brian said with a smile. "Is there a room where we can speak to Michael before we leave?"

"Yes, Mr. Wegner said you can use his conference room."

Mark Wegner was an assistant coach for Jeremy at North before he went into administration and before Jeremy became a counselor. Now a principal, he recently transferred from Horning Middle School to Butler.

He stepped out of his office, smiled at the three boys and O'Connor, and said, "I thought I heard some miscreants in the office." Once upon a time, the boys had teased that he looked and spoke like Tom Selleck. He did. It was an old joke that had begun during his coaching days.

He shook hands with all four boys and with O'Connor. He said, "Let's go in here."

Wegner held the door open, followed the boys and O'Connor in, and shut the door behind them. He stood in the back, out of the way.

George took one last look at Brian, started, but stopped, struggling with what to say. He didn't even know how to begin. He gave up and looked at Brian.

Brian sighed and said, "Michael, we have some news." He reached out and placed a hand on Two's shoulder, but Two stepped back and pushed Brian's hand off.

Brian gave George a *what-did-I-tell-you* look, and said, "An ambulance took Dad to mom's hospital. He fainted, and when he woke up, he said he had chest pressure and his left arm tingled."

Two's jaw dropped. When he recovered, he said, "Dad had a heart attack? Is he okay?"

"We don't know if it was a heart attack, and we don't know how dad is yet. Jeff took the other guys to the hospital. When we get on the road, I'll call mom for an update."

Two stared at his shoes, then back up at Brian.

Brian asked, "Are you ready to go?"

Two nodded.

"Then let's get going."

Mr. Wegner held Brian back and said, "When you hear something, anything, could you let me know? Your dad and I, we," he gave up and shook his head.

"Yes. I'll give you my cell number and if you text me, I'll have yours. When I hear something, I'll get in touch with you."

"You know many of us love your father. He's a good man."

Brian nodded and then followed the others out of the school.

CHAPTER FOUR

It had been uncomfortably quiet on the ride to the hospital. Brian held onto Billy's forearm for most of the trip, unless he turned or changed lanes. Billy stared out the side window, as did George and Michael.

There was little traffic, so Brian had no trouble following O'Connor. They arrived at the large hospital complex, and Brian pulled to the curb and dropped the three boys off, saying, "I'll go park the truck."

"Do you want us to wait for you?" George asked.

Brian shook his head and said, "No, go inside and find the others. I'll catch up to you."

George hesitated. He glanced at Billy and Two, who had crossed the road to the hospital emergency room, and then back at Brian.

"I'll be okay, George," Brian said. He tried to wear a smile, but it slipped off as quickly as it appeared.

George reached through the window, grasped Brian's arm and said, "This is not your fault."

Brian sighed and said, "You better catch up to Billy. I don't want him by himself."

Reluctantly, George turned and followed his two brothers. O'Connor stood outside the front door of the hospital, watching the scene at the truck.

George glanced back, watching Brian pull away and drive the short distance to the parking lot.

"Is he okay?"

George shook his head, but made no other comment. He entered the hospital, leaving O'Connor to wait for Brian.

Brian parked his truck in the visitor lot and sat quietly with his hands in his lap. There was no one else in the parking area, and that was okay with him.

He sat with his chin on his chest and his forehead on the steering wheel. As hard as he fought it, tears dribbled down his cheeks and along the side of his nose. He pushed his glasses up to wipe them away.

Despite what George had said, Brian knew he was at least partially to blame for his father's heart attack, or whatever it was. A part of him wanted to leave. Just drive off and head anywhere.

There was a rap on the window. Brian didn't look up because he knew who it was. He dried his eyes with his hands, and his hands on his jeans. He readjusted his glasses, took a deep breath, and opened the door. He got out and locked his truck by pushing the button on the key fob.

"Are you okay?"

Brian didn't look at O'Connor. He nodded and tried to walk past him.

O'Connor took him by the shoulders and wrapped him in a hug. Brian broke down again and wept against O'Connor's chest.

Pat let him for a minute and then took him by the shoulders so they could look at each other eye to eye.

"We don't know anything yet."

Brian nodded.

"I know you're worried about your father, but there is something else bouncing around your head, isn't there?"

Brian said nothing.

O'Connor said, "You've held it together this long. You'll need to hold it together a little longer. You've got to be tough for your brothers and your mom."

Brian nodded again.

"Can you do that?"

Brian nodded.

Then O'Connor smiled and said, "You're a tough young man, Bri."

"I don't feel tough."

O'Connor hugged him and said, "Tough guys never feel tough. They just are."

CHAPTER FIVE

Froedtert is the same as every hospital in most ways, but it is famous for its work on hearts. Victoria Evans was one of the head surgical nurses, so it was logical for her husband, the boys' father, to be taken there. Normally, she worked days, seven to three, but in a rare move, she swapped with a colleague who had a meeting with a wedding planner for her upcoming wedding. Vicky never minded helping her coworkers, but the late night and little sleep didn't mix well with the shock of Jeremy having a heart event.

It was what she referred to it as. She refused to use the words heart attack. She would not go there. Not yet.

She seldom wore makeup because she didn't need to. Her long brown hair hung past her shoulders and matched her brown eyes. She was dark-complected, and her two biological sons, Brett and Bobby, received their looks from her. Today, however, the lines at the corners of her eyes were pronounced, as were the dark circles around them. She tried smiling, but gave up. She wouldn't be able to fool the boys, so she figured, why bother?

With the blessing of her supervisor, she secured a conference room on the first floor, but away from the ER so she could meet with the boys and with the few adults who were considered family and personal friends. She wanted to tell them what she knew at one time rather than seven or eight different times. She and the boys waited, perhaps impatiently, for Brian and O'Connor to arrive.

There were two empty seats at the table. One between Billy and George, and the other between Bobby and Michael. When Brian and O'Connor stepped into the conference room, Brian chose the seat between Billy and George, which surprised Vicky, because she knew how close he and Bobby, and he and Two were. She was puzzled, but didn't question it.

She said, "Here's what I know. He is still undergoing tests, but the thought is that he did not have a myocardial infarction. An MI for short. We know his blood pressure shot up to 210 over 140, which is high. Too high. We know he had tingling in his left arm and tightness in his chest. He was sweating more than normal and had trouble catching his breath."

Brett breathed a sigh of relief and said, "That's good, right? I mean, the fact that he didn't have an MI."

Vicky bobbed her head from one side of the other as if she was deciding. She said, "Yes, but we don't know what happened. For sure."

She waited for other questions. When there weren't any, she said, "They gave him oxygen at school and again in the ambulance, and the paramedics put an IV in his arm so they could give him saline on a slow drip to keep the vein open. They also gave him a 324 milligram of aspirin to chew."

"Aspirin thins the blood," Brett said to her.

She smiled and said, "Yes, it does. The paramedics hooked him up for an ECG and determined nitroglycerin wasn't needed at that point. Once they got him here, they took him to the Emergency Department for another ECG, a blood draw for labs, and a chest Xray. Depending upon those results, he'll be admitted to a step-down unit. I don't have results on those yet."

"Wait! What's a step-down unit?" Brett asked.

"Sorry," Vicky smiled. She was so used to speaking nurse and doctor talk, it was sometimes difficult for non-medical people to follow. "An ECG is an electrocardiogram. And a step-down unit is another name for the Cardiac Unit. This is where your dad will be for the short-term."

She waited for questions. None came, so she moved on.

"Normal protocol would be for your dad to be here in the hospital for two or three days."

"Randy said, "Three days? That's a long time.""

Randy and Billy were identical twins. Like her own boys, they had brown hair and brown eyes, but were taller. The twins were a shade under six-three, while Bobby, younger than Brett by eighteen months, was six-one, and Brett was six-even.

Jeremy had adopted Randy first, when Jeremy was still single. Then came Billy.

It was easy for Vicky to understand why Billy had been so affected by Jeremy's heart event. His first adoptive father died of a heart attack. It was Billy who had found him after he had come home from school. His dad, Robert, had died in the upstairs hallway clutching two chocolate chip cookies. Vicky could only imagine the thoughts running through Billy's mind.

Brian held onto Billy's arm, sometimes shifting to Billy's hand.

Vicky smiled at Randy and said, "Honey, we have to stabilize his blood pressure. He'll be hooked up to a cardiac monitor, and the doctor might order an NTG patch."

When she saw the confusion on the boys' faces, she explained, "Sorry. An NTG patch is a nitroglycerin patch."

"But you said it wasn't needed," Brett said.

She reached out and took hold of Brett's hand and said, "I said he might. Whenever there is a heart event, there will usually be a daily Lovenox shot, daily aspirin, and blood pressure meds. Dad can't come home until they are certain he's in a good place." She nodded at Brett and then at the others and said, "All of this is a good thing. We know what we're doing here. He's in excellent hands. These are some of the best doctors in the Midwest."

"Can we see him?" Billy asked as he wiped away tears.

Sadly, Vicky said, "At some point, yes. I'm not sure about today. Possibly, but I don't know for sure."

She waited and then asked, "Do any of you have questions?"

There were head shakes, and a couple murmured, "No."

Vicky nodded and said, "I have some questions for you. I got home when everyone was asleep, including your father. I don't know what took place, but I think something did. There had to be a trigger or something that set him off."

She shook her head and said, "There isn't any history of anyone in his family with heart trouble. Your father isn't in the best shape. His diet is out of whack. I know he's a first-class worrier. But there had to be something that triggered this."

She glanced around the room and said, "I want to start at the beginning. How was Jeremy when you guys got home from basketball practice?"

Five of the boys were sophomores at Waukesha North High School. Bobby was a freshman, and Two was an eighth grader. All of them were in sports of one kind or another.

Puzzled, the boys looked from one to another, shrugged, and it was Bobby who said, "Fine. Like always." Then his eyes darted to Randy, Danny, and Brett, and finally landing on Brian.

"What?" Vicky asked. She, like most mothers, never missed much.

It was Jeff Limbach, Danny's father, who answered for them. "I noticed Jeremy getting more and more agitated as he listened to Jamie, Pat, and Paul fill us in on the fan mail investigation. Randy, Danny, and Bobby were with Jeremy and me at my house."

Vicky's eyes met Jamie Graff's. He nodded.

Graff, Jeff Limbach, and Jeremy were close friends dating back to North High School, when all three had worked there. Jeremy was a social studies teacher and head basketball coach, Jeff was an English teacher and budding author, and Graff was the school resource officer. Since then, Jeremy gave up coaching when he became a counselor. Jamie became a detective, and Jeff got out of teaching because of the enormous success he had with his books, especially those that had been turned into movies. He had written the screenplay for several and had a bit part in one or two.

"Can you fill me in?" Vicky asked. "I don't know where we are on the investigation."

Jamie knew it was the cherry on top of a shit sundae. He had little update to give. The information was sparse and incomplete when he presented it the night before. He didn't want to repeat it. Yet he knew he had to.

He shrugged and said, "There is no new information. The bottom line is, we don't have enough, and neither does the FBI. There has been no overt threat of bodily harm. Even the language in the letters or notes, whatever you want to call them, was determined by the behavioral science unit as benign."

"But a couple of months ago, you mentioned ViCAP and Cleve Batiste would be involved," Vicky said.

Graff shook his head. "He had been at the start, but there wasn't anything to investigate. Yet."

Graff recalled Jeremy sitting with arms crossed on his chest, staring out the window. He remembered Jeremy sighing and shaking his head. Graff knew him well enough to know Jeremy was fuming over the lack of attention the letters the three boys received were getting.

The detective looked at Jeff, who, just as he did the night before, sucked on the inside of his cheek.

Danny turned to his father, shrugged, and cocked his head. Jeff didn't respond to him. Jeff didn't look over at Vicky, choosing to focus on Graff.

Last evening, Graff felt fortunate Vicky wasn't there to ask the zillion questions she normally asked. She was mama bear when it came to the boys. To her credit, it didn't matter if they were adopted or almost adopted, or were her biological boys. In her eyes, all seven were her kids.

He wouldn't be so lucky now. Vicky wanted to know what triggered Jeremy's ride to the hospital, and she wanted to know how the investigation was proceeding.

Jeff turned to Vicky and said, "What Jamie is saying is that we don't need to worry about these letters."

"I didn't say that ... *exactly*. We need to keep collecting the letters as they come in." He nodded at Paul Eiselmann and said, "Paul will analyze them and make sure Skip Dahlke at Quantico is in the loop."

"That's the point where Jeremy got a little hot," Jeff said. "Jeremy leaned forward and perhaps more forcefully than he intended–or not–said, 'You've been analyzing them. We have a bunch of letters telling Bobby and Randy to get out of the band. The letters suggest Bobby and Randy are holding Danny back.'"

Graff was at a loss, and he didn't know how to respond to Jeremy the evening before. He didn't know how to respond to Jeff repeating Jeremy's statement now.

Jeff went on, "Jeremy wanted to know what the chances were that this sender goes after the boys like that piece of crap Alan Nelson did."

"Nelson was a psycho," Graff reminded him.

O'Connor watched Brian closely since it was Brian who had shot Nelson in the woods outside of their house. Brian hadn't moved. Brian stared at Graff, then at Jeff, and then at his mother. The concern, however, was all over Brian's face.

"Jeremy reminded Jamie that Nelson was a psycho who killed a half-dozen or more people, including a boy the same age as the boys, and he ended up in the woods because he was gunning for George and Brian." Jeff shut his eyes, shook his head and said, "I'm sorry. That came out way harsher than I intended."

"But Dad, that was what Jeremy said," Danny said. "Almost word for word."

"Nelson had a specific agenda," Graff said. "He didn't believe in adoption. He thought adopted kids ruined families."

Vicky said, "What's stopping this person from going after Bobby and Randy? Even Danny, if Danny continues to ignore these letters?"

"Vicky has a point," Jeff mumbled. "Using your words, these letters are benign. What happens if they amp up to something more?"

Danny spoke up and said, "Then Jeremy said he was only a counselor, but someone who fixated on Randy, Bobby, and me didn't seem rational."

Eiselmann jumped in to rescue Graff. He said, "That's why the FBI is paying attention to this case. They are sure the same person sent each letter, even though the postmarks are from different parts of the Milwaukee Metro area. The behavioral science guys said the same language is used, along with the same phraseology. Even the same type of paper and envelope."

"This person is smart enough to use self-adhesive envelopes and stamps, so we don't have DNA. There are some latent prints, but they aren't in the system," Graff said.

"It may not seem like it, but we are learning a lot about the sender," Eiselmann.

Vicky said, "Yes, but will you know enough to stop this sick," she bit her tongue and said, "*person* before he or she does anything to one of the boys?"

"The best we can say at this point is that we're working on it," Graff said.

Jeff said, "That's when Jeremy nearly lost it. He sat back in the chair, his jaw clenched, and his arms folded on his chest."

Jeff tilted his head first at Eiselmann and then at Graff, as if he had wanted to say something else. In the end, he shook his head and said nothing.

The only cop in the room who had contributed nothing to the case summary was Pat O'Connor. He sat in his chair and listened. O'Connor kept his eyes on the boys, particularly Brian, watching how each responded.

The boys were bright, intuitive. Danny's intelligence was in the stratosphere. O'Connor had believed whatever was said in Jeff's study would have been shared with the other boys in the Evans family. There were no secrets among the boys. They shared everything, and often, the boys seemed to know stuff before anything was vocalized. Yet, because of the body language and expressions of the boys, O'Connor suspected nothing much had been shared.

That was both good and bad. Good, in that they were a tight-knit group of friends raised as brothers, who would be quick to defend one another. They were the eyes and ears the cops weren't able to be. Bad, because the boys needed to know exactly what Danny, Randy, and Bobby might be up against.

Graff shared the one piece of information the three cops held from Jeremy, Jeff, and the three boys the night before.

He said, "The FBI believes the sender is someone at North High School, and we do, too. We believe the boys know this person, and we believe Jeremy knows this person." He turned to Jeff and said, "Jeff, you might know this person." He turned to the rest of the boys and said, "We believe this person had or has interactions with Randy, Bobby, and Danny. Perhaps with each of you."

O'Connor and Graff felt if the boys knew this information, they could be more watchful, especially George, Brian, and Brett. Those three had special abilities, and they seldom missed anything.

"What do we do?" Randy asked Graff. His eyes flicked to O'Connor and then to Eiselmann before settling back on Graff.

Graff looked over at O'Connor. Pat said, "Keep your eyes and ears open. You've read the letters. You know what's in them. If you hear someone mimic or parrot the same things in the letters, let us know. Let your parents know. Try not to be alone. Think of Noah's Ark. Two by two. More is even better."

Randy nodded.

"Danny, you have an eidetic memory, right?" Eiselmann asked.

"I have a pretty good memory," Danny said with a nod.

"You know those letters by heart. I would think it would be easy for you to pick up on what someone says that might match what is in them. Listen closely, and like Pat said, let one of us and your parents know right away."

"Pat, Paul, and I have to head back to the station. But before we do, are there questions before we leave?" Graff asked.

The boys shook their head or shrugged. Vicky and Jeff said nothing.

"One thing," Bobby said. He stared at his hands and he spoke slowly. "I've been thinking that maybe it might be safer if Randy and I drop out of the band. Maybe for a little while. You know, until this guy gets caught." He ended with a shrug. He made no eye contact with anyone as he spoke, and he laid it out there like a grenade with the pin pulled.

Jeff rubbed his forehead. He leaned forward and said, "Guys, perhaps more than anyone, I know about fan mail. I receive letters. My agent receives letters. My publisher receives letters. Most of them are positive, just like some notes or letters you've received. However, I also have my share of letters calling me names. They threaten me. I even have an evangelical church in Tennessee praying for me. They believe I'm going to hell along with anyone who reads my books. They call my books trash. I think one or two letters called them the words of Satan."

He smiled and said, "What I'm trying to say is that there will always be detractors. You will never please everyone. Not everyone will love your songs, or the music you play, or the way you perform."

"But what if this guy, whoever it is, starts ..." Randy didn't finish. He couldn't finish. "What if he ..."

"We're on it," Graff said. "So is the FBI. We won't let anything happen to you." He looked at each boy and said, "We won't let anything happen to any of you."

"But you can't guarantee it," Billy said.

Randy said, "You guys were all over that psycho asshole, sorry mom, but he was in our woods. If it hadn't been for Brian ..."

"Look," Danny said. "I can't stop you from quitting. I *won't* stop you from quitting. But we're good. Tim McGraw is putting three of our songs on his next album. We're making a name for ourselves. We sound great together."

"Better than great," Brett said.

Danny nodded. "Like dad said, we're going to get crap. But there will be plenty of people who will like what we do. If we're going to do this, we have to accept the fact that there will be good with the bad."

Jeff said, "You heard Jamie say they're on it. The FBI is on it. Right now, there is nothing in those letters threatening you. Nothing right now points to the fact that someone is out to get you."

"You don't have to quit yet," Danny said. "Maybe never. But if things ... get bad, you can always quit and I won't blame you."

Eiselmann said, "Guys, I love you just like you are my own. I know Pat feels the same way. I pledge I will do everything in my power to make sure nothing happens to you. Nothing."

Vicky sat with her elbows on the table, listening. She watched each cop. She watched Jeff. He was Jeremy's closet friend. Jeff was like an uncle to the boys. Danny was like a cousin, almost a brother.

She reached out and took hold of Bobby's hand and said, "Let's hold off on quitting. Let's give Jamie, Paul, and Pat some time."

Bobby nodded. So did Randy. Danny breathed a sigh of relief.

The band had been his lifelong dream. Danny, who had skipped two grades because of his intelligence, had spent summers at Julliard studying music. He could play any guitar, acoustic or electric, six string, twelve string, or bass. He played keyboards. Piano, organ, and synthesizer. He played any brass instrument. Recently, he picked up the mandolin and banjo.

Their band was called *Bits and Pieces* after the Dave Clark Five song. Jeff helped secure permission for the name from Clark's organization.

"Now I see why Jeremy might have been upset," Vicky said. She stared directly at Graff. "This family has been down this road before. Brian still has the scars. Both George and Brett have scars of their own. I want nothing more to happen to us. Enough is enough. Do you understand?"

Graff nodded and said, "I understand. If it were my wife and Garrett, I'd be just as upset as you."

"Same for me," Eiselmann said.

"Then we have an understanding. I want to know as soon as this turns south. I want to know immediately if any of my boys or Danny are in danger. I want your word. You've got to promise me that."

"You have my word," Graff said. There were tears in his eyes when he said, "Jeremy and Jeff are like brothers to me. If he wouldn't have adopted Randy and Billy, Kelly and I would have." He looked around at each boy and said, "I feel that way towards each of you. I won't let anything happen to you, and I promise to let your mom know if we come across anything that might place you in danger."

The three cops left shortly thereafter, leaving Jeff and Vicky with the boys.

Jeff said, "Last night after they left, I remember Jeremy tapping his chest. He said something like, this whole thing has given him a case of heartburn that won't quit."

"Isn't that one sign of a heart attack?" Brett asked.

Vicky nodded and said, "It could be."

"But it got worse when he came back to the house," Randy whispered. He glanced at Brian and Two, and then at his hands.

CHAPTER SIX

Alarmed, Vicky said slowly and deliberately, as if she would rather not know. "What happened?"

Brian remained stoic, not giving away anything. Two fidgeted in his seat. At first, George stared at the table, then at Brian. Billy reached over and held onto Brian's arm. It was Brett who spoke.

"You know how we do homework. If someone needs help with math, they go to Bobby, Billy, or me. Science, they go to Billy, George, or me. Social studies, they go to Brian. If someone needs help with a paper or English, they go to Randy, Bobby, or Brian."

Vicky nodded.

"Last night, Brian worked with Two on his paper for English. The five-paragraph essay crap they teach in middle school and freshman year. Brian worked Two through the first four paragraphs. Then dad came home. He went to the medicine cabinet and got some Gas-X. I figured he had heartburn or something."

Vicky waited for Brett to go on. Brett glanced around the room, mostly at Brian, who sat expressionless. Both Brett and Vicky noticed Billy tightened his grip on Brian's arm.

"Dad asked why Two hadn't gone to Randy or Bobby with his paper. Two said they weren't there, and that Brian was almost done with it."

"I told dad I had a ton of homework to do and I didn't have time," Randy said.

"What you *actually* said was that Two would have to *settle* for Brian because you were too busy," Brett said. "You have to admit it was pretty rude."

Vicky saw the hurt in Brian's eyes, but didn't know what to say to help.

"I know," Randy said quietly. "It came out wrong, and I didn't mean it like that."

"I knew what you meant. It's no big deal," Brian said, not making eye contact with anyone.

"Then dad told Two to ask Bobby for help. Bobby said he couldn't because he had math and social studies to do," Brett said. "By then, Brian was done, and was explaining how Two could fix up the conclusion."

Brett stopped, stared at Two, then at Brian, and said, "Then dad went off on Two and Brian. He asked why they were always hanging on each other. And Two was doing nothing we hadn't seen a million times. He had an arm around Brian's shoulders and his cheek on Brian's arm. Mostly, so he could see the computer screen. But that's just Two. And Brian. No big deal."

Vicky shook her head. She didn't understand. It was something she had seen Two do, not only to Brian, but to the others. Mostly with Brian. Two would get a piggyback ride everywhere from Brian. When they watched TV, Two would lean on Brian. It was both innocent and lovely. Brotherly love. As Brett said, it was no big deal. In fact, Vicky loved to watch the two of them together.

"Then dad stormed off to the office."

Vicky squinted at Brett, then glanced around the room and said, "Am I missing something?"

Brett puffed out his cheeks, leaned forward, and said, "That's what we thought. We figured dad reacted the way he did because of the meeting with Graff, Eiselmann, and O'Connor."

Vicky said, "Brian and Michael, I know what dad said hurt, but I want you to know there is nothing wrong with the way you are with one another."

"There's more," Randy muttered.

"More?" Vicky asked.

"Don't," Brian said as he shook his head.

Brett ignored him and said, "When we finished homework and got ready for bed, Brian went to hug Two, and Two pushed him away."

"I didn't push him," Two protested.

"Yeah, you pushed him," Billy said. "You almost did the same thing at Butler when Brian put his hand on your shoulder when he wanted to tell you about dad."

Two was George's half-brother and the newest member of the family. His full name was Michael Two Feathers, but the boys and Jeremy called him Two. The only ones who didn't were Vicky and Brian.

"Why did you push Brian away, Michael?" Vicky asked.

"Because I don't want anyone to think I'm gay."

Angered, Brian said, "You don't have to worry about that anymore, Michael. Or should I call you Two like everyone else? If I stay three to five feet away from you from now on, you won't catch any of my bisexual germs."

Two looked to be near tears. He loved Brian. Brian was more of a big brother to him than George was. He was torn between disappointing Jeremy, worried about what anyone thought of him, and worried about how his closeness with Brian looked to everyone.

"Billy, you'll probably have to scrub your arm and hand. We touched one another. You don't want to catch any of my germs, either."

"I'm not worried," Billy muttered.

"It was shortly after when Brian packed up some clothes and headed to Danny's to spend the night. He told me to take his truck, take Two to Butler, and he'd catch a ride with Jeff and Danny in the morning," Brett explained.

"But there's more," Billy said.

Randy, Bobby, Brian, and Two swung towards Billy, then at Brett.

"What?" Vicky asked.

Brett sighed. He first looked at Billy, then at George, and then he stared at his hands before he answered.

"I, we, wanted to fix things. Billy, George, and me. Me, mostly, I guess. After the others went to bed, we went to the office to talk to dad."

CHAPTER SEVEN

Vicky didn't know if she wanted to hear anymore. She had heard enough, but she knew what Brett was about to tell her might be the final straw for Jeremy.

Brett squirmed in his seat. He glanced furtively at Brian, sighed, and said, "It was mostly me. George and Billy were with me, but it was me."

Vicky nodded. To encourage him, she reached out and grasped his hand.

"I explained to dad how we divide up the help with homework. I explained what Two did to Brian." He glanced at Brian, who had trouble maintaining eye contact with him or anyone else.

"I told dad he's pushing Two away from Brian, and he's pushing Brian away from him and us. Dad asked George if he was okay with Two being closer to Brian than he was to him."

"I told him Brian is not only a great brother, he is also a great friend. I love him, and I am happy Two does also," George answered.

Neither Brian nor Two were comfortable. Both wanted to be anywhere else.

"How did dad respond?" Vicky asked.

Brett said, "He nodded. We thought he had accepted it, especially since it came from George."

Brett glanced at George, who stared at the table. Then he glanced at Billy, who had his head down.

"What?" Vicky asked.

"Brian, remember when I had to use your computer? My computer isn't connected to the printer in dad's office. Yours is."

Brian nodded.

"I had to do some research, and I checked your browsing history. I wanted to see if there was anything I could use."

Brian's jaw dropped. "You what?"

"I ..." Brett couldn't finish.

"I don't mind you using my computer. I don't even mind if you use my cell. But you had no right snooping into my browsing history," Brian said, glaring at Brett.

"What were you looking up?" Bobby asked.

Randy squinted at Brian and said, "Were you looking at porn?"

"Jesus!" Brian said. "Yeah! Guilty. You caught me. Every chance I get! I can't wait to come home from school so I can get my rocks off looking at porn sites. Guys, girls, animals, it doesn't matter."

He pulled his arm away from Billy, turned to Vicky and said, "That's why we're always out of tissue, mom. Sorry, but you know, after I watch a little, I have to clean myself off. Yeah, you caught me, Randy."

He turned to Two and said, "Lately, I've been planning on getting into your pants. Especially now, since Bobby said we need to take a break because dad might be upset. Our second break in what? Six months? So, it's smart of you to make sure you're never alone with me. And make sure you stay at least three to five feet away."

He took a deep breath, stared at Randy, and said, "What the hell, Randy? Because I'm bisexual, you think I'm a pervert, too? Fuck you!"

"Brian, please settle down," Vicky said. To Randy, she said, "Randy, what were you thinking?"

"You mean, what have Randy and everyone else been thinking?" Brian spat. "Now, Two."

To Randy, Brett said, "You idiot! No, it wasn't porn. Brian wouldn't do that. It was nothing like that."

"What was it?" Bobby asked.

Brian crossed his arms over his chest and glared at Brett.

"Brian was researching emancipation of a minor."

"No!" Randy said.

"What the hell do you care? You and Two think I'm a pervert, anyway."

"I don't think that," Two protested.

"Bullshit!" Brian said. "You pushed me away last night because I was going to give you a hug goodnight, something I've done since you moved here. This morning, you pushed my hand off your shoulder and stepped away from me."

"Mr. Wegner was there. I didn't want him to think …"

"Yeah, I get it. You didn't want him to think you were gay like me. I get it."

"Guys, Vicky, it's not what you think," Jeff said. "It was research."

"It's private!" Brian said. He stood up so fast his chair fell over. "Fuck it! I'm outta here!"

"Brian, please don't," Vicky said. "Please wait."

Brian never turned around. He didn't stop. He stormed out of the room.

Danny said, "Randy, what the hell were you thinking? You know Brian! You know him!"

"Jesus, Randy," Billy muttered.

"I'm sorry," Randy said. His eyes were downcast and filled with tears.

"A lot of good that does now," Brett said.

Jeff placed a hand on Danny's arm and said, "Guys, please stop."

He turned first to Brett and then to Vicky, and said, "If anyone were to look at my browsing history, given the fact that I'm a writer and I sometimes look up gruesome topics, they would think I'm a pervert or a mass-murderer or something. But Brian's research isn't anything like that."

He stopped and shook his head, considering whether to continue. He didn't want to break Brian's trust, but given the circumstances, he felt it was best to do so.

CHAPTER EIGHT

"Brian has been writing a book with my encouragement. He wanted to keep it a secret."

"He wanted it to be a surprise," Danny added, shaking his head.

"It's in a much different genre than mine. I write thriller/horror. Brian is writing a young adult novel, a coming-of-age story, about a boy who is forced to decide between living in his current situation or moving out on his own. He's almost half of the way into it, and I have to say his writing is terrific. So, no, he isn't looking at porn, and he's not looking to move out. Although, after what I heard ..."

"I wouldn't blame him either," Vicky whispered, more to herself than anyone else.

"I didn't know," Brett said. "I was just trying to help Brian with dad."

"I think that's why Jeremy showed up this morning to take Brian to school. He wanted to square things with him." Jeff shook his head and said, "Jeremy probably still thinks Brian was doing research so he could declare himself an emancipated minor."

"Could he do that?" Bobby asked. "I mean, would he leave our family?"

"Actually, yeah," Brett answered. "After seeing what Brian was researching, I did my own. Given Brian's finances, his grades in school, and everything else, he could easily become an emancipated minor."

"But he has no intention of doing that," Danny said in exasperation. "We talked about it. Dad, Brian, and me. He never brought that up. In fact, he talked about how hard it would be to live alone. Emancipation was one of the plot points of his book. The difficulty of his character on his own, living by himself and all."

"Danny's right. If Brian did anything, he'd move in with Danny and me, or move in with Big Gav and his mom," Jeff said. "But as of last night, he had no intention of moving out."

"Brian was hurting last night. He's probably devastated right now," Vicky said. "Does anyone know what was said between Jeremy and Brian on the way to school?"

"We never got the chance to talk about it," Brett said. He turned to George and Billy, who either shrugged or shook his head.

Vicky stood up and said, "I'm going to check on Jeremy. You boys are going to stay in the waiting area. Jeff, do you mind staying with them?"

"I don't mind at all."

"After I check on Dad, I'm going to find Brian and talk this out with him. *If* I can find him."

"Mom, I will look for him," George said.

She nodded and said, "Okay. Just George. No one else." To George she said, "I would prefer if you just locate him for me. I want to talk to him before anyone else does."

CHAPTER NINE

Vicky's eyes had to adjust to the darkened chapel. George found Brian kneeling in the second pew on the left, head bowed and hands folded. She knew his eyes were clamped shut. Every Sunday before mass began, this was Brian.

One Saturday a month, Brian drove to church to confession, most of the time face to face with Father Donahue. What he had to confess, Vicky didn't know. Perhaps Brian only wanted to talk.

Before he left for the church and without fanfare, he would mention where he was headed as a courtesy to Jeremy and Vicky. Brian, Jeremy, or Vicky would say nothing about it. It was as regular as doing Saturday laundry, only once a month.

Brian was a solid five-foot-eleven-inches carrying one hundred and sixty-five pounds. His nearly black hair hung to his shirt collar. A handsome boy, he was forced to wear glasses because of the damage to the cornea of his right eye. Even though the area around his right eye was scarred, he was handsome. His eyes changed colors depending upon what he wore. Either hazel or green. Along with the smattering of small freckles under his eyes and across the bridge of his nose, his eyes were Vicky's favorite feature.

She hesitated, not wanting to disturb him. She glanced at her watch. By her reckoning, it had been almost an hour since he left the conference room. She wanted to speak to him, and she thought he might have had enough time to pray about whatever it was he prayed about. Vicky didn't know for sure. She never prayed much.

She tiptoed up the aisle and slid into the pew next to him.

At first, Brian didn't move. Finally, he nodded, made the sign of the cross, and sat down next to her.

With his voice barely above a whisper, he said, "I'm sorry for the way I acted, Mom. I'm sorry for swearing, and for treating Randy and Two like I did. It wasn't right."

Vicky put an arm around his shoulders and hugged him. He scooted over to be closer to her, even resting his head on her. She kissed the top of his head, resting her cheek on the white patch of his otherwise black hair.

He received a scar on the right side of his head on the trip to Arizona, along with the scars around his right eye and the ones on his right hand, arm, and shoulder. They cut his hair to accommodate the staples to close the wound. His hair in that small area came back white as lamb's wool. The doctor told them it sometimes happens when there was a great deal of stress or some hormonal change.

Brian had a great deal of stress on the trip. Even before the trip, and certainly after they had come home.

"What happened in the car when dad took you to school?"

Brian shrugged, shook his head, and said, "He apologized for everything. I apologized. He talked some more, and I listened."

Puzzled, Vicky asked, "You apologized? What for?"

What he wanted to say was sometimes apologizing for shit, even if it isn't your shit, is a good way to go. Instead, he said, "It seemed like the thing to do."

"Brian, no one expects you to apologize to anyone, not to me, not to your father, not to any of the guys, if you haven't done anything wrong. And from what I heard, you have done nothing wrong."

The two of them sat there in silence. Brian staring at the cross above the little altar, Vicky staring off into space, deep in her thoughts.

"You mentioned you and Bobby are on a break. What does that mean?"

Brian sighed. He wiped away some tears. He said, "Bobby is worried we're making dad crazy. That we're causing him to be stressed out enough to cause his heart attack or whatever it is."

"It's mostly the letters Bobby, Randy, and Danny received." She paused and said, "But you love Bobby. You love each other."

Brian turned to his mom and whispered, "I have never loved anyone like I love Bobby, and I don't know if I ever will. I will always love him. No matter who I end up with, whether it's a boy or a girl, I will always love Bobby."

"Then why are you on a break?"

Brian shook his head, first turned his head from her, then dropped his chin to his chest and said, "Mom, it won't work between us. It won't. We tried. I know you and dad are uncomfortable with us ... doing stuff and loving each other that way. You and dad never accepted it. But it was always out of love when there weren't any words to express how we feel about each other. But you and dad don't want us to be in that kind of relationship. And as much as Bobby and I deny it, and say because we aren't actually related, we're brothers. Deep down, Bobby knows it. I know it. You and dad know it."

"I already spoke to Bobby. I wanted to get his side of the story, but he never told me any of this."

Brian shook his head. "It's because he doesn't know I feel this way. I have to talk to him about it." He thought for a minute and added, "Please let me talk to him before you or dad do."

"He's sorry he suggested it. I think he'd like to take it back."

Brian shook his head and said, "I love Bobby, Mom. I love him so much it aches. But I can't go through it again. The first time he told me we needed to stop, it tore me up. It tore up our family. I don't want it to happen again, not to me or our family. I love him. I'll talk to him, and as hard as it will be, I'm not going there again."

He paused, took a deep breath and said, "If there is one thing that ruined my relationship with dad, it was when Bobby and I became," he searched for the right word and settled on, "involved. That's when it all changed between me and dad."

"What does all this mean for you and Bobby?"

"It will be uncomfortable for us, especially if we're by ourselves, but we can't have that kind of relationship any longer."

"Just like that?"

Brian nodded, sighed, wept, and said, "It will be hard. He knows how I feel about him and I know how he feels about me. But I can't go there anymore. I can't. It will be better for our family."

Vicky wept. She had been against Brian's and Bobby's sexual relationship. She felt it was wrong. It wasn't because Bobby was gay and Brian was bisexual. She could and would accept it. But in her eyes, they were brothers, regardless of their adoption or not. They were family. Mostly, Bobby was her son, and she never wanted that for him. She would accept it and support him, though. She would support both of them.

After Bobby spilled it all out to her, she understood the struggle of emotions both boys had. The fear, the uncertainty. She understood how unfair and how judgmental she and Jeremy had become. Yes, their love by any family standard, biological or adoptive, was wrong in many ways. At the same time, their relationship was innocent and beautiful. Their relationship was loving and based upon a bedrock of friendship that gave birth to love. Neither she nor Jeremy had ever seen anything like it, and as a result, neither she nor Jeremy knew how to respond to it. Yet the other boys had accepted it. And Brian was right. They truly loved one another.

She said, "Brian, I want you to believe beyond any doubt I can and will support you for being gay. Bobby, too. I mean it."

Brian shrugged and said, "I know," even though he didn't believe it. He didn't know if he ever would.

After a long stretch of silence, she said, "You're sure about all of this?"

"I think so." In a much smaller voice filled with uncertainty, he said, "Yes, I'm sure."

"It hurts though."

Brian whispered and said, "More than you and dad will ever know. More than anyone will know."

"So, you're absolutely sure."

He nodded but didn't say it.

She kissed the side of his head, hugged him, and said, "What about Michael?"

"What he did, hurt. I never saw it coming. I love him, too." In horror, he turned to her and said, "Mom, he and I didn't do anything. Never. I wouldn't."

"I know that, Brian. I know that."

"He pushed me away. This morning, he pushed my hand away and stepped back. You heard him, Mom. He said he didn't want anyone to think he was gay. Like if anyone saw him with me, or saw me hug him or something, people would know he was gay because I am."

"I heard him."

"That is what hurt the most. I don't think it can be fixed. I don't think he wants to fix it." He sighed and said, "I don't know if I want to fix it."

"But you love him."

"Yes, but as a brother. I liked giving him piggyback rides and when he leaned on me. I liked it when he'd sit between my legs and put his head on my chest when we watched TV. Mom, I love him, but I would never do anything with him like I did with Bobby."

She smiled and said, "As much as I loved seeing you and Bobby together, I loved watching you and Michael together. It was special."

He nodded and wiped his eyes with his hands. He whispered, "It *was* special. But dad didn't think so. And now, Michael doesn't think so, either. Dad ruined it."

She nodded. "I know. I'm sorry. I think he was concerned that George felt left out. George and Michael are step-brothers."

"George and I talked about it, and you heard what George told dad."

She nodded.

"You don't think you can forgive him? Michael, I mean?" she asked, giving his shoulder a squeeze.

"Mom, I have forgiven him. And if he apologizes, I'll accept it. But from now on, he's just one of my brothers, like Brett or George or Billy. He's Two."

His words stung, and she knew deep down by saying them out loud, they stung Brian even more.

Maybe she could help fix their relationship. Time would tell, but she would not let their relationship die without trying.

"Is dad going to be okay, Mom? I mean, *really*, okay?"

Vicky nodded and said, "Yes. The doctors believe he is under stress. I think the stress came from the letters Randy, Bobby, and Danny received. The rest of the stuff blew up because of the letters. He's been suffering from stress. Add in a not-so-great diet and a lack of exercise. This is the result."

She kissed the side of his head and said, "I love your father deeply, Brian. Your father loves me. He loves each of you." She squeezed his shoulder and said, "Yes, Bri, even you."

Brian doubted it.

He thought for a minute and whispered, "Mom, would it help if I moved out? Maybe not permanently, but maybe for a little while? I could live with Jeff and Danny, so I'd be close by. I'd still come by the house and stuff, but maybe it would be better, you know, if I ..."

"No, Bri. If you moved out of the house, it would hurt me. I would miss you too much. Brett and Billy and George would miss you. I think it would hurt Dad more than you or I can imagine. He would blame himself. I think Randy, Bobby, and Michael would blame themselves. If you moved out, our family might never be the same."

Brian sighed, but nodded. He understood. And it was unwinnable.

CHAPTER TEN

"What about looking at staff to see if anyone had any prior dealings with Jeff or Jeremy?" Greg Gonnering asked. He had moved up the ladder quickly, starting as a patrol cop who worked his way to detective. Typically, he and Carlos Lorenzo were partners, just as Eiselmann and O'Connor were partners.

"For Jeremy, that would be the entire staff," Graff answered. "For Jeff, that would be a good portion of the staff." He wagged his head from side to side, and said, "Maybe more, since he still subs there occasionally."

"Besides, the letters aren't aimed at Jeff or Jeremy," Lorenzo said. "They are aimed at the boys."

"Yes," Eiselmann added. "At Randy and Bobby and Danny."

Gonnering, Lorenzo, Eiselmann, O'Connor and Graff sat in the captain's conference room brainstorming ideas to help solve the fan mail case. Normally, a case such as this wouldn't even qualify as a case. It wouldn't have garnered any attention from anyone. This was a unique situation, however.

Jeremy suffering a heart attack was one factor in the decision to look at this deeper. He, Vicky, and their boys suffered too much in too short of time. In any length of time.

The biggest factor was who the letters were sent to. Randy Evans and Bobby McGovern had to deal with far too much for any typical adolescent to deal with, and Danny Limbach was Jeff's son. The clincher was Jeff's celebrity as a best-selling author.

The band was Danny's idea, though he'd be the first to deny the band was his. He saw himself as one piece in the collective, but the other band members saw Danny as the leader based upon his musical genius.

They played covers, but their play list was gradually changing as they wrote more. Their sound was modern country with heavy guitars, laced with a rock and roll bass and keyboard riffs, and a huge dose of tight, intricate harmony. They sounded like no other band or group.

Bits and Pieces played at two fairs in Wisconsin. Their biggest gig was on the Briggs and Stratton stage at the Wisconsin State Fair for an hour and a half after one of the known acts had to cancel because of illness. Graff and Eiselmann brought their families, and O'Connor showed up. About half of the North student body and a good portion of kids from the other high schools showed up, and by the time their concert ended, the area was packed. Two encores later, the show ended.

Their trajectory was sky high.

To the casual observer and listener, Randy and Bobby would be considered the front men of the group. Danny, playing a boatload of instruments and mostly singing harmony, was content to be in the background. However, to the experienced eye and ear, especially those who knew music, Danny was the leader.

Randy or Bobby or both wrote most of the songs, but all of them had Danny's fingerprints on them. He was the producer, along with a high school friend, Garrett Forstadt. Garrett, or G-Man, as they called him, also doubled as their sound man. It was Danny who put together the play list and did the musical arrangements.

Danny played lead guitar, Randy the rhythm guitar, and Bobby doubled on lead guitar and piano when the song called for both piano and organ.

"Why don't the letters mention Sean, Troy, or Chris? The other three members of the band?" Lorenzo asked.

The question silenced Graff and the others causing them to think. It was a fair question.

"I think," O'Connor began and stopped. Thought for a minute and started again. "I think they seldom sing lead."

"Pat's right," Eiselmann said. "Think of any group. Stones. Metallica. AC/DC. The singer is the leader of the band. At least in the eyes of the audience."

"Randy sings lead the most. Bobby sings lead the second most. Randy has the physicality, the looks, and the voice. To anyone who didn't know better, Randy would seem to be the leader," Graff said.

"Paul, what do we know for sure?" Gonnering asked.

"We know the paper is twenty-eight-pound Hammermill. The school orders it by bulk and uses it in all their copiers and printers. It's probably common in every house where there is a computer. The envelopes are number ten regular self-adhesive envelopes. North doesn't use self-adhesive envelopes, so we know whoever sends the letters uses them. The stamps are self-adhesive. We can't get DNA off either, but we got partial latent prints on the paper, envelopes, and stamps. The prints aren't in the system. In anyone's system."

Paul and Skip Dahlke searched several data bases, FBI, and Interpol, and came up empty.

"Until this guy screws up and licks an envelope or stamp, we have squat," Eiselmann added.

"Let's play with Greg's idea of looking at staff who might have grudges against Jeremy or Jeff," Graff said. "Paul, can you interview Jeff and find out who on the staff might be envious, angry, or an asshole with something against him?"

"What about Jeremy?" Paul asked.

"Let's wait on him until he gets back on his feet. I don't want to deal with another heart attack, or worse."

"Um," O'Connor said and then stopped.

The other cops waited for him to finish his thought.

"It might not be someone with a grudge. This person could be a friend. Someone who cares about one or both. Envious, maybe. But someone who cares enough about Jeremy or Jeff to care about their kids. Danny, in particular."

Graff squinted at him, marveling at his insight and how his mind works.

Picking it up from him, Eiselmann said, "A friend who is protective of Danny. Someone who wants what's best for him, but in a fucked-up way."

O'Connor stood up, faced a wall as if it was a window, ran a hand through his long hair and said, "This person might not care about Jeremy or his kids. In fact, he might not like them a great deal or at all. Might see them as getting too much credit or the spotlight."

"Both literally and figuratively," Lorenzo said.

O'Connor nodded. "This person doesn't see it as fair to Danny, the musical genius."

He sat back down and jabbed a finger in the air towards Graff. "Who does the musical solos for band and jazz concerts? Who sometimes conducts the pep band? Who has even arranged music for the choirs and band?"

"Danny," Eiselmann said.

Graff picked it up. "This person wants Danny to get his due. He wants to make sure the spotlight is on Danny, not Randy or Bobby."

"We need to re-interview the boys," Eiselmann said. "Pat, you and I can do it?"

"I want to be involved, with Pat doing more observing. He's the best at that." He turned to O'Connor and said, "Catch facial expressions, their eyes, and their body language to see if a question triggers something."

O'Connor nodded, his mind already six steps ahead.

"When?" Eiselmann asked.

Graff thought it over and said, "In a day or so, but before Jeremy leaves the hospital. We interview the boys first. Then we go at Jeff. We go at Jeremy last, but we make sure Vicky is present."

"I think we need to include the other guys," O'Connor said. "More eyes and ears, the better."

"You may be right," Graff answered, already knowing what O'Connor intended to do and why, and he was okay with it.

It was Gonnering who said, "I can't help but feel we're missing something. Something right in front of us."

"Like what?" Graff asked.

Gonnering shook his head, his mind traveling in different directions at once.

CHAPTER ELEVEN

Vicky tried to prepare the boys for what they were about to see when they visited Jeremy, but Randy and Billy weren't ready. When Vicky led them into the room, Jeremy was in bed, hooked up by wires to every monitor possible. A thin tube, a cannula, ran oxygen directly to his nose. His eyes were closed, and he was pale, if not gray. It was at least a minute before he opened his eyes.

At first, it looked to the twins like he didn't recognize either of them. Then his eyes widened, and he smiled.

"Guys."

His voice was raspy, and he had to clear it twice. Vicky handed him his water, and he sipped it through a straw.

"Guys," he repeated, his voice soft.

Both boys wept, Billy harder than Randy. They had never seen Jeremy like this, and never wanted to see him like this again.

In Randy's mind, Jeremy was larger than life. His hero. Jeremy had saved him from a life no kid should ever have or grow up in. Mentally, Billy superimposed the image of his first father, Robert, dead in the upstairs hallway from a massive heart attack.

The twins were identical. Handsome, muscular, athletic. In terms of personality, Randy was quiet and reserved, gentle. Wise beyond his years. He could look right into someone's eyes and see their heart and soul.

Billy was outgoing, a joker. He was also the family peacemaker. Billy couldn't stand it if one or more of his brothers were angry with another. He did what he could to repair hurt feelings.

They stood a shade under six-three. Randy was the quarterback on the football team. Billy was one of the running backs with Brett, and a starting strong-side safety. He was also the long snapper, with Randy being the holder.

In basketball, Billy was one captain and the small forward. Randy came off the bench as a power forward. Both of them were leaders, not only in athletics, but in the school.

"I look worse than I feel," Jeremy said. "I promise."

He was embarrassed because of passing out at school. Embarrassed at being wheeled away on a gurney, and embarrassed at the ride in the ambulance. He felt weak, and not just because of his heart thingy, as he and Vicky called it. He didn't want the boys or Vicky to see him like this.

The boys looked at him doubtfully.

"Really. I'm going to be okay. I have work to do, and I need to take better care of myself."

He glanced at Vicky and said, "I need to process stress better, and I have to cut down on fatty foods."

"And exercise," Vicky added as she held one of his hands. "Consistently. We need you around for a long time."

Jeremy nodded, shut his eyes for a moment, and smiled at her and the twins.

Recalling the conversation he had with Vicky, he said, "Billy, none of this is your fault. Please believe that."

Billy neither nodded nor spoke. He felt he added to the stress Jeremy felt when he, George, and Brett confronted him the night before.

"I appreciate your honesty, and I appreciate you confronting me last night with Brett and George."

He turned to Randy and said, "Randy, the thing with the fan mail drove me crazy. It still does. I spoke with Jeff and Danny earlier, and they told me you and Bobby were thinking of quitting the band. Please don't. You guys are fantastic. It's like you are a different person when I watch you up on stage."

He turned to Billy and said, "Billy, this isn't like your father, Robert. I'm going to be okay. I don't want you to worry, okay?"

Billy finally nodded.

"Last night, I said some things." He shut his eyes and shook his head. "I was way out of bounds and inappropriate. I will make it up to you. To all of you."

Vicky stepped up between both boys, put her arms around their shoulders, and said, "Guys, I don't want your father to tire out before he speaks to the other guys. We'll have more time tomorrow after your basketball practice."

They struggled to give Jeremy a hug, being careful not to disturb the wires and electrodes, the IV, and the finger monitor the doctors and nurses hooked him up to.

"I love you guys," Jeremy said. There were tears in his eyes.

Both Randy and Billy started weeping again. They left quietly, with Randy turning around for another look. Jeremy lifted his hand in a small wave.

"I'll be back with Brett and Bobby," Vicky said as she followed the twins out the door.

Brett and Bobby looked similar to each other. When they were younger, they looked like twins, though Brett was eighteen months older than Bobby. People joked they looked like mini–Tom Bradys without the cleft chin. But as they got older, they lost some of that similarity.

Their hair and eyes were the same color as the twins. Brett had his styled the same as Randy and Billy, but Bobby let his hair grow out. It was the same length as Brian's, and not nearly as long as George's or Two's that hung down beyond their shoulders. Jeremy had joked that Bobby and Brian were two of the lesser known Beatles.

Their looks and dark complexion came from Vicky's side of the family, though Bobby's soft features came from his father, Thomas.

At six-one, Bobby stood an inch taller than Brett. Both boys were wicked smart and they could accurately be called brilliant. Brett was better at math and science, while Bobby was better at English and music. Both took an online Italian course for credit as one of their electives.

The conversation mirrored Jeremy's conversation with Randy and Billy. He reassured Brett that he had done nothing wrong. He thanked Brett for his honesty and for confronting him the previous night. He told Bobby exactly what he had told Randy.

"I'm going to be okay. Honest. I have to make sure I lay off the sweets and eat more salad, but I'm going to be okay."

Brett nodded. He had an arm slung around Bobby's shoulders. Bobby struggled to keep his emotions in check. He neither agreed nor disagreed with Jeremy.

Finally, Bobby said, "What if Randy and I don't quit, but take a break from the band? For a little while."

Jeremy shook his head and said, "I trust Jamie, Pat, and Paul. Those three cops are my friends. They're your friends, and they care a great deal about you. Let them do their cop thing. Right now, there is no need for either of you to quit or take a break."

Vicky noticed the numbers on the heart monitor jump. Not much, but enough for an alarm to go off. A nurse came into the room, read the monitor, checked the paper printout that looked like a slip from a grocery checkout, and turned off the alarm.

She glanced at Vicky and then left the room. The message in the nurse's prolonged eye contact was, *'Don't let him get too excited.'*

The medical team had been battling Jeremy's blood pressure all morning and into the early afternoon. It had been bouncing all over the place, no matter what the team had done. Currently, it was higher than they would like it to be, but steady.

Brett and Bobby left, and in came George and Two. Vicky thought about bringing Brian in with them, but decided not to because she knew Jeremy had too much to say to him. She felt Jeremy and Brian needed time alone. Brian appeared to be hurt by her decision, but she would explain it to him the first opportunity she had.

George and Brian were the quietest of the boys. George had an uncanny ability to *know* things before anyone else. Jeremy and Vicky referred to it as his *Navajo thing*. George and Two were full-blooded Navajo, born and raised in Arizona on the Navajo Nation Reservation. They were step-brothers, same father, different mother. Neither knew the other existed, or if they did, did not know they were related, much less step-brothers.

It was at the end of July when George, Brett, and Brian had traveled to Arizona to help find a missing childhood friend of George. By chance, George and Two met. Two, or Michael Two Feathers, came to live with George and the rest of the boys, since the man he had been staying with was in jail, and his mother had died of a drug overdose. The plan was for him to be adopted by Jeremy and Vicky.

Jeremy repeated to George what he had told both Billy and Brett. They had done nothing wrong, and he thanked him for his honesty and for confronting his behavior. In a typical manner, George never gave away what he was thinking, but he nodded respectfully. Neither Vicky nor Jeremy knew what he was thinking.

Jeremy turned to Two and said, "Two, I'm so very sorry for what I said to you and Brian. I was out of line. I had no right to question your relationship with Brian. It was wrong of me."

Unconvinced, Two stared at the floor, but nodded.

"You and Brian have a wonderful relationship. I hope I didn't damage it. If I did, I would like to help fix it. If you'll let me."

Two couldn't make eye contact with Jeremy. He dared not look at him. He was both sad and angry. Staring at the floor, he said, "You think I'm gay."

"No, Two, I don't."

"Yes, you do."

George placed a hand on Two's shoulder to get him to back off.

"No ... I ... I'm sorry," Jeremy said.

He swiped at his forehead. He shut his eyes and shook his head. He glanced at Vicky for support.

"It isn't like that. I didn't mean that. I," he searched for the right word, for any word. Nothing came to him.

He shook his head, unable to think properly.

Angry, Two raised his voice, pointed at Jeremy, and said, "Brian and I never did anything. I never even thought about doing anything with Brian. Brian never thought about doing anything with me."

Alarms went off. Jeremy shut his eyes, shook his head, and wiped perspiration off his forehead and upper lip.

He gave up. It had not gone the way he had wanted. He had hoped to mend fences, and he only made a mess.

Two nurses ran into the room with a doctor trailing behind them. Vicky ushered the boys out, telling them she would meet with all of them in the waiting area after they had Jeremy stabilized.

Two said, "It's my fault, isn't it?"

Torn between wanting to be with Jeremy and wanting to comfort and reassure Two, she gave him a hug, kissed his forehead, and said, "No, Two, it isn't. Your father has been struggling like this all day. It's not you. It's his heart."

George pulled Two away, and Vicky ran back into the room.

CHAPTER TWELVE

The boys had been weeping or crying, even sobbing in Billy's and Two's case, and Brian had enough. He wasn't sure what he should say, but knew something had to be said.

"Guys, come here." He waited until they gathered around him. "This isn't helping dad, and it's not helping mom."

Brian had his arms around Billy and Brett. All the guys, including Danny, stood in a tight circle in the waiting area. Jeff stood behind them, but in a position where he could see Brian's face and hear what was being said.

It was difficult to put his own hurt feelings on a shelf and concentrate on his brothers. As much as it hurt to be excluded from seeing Jeremy, Brian knew there were others suffering more than he was.

"Mom and Jeff both said Dad will have problems until the doctors get his blood pressure under control. But he will not die."

The guys nodded.

"Dad's being taken care of. We've got to take care of mom. We have to."

The boys nodded again.

"Randy and Bobby, you heard dad, mom, and Jeff tell you not to quit the band. Danny doesn't want you to quit, either. None of us do." He looked around the circle and said, "Right?"

Brett, George, Billy, and Two nodded.

"You guys are too good."

"Way good," Brett said.

"There are a couple of other things I need to say." Catching their eye, he said, "Brett, Billy, and George, I appreciate you sticking up for me last night. You didn't do anything wrong. What you did took guts."

He paused, turned to Randy, and said, "I said this already, but I'm sorry for jumping on you this morning. I was rude."

As hurt as he felt, and as much as he didn't want to, he looked at Two and said, "Two, same with you. I'm sorry."

Two stared at the floor and wept.

To all of them, he said, "The thing is, we've got to get it together for mom when she comes out here, because she can't see us like this. She can't worry about both dad and us. So, do what you have to do, but get it together. Okay?"

The guys nodded.

Brian took Randy by the shoulders and said, "Are you okay?"

Randy had trouble making eye contact, but nodded and said, "I was an ass this morning, Bri. I don't even know why I said what I did. I know you'd never look at porn."

"We're good, Randy. Honest."

"And I'm sorry for what I said last night about Two having to settle for you. It came out wrong."

Brian smiled, shook Randy's shoulders a little, and said, "I already told you we're good. I know that's not what you meant. You had a crap-ton of homework. Okay?"

Randy stared at Brian, tried on a smile, and said, "You know I love you, right? We all do. Seriously. We all do."

"Of course, I know that." Brian smiled and said, "But I need to remind you we're closer than three feet and I'm touching you, so you might catch my germs."

Randy laughed and said, "You're a shit."

They embraced for a long time. Brian said, "I love you, Randy. Always have. I know I don't spend as much time with you as I do with some of the others, and that's on me. I will work on it. I love you, though."

Randy nodded and said, "I love you, too."

The circle broke up. Jeff did more pacing than sitting. Brian sat down between Brett and George, facing Randy, Danny, and Bobby. The three of them whispered. Heads nodded. There was a smile or two. A chuckle here and there. Of the three, Randy was the most serious, while Bobby was the quietest, doing more listening than anything else.

Two sat next to George, and Billy sat next to Brett. They sat in silence. Some scrolled on their phones. Others texted. Billy and Two did neither. They sat and stared.

Brian worried about Billy and what Billy was feeling. He and Randy were the closest to Jeremy. Understandably so. They were his first sons.

Brian took out his cell and texted an update to the assistant principal, Bob Farner, to Coach Harrison, and to the Butler Middle School principal, Mark Wegner. Then he sent a longer text to O'Connor, Eiselmann, and Graff. He answered a few texts from friends wanting an update. It felt like half the school had texted him. He only bothered to respond to those he and his brothers were close to.

In most of the texts, he was fairly short and rather vanilla. Enough to get the facts to them with little detail. He felt his mom and dad would appreciate it. For as outgoing as both of them were, there was also a private side they wanted to keep.

Brett leaned over and said, "I'm sorry you didn't get to talk to dad. I know it hurt."

Initially, Brian had been upset. One more example of him being left out. But in truth, he wasn't ready to face Jeremy, especially alone, with or without Vicky in the room, and he knew he wasn't ready for what George and Two had witnessed. He didn't know how he'd react.

In answer to Brett, he said, "I'm okay."

Brett glanced at him, and then at George, who heard the question and the answer. There was a finality in Brian's response neither Brett nor George would question.

Two leaned forward, past George two or three times, to look at Brian. Brian saw it, didn't acknowledge it, and did nothing to encourage a conversation between the two of them. Brian also noticed Bobby glancing at him. Different reasons than Two. Yet, the reasons were similar to an extent. Brian reacted the same way towards Bobby as he did towards Two.

It was later afternoon when Vicky walked into the waiting area. The dark circles and worry lines around her eyes were more pronounced. Exhausted, her shoulders sagged, and she seemed smaller.

The boys stood up, eager to hear what was happening with their father. Brian was the last to stand and when he did, it was towards the back of the group next to Jeff. Jeff placed an arm around his shoulders and gave him a squeeze.

"Guys, your dad is finally stable. For now. He's resting comfortably, and he looked like he might doze off. He's sedated, but with nothing that would interfere with his heart function."

She glanced around the circle at the boys, expecting questions. Nothing came, so she said, "I'm going to spend the night here. Jeff, I know it's asking a lot, but can you stay with the boys tonight, and maybe bring me some fresh clothes in the morning?"

"Of course, Vicky. Happy to," Jeff said, nodding.

"Brett, can you and Bobby gather some things together for Jeff and put them into a small suitcase? Slacks, a blouse, socks and other things. I'll need my toothbrush, toothpaste, and deodorant. Maybe some shampoo."

"Yes, Mom," Brett said.

"Guys, I want to make sure you understand nothing has changed since this morning. Your dad will not die. As I said, it's stress. He's going to have to make some changes in his diet, and he's going to have to exercise regularly."

She let it sink in, turned to Two and said, "Michael, no matter what you think, you didn't cause your father's reaction. What happened was your father's heart and his blood pressure. He got agitated during Randy and Billy's visit, and a little more during Bobby's and Brett's visit. It was what I had worried about and what I thought might happen. But your father wanted to see each of you." She made a face and shrugged.

She turned to Brian and said, "Brian, I purposely held you back because I knew your father would have a tough time speaking to you. I'm sorry, but I felt it was best."

Head down, no eye contact, Brian nodded. He felt Jeff squeeze his shoulder.

"We'll see how he's doing tomorrow, and after basketball practice, if he's stable, you'll be the first to see him. Okay?"

Brian sighed and said, "Mom, it's okay. I would rather wait until he's fully recovered. I don't want anything to go wrong. And I'd want one of the guys with me. Brett or George or Billy. I don't want to go in by myself."

Tears filled Vicky's eyes. She glanced at Jeff and then back at Brian and said, "I would be with you."

"I know, but I'd want one of the guys with me, too."

She nodded and said, "Well, okay. We'll see what happens tomorrow."

Brett said, "Mom, you'll text us tonight and tomorrow to let us know what's happening?"

"Of course. I'll keep you all posted."

Jeff said, "Guys, why don't we go get something to eat, and then we'll stop by school and pick up your dad's car." He glanced around at the boys and decided Brett might be the most together, besides Brian, and said, "Brett, can you drive your dad's car back to your house?"

"Sure. No problem."

Brian said, "I'll text Coach Harrison and Mr. Farner and ask them to have dad's key fob handy. I'll have them look around his office to see if there's anything Dad might want at home or here in the hospital, but Brett, double-check once you get there."

Vicky smiled and said, "Thank you, Bri."

"Mom, you need to eat something," Randy said.

Vicky hadn't eaten anything all day. Once she got the call, she dressed hastily, jumped in her car, and drove straight to the hospital. She was more thirsty than hungry, but she knew she needed to eat something.

"I can go to the cafeteria and get you something," Bobby offered.

She nodded and said, "Something light. A sandwich and some fruit, maybe. Water and coffee."

Bobby turned to Brian and said, "Bri, do you want to go with me?"

"I think I'll text an update to everyone, and make sure Mr. Farner and Coach Harrison have dad's car and stuff ready."

Bobby looked disheartened, but nodded with a brave smile on his face. He'd try again when they got home.

"I'll go with you," Danny volunteered.

Vicky watched the interaction between Brian and Bobby. She would have more fixing to do. Brian and Bobby. Brian and Michael. Getting Jeremy healthy.

She took a deep breath, shook her head. For the time being, she knew she would have to shoulder the load with parenting. It was nothing new. Nothing she hadn't done during the last years of her marriage with Thomas. Nothing she hadn't done since her move to Waukesha before becoming involved with Jeremy.

Vicky loved her life. She loved her boys- all of them, not just Brett and Bobby.

Some months previously, she had a long talk with Bobby about his being gay, his feelings and his thoughts, and his relationship with Brian. She felt she understood what Bobby and Brian had been going through.

She had started a similar conversation with Brian, who said basically the same things, though she knew Brian was more guarded and less open than Bobby. Vicky still couldn't understand how Brian could be attracted to both girls and boys. Brian couldn't explain it, either. He had talked about his relationship with Cat, and he had talked about his relationship with Mikey, but he said little about his relationship with Bobby.

Vicky thought over the conversation she had with Brian in the chapel. She didn't know if it was going to be possible to end the sexual relationship with Bobby, because she knew their love for each other ran deep.

Vicky sighed. She and Jeremy were in a lose-lose situation. She could not and would not encourage their sexual relationship, but she also knew she couldn't discourage it, either. That would cause her relationship with Brian to disintegrate completely. She knew her relationship with him was vapor thin, especially after her decision to keep him from seeing Jeremy. It was probably a bigger set back than she first believed it was.

Just as Brian's relationship with Two was unique in its way, Brian's relationship with Bobby was even more so. Their friendship was beautiful, and she wanted it to last, just as she wanted Brian's relationship to last with Two.

If she wanted those relationships to continue, and she knew she did, she knew she had work to do. She was determined to find a way.

CHAPTER THIRTEEN

He had hesitated too long. George, Billy, and Brett climbed into Brian's truck, leaving him to ride in Jeff's with Danny, Randy, and Bobby. Two knew he had screwed up and hurt Brian. He wanted to fix it, but he didn't know how. He also didn't know if Brian would allow him to.

About halfway to school, Brett said, "I've been thinking about those letters Randy, Bobby, and Danny have been getting. We heard Graff and Eiselmann. Right now, the letters are just rude and obnoxious. I think we need to prepare for when they become more than that."

"I was thinking about that, too." Brian said. "I think one of us needs to be with them at all times." He glanced at Billy through the rearview mirror and said, "Billy, that goes for you, too, because you and Randy are twins. You shouldn't be by yourself."

"I'm hardly by myself, anyway. I'm usually with you guys." To Brett he said, "What were you thinking?"

Brett turned around and faced the back, holding his cell out in front of him.

"I found this app. It's a GPS locator. Parents use it for their kids and for their elderly parents. You've seen the commercial, maybe."

Billy shrugged, and George remained neutral.

"Okay, maybe you haven't seen it. Anyway, I looked it up and if we link our phones to one another, we'll know who is where all the time. Phones have to be on, and then all we have to do is activate the locator. It will lead us right to the person we're looking for."

"How will that help?" Billy asked.

Brian nodded and said, "Let's say the three of them go to a movie. Something happens. If they have their phone on, we can find them." He turned to Brett and asked, "That's what you're thinking, right?"

"Exactly."

"But one or more of us are usually with them," Billy pointed out.

"Yes, and we'll know right where everyone is all the time," Brett said.

George, who had remained silent but interested throughout the exchange, said, "We know whoever is sending the letters works at the school. The letters are personal to Danny, Randy, and Billy. That means the person knows them."

Brett nodded and said, "That's what Graff said."

"So, we need to watch and listen to everyone around us," George said. "Especially them."

"Teachers and staff, right?" Billy asked.

"Yes," Brian said.

George wasn't so sure. He said, "Maybe a student. We do not know for sure."

"I hadn't thought of that," Brett said. "Do we tell Randy, Bobby, and Danny?"

"Yes, I think so," George said. "And our phones will have to be on during school." He thought it over and said, "As a precaution."

"We'll have to clear it with Farner because of the no cell phone use in school rule," Brian said.

"I think under the circumstances, it shouldn't be hard to do," Brett answered.

"How much do they know? Mr. Farner and the school, I mean?" George asked.

The guys looked from one to the other. As far as they knew, nothing.

"Maybe dad mentioned it to someone. Farner or Harrison or someone," Brett said.

Brian thought for a minute and said, "I'll talk to Farner tomorrow. I'll find out what he knows. I'll talk to him about the phones. I'm pretty sure it will be okay."

"So, we agree we might try this thing?" Brett said.

George shrugged, then nodded.

Billy said, "It can't hurt."

"At least it's something," Brian added.

CHAPTER FOURTEEN

With dinner over, the boys dug into homework, if they had any. Jeff walked to his and Danny's house to take care of some chores and pick up their mail. Danny and Brett seldom had homework, and what little they had, they did at school. They sat at the kitchen table, helping the others. Finally, Brett got up and went to pack up some clothes and things for Vicky.

Danny knew his way around the Evans house as well as he did his own. Little things like where the glasses, plates, and silverware were located. Bigger things like knowing Brian, Bobby, Randy, and Two showered at night, while everyone else showered in the morning, and who slept with whom and where. Much of it was one of the great unknowns circling the universe of the Evans family.

Danny knew Bobby's preference was to sleep with Brian. Looking out the window in the door, he watched the two boys. They spent almost an hour talking in whispers on the back steps. He watched both wipe their eyes. Danny didn't think they would sleep together for a long time, if ever again.

Bobby came in first. Billy, George, and Two looked up and watched him cut through the kitchen, saying nothing to anyone. After he left, they went back to their homework, huddled around textbooks, notebooks, or laptops. Danny bet their minds were not on their work, however.

Danny heard Bobby climb the stairs to the bedrooms. He knew he and Randy would eventually find out what had taken place. Brian hadn't moved. He sat alone on the back step, shoulders hunched, elbows on his knees, head in his hands, and his fingers in his long black hair. Danny didn't know how long he'd be out there. He wanted to sit with him, but didn't know if he'd be welcome.

Not knowing what to do, Danny made his way up to Randy's bedroom and found him on his bed, on his back, hands under his head, staring at the ceiling fan. He didn't want to disturb him, so he stood in the doorway.

It was Randy who spoke. "Come in."

It wasn't the friendliest or warmest greeting he ever received, but given all that had transpired during day, he'd take it.

"I was just wondering where I'm sleeping tonight," Danny said as he shifted from one foot to the other.

"I think with Two in Brian's room."

Danny nodded and then said, "What about Bobby?"

"I think with me. He'll want to talk."

Randy had never looked at him.

"I think I'm going to shower tonight. Is that okay?"

"You know where the towels and stuff are, right? There's soap and shampoo in the tub."

Danny fished out a t-shirt and pajama pants from his duffle bag, started out of the room, but sat down on the bed next to Randy.

He said nothing.

"What?" Randy asked. Not angry, or even a bothered way. More out of curiosity.

"I'm just wondering how screwed up everyone is. You are."

Randy sighed. "I don't know. Really. We've never been through something like this. Dad, I mean. And then, throw in Brian and Bobby and Two. Who knows," this last he said almost in a whisper.

Danny's experience with a messed up family was his own. But by comparison, the two were different. His parents had divorced, and his mom lived in Omaha. He saw her on some holidays and part of the summer, but it was difficult. When he was with his dad, he missed his mom. When he was with his mom, he missed his dad. To lose either permanently, well, he didn't want to go there. While his situation differed from the guys, the feelings were similar.

He had lived with his father because Waukesha was where his friends were. In Omaha, he never had many. He never went to other guys' homes or hung out with anyone. He had been alone and lonely. It was far different in Waukesha.

Danny had grown, but was still on the small side. He had his mom's features and coloring, including her hair. His friends had debated the color. Depending upon how the sun hit it, his hair could be blond, brown, or reddish-blond. The only thing his father could claim was Danny's eyes, which were a piercing blue. Perhaps his smile, which Danny seemed to wear constantly.

"Are you going to be okay?" Danny asked.

At first, Randy didn't respond. Danny waited patiently, knowing Randy would process his question slowly, and only then answer. This is exactly what he did.

Randy rolled over to his side to face Danny, his head propped up by his pillow.

He spoke, shook his head, and started over. "Everything is messed up right now. Dad is in the hospital. Bri and Bobby are messed up. Bri and Two are messed up. Mom is worried about Dad, and probably about Bri, Bobby, and Two."

He stopped, looked directly at Danny, and asked, "How did all this crap happen? All at once? Damn!"

Danny shrugged and said, "I don't have an answer for you."

"I don't either. No one does, and it frustrates the hell out of me."

Randy scrunched up his face, pulled his mouth into a side frown, glared at the wall, and then asked, "Where is Bobby?"

Danny glanced at the open door, turned back, and said, "In his room, I think. His door is shut. Brett might be with him."

"Where is Brian?"

"When I left the kitchen, he was still outside sitting on the back step. He looked messed up."

"And Two?"

"In the kitchen doing homework with Billy and George."

"Two and Brian haven't talked yet?"

Danny puffed up his cheeks, shook his head, let the air out of his mouth, and said, "I don't think so. Bri spent most of the time with Bobby."

"Where's your dad?"

"He went to our house to do some stuff," he shrugged, "and he said he was going to get our mail."

Randy shut his eyes, sighed, and said, "Has anyone gotten our mail yet?"

"I ... I don't know."

"Crap!"

Randy got off the bed and headed out of his room. Danny knew where he was headed and didn't follow.

Danny watched Randy knock on Bobby's bedroom door. No one answered, so Randy stood in the hallway outside the closed door until he reluctantly walked down the stairs. Danny went to shower.

In the kitchen, Randy said, "Did anyone get the mail yet?"

The boys looked from one to the other and then shook their heads.

As Randy headed out the backdoor, Brian walked through. Brian's eyes were puffy and red. His shoulders sagged and his fingers were in his front pockets. They eyed each other cautiously.

Randy cocked his head, put a hand on Brian's shoulder, and said, "Wanna talk?"

Brian tried to smile, failed miserably, and said, "Not now."

"I'm going to go get the mail. We can talk when I get back."

"Maybe."

George spoke up and said, "Randy, you need rubber gloves, you know, in case ..."

Everyone knew what George meant.

CHAPTER FIFTEEN

Jeff saw the letter in the mailbox mixed in with flyers for a new roof, an urgent letter to get a car warranty before it was too late, and the propane bill.

Jeff sighed. He, as much as anyone, especially Vicky and Jeremy, wanted it to end. He also knew, without asking, that similar letters addressed to Randy and Bobby were in the Evans' mailbox mixed in with whatever mail or crap they had received. In his mind, the letters were somewhere below the car warranty advertisement, but somewhere above pond scum, though that was debatable.

Jeff had phoned Graff, who then phoned O'Connor and Eiselmann. Depending upon whose point of view, it was a fortunate opportunity that presented itself. In Graff's mind, it worked to his advantage to interview the boys that evening. In Jeff's mind, it only dumped more crap on an already shitty day.

It took thirty minutes for the three cops to arrive at the Evans house and sit down at the kitchen table with Jeff and the boys.

Without comment, Eiselmann used latex gloves and picked up each letter, still sealed in their unopened envelopes, and placed them in clear plastic evidence bags. The boys watched him with anxiety or disgust, depending upon whose face Graff and O'Connor looked at.

Eiselmann sealed the bags and made a note on each, as required, to secure a chain of evidence. Because the letters were unopened, he didn't know if the letters were derogatory, but no one wanted to take the chance.

They would be opened, read, and analyzed, and, if necessary, forwarded to Dahlke in Quantico for processing. If they were favorable fan mail, they would return the letters. If they weren't, the letters would be held onto. The undesirable ones may or may not be shared, depending on the content.

He then pulled up the spreadsheet noting the dates the various letters were received and postal locations from where the letters were sent. Like several others, these were postmarked from New Berlin, one county over to the east and south. With the letters noted and tucked away for safekeeping, he fired up the Word application, ready to take notes.

The boys looked worn out. Danny and Randy were dressed for bed, and their hair was still damp. Bobby and Brian looked like they hadn't slept in weeks. Two was anxious and jumpy. His eyes darted from the cops to Brian and back again, and his legs bounced rapid-fire under the table. Only Brett, Billy, and George remained, at least on the surface, calm and composed. Graff knew those boys didn't show what was churning on the inside. There was no sign on their faces or in their body language. But O'Connor watched them. He was better at reading the kids than he was.

Brian sat next to Bobby, even though it was uncomfortable for both of them. He, Bobby, Randy, and Danny sat on one side of the table, facing Brett, George, Billy, and Two on the other. Graff sat at the head of the table where Vicky normally sat, with Brian on his right and Brett on his left.

Jeff preferred to stand. He leaned against the kitchen counter near the sink with his arms folded and a mug of lukewarm coffee nearby.

Eiselmann sat at the end of the table across from Graff, while O'Connor leaned against the refrigerator so he could observe each boy. Graff had planned their positions on the ride over.

The four dogs looked to be sentries. Papa lay down at Brian's side. Momma lay in the hallway doorway. Jasper lay in the dining room doorway, and Jazmine lay next to George.

"Guys, we've already interviewed Randy, Danny, and Bobby, but we thought it would be helpful to interview all of you together. Just in case we missed something."

The boys didn't react, and Graff wasn't surprised.

He said, "I want to explore a couple of lines of thinking with you. First, I want to ask a question and before anyone answers, I want you to think it through. Okay?"

The boys nodded or shifted to a more relaxed position.

"I want you to think about anyone who might not like Danny, Randy, or Bobby. Someone who might have said something derogatory or mean about one of them. Someone who might have done something to them, ranging from questionable to more deliberate, or something that was uncalled for or unexpected."

"Anyone?" Randy asked. "Including teachers?"

"Yes, students, teachers, or staff members."

"He's not here anymore, but Dildo didn't want to give Danny any grade higher than a C on his English papers," Billy said.

"Dildo?" Eiselmann asked.

"Mr. Diddico," Randy said. "He got canned or resigned after Danny recorded him talking about it."

"When was that?" Eiselmann asked.

"Last year," Danny said. "I don't know what he's doing now."

Curious, Graff said, "Tell me about it."

"It's no big deal," Danny said. "He was my English teacher. There were a couple of things, comments he'd make about me, but not using my name. Things he'd say about dad, but not using his name. Everyone knew who he was talking about. It was uncomfortable. The big thing was he gave me a C- on a paper. I had never gotten anything lower than an A. I asked him why, and he said it was just as trashy as my dad's books. I wrote another paper, and this time, I had my phone on and recorded him. I asked him why I got a D+, and he said, 'You will *never* get anything higher than a C from me, so don't plan on it. You're used to getting things handed to you on a silver platter. That will never happen in my class.' I asked him why, and he said, 'To teach you and your father a lesson. Your work is as trashy as your father's. He writes shit that should never be published. Your work is just as shitty. Evidently, the old saying is true. The apple doesn't fall far from the tree.' I took the recording to Jeremy, and he took it to Farner or someone, and Diddico resigned or got canned."

"You also recorded stuff he said in class, too," Randy added.

"Yeah, he'd bag on dad and me without saying our names."

"When was this?" Graff asked again.

"Last fall. Honors English."

Graff furrowed his brow, cocked his head, and stared at Jeff to elaborate.

Jeff gave him a *whatever* look and said, "They hired him after I had already left. I never knew the guy. I had heard he wanted to write, so when I subbed, I'd stop in and chat with him, and he dismissed me. Said he didn't want or need my help, so I stopped trying. That was the end of it until Danny had him as a teacher."

"Did any other of you guys have him as a teacher?" Graff asked.

The boys murmured they didn't, and Billy said, "We had some friends who did. Troy and Van Boxtel hated him."

To Jeff, Eiselmann asked, "Any idea what he's doing now?"

Jeff shook his head and said, "No idea."

To Eiselmann, Graff said, "We'll look him up."

Graff checked his notes and said, "Anyone else you can think of? Any students who might not like Randy, Bobby, or Danny?"

The boys looked from one to the other, shook their heads, but otherwise, didn't respond.

O'Connor caught Brian frowning. "Bri, what are you thinking?" he asked.

Brian made a face, pulled on his earlobe and said, "I don't understand how this is helping. We should look at anyone who likes Danny, but doesn't like Randy or Bobby. But everyone likes Randy and Bobby."

"Everyone?" Eiselmann said.

"Yeah, pretty much," Brian said. "Are some people jealous of Randy because he was the quarterback? Sure, probably. Are some jealous because of Randy's or Bobby's singing or Bobby's poetry? More than likely. But I don't know anyone who would send stupid letters to them or to Danny. Everyone loves Danny. He's everybody's little brother."

The others nodded in agreement, except for Randy, Bobby, and Danny.

"What you're saying is that there is no one in the school, teacher, staff member or student who doesn't like Randy, Bobby, and Danny," Eiselmann said.

Brian shook his head and said, "That's not exactly what I said. There might be someone who is jealous, but I don't think anyone is jealous enough to start a letter-writing campaign."

Randy leaned forward and said, "Are there students who like Danny better than Bobby or me? Probably because everyone likes Danny, but not everyone likes Bobby or me."

"Why?" O'Connor asked.

Randy puffed up his cheeks and then let the air out as he shook his head. "Like Brian said, I sing a lot of solos. I'm the sophomore class president, and I'm in a couple of clubs, and I was the quarterback and got all-conference. I play basketball and baseball. Bobby plays football and now basketball. He got an all-conference as a receiver as a freshman. That's a big deal. He and Sean play piano for the choir concerts. Some students might be jealous."

Graff nodded and said, "Okay, let's go this route. What students like Danny enough to think he might not be receiving the credit he deserves for his ability in music or with the band?"

Billy stifled a laugh and said, "There's this girl."

Danny turned beat red and said, "I know what you're going to say, but she's just different."

"Who?" Graff asked.

"Her name is Nada. She's always bringing him homemade cookies or stuff. He doesn't eat much of it and gives it away," Billy said.

"To you, mostly," Randy said.

"She's harmless," Danny said. "She's just awkward."

"She doesn't have social skills," Brett said. "She might be special ed, maybe." This last he said with a shrug.

"Do you know her last name?" Eiselmann asked.

The boys looked from one to the other, and finally Danny spoke up and said, "Nada Sherry."

"How did she meet you?" Eiselmann asked.

Danny chuckled and said, "I have no idea. I don't have her in any classes. She must have seen me in the hallway or something. Maybe at a concert or pep rally or something."

"She's harmless," Brett said.

"I don't think she has any friends," Randy said. "Kind of sad."

"You haven't done anything to lead her on? Make her think you are a friend of hers?" Graff asked.

Billy laughed and then said, "Sorry." He covered his mouth with the back of his hand.

"No," Danny said as he shook his head. "No way."

"Because ..." O'Connor said.

"She's weird," Danny answered.

"Okay, so we have one weird girl with no friends who brings Danny cookies," Graff said. "Anyone else?"

"There's this girl in chorus. Maryanne Sturgis," Bobby said.

"What has she done?" Danny asked.

Brett laughed and said, "Danny, you're about as aware of stuff like that as Brian is."

The boys laughed, and Brian protested and said, "Hey! I'm aware."

"Uh, huh. Sure," Billy said.

"I'm aware!" Brian repeated, this time turning red.

"Seriously, dude!" Brett said, causing everyone to laugh, even Brian.

"You've got to admit I'm getting better."

"You couldn't get any worse," George said.

"We're talking about Danny, not me," Brian said as he laughed along with everyone.

"Okay, okay," Graff said as he tried to regain some order. "So far, we've established that a weird girl brings Danny cookies; a girl in chorus has a crush on Danny; and Danny and Brian are oblivious to anyone who has a crush on them."

The boys and cops laughed, even Brian.

"Hey! No one used the word oblivious," Brian protested.

"We were being polite," Brett said. "But figuring out if someone likes you, you are oblivious."

"You've got to admit I'm better than Brian," Danny said with a laugh.

Billy pretended to cough into his hand and muttered, "Bullshit," and everyone laughed.

Graff said, "Bobby, tell me about this kid in chorus."

Bobby frowned, sat back in his chair, and said, "I don't know how to explain it. It's like if Danny said the room is purple, she would not only agree with him, but add it is a dark purple. If he said something about the sopranos being flat or sharp, she would agree with him and point out where it was coming from. She's always quick to say his hair looks nice or his shirt matches his eyes. Stuff like that. Little stuff, but ..." he shrugged.

"So, this Maryanne Sturgis wants to make out with Danny," Graff said with only a slightly straight face.

"Oh, come on!" Danny protested, but laughed along with everyone else.

"Is there anyone else?" Graff asked.

The boys settled down, thought about it, and it was George who spoke up.

"There's this boy." He turned to his brothers and said, "You've seen him. I don't know him, and I don't know his name. But he is around us."

"Describe him," Brian said.

To Brian, George said, "About my height, but your build. Short blond hair. Brown eyes. He dresses like Danny."

"Kind of preppy," Randy said.

Danny looked at him questioningly, and Randy said, "It's not a bad thing. Bri, Brett, and Bobby dress like that sometimes, too."

"What does this kid do?" O'Connor asked.

George frowned, thought for a minute, and said, "Nothing. I see him glancing at Danny now and then. Not quite stares at him, but maybe more than a glance. He'll look at Randy and Bobby, too, but not in the same way."

"Where does he do this?" Danny asked.

"Before school in the cafeteria. He sits a couple of tables away, usually by himself. Then at lunch. Same thing. A couple of tables away, but there will be other kids with him, but *not* with him."

Brett said, "At the same table, but he isn't a part of the group."

"Yes, like that."

Eiselmann asked, "Does he ever talk to Danny or to any of you?"

"I don't know who he's talking about," Randy said.

Billy and Brett agreed with Randy.

"I've never seen him talk to any of us. He only looks at us, mostly at Danny. Sometimes at Randy and Bobby," George said.

"Okay, don't take this wrong," Graff said, "but could this kid be gay? Maybe interested in Danny?"

Brian leaned forward, and Papa raised his head. Brian said, "Why would he have to be gay to be interested in Danny? Or Randy or Bobby?" He answered his own question by saying, "Maybe he's lonely and wants to be friends with Danny or with us. He wouldn't have to be gay."

There was frustration in Brian's comment. Everyone picked up on it, especially Graff.

O'Connor said, "No, he wouldn't have to be gay. I don't think Jamie meant that."

"But that's the word he used," Brian said. "But he doesn't have to be gay."

"You're right. He wouldn't have to be gay. He just might be a kid who is interested in being a part of the group, a friend of Danny's," Graff said. "I misspoke and I'm sorry if I offended you or anyone else."

Brett said to George, "But you don't know his name, and you don't think he ever talked to Danny or to us."

George nodded and said, "Yes, that's right."

"Tomorrow, can you point him out to us without him noticing?" Randy asked.

"Yes, I can."

"If you can, find out his name and text me," Eiselmann said.

Randy leaned forward and said, "I don't feel right pointing out a kid who doesn't have friends and who seems lonely. I don't like any of this."

Graff leaned forward and said, "I understand how you feel. We're not going to throw any of these kids in a locked room, turn on bright lights, and grill them. We want to find out a little more about each of them. That's all."

"Mostly, now we have a starting place, and *you* have a starting place," O'Connor said. "Be alert. Watch. Listen. You are in better positions than we are. I think the person responsible for the letters might not be dangerous. I think ..." he paused, ran a hand through his long hair, and said, "using someone's words, awkward, perhaps. Not a lot of social skills. Watch and listen. Let us know. If you hear someone saying some of the same stuff in the letters, it could be important. Let us know."

"It's getting late, and I think we did all we can do tonight," Graff said. "Bri, I didn't mean to offend you or anyone else. I'm sorry."

Brian shrugged noncommittally and said, "No big deal. We're good."

Jamie stood, and Eiselmann turned off and packed up his laptop. George stopped them.

"May I ask a question?"

"Sure. What?" Graff said.

"About a month ago, there was an explosion in the stadium parking lot. It was after the conference championship. Brian and the guys won on PKs and were walking off the field when the explosions occurred. Three of them."

Graff nodded, and O'Connor placed a hand on Eiselmann's shoulder.

"You investigated it."

Graff said, "We had a hand in it, but the FBI, out of Milwaukee, did most of it, especially the crime scene forensics."

"Jeff's car was totaled."

"Along with two others," Eiselmann said. "It was determined the car next to Jeff's started the explosions. Like dominoes."

"Yes, I know. Did anyone think it might be a part of this? The letters, I mean?"

George looked up at Jeff, who was taken completely by surprise. Recovering, he smiled and waved it off. He hoped the concern he felt was not evident on his face.

Graff and Eiselmann sat back down. Graff said, "How?"

George blushed, but said, "Perhaps the timing was off. Jeff wasn't near his car. Neither was Danny."

"That's a happy thought," Brett muttered.

To Jeff, George said, "I am sorry."

Jeff didn't hear him. He stared intently at Graff.

Graff scratched his cheek, his eyes far away. Eiselmann stared at George, then at Graff.

It was apparent to everyone in the kitchen they had not put the explosions and the letters together.

CHAPTER SIXTEEN

After a quick discussion on the car explosions, the cops left. Graff tried to reassure the boys and Jeff the explosions were separate and had nothing to do with the letters. He explained the MOs weren't the same. Nothing remotely alike. They did their best, but Jeff wasn't so sure, and neither were the boys, especially George.

Still gathered in the kitchen, Brett said to Jeff, "Bobby and I changed the sheets in Bobby's room. You can sleep there, and you can use Mom and Dad's bathroom. I put a towel and washcloth on the counter."

"Thanks, I appreciate it."

The guys got up to leave the kitchen when Brian stopped them.

"Did everyone get their homework done?"

Heads nodded.

"Two, did anyone look over your English?"

Of the seven boys, Two struggled the most with school. He pulled Bs and an occasional A or C, but it didn't come easily for him. It wasn't because Two was dumb. On the contrary, he was bright. It was just that in the last year or so, his education and schooling were spotty.

Two glanced at him and at the others, and said, "I didn't have anything in English."

"How about math?"

Two shifted from foot to foot, and said, "Brett did."

"It was perfect. Not one problem wrong," Brett said, throwing a fake punch at Two's stomach, causing him to flinch.

"Excellent," Brian said. He changed the subject and asked, "Do we know who is traveling with whom tomorrow?"

Heads nodded, and Billy said, "Same as always."

"Okay," Brian said. "Whoever is riding with me, we have to leave a little earlier. Mrs. Beatleman wants me to show a new kid around the school before first period."

"Why did Beatle pick you?" Brett said. "I mean, with everything going on with our family, couldn't she have picked someone else?"

"I don't mind," Brian answered. "Besides, the kid is probably nervous about coming into a new school this late in the year. I want to make sure it's done right."

Brian was on a list of twenty students, both boys and girls and all grade levels, called the Star Team. Randy and Bobby were on it, too. That Brian was asked meant the new kid was a sophomore and a boy. It didn't always work out, but the counselors and Kristi tried matching grade level with grade level, and gender with gender.

He and Brett playfully hip-checked each other as they climbed the stairs. Billy joined in by tackling both of them from behind, and then George tackled Billy. Papa jumped on top of George and Billy and licked their faces.

Jasper and Jasmine jumped over the pile and raced ahead. Momma sat down at the foot of the stairs and it looked to Brian she disapproved of the tangle of bodies.

The boys separated into their own rooms. Randy's door was closed, and Brian suspected he was getting the details of the conversation he had with Bobby. He assumed Danny was in there, too.

He heard the shower running in the bathroom he shared with some of his brothers, and by a process of elimination, he figured Two was in there. Brian could have used the other bathroom at the end of the hall, but waited. He still had not spoken to Two about what took place, and he wasn't looking forward to it. Mostly, he didn't know what he was going to say, but he couldn't put it off any longer.

He sat down on the floor next to his bed, scratched Papa and Jasper behind their ears, while kicking off his shoes and taking off his socks. After giving the pups- his buddies- the attention they demanded, he stood up and stripped down to his boxers, waiting to shower. He sat down on his bed, grabbed his copy of *Lord of the Flies* and thumbed through the two chapters Penny Rios, his English teacher, wanted them to read for the next class.

Because he had read the entire book and thought about it often, he knew what was in those chapters. So, instead, he fired up his laptop, and reread the chapter he wrote the night before. He liked his book, because it was an interesting story, and he loved his characters. Jeff pointed out that conflict in and between the characters kept the book alive, and placed readers on the edge of their seat. Jeff had a long conversation with him about character development. That conversation had helped him in English class, too.

He never heard Brett enter his room.

"Are you sleeping in here tonight?"

Brian shook his head and said, "I was planning on sleeping with you, if it's okay."

"Sure, no problem." Brett suspected as much and already knew where Two would sleep.

He leaned over and rested his chin on Brian's shoulder, and read along with him. He said, "When do I get to read the whole thing?"

"When I'm done with the first draft, and after Jeff looks it over."

Brett stood up, placed his hand on Brian's shoulder and said, "It's pretty cool you're writing a book."

Brian shrugged. He was uncomfortable with the attention, because while he enjoyed writing the story so far, he didn't know if it would turn out the way he envisioned it, and it didn't know if anyone other than his family or a few friends would read it. Mostly, just as he said at the hospital, he wanted it to be private.

"How autobiographical is it?"

Brian saved what he had written, turned off the laptop, and said, "It's not. I mean, the main character is like me in some ways, but not in others. Probably more unlike me. The other characters are from my imagination."

"Pretty cool," Brett said, giving his shoulder a squeeze. "You know I love you, right?"

"Of course. Me, too." He caught Brett at the doorway and asked, "Hey, any word from mom?"

"Nothing yet. I hope we'll hear something yet tonight, though."

Brett left, and the shower turned off. Brian sighed and decided to get it over with. Needed to get it over with. He sat back down on the bed to wait. The bathroom door was slightly open, and he heard the faucet in the sink running, and he knew Two was brushing his teeth.

Several minutes later, the faucet turned off. The door opened up, and Two entered the bedroom, still toweling off his long black hair. He had another towel around his waist, and Brian could see Two was still damp on his chest, back, and legs.

On any other night, Brian would have taken the towel from Two and dried him off. No chance of it happening this evening. He took a deep breath and waited.

Two stopped just inside the door, stopped drying his hair, and stared at Brian. Eventually, Two said, "Do you mind if I sleep in here tonight?"

"Nope," Brian said as nonchalantly as he could. "I'm sleeping with Brett. You'll sleep with either Bobby or Danny. Probably Danny."

Fighting back tears, Two said, "I said I was sorry."

Brian nodded and said, "I heard you, and I accepted your apology."

"Then why are you still angry with me?"

"Because what you said and what you did hurt, Two. I had done nothing to you. I haven't thought of doing anything sexual with you. No one thinks you're gay. Not even dad. He's just pissed at the letters or just weirded out or something. He'll get over it."

"I just don't want dad or anyone else to think I'm gay."

"Yeah, you made that pretty clear. And by hanging out with me, people might think that, right?"

Two started and stammered. He didn't know how he could explain himself. He thought about Lou, the man he stayed with in Arizona on the Navajo reservation.

"Can't we go back to the way we were?" Two asked in a near whisper, a tear running down the side of his nose.

Brian's voice rose, and he didn't care. He said, "Did you even listen to yourself? You think by being around me, or messing around with me, someone is going to think you're gay because I am. That's what you're saying."

"It's not what I meant," Two said as he wiped tears off his face.

Brian calmed down, feeling guilty about making Two cry.

"That's what you said. So, no. We can't go back to the way we were. At least, not right now. Maybe never. I don't know. Yet. What you said and did hurt. It hurt a lot. I loved you, Two. You were my little brother. That's the way I treated you. Nothing more and nothing less."

"I know."

"Yeah, well," the steam ran out of Brian's sail. "It's going to take time, Two. That's all I can say right now."

He side-stepped around him, went into the bathroom, and shut the door behind him.

CHAPTER SEVENTEEN

The silence in Graff's car was deafening. No one spoke until Graff pulled into the station and turned off the engine. Still, none of them had moved.

It was Eiselmann who broke the silence. "Who did the initial investigation?"

Graff understood the implication in the question. He also knew the three of them were the first on the scene, since they were watching the soccer game.

"Paul and I were wrapped up in the Chicago thing. The second trial on the Andruko bust," Pat said, his mind rolling back.

Graff shook his head in disgust. "Vukovich and Tresman." He shook his head again. "I should have pulled Gonnering and Lorenzo off the Carroll College B and E."

"Well," Eiselmann said, "the good news is the FBI were in on it the same night. Not much time for a fuck up. Excuse my language."

Both Graff and O'Connor knew what Paul meant. Gordon Vukovich was lazy, and Rich Tresman didn't care for details. There were bound to be gaps in the report, not to mention holes in the investigation. It was a perpetual problem that someone, usually Graff, would have to clean up. Both of the detectives were biding their time before they could retire. It wasn't soon enough to suit Graff.

"That's going to be part of the problem," Graff said. "Because the FBI took the case, there won't be much in our file. We'll have to rely more on the FBI files."

He stared out the side window and said, "I'm going to read over what's in the file, and then I'll pull what the FBI has and look for gaps."

"When?" O'Connor asked.

Graff glanced at his watch. He'd like to get home before Garrett went to bed, and he wanted to spend some quality time with Kelly, pregnant with their second child.

"Tonight, at least Vukovich and Tresman's report. I'll save the FBI file for tomorrow morning."

Eiselmann chuckled and said, "Well, at least you won't be spending hours reading through it. I figure five- or ten-minutes max."

"If that," Graff muttered as he pushed open his door.

"I have nothing to do," Pat said. "I'll join you. Help you understand the big words."

Eiselmann laughed. "There won't be anything over two syllables."

CHAPTER EIGHTEEN

Brian left the bedroom door ajar, just as Brett wanted it. Of the brothers, Brett had the most trouble of anyone shutting his door completely. A shut bedroom door reminded him of the two years he spent confined to a bedroom in the brothel in Chicago.

Momma, who normally slept just outside Brian's room, had repositioned herself to outside of Brett's bedroom facing the stairs. Papa and Jasper lay on the floor in the bedroom, Jasper on Brian's side of the bed, and Papa at the foot of the bed.

After Brian slid between the covers, Brett lifted the t-shirt Brian wore and inspected him.

"What?"

"Just looking for any blood or bruises. It doesn't look like either of them ripped your dick off," Brett said with a smile. "Do I need to check Two or Bobby to make sure they're intact?"

"You're a dork." Brian pulled his shirt down and said, "We're okay. Maybe not right now, but we will be."

Brett tapped Brian's chest with his finger and said, "That's one thing I'm sure of. You forgive easily because you have a good heart."

Brian's eyes were open, and Brett wasn't ready to sleep, either. Brett said, "I've been thinking."

"A scary thought," Brian said through a yawn.

"I think the reason you and dad butt heads is because you two are so much alike."

"I think you have me confused with Randy."

Brett bounced his finger on Brian's chest and said, "Even Randy agrees. We all do. Did you know Billy calls you 'Little J' behind your back? And the thing is, everyone knows who he's talking about."

Brian turned and stared at him. "In what world am I like dad?"

"You think like he does. You're slow to respond when someone asks a tough question because you think your answer through just like dad does."

"So does Randy. Even you and George."

"Who decided who was driving with whom to the hospital this morning? That's something dad does. Dad, mom and you would give their own life to keep us safe. Think back to Arizona. Who was it who made sure I was safe behind a boulder, and who sent Two away from the mesa to keep him safe? This afternoon at the hospital, who was the cheerleader who worried about both mom and dad, despite how you were feeling? Again, something dad would do."

Flustered, Brian said, "I didn't ... I mean ... oh, whatever."

Brett smiled and said, "You know, it's okay to be like dad."

"But I'm not. I'm nothing like dad."

Ignoring Brian's protests, Brett said, "Dad's a pretty good guy. He cares. He'll do just about anything to make sure everyone's okay. Dad would walk through hell with a target on his back if it meant everyone was safe. He's pretty damn smart. Dad makes mistakes, just like everyone else, but nine times out of ten, he's dead on." He tapped Brian's chest again and said, "Just like you."

Brian turned back to Brett and said, "I'm way different. I don't see it."

"You *don't see* it, or you *don't want* to see it?"

Brian shook his head. He didn't have any kind of retort ready, and clamped his mouth shut before he said anything he couldn't take back.

He rolled onto his side to face Brett and said, "Mom and I talked at the hospital, and I told her dad's and my relationship changed when Bobby and I got involved. It's never been the same since. It's the only thing I can think of."

Brett remained silent, giving Brian room to get whatever it was off his chest.

"I don't know if it's because I'm gay and he doesn't like gay people, or if he doesn't want any of his kids gay. Maybe because I'm gay, he thinks I've contaminated Bobby and might contaminate Michael."

Brett sighed, but knew nothing he would say would be listened to.

Brian went on, and said in a whisper, "I think he regrets letting me move in, and I think he regrets adopting me."

Brett reached out and pushed Brian's bangs off his forehead and said, "He loves you."

A tear slid down the side of Brian's nose, and he whispered, "How can he love me when he doesn't even like me?"

Brett thumbed the tear off Brian's face, and then he kissed his forehead. He said, "Bri, dad does like you, and he loves you." He added for emphasis, "He does. We all do."

"It feels like I fucked up this whole family. We've not been the same since I moved in and got into a relationship with Bobby. And now dad's worried I might be after Michael. I've never been interested in Michael like that. He's only a little brother to me."

Brett shook his head and said, "He's concerned about the letters. We all are. The letter thing fucked him up, that's all."

"Screw it. From now on, I'm staying away from all guys and all girls. I'm not dating anyone, not even as friends. It's not worth it."

"You worry too much, Bri. Especially about stuff you can't control. Besides, you have every right to love whoever you want. No one- not dad or mom, or anyone else should dictate who you love or not."

"But dad ..."

"But dad nothing. You love who you love. No one can control it. Not even you."

Brian nodded, though he wasn't so sure.

Brett tweaked Brian's nose and said, "Besides, we have your back. All of us. That's a promise."

"Thanks."

"I love you, Bri. All of us do. Don't forget that."

Brian nodded. He was certain of that in the same way he knew the sun would rise in the morning. Maybe not dad, so much, but his brothers, for sure.

Brett threw an arm across Brian's chest and his head on Brian's shoulder. The last thought Brian had before he fell asleep was wondering if the love of his brothers would be enough until he moved out and went to college.

CHAPTER NINETEEN

Graff tossed the file across the shiny table in the captain's conference room. It slid off and onto the floor before Eiselmann could catch it. Eiselmann picked it up and placed it on the table after tucking away two sheets of paper back inside the manila folder.

The detective squad room was empty, except for Jorgy and Lisa Vickers. Both of them had played essential roles in the capture of the assassins contracted by Andruko to kill O'Connor and Eiselmann.

"This was a waste of time," Graff muttered.

"About what I expected," O'Connor said. "To be fair, Tresman and Vukovich were happy to have handed it off to the FBI. After they did, they stopped investigating."

"But you or Paul or I wouldn't have quit on it," Graff said.

O'Connor nodded his agreement.

Eiselmann had his eyes planted on his laptop, frowning and rubbing his chin.

"What are you thinking?" Graff asked.

Intent on what he read, he never heard him.

"Yo, Paul, what are you thinking?"

Eiselmann looked up slowly and saw both men staring at him. "What?" he said.

O'Connor chuckled. "What are you thinking?"

"I've come up with a list of things I want to see and read."

Before Graff or O'Connor asked what they were, Paul said, "I want to see the video from the stadium parking lot. The FBI has ways to enhance the picture so it won't look dark and grainy. The school's camera system is digital, but the cameras themselves pretty much suck. I also want to read the FBI report. I want to go over the report on the vehicles. We know the device used was a pipe bomb, but I want to know how it was constructed, where it was placed, and how it was set off. It might tell us who made it and planted it."

He nodded as if he agreed with himself and added, "Things like how sophisticated or knowledgeable he or she is. Depending upon the sophistication of the device, it might tell us how old he or she is. I'm having doubts it is a high school kid, and not to sound sexist, I have doubts about it being a girl. I mean, statistically speaking."

"I thought that, too. About it not being a high school kid," Graff said. "The post office markings on the letters tells us the sender has wheels and is mobile. Whoever it is, the shithead is going out of his or her way to be careful. That doesn't sound much like a high school kid. They're more ..." he wagged his head from side to side and settled on, "unsophisticated. Sloppy, or at least, haphazard."

"You're not suggesting the interview with the boys was a waste of time," O'Connor said, his eyes narrowing.

"No, I'm not saying that. It gives us a starting point. Or like you said, it gives the boys a starting point. Knowing them, they will be careful. They will listen to conversations around them, especially George, Brett, and Brian."

"I'm betting Danny will be key. He has an eidetic memory and he won't miss anything," Eiselmann said.

"One thing we need to do, and you can add this to your list, is to check out the kids the boys told us about," Graff added.

"And the teacher, though I think he's a longshot," Eiselmann said.

"Have you thought about asking Bob Farner or Chuck Gobel to provide us with a list of staff members who live in or drive through the cities where the letters came from?" O'Connor asked.

Graff sucked on the inside of his cheek and said, "Actually, I have. But I'm not going to yet. I know both are friends of Jeremy and Jeff, and Farner is especially fond of the boys. But we can't rule them out, either."

O'Connor frowned at him and said, "I never considered them. I can't see it."

"But we don't know for sure," Graff said. "Not yet."

O'Connor shrugged and said, "True, I guess. I just don't see it."

Eiselmann stretched his arms over his head, yawned, and said, "We don't know if the car bombing has anything to do with the letters. The two might or might not be related. We have to get the FBI report and view the footage. It will give us a better idea."

"The oddity is that it was awfully coincidental," Graff said.

"No such thing as coincidence," O'Connor said. "We either have two separate cases or they are related."

"If the car bomb has anything to do with the letters, we have a whole other level of ugly," Eiselmann said.

Graff shook his head. He had promised to inform Vicky and Jeff, and by extension, Jeremy, if anything came up in the investigation placing the kids in harm's way. He said, "I don't want to go there yet."

Eiselmann sighed and said, "What disturbs me is that George thought of it before we did. Before anyone else did. It pisses me off." This last he said as he waved his hand at the anorexic manila folder containing the report of the car bombing.

O'Connor nodded and said, "George is some kind of special."

Graff nodded and said, "Agreed. I'm thinking a hell of a lot more special than Vukovich and Tresman." Then he added, "Look, we've done enough damage tonight. I'm heading home. I want to be with Kelly and Garrett. I have a feeling it's going to get busy really quickly, and none of us will have time for much else."

"Hunch?" Eiselmann asked.

"It's just bound to. Especially if we tie the car bombing to the letters."

CHAPTER TWENTY

The guys scrambled to get going. They brought over their dirty breakfast dishes, and as Brian rinsed them off and placed them into the dishwasher, he said over his shoulder, "Everyone almost ready? Those of you who don't have lunches, do you have enough money in your lunch account?"

Most had lunches, except for George and Billy. Billy said, "I might be low."

"Take a five or a ten out of my wallet. That should cover it."

Jeff laughed and said, "Brian, I've got it." He handed Billy a ten and laughed again. "George, how about you?"

"I'm okay, thank you."

"Michael, do you have lunch money?" Brian asked.

"I packed one."

"Did you pack enough?"

"I think so."

"Brian, what do I do with the dogs before I leave?" Jeff asked.

After handing the money to Billy, he went back to reading the newspaper and sipping his coffee. The night before, Brett packed a small suitcase containing Vicky's clothes and other items, and it sat off to the side. Jeff wanted to get going fairly early.

"I let them out this morning, Mr. Jeff," George said.

"And I gave them food and water," Two added. "Brian, we're almost out of dog food."

"I'll stop and get some on the way home after practice."

George said, "Mr. Jeff, if you let them out before you leave, they should be okay until we get home."

Jeff looked up and smiled at him. "Do you think you'll ever call me anything other than Mr. Jeff?"

George blushed, smiled, and said, "I don't think so."

Brian dried his hands off on the red towel hanging from a handle of the oven, and said, "Okay, everyone ready to roll?"

"Yes, mom," Brett said with a laugh. "Or, should I call you ..."

"Don't start," Brian muttered. "I'm just checking on stuff that needs to be checked."

Billy laughed and said, "Little J, we have it covered." The others laughed with him.

"Stop," Brian said, glaring at Billy, and then at Brett.

They were about to walk out the door when Brian placed a hand on Two's shoulder.

"You're wearing syrup."

Brian licked his thumb and wiped off whatever it was on his cheek. Two then dried his cheek off with the sleeve of his sweatshirt.

"That's gross, Bri," Randy said. "Using your spit on Two's cheek?"

Brian shrugged, and Two said, "It's okay. I don't mind."

He stared at Brian, and Brian sighed, softened, and said, "Michael, listen. Sorry about the spit thing. And I'm sorry for ... you know, whatever."

Two nodded, his eyes downcast.

"Look, we can't go back to where we were, but we can start here and now, and move forward. If you want to."

Two looked up at Brian with tears in his eyes. Brian smiled, thumbed the tears away, and said, "Are we okay?"

In answer, Two hugged him and held on. Brian did the same.

"George will pick you up after school. Are you working out with him?"

Two nodded.

"Do you have your workout stuff and running shoes?"

"All set."

"What about slides or flip-flops for the locker room and shower?"

Two smiled and said, patting his duffle bag, "Packed."

They embraced again and Brian said, "Love you, Michael. Always will."

"Me too."

CHAPTER TWENTY-ONE

Jeremy's color was back. He still looked tired, and he still felt embarrassed about 'all the fuss' but he also felt better and stronger. The doctors had stabilized his blood pressure, though they were reluctant to release him. Vicky and Jeremy were still in discussions with them, with Vicky wanting to err on the side of caution and keep him in the hospital one more night.

Jeremy first met with a registered dietician to discuss his diet. A meeting with a physical therapist would be later in the day to discuss a safe way to increase physical activity. Both he and Vicky understood he needed to take better care of himself. He also understood Vicky would be a strict disciplinarian to help him get whipped into shape.

Jeff stood at the foot of the bed, and Vicky sat in the chair at his bedside.

"How do you feel?" Jeff asked.

"Stupid. Embarrassed," Jeremy muttered. He had trouble maintaining eye contact with either of them. "A little weak and tired, but not bad."

Jeff said, "You would have been proud of the boys. They are pretty self-sufficient. Brian took charge, and the boys followed."

Puzzled, Jeremy looked at Vicky and then both looked at Jeff. Jeremy cocked his head and said, "Brian?"

"Absolutely. Yesterday at school, he organized who drove with whom. After your episode yesterday afternoon, even with all the ... stuff that had happened and was said, it was Brian who gathered the boys together and urged them to keep their emotions in check because, as he said, it wouldn't help either of you. It was quite the pep talk. He had a long conversation with Bobby when we got home. I think both boys are still unsettled, if not upset, but I think things are going to be okay between them. And he and Two patched things up before they left for school."

"I was worried about Brian and Two," Vicky said.

"When you say Bobby and Brian will be okay, what do you mean?" Jeremy said.

Jeff shrugged and said, "They love each other. They're brothers and friends, and that won't change. Their ... *relationship* will be different, but that's to be expected."

Jeremy and Vicky locked eyes. Jeff knew something had passed between them, and he wanted no part of it. He said, "Last night, Brian went from room to room to check on everyone to see how they were doing." He laughed and said, "This morning, he made sure all of them had lunches or lunch money. He's a great young man."

"Brett and Randy are the leaders among the boys. I never pictured Brian as a leader," Jeremy said, more to Vicky than to Jeff.

"I can only tell you what I saw and heard last night and this morning. Randy spent most of the time in his room talking to Danny and Bobby, but other than that, he kept to himself. Brett was more like Brian's wingman than a leader."

"Who slept where?" Vicky asked.

"Bobby with Randy. George with Billy. Danny with Two. And Brian with Brett."

"Hmmm," Vicky muttered. Her face clouded over, and her thoughts took flight to a million miles away.

"George is picking up Two from school and then the two of them are heading back to North to work out. Brian picked up the kitchen before they took off, and he is picking up dog food on the way home after practice. Like I said, he took charge yesterday and today."

"I have trouble picturing it," Jeremy said. "Not that I doubt you. It's just not something I've seen from him."

Jeff frowned and shook his head. He said, "Jeremy, you're like a brother to me. My best friend. You've helped me through a dark time during my divorce. Without you, I don't know if I would have remained sane. I mean that. But I'm going to say something I hope won't upset you too much. I need you to hear me out."

Jeremy nodded slowly and said, "Okay."

Vicky looked alarmed, glanced at the monitor, and looked at Jeff sideways.

Undeterred, Jeff said, "Last night, I was going to pop into Brett's room and thank Brian for everything, but I never did. I stopped when I overheard Brett and Brian talking. It was emotional, and I have to tell you, it choked me up."

He paused, thinking back to the night before, and wanting to choose his words carefully.

"This isn't going to be easy, Jeremy, but you have to know Brian doesn't feel you love him. He doesn't feel you even like him."

Jeremy sighed, and said, "I've heard all this before."

"Let me finish. It's not about your feelings. This is about Brian's feelings."

"It was his idea to break up with Bobby, for lack of a better word," Vicky said. "He told me he believed your relationship changed when he and Bobby got involved."

"I know," Jeff said. "He told Brett the same thing last night. He feels you think he turned Bobby gay, and now he's working on Two."

"I ..." Jeremy said, shaking his head.

"Let me finish. Please."

Jeremy held up his hands in surrender. Vicky glanced at the monitor. So far, the numbers hadn't climbed much higher than normal. Only a little, but not the leap it took the previous afternoon after Two and George's visit.

"Brian doesn't know if you don't like gay people, or don't like the fact that he's gay, or don't like the fact that one of your sons is gay. Technically, two of your sons."

He paused and stared at Jeremy to see if anything had landed. He was pretty sure what he said amounted to nothing more than glancing blows.

"He feels you regret letting him move in, and you regret adopting him. Brian feels he single-handedly ruined your family the moment he moved in. Again, his feelings. Accept that."

"Why do you say that? 'His feelings, accept that.'"

"Because even though you're a smart man and an even better counselor, sometimes you can't find your ass with both hands and a compass. Sometimes you interject your own feelings instead of listening and feeling what someone else is saying and feeling. In this case, Brian."

"I ... shit. I don't know," Jeremy said, looking past Jeff at the far wall.

"You and Brian butt heads because you two are so much alike. Both of you are stubborn as hell. You talk the same. You walk the same. He approaches life the same way you do. The two of you would do anything to protect the family. Nothing and no one is more important than family in either of your eyes. Both of you feel the same way."

Jeremy looked down at his hands and nodded.

"Both of you are passionate. About people. Your boys, his brothers. Vicky, your wife, his mother. Life. But Jeremy, if you don't turn this around and get your head out of your ass, you're going to lose him. You might have already."

Jeremy blinked and glanced at Vicky.

"You think I, we, were wrong to stop the sexual relationship between Brian and Bobby? Would you have reacted any differently if you were in our shoes and Danny was involved?"

Jeff sighed and said, "To answer to your first question, I can see both sides pretty clearly. Yes, both boys are raised as brothers. But they aren't brothers. They are friends who truly love one another. People love who they love and there is nothing you can do about it. Nothing. Not you, not Vicky, not anyone but them. I don't believe being gay is caused by any event. It's DNA and the way a brain is wired. It's science. Yes, I believe in science even though the previous moron in the oval office didn't. I know Brett questions his sexuality because of the crap that took place in Chicago. But I believe he'll come around because he never had sexual feelings towards any guy before Chicago."

Jeff laughed, shook his head and said, "Maybe you already know, maybe you don't. But do you know Brett tried to be involved with Brian?"

Vicky blinked, and Jeremy squinted at him.

"You heard me correctly. Brett told me Brian had rebuffed him several times. As close as Brian and Brett are, Brian had no desire to do anything with Brett, because in his mind, they were friends. As close friends as they could be. It was different with Bobby. They were more than friends. He couldn't control it, and neither could Bobby. They fell in love. They probably still are, though they would never admit it to anyone. Not even to each other after last night."

"Did you know about Brett and Brian?" Jeremy asked Vicky.

"Maybe, possibly." Her voice trailed off. She suspected Brett felt that way. She didn't know if he still felt that way.

"I don't know what Brian's and Bobby's friendship will look like. In time, it might be just fine. But if I had to guess, their friendship is broken and nothing can be done to repair it. I don't believe they know how, and if they don't," Jeff let it end there, and he shook his head sadly.

He knew he had walked in a minefield, but he didn't care. He was willing to take the chance because what he said needed to be said. Deep down, he believed Jeremy and Vicky knew everything he said was the truth.

"The answer to your second question is Danny and I have had long conversations about Brian and Bobby. We talked about Danny's feelings. He isn't gay, if that's what you're thinking. He knows it's all about brain chemistry and science. But he also understands the friendship coin is razor thin and has two sides. It doesn't take much for the coin to flip from one side to the other. And if it flips, both he and I can and will accept it. As I said, it's his feelings and his heart. No one has the right to decide who he should love, but him. Not me or anyone else."

Vicky looked down at her hands. Jeff could tell she wept. He saw tears in Jeremy's eyes, too.

"The letters are driving you crazy. I get it. Probably driving you and Vicky crazier than me." He shrugged and said, "I'm used to it. You don't have the experience I have with crap like this. But the letters are just one thing going wrong in your life right now. Mainly, you don't take care of yourself like you should. You haven't for a while now. I should have said something to you a long time ago. But right after getting yourself healthy and back on your feet, you have to fix your relationship with Brian before it affects your family more than it has already." For emphasis, he added, "You have to."

Jeremy cleared his throat and in more of a whisper, said, "I'm not sure I know how."

"Talk to him. Really talk to him. But listen more than you talk. It won't be easy, but I know Brian will be honest. Remember, he chose to live with you and Vicky, and he chose to be adopted by you. That means something."

CHAPTER TWENTY-TWO

The Evans boys and Danny hadn't made their way out of the parking lot without stopping every few steps. Everyone, it seemed, wanted to know how the boys' father was doing and if he was going to be okay. Most of the time, the boys knew who they spoke to. Other times, they were clueless who had walked up to them to ask about Jeremy.

Their answers were the same. *"He's doing fine." "He'll be home today or tomorrow." "No new updates yet."*

They kept it bland, mostly because they didn't know any more than what they told them. They were still waiting for an update from Vicky.

Brian kept his head down and his pace fast as he made his way to the guidance area. He saw Kristi and said, "Hey, how are you doing?"

She got up from behind her desk and hugged him. "Chuck and Bob told me you had asked about me. That was thoughtful. Thank you."

"I saw you crying and I know you and dad are friends."

She kissed his cheek and said, "Thank you."

Brian filled her in using some of the same words used in the parking lot, but also told her Jeremy's blood pressure had finally been stabilized. Things were looking up.

"That's good to hear. The staff has been worried sick. I think Mr. Gobel is going to put out an email to the staff to reassure them. He might want to consult with you and your brothers."

"Okay, but I have to show a new student around first, though."

"I think he's in Mrs. Beatleman's office already. He and his parents got here before I did."

Brian had hoped she could provide some insight on the kid, but no such luck. That was okay. This way, he could form his own opinion.

He dropped his backpack behind Kristi's desk, rounded the corner, and walked down the short hallway to Beatleman's office. He rapped a knuckle on the door and waited until Beatleman opened it.

A family of curly or wavey blond hair smiled at him.

"Everyone, this is Brian Evans, the young man I told you about," Beatleman said, ushering him into the small office, crowded with extra chairs and extra bodies. "Brian, given everything happening right now, I appreciate your taking the time to show Tony around the school."

"No problem at all."

Brian couldn't hide the surprise, or perhaps shock, on his face.

Tony stood up to shake hands, blushing as he did. His curly white-blond hair hung just to his shirt collar. He had a heart-shaped face with full lips, and eyes the brightest, palest blue Brian had ever seen. Captivated, Brian had trouble looking at anything else.

His complexion was dark, like Brett's and Bobby's. He was about two inches shorter than Brian, putting him around five-foot-nine. He was slender with fine features, long thin fingers, and soft hands. Built like George and Two, Brian wondered if he was a runner.

He wore an off-white Henley, with fashionably faded jeans with holes in his knees, a shell necklace like a surfer would wear, a Fitbit on his right wrist, and two leather bracelets on his left. Brian pegged him as a lefty.

"This is Mr. and Mrs. Vittoria, Tony's uncle and aunt, and these are his cousins, Benny and Sophia."

The little girl turned her head away, hiding from him. Benny smiled broadly and waved. Brian gave him a fist bump.

To Benny, he said, "So you're starting high school today? I'm showing you around, right?"

Benny laughed and his parents smiled.

"I'm only five," Benny said shyly.

"Only five?" Brian faked dismay. "You look way older than five. And your pretty sister looks like she's an eighth grader."

Sophia giggled and said, "I'm only three."

"Well, you're a very cute three-year-old."

Sophia and Benny giggled.

"We're sorry to hear about your father, Brian. We hope he's okay," Tony's uncle said.

"Yes," his aunt said. "Thank you for taking the time to show Tony around the school this morning."

Brian was taken with them. His first thought was *nice people*. And his second thought was *Tony must be nice, too*.

He smiled and said, "It's no problem. My dad is doing well. He'll be discharged either today or tomorrow. We're just waiting on word from our mom." He turned to Tony and said, "I normally get to school about this time, and I'm happy to show you around."

Brian and Tony left the small office, walked to the main guidance area, and sat down at a table. The office was empty except for Kristi working at her desk.

"Can I see your schedule?" Brian asked.

Tony handed it to him as Brian wrote names across from each of the classes.

"I know at least one person in each of your classes, except for art. But you have one of the best teachers in the school. Mrs. Arney is awesome. Everyone likes her. And my brother George and I are in your PE class. The teacher is our basketball coach. He's a good guy."

Brian looked up and smiled at Tony and said, "Did you bring a swimsuit or anything for PE? Slides or flip-flops?"

Tony blushed and said, "No. I didn't know."

"No problem. If you catch your aunt or uncle before they leave, they can bring them to the front office and we'll pick them up at lunch."

"We have the same English teacher, Mrs. Rios. She's awesome, too. Probably my favorite teacher. But we're in different periods. I have her first period when you're in art. We're reading *Lord of the Flies*, and I can give you my notes and get you caught up. No problem."

And it went just like that. The two of them talking about Tony's classes, things that interested him, and clubs or sports he might want to be involved in. To those who might have listened in, like Kristi, it looked like they had known each other for years and were best friends.

As they walked the hallways, Brian pointed things out, and explained how things worked. Sometimes Brian put an arm around Tony's shoulder or held onto his forearm as he explained the ins and outs of North High School. If it bothered Tony, he never let on. In fact, several times, Tony took hold of Brian's arm, too.

"Why do you have a patch of white hair?" Tony asked.

"Long story. Give me your hand," Brian said. He took Tony's fingers and ran them over the scar under the white patch. "It's a scar I got in the summer, which is another long story. The doctor said sometimes, stress can cause hair to change color."

"You're under that much stress?"

Brian laughed and said, "No more than anyone else. Sometime, I'll tell you the whole story. I got the scar along with this one," he pointed to his right eye, "and these," pointing to the scar on his right hand and arm. "I have one on my shoulder, too. The glasses have no prescription. I wear them because the doc wants me to protect my right eye. I almost lost it."

"Must be quite the story," Tony said as he stared at Brian's eye.

"Can I ask why you live with your aunt and uncle? If it's none of my business, it's okay."

Tony blushed and said, "It's a long story."

Brian laughed and said, "Looks like we have some stories to tell each other."

Tony chuckled. Brian couldn't tell if he was uncomfortable or shy. Maybe both.

To change subjects, Brian said, "George will like you. You're a runner. He's in cross country and track. And we can ask Mrs. Arney about the art club. What kind of art do you do? Mostly, I mean?"

"I like drawing in pencil and pastels. I like painting, but watercolor can be difficult."

"My brother, Brett, is in photography. He's super. He likes black and white the best because he says it brings out shadows. Something about contrast."

"That's why I work in pencil. Same thing. Color can hide flaws, and feel unnatural." This last he said with a shrug.

Brian liked the sound of Tony's voice. It was soft and light, almost musical, and it brought a smile to Brian's face.

"What?" Tony asked.

Brian smiled, blushed, and said, "Nothing. I think you'll like it here. Can you give me your cell number? I'll give mine to you. That way, if you have questions or need anything, you have someone you can ask. And we can talk about stuff. If you want to." He was hopeful, but he didn't want to push.

Without hesitation, Tony snagged his cell from his back pocket and the two boys exchanged numbers.

The hallways had filled up with students moving in both directions. Brian glanced at his watch and noticed they had three or four minutes before first period. His cell buzzed, showing a message. He saw it was Vicky, and he shut his eyes and took a deep breath before reading the text.

Guys, your dad is doing fine. I think he's going to stay one more night and then he will be discharged sometime tomorrow. To be cautious, he won't have visitors. Hope that's okay. Love you guys. I'll text again later. I'll probably spend the night here.

Brian slumped against the lockers. He wasn't sure if he was relieved or hurt. He was the only one who didn't get to see or talk to Jeremy. Not that he minded all that much, because when they would, it would be uncomfortable.

Tony placed a hand on Brian's shoulder. He said, "Everything okay?"

Brian nodded. "I think my dad is getting out of the hospital tomorrow sometime."

Tony cocked his head and said, "That's a good thing, right?"

Brian sighed. "He can't have visitors, and I was the only one who didn't get to see him. That's all." He shrugged and said, "We better get you to your first class."

They walked the rest of the way in silence, and just outside the door, Brian stopped him. Tony leaned against the lockers, and Brian saw anxiety on his face.

He reached out and put his hand on Tony's shoulder, letting it slide to his forearm. He said, "I know you're nervous, but I'm here. My brothers, six of them, are here, and there are guys and girls in each of your classes who will look out for you. If you need anything, text me. Okay?"

Tony nodded, but Brian saw he was still nervous.

"I'll meet you at lunch right where I showed you, okay?"

Tony nodded again.

Without thinking about it, Brian embraced him, and Tony let him. They clung to each other like old friends.

"You got this."

"Thanks for everything."

"That's what friends are for," Brian said with a smile.

CHAPTER TWENTY-THREE

"Mr. Dildo, Danny's old English teacher, lives in the Twin Cities. He teaches English at a private school and is an adjunct professor at the University of Minnesota," Eiselmann said from his desk in the detective room. "That removes him from the suspect pool, considering there have been zero postmarks from the faraway land on the other side of the Mississippi."

"Minnesota sucks," O'Connor said dryly. "Home of the Vikings."

"I agree with you," Eiselmann said. "Do you know where Jamie is?"

"No, why?"

"I have the video of the car bombings, and Skip Dahlke sent me the preliminary report on the latest letters. I think you guys need to look it over."

O'Connor squinted at him and slowly got out of his seat. He ambled over to Eiselmann's desk, pulled a chair over from the empty desk, and sat down.

"Should we wait for Graff?"

O'Connor shook his head and said, "You've got my curiosity up."

Eiselmann handed him the report from Dahlke along with a copy of the letter to Danny, and O'Connor read them through twice, accompanied by a "huh" and a "hmm".

Danny-

I tried to make you see how those two are dragging you down. You don't need them. If something was to happen to them, you'd still be a star. Maybe something should happen to them. You are a star without them. You don't need them.

But you aren't listening. You're ignoring me. Maybe I need to do something to get your attention and show you I mean what I say. I will if I have to. It's up to you.

I only want what's best for you. Why don't you listen? Why? Don't you care? Maybe I need to show you how much I care. Is that what you want?

Love,

Me

"It's different from the others," Eiselmann said. "Darker. Not quite threatening, but almost, if you know what I mean."

O'Connor nodded and said, "Desperate. Wants Danny's attention."

"Yeah, but you heard the guys. He probably doesn't recognize it. Oblivious."

"The kid, and I think it's a kid, isn't using a program that prompts for grammar or sentence structure. A thing that checks for multiple word usage."

Eiselmann said. "Maybe the kid is bright and doesn't need it."

"I use it, and I'm pretty smart."

"Since when were you ever good at English?"

"Hey, you sucked worse than I did!"

Graff walked up and said, "You both suck. What's going on?"

"We have Skip's report on the letters, along with copies of the letters, and we have the video of the car bombs from the FBI," Eiselmann said. "What do you want to start with?"

"The report and then the letters."

Graff sat on top of the empty desk next to Eiselmann and read them both. He looked up, frowning.

"Not quite a threat, but almost."

"The same thing Skip, Pat and I thought," Paul said.

"What about the letters to Randy and Bobby?" Graff asked.

Eiselmann handed one copy to Pat and the other to Jamie. They were identical.

Randy,

Your not listening to me. Your ignoring me. Why?

Don't you see your hurting Danny's chances of being a star? You aren't and you never will be. I tried, but you don't ever pay attention to me. I might have to do something to show you how serious I am.

Not a fan of yours!

"This is a kid," O'Connor said. "The first two sentences, *your* is misspelled. It should have been *y-o-u-apostrophe-r-e*. Typically, that's a kid's mistake."

"I caught it," Graff nodded. "Randy's letter is identical to Bobby's letter. Both are ... somewhat threatening. I'm concerned things could escalate against Randy and Bobby. Danny, too."

O'Connor nodded and said, "The threat is there. Vague, but there."

"Like the writer has a thing for Danny, but not for Randy or Bobby," Paul said.

"I'm thinking, girl," O'Connor said.

Graff wagged his head from side to side, considering it. He thought it could be a boy who might have a thing for Danny, but after sticking his foot in his mouth the night before, he kept that thought to himself.

"The wording is almost middle school," Paul said. "My daughter, Alex, has friends who talk like this. I can see them writing these letters."

"So, it's possible the writer might either be younger than the boys, or not as bright as the boys," Graff said. "And those boys are damned smart. That puts the suspect pool too damn large."

O'Connor squinted at the wall and said, "Not necessarily. I think the writer knows them and they know the writer. The writer is more comfortable writing his or her thoughts than speaking them. And if you had a gun to my head, I would say the writer is a girl. Kinda shy. Quiet."

"A shy, quiet girl with a crush on Danny," Paul said.

"Something like that," Pat answered.

Graff pulled at his earlobe and chewed the inside of his cheek. He said, "I'm not ready to say if it's a boy or a girl. Not yet."

"You want to see the video?" Paul asked.

"Yes, but let's use the screen in the conference room," Graff said, already moving in that direction.

Paul set up his laptop and connected it to the large screen TV monitor in the captain's conference room. He brought up the video and said, "Here we go."

The video was dark, but not grainy. From the top of the press box, the parking lot was miniaturized, but clear. The parking lot lights had a star-like corona, creating some shadows in the rows of cars. The cars themselves were on the small side, but the makes and models were fairly easy to make out.

"It took me a while to figure out the orientation, but over on the right towards the top of the screen, you can see Jeff's SUV." He stood and pointed to the vehicle to the left of Jeff's vehicle, and said, "This is the vehicle where the pipe bomb was placed."

Eiselmann sat back down and picked up the FBI report and read from it.

"A crude pipe bomb was attached to the gas line of a 2005 Nissan Sentra."

"Wait," Graff said. "Crude?"

"That's what the report said," Eiselmann shrugged off the question. "Their words, not mine."

"Okay, go on," Graff said with a frown.

"The fuse was lit, and the flame traveled fifteen yards to the bomb. The fuel door was pried open and the gas cap removed on all three vehicles. The video tape shows the suspect prying open the fuel door of the 2006 Chevy Impala to the right of the black Escalade, then prying open the fuel door of the Escalade, and then spending at least six minutes on the side of the Nissan Sentra."

Eiselmann looked up and said, "The FBI believed the suspect used that time to place the pipe bomb on the fuel line, pry open the fuel door, remove the gas cap, and set the fuse."

"Wait, wait, wait!" O'Connor said, running his hand through his long hair. "Why not just push the fuse into the gas tank, light it, and run? Why go through all the trouble of building a *crude* pipe bomb, using their words, when a fuse in the gas tank would take less time and be just as effective, if not more effective?"

Eiselmann and Graff stared at each other, then at O'Connor. It was Graff who answered.

"Not a fucking clue, Hoss."

"And assuming Jeff's caddy was the target vehicle, why set off the pipe bomb on the Sentra? Why not attach it to the caddy and be done with it?" He shook his head and said, "It doesn't make sense."

"Who owned the Sentra?" Graff asked.

"TJ's uncle and aunt from Buffalo. They came down to watch TJ play," Eiselmann said. "We can assume their car was collateral damage and not the target."

"We need to interview TJ's aunt and uncle. Find out more about them. See if anyone had a beef with them. That sort of thing."

"Road trip?" Eiselmann asked.

"Maybe." Graff thought for a minute and said, "For the time being, let's assume Jeff's Escalade was the target. What was the makeup of the pipe bomb?"

Eiselmann dug through the FBI report, licked his thumb and index finger, flipped a page and found it. He read it as he pointed to it.

"One- and one-half inch PVC pipe, one foot long. Gun powder, nails, nuts, and bolts."

Eiselmann looked up from the report and said, "There was enough gun powder to cause the flame and explosion, which set off the gas tank. The flames and concussion set off the explosions of the other two vehicles."

"I understand why they said it was crude," O'Connor said.

"Certainly not professional," Graff said. "Roll the tape through, then we'll watch it a second time in slow motion."

Eiselmann didn't move. O'Connor worked with him long enough to recognize the look. "What?" he asked.

"The car bomb took place, what, a month ago? But the letters arrived last night. They suggested something might happen to catch their attention. Wasn't the car bomb enough of an attention getter?"

"Dammit!" Graff said, running a hand over his face. "What else does this kid have in mind?"

O'Connor knew they promised to let Jeff, Jeremy, and Vicky know if something bigger and bolder might be coming at the kids. What he didn't know was if this warranted a warning.

Eiselmann ran the video through once and then slowed it down.

"There, right there!" O'Connor said. "Someone, a kid based on size, by the cars."

"Like he or she doesn't want to be seen," Eiselmann said. "Dressed in black with a hoodie."

"It might not be a kid. Can you blow it up?" Graff asked.

"Doubt it," Eiselmann said as he shook his head. "If it could have been done, the FBI would have done it."

"Look at the hands," O'Connor said. "Gloves?"

"Looks like it," Graff said. To Paul, he said, "Can you get a still shot of the suspect and print off a couple? Maybe try blowing it up that way?"

"I can try, but it might be grainy."

"Let's see what you can do," Graff said.

They watched the tape through, and then again in slow motion. They watched the suspect run off through the parking lot, dodging cars. He or she kept low, almost out of sight.

"Where did he or she run off to?" O'Connor asked.

"I know the system, and they don't have cameras the length of the entrance," Eiselmann said as he scratched his cheek.

"What about on the street? ATMs. Shops."

O'Connor shook his head and said, "The area is residential. Nothing nearby."

"We need to find out where these three kids live. Maybe whoever it was just ran home," Eiselmann suggested.

"Good idea, but again, it might not be a kid. Put it on your to-do list," Graff said. "Now, how do we approach the three kids the boys mentioned?"

O'Connor shook his head and said, "I don't think we do. Not yet. We need to see what the boys find out."

Reluctantly, Graff agreed, hoping they would find more information sooner rather than later. "That's placing a great deal of responsibility on those boys. Jeremy, Vicky, and Jeff aren't going to like it."

Eiselmann shrugged and said, "Pat's right, though. There isn't much we can do without any information to go on. Besides, the kids are going to be kids. All they're doing is listening and paying attention to anyone around them. No harm in that."

O'Connor and Graff exchanged a look, and Pat said, "I think we check in with the boys each day after school. See what they find out, if they find out anything."

Graff nodded and said, "We also need to hook up with Jeff, Jeremy, and Vicky. It's possible Jeff or Jeremy might know the kid." He shrugged and said, "Or the adult. At least it's worth a shot."

CHAPTER TWENTY-FOUR

George saw the boy before the others did. He followed the Apache belief that if you stare at the enemy, the enemy will see you. Instead, George kept his head down and took small glances in the boy's direction out of the corner of his eye.

Like always, the boy sat alone at the same table, fairly close to where George and the others sat before school and at lunch. It looked to George like the boy worked on math, judging by the open algebra book, the pencil in his hand, and the notebook in front of him. George also noted earbuds in his ears. He assumed the kid was listening to music.

"Danny, look this way," George said as he held his cell out, ready to snap a picture. George wasn't interested in a picture of Danny. He aimed his cell just over Danny's left shoulder and enlarged the screen so he could get a closeup of the boy.

Danny was smart enough to see what George did, but he played along. After the picture was taken, he casually turned and glanced over his shoulder. It was a brief moment, but Danny took the boy in. He had never seen or noticed the kid before.

He pursed his lips, looked up at George, and shook his head slightly.

Billy and Brett were too busy eating the last bites of a cinnamon bun and reviewing for a quiz in English to notice. However, both Randy and Bobby saw the exchange between George and Danny.

First Randy, then Bobby, looked over their shoulder to take a peek at the boy. They shook their head at each other, then at George and Danny.

"I don't know who he is," Randy whispered.

"We don't either," Danny whispered back. "What do we do?"

George answered, "We watch and we wait. At lunch, I might go talk with him."

"Do you think that's safe?" Randy asked.

George glanced at the boy again and noticed the boy looking back at him. It was awkward, so George covered himself by laughing. He pointed at Randy and said, "Good one." In a whisper, he said, "Don't turn around. Laugh."

The boys did, and Danny added a punch to Randy's arm. Randy smacked him back, playing along.

The small blond boy stuffed his algebra book and notebook into his backpack, and got up and left without looking back. George watched him go, wondering if the boy had caught on to them watching him.

"That him? The boy you talked about?" Brett asked.

George nodded.

"Did you guys see mom's text?" Billy asked.

The boys made faces or nodded.

"If he isn't coming home until tomorrow, does it mean he's not okay?" he asked.

"Not necessarily," Brett said. "I've been reading up on stuff, and it isn't unusual for someone who had a heart attack to spend two or three nights in the hospital."

"Is that what it was?" Bobby asked.

Brett shrugged and said, "Mom and dad and Jeff aren't saying it, but from what I've been reading, everything points to it."

"So, it's just a precaution? I mean, dad staying one more night at the hospital?" Billy asked.

"I think so," Brett said. "Mom made it sound like they had a hell of a time getting his blood pressure stable. He'll be okay, though. Mom would have told us if he wasn't."

To Brett and Billy, Danny said, "When you and Billy were getting your rolls, Farner came in looking for Brian. He wanted to run the message to the staff by him."

"Bri is still with the new kid," Billy said.

"That's what we told him, and he said he'd try to find him," Bobby said. "The message looked fine to us. Nothing special. Just stuff we already know. Bland."

"Mom and dad would probably prefer it that way," Brett said.

"That's what we told him," Randy said.

"Danny, here comes that one girl, Nada Sherry," Billy muttered under his breath. "She has cookies."

"Shit," Danny said. He hustled stuffing things into his backpack, and he picked up his trumpet case, and tried to leave before she got to him. He wasn't fast enough.

"Hi, Danny. I brought you some chocolate chip cookies."

She was small and narrow, with stringy brown hair, which may or may not have been washed. The frayed sweater she wore was too large and the sleeves almost swallowed her hands. Her glasses were too large and threatened to fall off. She kept pushing them back from the end of her nose. A constant battle caused by gravity, oily skin, and a narrow face.

"Nada, I appreciate it, but I try not to eat too many sweet things. And you don't have to keep bringing me stuff." To soften it, he repeated, "I really appreciate it, though."

Flustered, she flapped one arm, pushed her glasses up on her face and said, "What am I supposed to do with them?"

Billy stepped forward and said, "I'll eat 'em."

He reached for them, but she snatched them back, and said, "No, they're for Danny."

She hustled away, crushing the four cookies in the little sandwich bag, and then threw them in the trash.

"What the hell?" Bobby said.

"I think you broke her heart," Brett said with a smirk.

"I thought I was gentle," Danny said.

Brett put an arm around Danny's shoulder and said, "You were, but you still broke her heart."

"No more cookies or cake," Billy said. "Nice going, Danny."

The guys gathered their books, notebooks, and things, cleaned off their table, and headed to the arch leading to the hallway for their classrooms.

George hung back and waited until they had left. He walked to the large gray barrel that served as the garbage can and fished out the bag containing the crumbled cookies. Spilled milk and remnants of someone's morning latte made the bag damp in spots.

Gingerly, he carried the bag of cookies to the restroom, where he washed and dried it off. As he walked to guidance, he texted a message to Graff.

In guidance, he walked to Kristi and said, "Ms. Johnson, Detective Graff is going to pick this up. Can you keep it safe until he comes to get it? Don't let anyone touch it and don't let anyone eat it."

The smile fell off of Kristi's face, but she managed to say, "George?"

George smiled, nodded, and said, "Please put it somewhere safe where no one will touch it. Detective Graff will be here shortly."

He nodded again, and then he left.

Kristi stared after him, and then stared at the bag, not wanting to touch it, either.

CHAPTER TWENTY-FIVE

In response to Eiselmann's question, Graff said, "It went about the way I thought it would. From what we got from Jeremy and Jeff, we're looking at a kid, but they didn't rule out a small adult."

He was silent for a beat and said, "We need to stop by North and pick up cookies a girl brought to Danny. We're supposed to talk to George when we get there."

O'Connor privately wondered if the car bomb had anything to do with the letters. He couldn't, however, get rid of the *tickle* at the back of his mind.

Tickle was a word used by George, who got it from his grandfather. O'Connor adopted it. The *tickle* was a nagging thought that they were missing something. Something they had overlooked. He knew it would come to him. He made a mental note to review the tape and the letters when they got back to the station.

"Guys, I can't help feeling we're making something out of nothing," Eiselmann said.

"I mean, other than the car bomb, which may or may not be linked to the letters, the only thing we have are letters that don't really threaten anyone. Like Jeff has said all along, they come with the territory of notoriety and being in the limelight. Even a small spotlight like the three boys find themselves in."

Graff nodded. "The thing is, on the face of it, the bomb targeted Jeff's car and Jeff. Not necessarily the boys. Unless the kid wanted to get Jeff's attention. If the kid got Jeff's attention, then perhaps the bomb would get the boys' attention."

O'Connor shook his head, and it wasn't lost on Graff, who caught it through the rearview mirror.

"What?"

O'Connor shook his head again. "I don't think they're related. But it's convoluted enough to be a design and work of an inexperienced kid for all the reasons I pointed out this morning. The kid wanted to get the boys' attention. The thing is, it didn't work. Because the whole thing is convoluted, it sounds and looks like the work of an inexperienced kid. A kid who writes letters to proclaim affection, and threaten anyone who gets in the way."

"Like Randy and Bobby," Eiselmann said.

Pat had the tickle again. He frowned.

Eiselmann was about to say something, but Graff stuck out an arm and held onto Paul's arm as he said, "Pat, what?"

O'Connor pursed his lips and said, "There is something we're missing. I don't know what it is, and I don't know if it's big or small. But it's there. I can feel it."

O'Connor's comment and feeling produced a look of consternation on Graff's face, and a cloud of thought on Eiselmann's. Graff trusted O'Connor and Eiselmann more than anyone on the force. They worked well individually and as a team. Individually, both were smart and insightful. They put two or three abstract, seemingly unrelated things together, and got a result. Together, they were a force of nature.

Paul said, "Is it the letters, the bomb, or what?"

Pat stared out the back side window and said, "Something."

CHAPTER TWENTY-SIX

Music had always been Danny's love. He began pecking away at a piano at age seven, playing by ear flawlessly. So much so, his amazed parents took him for lessons and he was soon playing the classics using a blend of sight reading and his ear. He wouldn't stick to the sheet music, though. He would add what he wanted and when he wanted it, much to the dismay, frustration, and pleasure of his instructors.

Guitar came next at age eight. He'd watch YouTube videos of Hendricks, Van Halen, Brad Paisley, and Keith Urban, and anyone else who caught his ear. He'd watch their quick fingers over the frets and as he watched, his mom and dad watched his own fingers mimic the movements at first in the air, then on his guitar, to where he could match note for note what he heard on YouTube.

Lessons began within a week. Classical guitar lessons, but Danny loved a mix of older 60s rock and roll and modern country. His parents made him stay with the classical lessons, however. It was Jeff's idea that it would strengthen his skill, and it proved him right.

Because music was his first, and perhaps only, love, the choir room and band room were a home away from home, outside of the studio Jeff built for him. He was one among the other music geeks, many of whom were friends. They shared similar interests, though none approached the ability Danny had.

Danny was gracious and humble, willing to help whoever needed it. He took on additional tasks of arranging choral music and band arrangements.

It took something off his teachers' plates and gave him something to do. Eddie Steenstra, the band instructor, had Danny lead sectionals and the pep band. Joe Eveler, the choir instructor, had Danny work with the tenors and baritones on parts as they neared concerts.

Most everyone liked Danny, who saw him as a little brother. While the letters didn't bother him as much as they did Randy or Bobby, he was still aware of what was said around him and especially who said it. While he worked with a boy and girl duet in the corner, he picked up most of the conversation between Randy and a girl, Sonya Fulton. Danny knew they had a crush on each other.

"Randy, I was wondering if you could help me on my solo for Broadway night. I'm having trouble with some of the phrasing."

Randy smiled and said, "Sure. I'd be happy to."

Maryanne Sturgis overhead, shook her head, and said, "No offense to you, Randy, but Danny's better at it than you are."

Randy blinked, recovered, smiled and said, "I know he's better at it than I am." Not wanting to include her, he turned to Sonya and said, "If you still want me to help, I'm happy to."

Sonya glared at Sturgis and said, "Yes, if you don't mind."

Maryanne shrugged, made a face, and sat waiting for the class to begin with her music folder on her lap and her hands folded on top of it.

Bobby walked up to Randy and said, "Did you get Brian's text about the new kid? He's not in choir with us because of art. He's in band, though."

"Yup, I saw. A Tony something."

Bobby said, "Vittoria. Sounds Italian."

"Brian said he's nervous."

"Shit, I'd be too." With a wry smile at Randy, Bobby added, "You two look busy."

Both Randy and Sonya blushed and then moved away to a corner to work on her part.

"I told them Danny would do a better than Randy, but they didn't listen."

Bobby frowned at Maryanne, shook his head, and walked away.

CHAPTER TWENTY-SEVEN

The cafeteria, the locker room, and the restroom were the scariest places for new kids. Even with a thousand other kids floating through the hallways, new kids were an easy mark. It would begin with a bump, sometimes on purpose. It would graduate to a shove. The kid would be cornered and questioned. If the answers to the questions weren't acceptable- and who in the hell knew what the acceptable answers were- slaps and punches would follow. Money demanded. Other items taken. And the new kid would be left alone to fend for himself, only to have the process repeated each day, until the novelty wore off. Sometimes, the novelty never wore off.

The funny thing about new kids. They knew other new kids went through the same thing. When in the same restroom or locker room, they didn't stick around to watch, certainly not to intervene. They just hoped they could escape this one time, maybe guilty it was happening to someone else and not to them. A life cocktail that was difficult to drink.

Tony had seen and lived it.

The worst was the spring of eighth grade. The name calling. Taunts. The humiliation. Abandonment by friends, or rather, who he thought were friends. The utter aloneness. He managed to tough it out, though by the time the school year ended, Tony lost his smile. Maybe his reason to smile.

Quiet and reserved by nature, he went to school. He managed good grades. His teachers liked him. One in particular, Shelly Wilson, his art teacher, took time to talk to him, encourage him, and worry about him. The other teachers saw him as they did any other student. Just another kid.

All of this ran through Tony's mind as he waited for Brian. Hoping Brian wouldn't forget.

Tony leaned against the bank of lockers, wishing he would sink inside. If he just stood there and didn't move, maybe no one would notice him.

Five minutes, inching towards six. At this rate, he wouldn't have time to eat.

Hands sweaty, he rubbed his jeans, first one hand, then the other. His mouth, dry. His instinct was to find a quiet corner and eat lunch by himself.

Tony saw Brian. He didn't realize he had been holding his breath, hoping, worrying, scared. Tony relaxed only a little.

As Brian walked towards him with a grin on his face, he held up a plastic grocery sack.

"I stopped by the office and picked up your swim stuff for PE." He noticed the worry on Tony's face and said, "Everything okay?"

Tony licked his lips, swallowed, and nodded.

"Did something happen?"

Tony shook his head again.

Brian suspected Tony's anxiety, gripped his shoulder and said, "Hey, it's going to be okay. My brothers and my friends are in there. You met a bunch of them already. I'll be with you. We have this, okay?"

Tony tried to smile, but only shrugged.

With an arm across Tony's shoulders, they walked into the cafeteria to the group of tables where he and his friends sat. Tony wanted to bolt, but his legs felt like jelly. Like he did with most everything else and as he did so often, he toughed it out.

The cafeteria was just like any other cafeteria. Few students even acknowledged his existence, which was okay with him. He preferred it that way.

Kids seemed to be grouped by grade or by interest. Gamers pecked away at their cells and were clustered at tables off to the left of the doorway. Jocks, sporting letter jackets with duffle bags under their tables, were up front near the serving lines. Other tables were a mix of just boys, just girls, or mixed. Some things never change. Only the players.

"Hey, everyone! I want you to meet Tony Vittoria."

There were waves and hellos, along with, *"We met in ..."* reminding him in which class he had met them. Overwhelmed, Tony did not know who was who or how he would remember them all. There had to be almost twenty guys and girls sitting at the tables. All were smiling or mouths covered because they chewed chunks of sandwich, spoonfuls of yogurt, an apple or baby carrots. They seemed friendly and at least nodded and waved. A couple he recognized from his classes.

"I saved you two a seat," Brett said, showing them two empty chairs at his table. "Vittoria. That's Italian."

Tony smiled and said, "Yes."

"Are you Antonio or Anthony?"

"Antonio."

"Thought so," Brett said. "Your family must come from Northern Italy."

Surprised, Tony said, "From a small town near Torino."

"Probably a stereotype, but a lot of blond Italians come from the north." He pointed at Bobby sitting one table away and said, "That's my brother Bobby." Bobby waved with one hand, held a sandwich in the other, busy chewing. "Our family, the Dominico side, come from the south, near Torretta." He pointed to a smallish kid with long black curly hair and said, "See that kid? His name is Mario Denali. His family comes from Sicily, near a town called Salemi."

"He's a helluva soccer player," Brian said. Mario and another boy waved at him.

"Are you a surfer?" Billy asked.

Tony laughed and said, "I boogie board. I snow board and I ski, but I've never surfed."

Billy laughed and said, "You look like a California dude with your hair and tan. Even the shell necklace."

Tony laughed again and said, "I've never been to California."

Brett said, "Brian said you're in art? What kind do you do?"

"I like to draw with pencil and pastels. But I like to paint, too."

"I'm in photography. Can I see some of your work?"

Tony pulled out his phone, hit the Gallery app, and found the folder containing pictures of his drawings. Brian and Brett leaned over to see them.

"These are terrific," Brian said. "I didn't know you were this good."

"I won a couple of awards," Tony said, as he blushed and shrugged.

"Brian said you're taking photography. Can I see some of your photos?" he asked Brett.

Holding his cell out, "Here are three of my favorites." He showed them a picture of Bobby sitting between Brian's legs, with Bobby resting his head on Brian's chest, with Brian resting his head on the side of Bobby's head. Both boys stared straight ahead. "They were watching TV and didn't notice me taking the shot."

He flipped to a photo of Brian giving Two a piggy-back ride, both boys laughing. "That's our brother, Two. He seldom goes anywhere except on Brian's back."

The last picture was of Brian in the stable on the Morning Star ranch on the Navajo Nation reservation. Brett snapped it on their trip west in late summer.

Brian had his shirt off and his cowboy hat on. Beads of sweat on his back, chest, and arms. Some rivers of sweat ran down his side and stomach. He leaned on a pitchfork and his expression was far, far away. Sad, it looked to Tony.

He glanced at Brian and said, "What were you thinking?"

Brian turned away from the picture and muttered, "It was a shitty trip and I wished I was back home."

Tony didn't understand the comment, not knowing the context.

"It's a long story," Brett said.

"Hey, where's George?" Brian asked. "I wanted him to meet Tony. Tony runs cross country and track."

Brett motioned with his head as he took a sandwich out of the plastic bag.

"Talking to the kid over there," Billy said. He introduced himself to Tony and said, "I don't have any classes with you, but we eat lunch together. My twin brother is over there," Billy said, pointing to a nearby table.

"Who's older?" Tony asked.

"I am," Billy said proudly. "Randy is Xeroxed."

"A newer and improved model," Randy said over his shoulder. "We met when you were on your way to band."

Tony looked at Brett and then at Bobby and said, "You two are brothers?"

"Yup, I'm older, smarter, and better looking."

"You wish," Bobby laughed. "He's only eighteen months older than I am. I was with Randy when we met."

Tony smiled at the remark.

Brett leaned around Tony and said to Brian, "Do you know who the kid is?"

Brian squinted at him. "He's new. About a month ago, I met him in guidance. A freshman. I think his first name is Andrew. I can't remember his last name. Kind of quiet." He thought for a minute and asked, "Is that ...?"

"Yeah, I think so," Brett said.

The exchange puzzled Tony, but he didn't ask about it.

George wandered back to the table, introduced himself to Tony, and offered to work out with him after school.

"I didn't bring anything," Tony explained.

"It's okay. I have to pick up our brother after school, and we can swing by your house to pick up what you need, and come back to North and work out."

Tony made a face and said, "I don't want to put you through too much trouble."

"It's not. I'm happy to."

The boys ate their lunches, talked about this and that, and got ready to head to their classes.

Quietly, so only George could hear, Brett asked, "What did you find out about the kid?"

George made a face, eyes darting around the table, and said, "Nothing much. I invited him to sit with us, but he said he was fine where he was."

Brett glanced that direction, but the kid was nowhere to be seen. He made a face and shrugged. "Just as well, I guess."

Before they left, Brian said to Tony, "George and I'll see you in PE. Wait by the locker room door. I'm coming from the other side of the building, so it will take me longer to get there. I'll introduce you to coach and get you a locker and a lock."

Tony smiled and said, "Thanks."

The two boys embraced briefly, while George, Billy, and Brett looked on, and then the boys went their separate ways.

Tony smiled to himself, glanced over his shoulder, and saw Brian smiling back at him. He gave Tony a little wave. Tony smiled and blushed, but waved back.

"Nice guy," Brett said.

Brian smiled, and said, "Yeah. I like him."

"I can tell."

CHAPTER TWENTY-EIGHT

Brett barked directions during the five-on-five drill. Mikey guarded Brett as best he could. He could almost match Brett's quickness, but his inexperience showed. Brian squared off against Bobby, and Troy against Big Gav, but it was no match at all. Gavin did whatever he wanted, when he wanted, and how he wanted. At six-six with guard skills, Brian thought Gav was the best player on the court.

Billy played against Randy, and in Coach Harrison's eyes, Billy took it easy on him.

"Everyone get water. Billy, come here a minute," Coach said, walking off the court away from the others.

Billy joined him and Harrison said, "Billy, you're not doing Randy any favors by playing soft. The only way he's going to get better is if you play him as hard as you do anyone else."

Billy looked down at his shoes and said, "It's hard. He's my brother."

"He's just another guy when we're on the court. You don't see Brian or Bobby taking it easy on each other."

"Yeah, I know."

"When Randy gets on the court, I need him to be ready. The only way it's going to happen is if you play him hard."

"I know," Billy said, nodding.

Harrison watched Brett work with Tony on his running form, showing how to position his hands. He could almost hear him say, *Your hands are like blades slicing through butter,* which was something he had heard Brett tell other runners. Harrison knew that first statement would be followed up with, *You can only run as fast as you pump your arms. The faster you pump your arms, the faster you run. Keep your head as still as possible. Don't let it bob.*

"What's the new kid like?" Harrison asked Billy.

Like he and Randy did during timeouts and during free throws, Billy had the top of his jersey clenched between his teeth. After releasing it from his mouth, he said, "Good guy. Brian's taking care of him."

"I noticed. Seems to be good for each other."

Billy glanced at Brian, who spoke with Mikey and Bobby. "I think so too."

As they walked back to join the others, Harrison said, "Play hard, Billy. I'd like to go ten deep this season."

"Got it, Coach."

Harrison put them through several more drills and ended with a series of sprints between free throws. He took the time to walk to each basket and speak with each player. That done, he called them all to center court.

"Our first game is Friday night. Tomorrow will be a lighter practice, more of a walk-through with a lot of shooting. Make sure you're eating right and getting enough sleep. We need everyone healthy."

Brett waited until Harrison finished talking, and then he said, "Everyone showers after practice and after games. You don't leave the locker room sweaty. That's a good way to get sick. And Vitamin C is always good."

Coach Harrison finished with, "Good practice, guys. Keep it up. Take nothing for granted. One game at a time."

Billy tried to keep a straight face when he said, "Any other cliches' you want to add?"

The guys laughed, and Harrison said, "Sure. How about another ten sprints?"

"Ahh, that's okay, Coach. Use all the cliches' you want," Billy said.

"Then get out of here before I run you to death."

Brian waited just outside the locker room for George, Michael, and Tony.

"Good workout?" he asked, more to Tony than to George or Two.

"I don't think George or Two broke a sweat."

Tony was as sweaty as Brian and the other basketball players were.

"They've been working out since cross country ended, so they have a head start on you. That's all."

"You kept up just fine," George said. "Tomorrow will be a lighter day."

Brian slipped an arm around Tony's shoulders and said, "From what I saw, you did well."

Tony smiled at him as they walked to their lockers. Two grabbed an empty locker next to Brian.

"Make sure you wear your slides. The shower and the locker room floor can be gross. Towels are in a bin just outside the shower." Brian bent closer to Tony and said in a quieter voice, "Make sure you lock your locker. Stuff gets lifted in here."

"Um, I forgot shampoo, soap and deodorant," Tony said.

"Got you covered. We'll share mine," Brian said with a smile.

Like most other schools, the showers comprised of two large center poles, with shower spigots around the pole. Each center pole could accommodate six people, which made it cozier than the boys would have liked. And like most school showers, the water was only lukewarm. The boys theorized that kept everyone moving.

The boys kept their distance as best they could, given the cramped area. Most everyone shared body wash and shampoo. Talk was of the upcoming game, who was doing what after it, and who had plans for the weekend. There was hardly any talk about school.

Done, the boys grabbed towels and dried off. They dressed quickly and filed out of the locker room door, spilling out onto the parking lot.

"You can ride with me," Brian said to Tony.

The boys split up with Tony, Two, Billy, and Brett riding with Brian. George took Bobby and Randy, and told Brian he'd stop and pick up the dog food on the way home.

"We're having tacos for dinner," Brett announced.

"I'll grill the chicken, and Michael can shred it," Brian said, glancing at Two in the rearview mirror.

"Sure. I might make dessert, too," Michael said.

"Fritters!" Billy said.

"Sure. Strawberry and blueberry."

To Tony, Billy said, "Two is the dessert king." Then he asked, "Are Jeff and Danny eating with us?"

"I'll text them and ask," Brett answered. His fingers already pecking away on his cell.

After a quick ride into one of the newer subdivisions, they arrived at Tony's house, and Brian pulled into the driveway.

"Thanks for the ride," Tony said.

"No problem. I usually drop Michael off at school each morning, so if you want, I can pick you up."

"You don't have to," Tony said.

"I don't mind," Brian answered.

"Well, if you want to."

"Sure. I'll call you tonight after dinner. Face Time."

Goodbyes, followed by waves and a *"See you tomorrow"* or two, and Brian pulled out and drove off.

"Seems like a nice guy," Billy said.

Brian nodded with a smile to no one in particular. Brett noticed, smiled, but otherwise said nothing.

CHAPTER TWENTY-NINE

Jeff scrubbed his hands with dish soap, the kind that is especially strong on grease. Then he ran to the bathroom and poured hydrogen peroxide on his hands, and then washed them again with soap and water.

After drying his hands, he called Brian. Trying to keep the fear and urgency out of his voice, he asked, "Brian, has anyone gone to your mailbox and picked up the mail yet?"

Brian stood at the sink, getting ready to pack the dishwasher, and then wash dishes and pans that wouldn't fit. He looked over at the counter and other places the guys put the mail, and not seeing it, he said, "I don't think so. At least, I don't see any."

"Ask the others, please."

Brian stared at the phone, shrugged, and then said, "Guys, did anyone get the mail yet?"

Buried in homework or helping with homework, heads shook while one or two muttered, "No."

"Nope. No one picked it up yet."

George stood up from the table, went to the cupboard where the latex gloves were, and pulled out a left and right.

"Looks like George is going to go get it."

Almost climbing through the phone, Jeff yelled, "No! Don't let him! No one goes near it!"

It was so loud the guys sitting at the table looked up at Brian. George froze where he stood.

"Eiselmann, Graff, and O'Connor are on their way. I'll call them and have them stop for your mail, too."

Alarmed, Brian said, "Jeff, why? What happened? Are you and Danny okay?"

Calming some, but not much, Jeff said, "Yes, we're fine. Just don't go anywhere near your mailbox."

CHAPTER THIRTY

Eiselmann, O'Connor, and Graff stood in the driveway with Jeff, well back from the letter on the porch. Jeff had ordered Danny not to come outside and not let any of the Evans' boys know what was happening. Danny contented himself by fiddling with homework and glancing out the window at the commotion.

"I never brought it in the house. Once I felt what was in it, I dropped it on the porch, ran inside and cleaned off my hands." He shrugged and said, "I'm not sure why I scrubbed my hands like I did. I wore latex gloves."

"Better to be safe than sorry," Eiselmann said as he climbed into a Tyvek suit.

"Tell me again what you felt when you looked over the envelope," Graff said.

Jeff shook his head and said, "It felt like powder. Not much, but something is in there."

"The envelope is completely sealed," Eiselmann said. "I don't see any openings. Whoever sealed it made sure it wouldn't leak. Someone meant business, both with the letter and in sealing it."

He pulled out a camera and snapped photos. That done, he grabbed a plastic bag and placed the envelope inside it, and sealed the bag. As a further precaution to minimize exposure, he placed the plastic bag inside yet another plastic bag and sealed it. Following protocol, he wrote the time, date, location, and signed it.

Eiselmann didn't realize he had been holding his breath. "Damn, I was more tense than I thought."

"I'd rather you be tense and thorough than not tense and sloppy," Graff said.

Noting Danny peering out the window, Graff turned to Jeff and asked, "Who knows about this?"

"If we're talking about the envelope, Danny and me. I already told Danny not to mention anything to the Evans' boys. Brian and the boys know not to go near their mailbox. They don't know why, but they're smart enough to figure something is up."

"Paul, are we safe out here?"

Paul was stepping out of the Tyvek suit. "Should be. I think so." To himself, he muttered, "I hope so."

Graff motioned for Danny to come outside.

It only took a minute or two. Danny stood on the porch in his socks, and his fingers stuffed into his front pockets.

Graff said, "You received another letter. We're upping our precautions just to be safe. We're not worried, and you and your dad shouldn't be. Okay?"

Danny glanced at his dad, shrugged, and said, "Okay."

"Have you spoken to Bobby or Randy, or anyone else since your dad found the letter?"

Danny shook his head and said, "No."

O'Connor smiled wryly and said, "That would include texting, Instagram, Snapchat, or TikTok."

Danny laughed and said, "As far as I know, no one knows you guys are here. No one knows I received a letter. And no one knows Paul dressed up in a space suit like the letter had something contagious inside of it."

"You are a smartass," O'Connor laughed.

"He gets it from his dad," Graff said.

"Hey!" Jeff laughed. He sobered up and said, "I told Brian you guys were on your way, though."

"Okay, we're off to see whether Randy or Bobby received similar letters. Please keep this under your hat," Jamie said.

"I don't wear a hat," Danny said with a barely straight face.

"I would suggest somewhere else to keep it, but that might be inappropriate," O'Connor said. "And I'm seldom inappropriate."

"Yeah, right," Danny said, already turning back and heading into the house.

CHAPTER THIRTY-ONE

They stopped at the top of the driveway, got out, and inspected the contents of the mailbox. Other than what they might find in anyone's mail, there was nothing. No letters to Randy or Bobby. Just assorted junk mail, flyers, and a couple of bills.

"Huh," O'Connor said.

Graff screwed his face up in thought and said, "What do you make of this?"

It was O'Connor who answered. "A couple of possibilities. It could be the mail is late. Again. With this new idiot in charge of the U.S. Postal Service, anything is possible. So, we'd have to check tomorrow. The other possibility is that whoever sent the letter to Danny didn't intend to send one to Randy or Bobby. More of a message designed specifically for Danny."

"Like, 'You aren't paying attention to me, so now I'll really get your attention!'" Eiselmann suggested.

"Something like that," O'Connor said.

Graff stared at his feet and toed a small stone near the mailbox. He didn't like where this case was heading. He had hoped to have it solved before Jeremy got out of the hospital, but with Jeremy's discharge in the morning, it didn't seem likely.

"Okay. Let's deliver this pile of garbage to the boys and see if they found out anything from any of the kids or staff at school."

They climbed back into Graff's car, but O'Connor stopped him from driving up to the house.

"Wait a minute. The letter Danny received. This escalates it a bunch. Some sort of substance in the envelope?" He shook his head. "This doesn't seem like a kid anymore."

"Almost too sophisticated to be a kid," Eiselmann said.

"I thought that, too," Graff said.

"But I don't think we should say anything to the boys. I mean, it would give them tunnel vision and they might not pick up anything from kids," Eiselmann said.

"Good point," Graff said. "Okay, we'll see what the boys have to say."

"Should take us all of three minutes," O'Connor muttered as he stared out the side window.

They pulled up in the circle drive near the door, got out, and Graff rang the bell.

Billy met them. "What's the password?"

"I think it's something like, get out of the way or I'll flush your head in a toilet," Graff answered.

"After I pee in it," Eiselmann said.

"That's rude," Billy laughed.

He held the door open to them.

Brett sat next to Two working on what looked like math. George and Billy were doing science. Graff heard singing and the sound of guitars from a different part of the house. Probably the living room. He didn't recognize the song.

"Where's Brian?" O'Connor asked.

"He's upstairs talking to a new kid," Brett said.

"Still?" Randy asked as he and Bobby walked into the kitchen. He looked at his watch and said, "It's been almost an hour."

"It's no big deal," Brett said. "Tony is new to the school, and he and Brian seem to hit it off."

"I'll say," Randy muttered.

"What's your problem?" Brett asked.

"Nothing. No problem," Randy answered with a frown.

"I'll go get Bri," Two said.

George and Billy watched the exchange between Randy and Brett, but didn't comment on it. Neither did the three cops.

A few minutes later, the boys and the cops heard laughter and banging down the steps. Two, on Brian's back, laughed along with Brian as the two boys ran into the kitchen. Brian banged Two into a wall and the refrigerator, making them laugh all the more.

"Who let you in the house?" Brian said with a laugh.

"There are times when you need a good butt whooping," O'Connor said.

"First, you'd have to catch me, and there's no way you would. Second, I'm tougher than you, so there's that." Brian couldn't keep a straight face and laughed.

"You're a little shit, Evans. If you didn't have a game on Friday, I'd teach you a lesson."

"Okay, okay," Graff said. "Before Pat goes WWF on Brian's ass, we stopped by to bring you your mail and to ask if any of you heard anything today that concerned you or sounded fishy. Maybe someone did something you thought was questionable or strange."

"What about the cookies I gave you?" George asked.

"Nada's cookies?" Billy asked.

"Yes," George answered without further explanation.

"We won't know anything about them for another day, maybe two. It takes time," Graff said.

"What happened to them?" Eiselmann asked. "There was nothing but bits and pieces and crumbs."

Billy laughed and told them the story of Danny rejecting them and his offer to eat them, and Nada getting pissed and throwing them away.

"Danny broke her heart," O'Connor said. "Again."

"He was nice about it. He thanked her and all," Billy answered with a shrug.

"Her reaction was extreme, don't you think?" Graff said. "A little weird?"

Two, Brian, Brett, and Billy laughed. Brett said, "She is weird."

"But her cookies and stuff are good," Billy said.

"Anything else?" Graff asked.

Bobby and Randy exchanged a look, and then Bobby said, "It's not much. Probably nothing, but a girl in chorus, Maryanne Sturgis, was rude to Randy and Sonya Randle."

"How so?"

Bobby explained what he had heard, and then Randy explained what Sturgis had said. After Randy finished, Bobby said, "But it's not a big deal. She's weird like Nada, but in a different way."

Graff nodded thoughtfully and said, "But neither girl threatened any of you."

The boys shook their head or said, "No."

"Nothing more than something that might take place in middle school," Eiselmann said.

The boys nodded or said, "Yeah."

The cops looked from one to the other and Graff said, "Anything else before we go?"

Like he was in school, George raised his hand and said, "I spoke to the boy today at lunch. The boy who watches us from another table."

"Oh? How did it go?" Graff asked.

"He's a freshman. His name is Andrew Westlake."

Brian snapped his fingers and said, "I met him in the counseling office about a month or two ago. He's new to North."

George said, "I sent you a picture of him."

To George, O'Connor asked, "How did the conversation go?"

"I asked him how things were going for him, being new to the school. He said things were fine. He said no when I asked if he was making friends. I asked him if he wanted to sit with us at lunch or in the morning. He said no. I walked away and almost right after I got back to our table, he had left the cafeteria."

"Huh," O'Connor said.

Graff squinted at George and said, "Was he angry you spoke to him? Embarrassed, maybe?"

George shook his head and said, "Maybe embarrassed. A little. He didn't seem angry. I think he's shy. Quiet."

"Did he make any threatening statements?" Eiselmann asked.

"No, nothing."

"Have any of you heard or seen any staff member saying or doing anything concerning?" Graff asked.

"Mr. Farner asked me if the group could sing the anthem Friday night," Randy said. "Nothing else."

Shrugs. Shakes of heads.

"Well, okay then. Your mail is on the counter," Graff said. "If something comes up, text or call one of us."

After O'Connor put Brian into a headlock and rubbing his knuckles on his head, they left.

Brian went to the refrigerator, took out the milk, and poured himself a glass. He said, "Anyone want anything while I'm up?"

"Throw me an orange, please," Brett said.

"As long as you're there, I'll take orange juice," Bobby said.

"I can pour you a glass."

"No, I've got it. Thanks, though." Bobby stood up, went to the cupboard, grabbed a glass and poured himself some. Brian and Bobby hip-checked each other at the counter and chuckled about it. After, he put the juice back into the refrigerator.

"What were you on the phone so long with Tony about?" Randy asked.

"I wanted to find out how his first day went," Brian said with a shrug. "Getting to know you kinds of things. We talked about *Lord of the Flies*. Other than that, not much."

He drained his glass of milk, wiped his mouth off with his hand, and rinsed the glass in the sink. After, he put it in the dishwasher. Then he handed Brett a napkin and a plate for the orange.

"He's going to get something to eat with us after the game, and then he's spending the night." He turned to George and said, "I told him about running Saturday morning, and he said he's up for it. I invited him to go riding with you, Two, and me, and he said he would."

"You invited him to spend the night after, what, one day?" Randy said with a humorless laugh. "It didn't take long for you to try and get in his pants."

The boys, especially Brian, were stunned. No one knew how to react. It was both what he said and the way he said it.

"What the hell is that supposed to mean?" Brian said.

"You know what it means," Randy said. "You break up with Bobby one night, and the next night, you invite a new kid, someone none of us knows, including you, to spend the night."

"What's wrong with you?" Bobby spat at Randy. "Brian and I agreed to end that part of our relationship because we knew mom and dad were against it. It might have been Brian's idea, but I agreed to it. And just because a guy is coming over to spend the night, like Troy or Chris or Sean do, doesn't mean Brian is going after him."

"Didn't you see him at school? He and *Tony*," Randy purposely changed his voice to ridicule Brian. "They were hanging all over each other."

"Fuck you!" Brian said.

"I like him," Brett said.

"Of course you do," Randy said. "You're always sticking up for Brian."

"Because lately, you've been on his ass for no apparent reason."

"I like him, too," Billy said, glaring at his twin.

"So do I," Two said.

"Great! Everyone loves Tony. Brian will get in his pants and we'll see where that goes."

"If Brett or Billy invited him over, no problem, right?" Brian barked.

"They aren't interested in his dick!"

"Fuck you!" Brian said, as he charged Randy.

Randy stood up, hands in fists. Bobby pushed Randy out of the room, while Billy and George blocked Brian's path.

Brett ran over, put both hands on Brian's shoulders, and said, "Let it go, Bri. He's acting like a tool."

"What did you call me?" Randy asked from the hallway, trying to push Bobby out of the way.

"I said you're acting like a tool, which is slang for a dick, which is slang for a penis. I can think of other things to call you, but a tool will suffice."

"Fuck you!"

"And fuck you right back."

Brian's face was fire engine red. His breathing was short and rapid. His hands in fists.

"Brian, let it go," Brett whispered. "It's nothing."

Brian shook away from Brett and walked outside, and slammed the door behind him. He didn't know where he was headed, only that he had to get away.

CHAPTER THIRTY-TWO

He sprawled on a bale of hay. Still seething, he had trouble controlling his breathing and his shaking hand. Ironically, it was Randy who had taught him yoga and basic meditation. Now Randy caused his anger and the shakes.

The stable was warm and smelled of horse and hay. Brian found it comforting. He had never grown up with horses. Not even dogs or cats. Yet, he could ride as well as George or Two, and three of the four dogs in the house favored him over any of his brothers or his parents.

He could ride with a saddle or bareback, and he had ridden each of the horses. His favorite was Nochero, George's stallion. He wandered over to him. Sleek and black, his main and tail matched the color of its body. Bigger, faster, and stronger than Jeff's Bay or Danny's Buckskin, the next two largest horses of the little herd. He stroked the big horse's smooth neck and spoke in a calm, quiet voice. It soothed Nochero as much as it did him.

It wasn't any of Randy's business who he hung out with or who he invited over. But what angered Brian the most was that Randy wasn't totally wrong. It was a tough pill of truth to swallow, and Brian choked on it.

Brian was interested in Tony. Tony was easy to talk to. He laughed easily. He was quiet and reserved, like Brian was, and Tony was gentle, like Bobby and George. While Brian wasn't into art or track or cross country like Tony, it didn't seem to bother either of them. Brian had other friends who were into other sports or activities and he got along with them just fine.

Brian also recognized an attraction to Tony beyond friendship. He didn't know if Tony shared that attraction. Brian would never ask him, and Brian doubted he'd ever admit his feelings for him. Still, he had a crush on Tony, and Brian hoped it was reciprocal. He didn't know, and Brian was smart enough, and cautious enough, to realize he might never know.

Brian heard the door open and close. He glanced over his shoulder and saw it was Brett.

Brett walked over and stood next to Brian. Nochero eyed him and snorted.

"He scares me."

"Maybe because you don't ride him. He looks mean, but he's gentle."

After a beat, Brett asked, "Are you okay?"

Brian thought for a minute and said, "It's none of his business who I invite over."

"I know that. He does too."

"Why did he come at me like that?"

Brett climbed up on the wooden door of the stall, and sat down, his back to Nochero, and facing out over the stable.

"Because he cares about Bobby. He doesn't like seeing him hurt."

Indignant, Brian said, "I'm hurting as much as Bobby."

"I know that. He knows it. We all know it."

"I don't understand why he's pissed at me. We broke it off because of dad and mom. I didn't want to. Bobby didn't want to. But we ended it for the sake of the family. For dad. Yes, it was my idea, but Bobby agreed to it."

Patiently, Brett said, "We know, Bri."

The silence, as comfortable as the two boys were with each other, dragged on slowly. It was Brian who broke it, though he didn't make eye contact.

"Randy wasn't entirely wrong."

Brett didn't respond.

"I'm kinda falling for him. Tony, I mean."

"We know."

Brian looked up and asked, "What do you mean, we know?"

Brett shrugged and said, "One of the cool things about you, Bri, is that you are transparent. You don't hide shit most everyone else hides. That's a good thing. Most everyone hides shit like it's fucking treasure or something. You're way more honest than most everyone."

"Fuck."

Brett chuckled.

"Do you think Tony knows? I mean, that I have a crush or something on him?"

Brett laughed and said, "Unless he's more unaware than you or Danny are, probably."

Brian started to protest, but gave up. It was an argument he would not win.

"Now what?"

Brett hopped down off the gate, took Brian by the shoulders, then placed his hands on Brian's cheeks. Like they did often, their foreheads rested on each other.

"You be you. You don't have to apologize to anyone about what you do or why. Don't hide who you are from anyone, including Tony. If Tony is as smart as I think he is, he will see what I see."

"What?"

"You're one of the coolest, nicest, most genuine guys I know. He'll be lucky to have you as a friend."

He thought for a minute and added, "Be satisfied with friendship. If it grows into something else, that's the cherry on top."

"What about Randy?"

Brett hugged Brian and said, "He'll probably apologize to you. Bobby and Billy are all over his ass as we speak. Whether you accept his apology is up to you. In the end, whatever is or isn't between you and Tony is none of his business, and it's none of our business, either."

CHAPTER THIRTY-THREE

While one was in the shower, another might be at the sink brushing teeth or combing hair. Multiple bathrooms helped. All of them had showered after basketball practice, or in George's and Two's cases, after they worked out. It meant only having to get rid of bed head or sprucing up pits and crotches. What helped even more was that none of the boys took any more time than needed. Today was no different from any other day. Perhaps more special since Jeremy was coming home.

"Guys, make sure you pick up the bathroom and your bedrooms," Brett yelled. "Mom and dad shouldn't come home to a messy house."

"I'll take care of the kitchen," Brian yelled back. "Michael, can you take care of our room? Make the bed?"

"Got it." After a beat, he said, "Do I look okay?"

Two wore a red Wisconsin Badgers long-sleeve shirt with black Nike nylon sweats. He topped his outfit off with white Air Jordans.

"You look fine. Will you be warm enough? Butler can get cold."

"I'll bring a sweatshirt, just in case."

"Are you working out with George and Tony after school?"

Two was already putting his running and shower gear into a duffle bag. "Yup. George wants to do an easy eight. We're doing hills tomorrow." This last, he said, wearing a face of disgust.

"Hills will get you in shape. Listen to George. Watch him. He's a master at them."

Two laughed and said, "I know. I just don't like running them unless I'm in a race."

Brian laughed along with him and said, "I don't like running hills, either. In fact, I'm not a fan of running."

Both boys laughed, and Brian added, "Hey, remember. Stay close to the doors while you wait for George."

"I always do."

"Good. I want you to stay safe. You're pretty ugly, so you should be safe. You never know, though."

"You're a dork!"

"Takes one to know one."

With than, Brian picked up his backpack and duffle bag, and bounded out of the room and down the stairs to the kitchen.

Billy and George were just finishing up their breakfast. Billy walked their dishes and placed them on the counter next to the sink. That was where Brian wanted them.

"I made you an egg sandwich on a bagel with extra bacon. No cheese," Billy said.

"Awesome, thanks."

He began rinsing off plates, forks and knives, and loaded up the dishwasher as George brought his dirty dishes over to the counter.

George said, "The dogs have been out, and I fed them and gave them water. I'll take them out again before we leave."

"I owe you money for the dog food. Thanks for picking it up. I think Brett is double-checking the upstairs."

"We made a sandwich for him, too. And Two," Billy said. "Shoot, didn't think of Randy or Bobby."

Billy grabbed the dirty pan and started in on eggs and bacon for them. George brought the toaster back out, pulled out the bread and butter, and made them toast.

Brian searched for anything else needing washing, found nothing, and shut the dishwasher door, and turned it on.

"Don't you want to wait for the pan and spatula?" Billy asked.

"Nope, I'll do them by hand."

He filled up the sink with warm water and dish soap, and wiped down the counters and table.

Bobby, Randy, Brett and Two trooped in and set their backpacks and duffle bags by the door. In Randy's and Bobby's case, neither looked like they got much sleep.

"Breakfast will be ready in a sec," Billy announced.

"Aren't you going to eat?" Brett asked.

"Did already. Two, your sandwich is in the oven warming up with Brian's and Brett's."

Two went to the refrigerator and said, "Who wants what to drink?"

Water all around. Bobby added a glass of orange juice, and Brett asked Two to throw him an orange.

"On our way in, I'm stopping at Speedway for donuts or muffins. Make sure you text me your order. I'll bring them to the cafeteria," Brian said as he dried off the counter.

He finished up the dishes and placed them in the sink to air dry. Brett grabbed a towel off the handle of the oven and began drying them off.

"I'd rather mom and dad walked in and not have to do anything extra," he said as an explanation.

"Smart," Brian said.

Dishes done and put away, the guys got ready to leave.

Brian laughed, and said, "Michael, I can always tell what you ate by looking at your face or your shirt."

Two grinned at him.

Brian licked his thumb and wiped off Two's cheek. "The rest of you looks good, even though you're kinda ugly."

"You're a dork," Two said with a laugh.

Brian turned around and said, "Hop on."

Randy was the last to leave the kitchen, and he said, "Brian, can I talk to you for a minute?"

"Michael, why don't you head to the truck? I'll catch up. And remind everyone to text me their donut or muffin order."

Brian turned to face Randy. He wasn't ready for this. One more apology. One more promise to do better. Only to be repeated in a couple of days.

When Two was out the door, Randy said, "Look, Brian. Last night I was out of line. I never should have said anything. Your friends are your friends. Your business is your business. I just know how hurt Bobby is."

"And I'm not hurting?"

"Well, yes. Of course, you are. I just ... Bobby," he gave up and shrugged. "I'm sorry about last night. I've been an ass lately. I'll do better."

Brian didn't know what to say. He didn't know if he was ready to accept Randy's apology, but he knew he needed to. If not for his and Randy's sake, then for their parents.

He said, "Mom and dad, especially dad, can't afford to see us, any of us, fighting and not getting along. It's no good for them, and it's no good for the family."

Randy nodded, but didn't, perhaps couldn't, make eye contact.

He paused, and then he said, "We better get going," and he turned and walked out of the house.

Randy blinked at the empty doorway, wondering if his apology was accepted.

CHAPTER THIRTY-FOUR

Even though he didn't receive a donut or muffin order from Randy or Bobby, Brian made sure he bought them something. He and Tony walked to the art room, while Billy and Brett walked to the cafeteria carrying donuts and muffins with them.

The guys sat around tables like they always did, eating and drinking their water or juice. Farner, the assistant principal, came up and made sure the group was ready to sing the anthem, teased them about not getting him a donut or muffin, and left to patrol the crowd in the cafeteria.

George had an idea.

Instead of eating his muffin, he carried it over to the new kid, Andrew Westlake, who sat at his table in his usual seat.

"Hi, Andrew. We stopped at Speedway and got muffins and donuts, and I have one for you."

Andrew blushed, got flustered, and said, "You didn't have to. I ate breakfast."

George smiled and said, "We did, too. We just wanted a snack before class. This is for you. If you want to join us, come on over. If you don't want to, that's fine."

George placed the muffin on the napkin and set it on the table within Andrew's reach and then walked away. He rejoined the group and took part in the conversation and laughter, glancing every so often at Andrew.

At first, the muffin remained untouched. Little by little, Andrew would reach over, break off a chunk and eat it. It wasn't long until the muffin was gone and Andrew wiped his mouth on the napkin.

Curiously, Danny watched from where he sat with Mikey, Stephen, and Garrett. He decided he was going to stop over and talk with Andrew at lunch, just as George had done.

"Billy, you eat everything I bring Danny, so I made these especially for you."

Nada Sherry, wearing the same sweater and most of her clothes from the day before, stood behind Billy, startling him. She set a paper plate of what looked like double chocolate chip cookies in front of him.

"I'm sure you won't share with anyone, but if you do, I hope you and anyone else chokes on them." She turned and stalked out of the cafeteria.

The boys stared at the plate as if it were about to grow legs and follow her.

The cookies looked good. Delicious, actually.

"Shit! Now what?" Billy muttered.

Danny walked over and said, "Don't touch them. Throw them away."

Bewildered, Billy said, "Why?"

Remembering Eiselmann in the Tyvek suit the night before, he said, "I don't trust her."

George stood up and said, "I'll take care of it."

CHAPTER THIRTY-FIVE

As he created it the evening before, Tony felt good about it. Two of his best drawings, he thought. They were small, of course. He had taken a piece of his special paper he used for his drawings, and folded it in four squares.

In the first square was a pencil drawing of Brian. It was just after he had received the text from his mother letting him know his dad wouldn't be home that evening, and no visitors would be allowed. The drawing showed Brian with his right hand in his hair, his left holding his cell, as he leaned against the locker. One leg straight, the other balancing on his toe. Brian's expression was sadness. It was an easy drawing for Tony.

In the third square was a pencil drawing of both Brian and Tony as they stood facing each other just outside of the art room. Tony debated whether to include Brian holding his wrist or with his hand on his shoulder. He had wanted to portray Brian holding his hand, but because it didn't actually happen, he settled for Brian holding his wrist. The figures stood almost toe to toe, Tony shorter. Tony looking anxious, as he knew he was. Frightened. Brian working hard to reassure him. There was an intimacy to the drawing Tony hoped Brian would like.

Unique to Tony's drawings was that while the drawings were always black and white with shades of gray mixed in, he used colored pencils to match the figure's eye color. For Brian, his eyes were a beautiful hazel, a mixture of green, gray, and brown. They sparkled. For Tony, his eyes were ice blue, vibrant. At least, that's what he saw in the mirror and how people described them to him.

What he struggled with was the message on the second square. He thought long and hard, went through several drafts on copy paper, not in love with any of them. He wanted something matching the intimacy of the second drawing, without it being too ... in Brian's face. Tony didn't want to push him away or make him feel uncomfortable. He wanted to hint how he felt, but didn't want to put it all out there. Not yet. Maybe never. He'd have to see. He settled on his third try, printed in an artistic freehand, italic.

Brian,
Thank you for taking all the time you did with me, showing me the school, and introducing me to your friends. That never happened before, and I've never had a friend like you. I appreciate it. I'm hoping our friendship grows and that somehow, I can make it up to you.
Thanks again,
Tony

Tony wasn't sure if it was enough, but it was, at the least, simple and direct.

Brian sat with his laptop open, tongue slightly out to the side, leaning over it, and concentrating on what he was writing. It looked like a story, but Tony wasn't sure.

Tony looked at the clock. In less than five minutes, students would file in for class. For now, it was just Mrs. Arney, busy at her desk, Brian with his laptop, and him.

Now or never. He decided to give it to him before he chickened out and before anyone else came into the room.

Tony sat down next to Brian, who looked over and smiled. Tony loved Brian's smile. It was warm and friendly. Genuine.

"I made something for you. If you don't like it, you can always throw it away," Tony said with a shrug.

He handed him the note anxiously, afraid Brian would bolt out of the room. The end of that friendship, or whatever it was.

Brian took the note and stared at the cover.

"You drew this?"

Tony nodded.

"That's me."

Tony smiled. He had worked hard to get it just right.

"How ...?" the question trailing off. "This is awesome. Seriously, dude."

Tony blushed, shrugged, and smiled.

Brian opened it and stared at the second drawing. Surprised, he blinked. He didn't understand why this drawing hit him the way it did. Maybe it was Randy attacking him the night before. Maybe it was how he felt about Tony, or maybe it was Brett reassuring him. Whatever it was, it was a visceral feeling, like a wrench tightening on his heart and a lump growing in his throat.

"Us," he whispered. "Yesterday, just before art."

Tony nodded.

Brian stared at Tony briefly, then at the picture, then back at Tony. Tony couldn't read Brian's reaction, and that frightened him. It was as if Brian wanted to say something, but thought better of it.

To break the tension, Tony said, "I just wanted to say thanks for all you did for me yesterday. I appreciate it."

Tony didn't know if Brian had heard him. Brian was too busy reading the note and staring at the drawing of the two of them. He watched Brian closely. It looked as though Brian blinked back tears, but Tony still didn't recognize his reaction. He only hoped he didn't blow it.

"This is really cool. One of the best things I ever received."

Tony smiled and blushed. Relieved.

"Brian, the bell is about to ring, and I don't want you to be late for class. But if you don't mind, may I see it?"

This whole time, Mrs. Arney had been watching and listening to them. Neither knew it, and they seemed to have forgotten she was even there.

Arney was a short ball of fire. She was a young thirty-something, popular with the students and staff. Seldom without a smile or an encouraging word. An excellent teacher who always gave more than she received.

Both boys stood up, and Brian embraced Tony.

"Thank you," he whispered.

The embrace lingered, and then they stepped back, with Brian still holding onto Tony's wrist, then briefly, his hand. "Thanks."

Tony smiled, eyes shining.

"Look at this, Mrs. Arney. It's really cool."

She took it. Nodded at the first drawing, opened it, nodded and smiled at the second drawing. It didn't appear she had read the note.

"Tony, you need to draw these bigger. Maybe ten by thirteen. Even larger. These are fantastic."

"Thank you. I am actually. Drawing them larger, I mean."

"Can I have the one of the two of us?" Brian asked. "I'll even pay you for it."

"After I see it, grade it, and display it," Arney said. "If you want me to display it. It's up to you."

"You might want to keep it, but if not, I'd like it," Brian said hopefully.

"You can have it, and you don't have to pay for it."

They embraced again, and Brian whispered so only Tony could hear, "Thank you. I mean it. It means a lot to me."

He packed up and left the room after Arney gave him back the note. At the door, Brian turned around, smiled at Tony, and left.

Arney said, "You know, Tony. If I were a student and if I could only have one friend in this school, I would choose Brian Evans. He's one of a kind, and you won't find anyone better." She smiled, fussed with some projects on her desk, and added, "But hey, that's just me. I'm an old lady, so what do I know?"

Tony smiled at her, thinking the same thing. About Brian, that is.

CHAPTER THIRTY-SIX

Graff and Eiselmann sat in Bob Farner's office. Bigger than some, smaller than most. A stack of half-page printed notes in triplicate sat on a corner of his desk. A stack of manila folders sat on the other side. In the middle of the desk was a large calendar with scribbles Graff couldn't read, caused by a combination of Graff's angle and because of Farner's small handwriting. Notes were all over it. Some in pencil. Some in black or blue ink. Some in red. Here and there were yellow, pink, and light blue sticky notes on his desk or on the little board on the wall next to Farner within arm's reach.

Farner was a round man with a ready laugh. He had a penchant for poking fun, especially with the kids, with a great ear for news and gossip honed from years listening to kids in the classroom, cafeteria, and hallways. His go-to colors were brown, tan, and yellow in various combinations.

Originally, he was hired as a hammer. They found discipline lacking at North. As a result, the principal and two assistant principals were fired. In came new principal, Chuck Gobel, and two new assistant principals, Farner and Liz Champion.

Champion didn't last long. Married, she had an affair with a business teacher. Both of them ran a drug operation using high school students as couriers, and middle school kids as guinea pigs, almost all of whom had died. The business teacher died a nasty death at the hands of an enforcer from MS-13, and Champion was arrested and sentenced to forty years in prison without parole for her part in the drug ring and the deaths of kids.

Cathie Tobin, a former English teacher and counselor, currently filled the position. By all counts, especially those in the positions to hire and fire, Tobin was spectacular. Rumor had it she was going to be the next principal when a position opened up.

Young, she had a dry, sarcastic wit, and was smart and insightful. A mother herself, she used her every-mother's antenna to her advantage. She had an uncanny ability to, without tangible evidence, arrive at a conclusion and be dead on.

In his lap, Eiselmann had a pad of paper tucked nicely into a leather cover with a pen at the ready.

Graff asked, "Bob, what can you tell us about Nada Sherry?"

Farner threw his head back and laughed.

"That she's weird."

"That's what the Evan's boys said about her. Anything else you can share? Anything that might tell us why she's weird?"

Farner laughed again. "I mean, she is a full six pack of weirdness. Everything about her is strange. I met her mother." He rolled his eyes and shook his head. "The kid comes by it honestly. If Nada is the six pack, her mother is the freakin' truckload."

He reached for his phone, punched in a couple of numbers, and said, "Gloria, do you have a couple of minutes? I would like to speak with you in my office. And please bring everything you can on Nada Sherry."

As they waited for the counselor to arrive, Farner asked, "It's been a while, but I was wondering if you found out anything on the car bombings?"

Eiselmann, a perfect poker player, didn't move. Not even a facial tic.

Graff shook his head and said, "The FBI are handling it. As far as I know, the case is still open, but I suspect there aren't any leads."

Farner shook his head and said, "I keep thinking, what if kids or parents were in the lot when they went off? How many deaths and injuries?"

Graff remembered the explosion at the nightclub in downtown Waukesha and the shooting at the soccer field two or so years back. On the same night, within minutes of each other. A needless waste of life.

Farner shook his head again. "Most of my time as an assistant principal is with about ten percent of the student body. Only ten percent. I look at some of those kids and I know in five or ten years, they will be in the newspaper or on the news, and it won't be for something good. And the thing that concerns me is that I think those kids know it. They've given up and don't give a damn, and neither do most of their parents. Not all. There are some who would do anything to turn their kids' lives around. But others?" He shook his head and didn't continue.

Gloria Beatleman knocked on Farner's door, and then entered. Before she was seated, she said, "I found what I could, but there isn't much."

She handed the file to Farner, turned to Graff, and said, "Any news on Jeremy?"

"Good news. He's coming home today at some point. I'm guessing he might be back at work on Monday."

"That's great news," Beatleman said.

"Gloria, in looking at the file and what you've observed in your contacts with her, what can you tell us about Nada?"

"She's weird."

Farner gave Graff and Eiselmann a look that said, *what did I tell you?*

"What can you tell us about her friends? Things she's into? Stuff like that," Eiselmann asked.

"She doesn't have many friends. She's not into any clubs or athletics. She doesn't take band or choir. She's not in any theater class or in any school plays. It is good she hardly misses any days. She comes to school, goes to her classes, and leaves. She's like a ghost. What I would call an invisible kid."

"You might not be permitted to tell us, but is she in special ed?" Graff asked.

"Bob, can you hand me her file, please?" Beatleman asked.

When she received it, she licked her thumb and paged through it, and found what she was looking for.

"There was an SEC meeting." She looked over at Graff and Eiselmann and said, "That's a committee made up of teachers, a counselor, and special ed staff. They looked into a placement for giving her special education services, but there was no basis. Reading scores are below average, but not too low. Social and emotional scores were low, but not too low. They even looked at a 504 plan."

She looked over at the two cops and said, "It's like a special ed IEP, an individual educational plan, but on the medical side of life. For kids with diabetes, ADHD, things like that. But again, there wasn't any basis."

Graff pursed his lips and then said, "Let me ask this question in all seriousness." He waited for a beat and then asked, "Could she be dangerous? To anyone. A student. A staff member. Anyone."

Farner sat back in his chair and frowned. Beatleman blinked, opened her mouth, and then shut it.

Farner said, "To herself, maybe. To anyone else?" he shook his head, answering his own question.

Beatleman shook her head and said, "Honestly, I can't see it. I might be wrong. There have been kids who surprised me, but Nada Sherry? No way."

Eiselmann asked, "Does she drive?"

"No. She's only a freshman," Farner said. "She doesn't take driver's ed until next year."

Beatleman consulted the contents of the folder and said, "She won't turn sixteen until April of next year. She wouldn't get her license until next summer."

Graff tried a different track. "Would she be the type to send letters to other students? Sort of fan mail, but not quite. Specifically, to Danny Limbach, Randy Evans, or Bobby McGovern?"

Both Farner and Beatleman gawked at him.

"Seriously?" Farner asked. "Not to sound unprofessional, but I'm not sure she could string words together to make sentences, unless the letters were elementary or middle school level."

He looked at Beatleman, who shook her head. "Why them? They don't come close to traveling in the same social circles."

Graff pulled the plate of chocolate cookies out of the paper bag and set them on the calendar on Farner's desk.

"These look exceptional!" Farner looked up from the cookies, smiled at Graff, and said, "Are you offering?"

"Mmm, not really. Nada made them for Billy Schroeder. It seems from time to time, she makes cookies or cake and brings it to Danny. He doesn't eat it, but others do, primarily Billy."

Farner pushed his chair back, grimaced and said, "She made these?"

"Evidently. She brought them to Billy this morning before school. We can confirm it with the security cameras, which we might need to do."

Eiselmann broke in and said, "We're taking these to the FBI for analysis to make sure they are just cookies."

"Jesus! I think I want to disinfect my desk."

Graff thought for a minute and said, "Do you have time to talk about two other students? One is Maryanne Sturgis, and the other is a new kid, Andrew Westlake. What can you tell me about either of them?"

Farner shrugged and said, "Not much about either." He looked over at Beatleman and shrugged again.

"Maryanne is quite bright, but not as bright as she thinks she is. Can be a snob. Has a few friends in the choir and in theater. I can't say much about Andrew. He's only been here a short time. Came from Racine."

"Would either of them hang around with Nada Sherry?" Eiselmann asked.

Both Farner and Beatleman shook their heads.

"No way," Beatleman said. "Maryanne would think Nada is beneath her. And I don't see Andrew hanging with either. He seemed shy when I registered him."

"Do either of them drive?" Graff asked.

Farner punched some keys, found what he was looking for, and said, "Sturgis does. Westlake is too young. No license."

Graff looked over at Eiselmann, who shrugged. Graff said, "Well, I think we took enough of your time. I would like this conversation kept between the four of us, please. We're following up on a couple of things."

Both stood, as did Farner and Beatleman. Everyone shook hands.

Eiselmann said, "Can I offer either of you one of these delicious looking cookies?"

"Oh hell, no!" Farner said.

CHAPTER THIRTY-SEVEN

The drive into Milwaukee wasn't as bad as Graff and Eiselmann thought it would be. Traffic congestion around the Zoo Interchange was a given because I-94 converged with I-894, coupled with road repairs, which lasted forever. The next traffic hotspot was the Airport Interchange, where I-43, I-894, and Highway 45 joined. The last hurdle was the Mitchell Interchange, where I-43, I-894 hooked up with I-94 and Highway 41. Graff switched to surface streets to reach St. Francis, the city on the outskirts of Milwaukee, where the FBI office sat on Lake Drive.

Graff was fine as long as traffic kept moving and he had a travel mug of warm coffee. Eiselmann drank a Coke and munched on a power bar.

Graff glanced over at him, smirked, and said, "You could always try one of the chocolate cookies."

"Fuck, no!"

They had the radio dialed to FM106.1, the country music station in Waukesha serving the Milwaukee area. Graff tapped the steering wheel to the beat of a Chris Young song.

"I'm hoping the phone call from Skip Dahlke to the FBI lab will get them moving. Especially on the envelope of mystery powder," Eiselmann said between mouthfuls.

"If not, I'll have Pete Kelliher ask Summer Storm to light a fire under them," Graff said. As an afterthought, Graff asked, "What do you know about this Gordon Pasquale, the lab guy we're supposed to hook up with?"

"Pasquale is good. He's thorough. He won't small-talk you to death. He does his thing. When he's ready, he'll fill you in. You combine your IQ score with mine and O'Connor's, and we still wouldn't get as high as his is. If he's not in Mensa, I don't know who is. He might have a pocket protector. Not sure, but I think so." Eiselmann chuckled and said, "You remember Leonid Brezhnev, the Russian dude?"

"Yeah," Graff answered, puzzled by the question.

"You might see a resemblance," Eiselmann chuckled. "Of course, he doesn't carry the three hundred pounds Brezhnev had."

Graff thought for a minute and said, "You have a pocket protector."

"Bullshit."

They pulled into the lot, and Graff popped the trunk. They got out of the car and stretched. The day was pleasant enough, but there was a cloud build up to the northwest, indicating the possibility of a late afternoon rain shower. As the saying went, if you don't like the weather in Wisconsin, wait an hour.

"I'll take the cookies," Graff said. "You can carry the letter with the mystery powder." He shivered involuntarily and said, "Just having it close by gives me the willies."

Eiselmann smiled and said, "It's sealed tight."

"Still," Graff answered, shaking his head.

They showed their creds, waited for about ten minutes, and Pasquale arrived to escort them to the lab.

Pasquale was a middle-aged man with black, thick, bushy eyebrows making him look older than his thirty-three years. He had thick, black, unruly hair matching his eyebrows. Graff understood Eiselmann's comment about Brezhnev. Graff didn't see a pocket protector.

"My lab is this way, if you'll follow me."

He glanced at the plate of cookies and said, "They look good. Nothing unusual in the chocolate chip cookies. Or the crumbs, I should say. Someone was pissed he didn't get one from the looks of them."

"The baker got pissed when they were rejected," Graff said.

"And the baker tried again with this batch?" Pasquale bobbed his head from side to side, throwing his mop of black curly or wavy hair from side to side.

"That's what makes us believe these might be different," Eiselmann answered.

"Nothing worse than a pissed off baker. Maybe a butcher."

They walked to his office off the lab. It was on the small side, but efficient. It resembled Farner's office, though Pasquale had a bank of three computer screens, and a laptop on his desk. A pad of paper and a mechanical pencil on top of it sat off to the side, near his telephone. An MIT pennant hung from the wall. His diploma in an expensive-looking frame hung next to the pennant. The diploma was also from MIT.

"I shoved some other things aside so I can tackle your projects. I am going to begin with the cookies. The letter and powder will take longer, most of the afternoon or longer. The cookies should take me about an hour. You can wait here or you can wait in the lobby or you can wait in the small break room. You can also leave, and I can call you when I the tests are completed. Up to you."

Graff checked his watch and said, "Is there a diner or something close by?"

"A Panera about a half a mile away. Across from Panera is a Starbucks. Turn right out of the parking lot. Stay straight, and you'll see them."

Pasquale already had Eiselmann's number, and Graff gave Pasquale his, and said, "Call when you have something. And thank you for rushing it. We appreciate it."

"I enjoy interesting projects and puzzles."

Graff thought, *I bet you do!* as he and Eiselmann left the office. *And I bet you're damn good at them.*

CHAPTER THIRTY-EIGHT

Graff and Eiselmann sat at a table in the back where they could watch both exits. They also had a view of the patio and the street beyond. It was nice to get out and away from the office. Graff especially sought to escape paperwork, but knew the pile would only grow.

"The Westlake kid's father works at Hi-Mar Specialty Chemicals on McKinley Avenue in Milwaukee. It has 203 employees and does basic chemical manufacturing, whatever the hell that means," Eiselmann said without taking his eyes off his laptop. "Basic chemicals is all the website reads."

"I'm thinking he's a longshot, anyway. He's so new to the school. The letters were sent before he arrived. Some of them, anyway. Months ago," Graff said. "And he doesn't drive."

"We need to hold off judgment until we get the results back on Danny's letter, at least."

Graff shrugged and said, "Probably right."

"Maryanne Sturgis' mother works at Waukesha County Technical College." He looked up and added, "Security."

Graff pursed his lips and said, "Access to a gun?"

"Maybe. Don't know. I'll check it out."

Eiselmann pushed the laptop to the side and took a bite out of the chipotle chicken sandwich. He swallowed most of the bite and said, "I don't think we're any further along than we were a month ago." He swallowed the rest of the bite, took a swig of his acacia hibiscus tea, and said, "We have three suspects so far. A weird girl who doesn't drive and who can't write a coherent sentence. According to Farner and Beatleman, that is. Sturges drives, and is in the same chorus class as Danny, Randy, and Bobby. But all we have on her is that she says rude shit to Randy and Bobby, and is an elite snob. Again, according to Farner and Beatleman. Then we have one shy kid who just moved here." Eiselmann jabbed a finger at Graff and added, "What we don't have is any evidence they associate with one another."

"All true. But, and this is a big but, we don't have any proof they don't associate with one another. And we still have the weird girl delivering cookies to Danny and now, Billy."

"I guess we wait until we have the results of the cookies and the letter and go from there."

Graff nodded as his cell went off. He checked the caller ID, didn't recognize it, answered it and said, "Graff."

"This is Gordon Pasquale. I have the results for your cookies. Come back and I'll walk you through it."

Graff hoped for a preview, but he didn't get it. He said, "Let's go."

CHAPTER THIRTY-NINE

There were three open chairs at the table where Andrew Westlake sat. Two girls sat across from him, but they never interacted with him. As they ate their lunch, they shared a cell between the two of them, listening to music with one earbud apiece. Danny couldn't tell what music they listened to.

They sat down, with Danny sitting next to Westlake and Garrett sitting next to Danny.

Danny smiled and said, "Hi, I'm Danny Limbach. This is Garrett Forstadt, but we call him G-Man. You're Andrew, right?"

Two bright red circles the size of half-dollars appeared on the boy's face. His dark blue eyes grew wide. He didn't speak, but nodded.

"You met our friend, George. We thought we'd come over and eat with you," Danny said.

The boy drank from his carton of chocolate milk. He set it down, and said, "I think I have a YouTube clip of you singing and playing *Roll With The Changes* by REO. I think it's you, anyway."

Danny smiled and said, "May I see it?"

Westlake picked up his cell, unlocked the screen by tapping in four numbers, and scrolled through it until he found what he was looking for. He put the cell on the table between the two of them. Garrett leaned over to see it.

"I made this just before I turned ten." Danny checked the number of views and saw it was over a thousand. Almost 100% gave it a thumbs-up.

"It's one of my favorite songs," Westlake said. "I like rock and roll."

"So do I." Danny tapped the search bar on Westlake's cell, typed in Letterman and Limbach, and found another video. "Have you seen this one?"

It showed Danny with Paul Shaffer and his band performing the same song.

Westlake and Garrett leaned in to watch and listen.

"Paul Shaffer saw the YouTube video you have and called my dad's agent, who put him in touch with my dad and me. That was one of the best times. I mean, performing with him and his band."

"You were on David Letterman?" Andrew asked.

Danny smiled and said, "Two or three times." He was going to add that he and Shaffer text each other. He was going to say Shaffer was one of the first set of ears to hear his new music, but decided not to.

Westlake clicked the save button and the like button and said, "Why haven't you tried out for *The Voice* or *American Idol*? I think you'd win."

Danny smiled and shrugged and said, "I don't want to be a solo artist. I enjoy being in a band. And honestly, Randy and Bobby have better voices than I do. If the song is more of a blues-type of rock, then I sing it."

Garrett said, "You know he's in a band, right?"

Westlake shook his head and said, "No, I didn't know. What kind of music?"

"Most would describe us as modern country. I would say it's a fusion of modern country and rock and roll."

Garrett added, "Think Jason Aldean hooks up with Bob Seger, Mellencamp, and Springsteen."

"With big guitars and harmony," Danny said.

"Do you have a name?"

Danny smiled and said, "Bits and Pieces."

"Like the Dave Clark Five song," Westlake said. "I like that group."

"Exactly," Danny said.

Garrett pulled out his cell, punched some keys, and gave his cell to Westlake. He said, "Listen to this with your earbuds. It's one of their originals."

"Which one?" Danny asked.

"*Digging a Hole.*" To Andrew, Garrett said, "Randy, Danny, and Troy wrote it."

"Who are Randy and Troy?"

Danny turned around and pointed, and said, "Over there, the table with the blond kid? The guy sitting to his left is Troy Rivera. He plays bass and sings middle harmony. Randy is sitting to his left. He plays rhythm and sings lead vocals. He and Bobby alternate lead vocals. The kind of skinny kid with kind of long blond hair is Sean Drummond. He sings high harmony and plays keyboards. The brown-haired boy sitting next to Randy is Bobby. He plays rhythm and lead guitar, and plays piano. The bigger, other blond-haired boy is Chris Granger. He plays drums and sings the low harmony."

Andrew turned on the song and listened, his head bobbing to the beat. He smiled. Glanced at Danny and at Garrett, and smiled again.

"This is great," he said, a little too loudly.

"You said you like rock and roll, so I thought you would," Garrett said proudly. "It's one of my favorites."

To Garrett, Andrew said, "What do you do?"

Garrett scratched his head, blew out some air through pursed lips, and said, "Mostly, I run their sound. I'm also the guitar tech. You know, if someone breaks a string, I have to change it."

"But G-Man also co-produces our songs," Danny said, taking a bite out of his sandwich.

"You're making a record?" Westlake asked.

Danny bobbed his head back and forth and said, "Kinda, sorta. We're stacking songs for a demo."

"Tim McGraw is recording three of our songs on his new album," Garrett said proudly.

"No shit?"

Farner walked up behind them and said, "I hope no one shits in the cafeteria."

Danny and Garrett laughed, while Andrew blushed and looked horrified.

To Farner, Danny said, "On Monday, we'll have a CD for you. We're writing Saturday morning, and recording Saturday afternoon."

"Excellent." Farner studied Andrew and said, "And who do we have here?"

"Oh, sorry," Danny said. "Mr. Farner, this is Andrew Westlake. He's new here." To Westlake he said, "About a month?"

Westlake nodded.

"This is Mr. Farner. He's one of the APs. He's also one of the first ears we give our songs to, besides Randy's and Bobby's dad and my dad."

Farner and Andrew shook hands.

"Welcome to North. I think you'll like it here." He smirked, shielded his mouth from Danny and Garrett and said, "I would pick better friends, though. These two characters ..." he trailed off and shook his head.

Andrew didn't know how to respond, but Danny and Garrett laughed. Garrett said, "You know you love us."

Farner faked coughing and said, "Bullshit."

The boys, including Andrew, laughed.

"You guys set for the anthem tomorrow night?"

"Yup. What kind of mic set up will we have?" Danny asked.

"What do you need?" Farner asked.

"Two would be ideal. On mic stands. I'm playing acoustic electric, and I can bring an amp."

"We can arrange that," Farner nodded.

"Awesome," Danny said.

"Are you singing too?" Farner asked Garrett.

Danny laughed and said, "He'd clear the gym in seconds. Some might throw up on the way out."

"I'm not that bad!" Garrett protested. "Okay, maybe I am. A little."

"A lot," Farner deadpanned.

He strolled off and said over his shoulder, "Need anything, holler. You know where to find me."

Westlake watched Farner walk away and while still watching him, said to Danny and Garrett, "You guys are friends with the assistant principal?"

The boys laughed, and Danny said, "Not friends, really. But we like him and he likes us. Most everyone likes him."

Garrett added, "Most of the teachers and coaches are like that. You're going to like it here."

Back at the other table, Billy said to Tony, "I have to give a presentation in my drafting class. I have to present a landscaping design on the house we're building up north on a lake."

"It's really cool," Brian said. "Billy designed the whole thing. They began construction on it last month."

"I might have designed it, but all the guys gave me input. Mom and dad, too."

Tony first looked at Billy, then Brian and said, "Wait. You designed a house and you're building it? You're moving away?"

Brian, Billy, and Brett detected sadness in Tony's voice.

Brian slipped his arm around Tony's shoulders, gave him a squeeze, laughed and said, "No, no. It's a vacation home on a lake. A year-round home."

"Oh, okay. Good."

The boys smiled at him.

"Anyway, I have to come up with a design for the landscaping. It's a major grade. You're in art, so I thought you could help. If you want to, that is."

"Sure, but are you allowed to have help like that?"

Billy smiled broadly and said, "Actually, I already spoke to Mr. Jett about it. As long as you join Skills USA and help me with the presentation in class, he'll allow it. Others in the class are doubling up with each other, but none of them are in art like you."

"What's Skills USA? What would I have to do?"

"It's a club through CTE. Like drafting, carpentry, business, and culinary arts. Dues are $25 bucks, but it pays for a polo shirt. It's a good club."

"Okay, I'll do it."

"Awesome! I thought as long as you're sleeping over tomorrow night, we could work on it Saturday afternoon."

"Sure," Tony said with a smile.

"And Saturday night is game night at our house," Brett said. "You might have to stay over for that, too."

"If we play Pictionary, I want to be on Tony's team," George said.

Brett leaned over and said, "George can't draw at all." He said this loud enough for George to hear it, and the guys laughed.

"I'm a good guesser, though," George responded.

"You guys want me to spend two nights at your house?"

The four boys laughed and said, "Yeah, why not? Game night is fun."

"I'll have to check with my aunt and uncle, but I think it will be okay."

"Great!" Brian said. "On Sunday, we go to church, and then we go out for breakfast."

"You're Catholic, right?" Brett asked.

Puzzled, Tony said, "Yeah. How did you know?"

He chuckled and said, "You're Italian. There are a lot of things I can say about being Italian." He chuckled again.

"Don't get him started," Brian said with a laugh.

CHAPTER FORTY

"Did you think it was smart eating lunch with the kid?" Randy asked as he, Bobby, Danny, and Garrett walked to their classes after lunch.

"He's a nice guy," Danny said.

"I'm picking him up for the game tomorrow night," Garrett said.

"He's coming to the practice on Saturday. I invited him," Danny said. "We're going to check him out to see if he can run lights and help Garrett on the soundboard."

Horrified, Randy said, "Danny, we know nothing about him."

Puzzled, Danny said, "That's why we ate with him. We wanted to get to know him. At least I did. Garrett came with me."

"I like him," Garrett said.

Bobby chuckled and said, "You like everybody, G-Man. So does Danny."

"I don't think it's smart," Randy said, turning into the hallway towards his science class.

Bobby held Danny and Garrett back. He waited until Randy was well ahead and said quietly, "Don't mind him. He has a bug up his butt."

Danny thought for a minute and said, "He better lose the bug, because Andrew is my guest."

Bobby watched Randy enter his classroom and said, "I think he'll be okay." But even he didn't know for sure.

CHAPTER FORTY-ONE

"A laxative? Like Ex-Lax?" Eiselmann said with a laugh.

"Exactly like Ex-Lax," Pasquale said. "In fact, I'm pretty sure it's the key ingredient in these."

Graff had trouble keeping from laughing.

"There is so much Ex-Lax in these cookies, one of them would turn your underwear into a fudge factory- to quote Teddy in the movie *Stand By Me*."

Eiselmann and Graff couldn't hold it together any longer.

Graff turned to Eiselmann and said, "Can you imagine Farner or Beatleman ..."

"Stop! Stop!" Eiselmann laughed.

Pasquale was perplexed. He didn't mean to make them laugh. He said, "Guys, this is far from a joke. It's quite possible one of these cookies could put someone in the hospital."

This made the two cops laugh harder.

"Oh my God! Stop!" Graff said.

Pasquale crossed his arms on his chest, frowned and said, "This isn't funny."

"But it is," Eiselmann said.

Angry now, Pasquale said, "Taken by the wrong person and not caught right away." He stopped and shook his head. "It could have been lethal."

The laughter stopped.

"How so?" Graff asked.

"Dehydration for one. Someone with a heart condition, stomach ailment, kidneys and such," Pasquale stopped, shook his head and said, "It isn't a joke, and it shouldn't be treated like one."

Graff held up his hand and said, "We get it. We're sorry. It just hit us wrong."

Still miffed, Pasquale fiddled with some papers on his desk.

"Can we get the remaining cookies back? We'll need them as evidence," Graff said.

Pasquale nodded. "I already signed the evidence bag per protocol. I'll go get them."

When he left, Eiselmann said, "I feel kind of bad."

With a straight face, Graff said, "I feel kind of shitty."

Both men lost it again, but recovered before Pasquale came back into his office.

"Do you know when you might have the results of the contents in the envelope?" Graff asked.

"I'm doing that next. It will take time, though. Just the safety precautions, but I hope to have it done yet today."

Graff nodded and said, "Please be safe, Gordon. Thanks for the rush on this one. We appreciate it."

"And sorry for laughing. We realize it isn't a joke. It just hit us wrong," Eiselmann said.

Pasquale said, "Yeah. These things can have a crappy outcome."

Stunned, Eiselmann and Graff stared at Pasquale, and then all three ended up laughing hysterically.

CHAPTER FORTY-TWO

Traffic snarled at the normal spots. Rush hour is rush hour.

"At this rate, we won't get back before the end of the school day," Eiselmann said.

"Yeah, I know. I think we go at her first thing in the morning. No tip off tonight. I don't want her to prepare, and I want her isolated when we interview her. We don't even let Farner know."

"Are you looking at charges?"

Graff pursed his lips and said, "My gut tells me no. Let the school handle the discipline. Our job is to scare the shit out of her, no pun intended, so the letters and the baking stop. She needs to understand her attention is unwanted."

Eiselmann stared out the side window and casually pulled at his ear.

"What? You think I'm too soft?"

Eiselmann shook his head and said, "No, it's not that. I was thinking what you are thinking. Let the school handle the discipline. It's just," he stopped and shook his head.

"It's what?"

Eiselmann cocked his head. "It's like ... if we listened to Beatleman and Farner describe her, it seems like she isn't capable of writing the letters. She doesn't have wheels. Is mom the one who mails them?" He shook his head and said, "I don't think so."

"And according to Beatleman and Farner, she wouldn't be capable of putting together a bomb and blowing up three cars. If the letters and the car bomb are related."

"I agree."

Graff nodded and said, "Let's say you're right. If that's the case, we either have two kids acting together or we have two separate kids acting on their own without knowledge of each other. Or we have an unknown adult."

Eiselmann sighed and said, "Or any of those combinations. Our case just got more complicated."

"Shit!" Graff glanced over at Eiselmann and said, "Pun intended."

Neither man laughed at Graff's joke.

CHAPTER FORTY-THREE

The boys were surprised Jeremy and Vicky hadn't been there when they got home from basketball practice. Brett and Brian did a once-around the house to make sure the boys had picked everything up.

When Jeremy and Vicky arrived home, everyone was silent. Everyone waited expectantly, not sure what to do next. Vicky walked through the door first, with Jeremy trailing behind. To the boys, he looked the same. Maybe smaller. Maybe more tired. The boys greeted both of them with hugs and kisses.

Brian waited at the back and was the last in line. He tried to put on a brave face, or at the least, a neutral face, but the anxiety and apprehension were visible. Brett could feel it oozing off him in relentless waves. Brett was pretty sure the others noticed it, too.

That over with, Jeremy said, "Guys, let's sit down. Mom and I have to talk to you. Me, mostly, I guess."

They sat at the kitchen table because that was where everyone could sit comfortably, as well as be seen and heard. Jeremy sat at one end near the refrigerator, his usual seat. Vicky sat at the opposite end near the dining room. Randy, Billy, and Bobby sat on one side. Brett, Brian, Two, and George faced them. Everyone was in their normal spots for meals.

"Are you sure you want to do this, Dad?" Randy asked. "I mean, you just got out of the hospital."

Jeremy smiled, and said, "Yes, I need to. I'll be fine."

Vicky smiled encouragement, but she privately worried what the result might be.

He rubbed his brow and then his mouth. He started, stopped, and began again. "Guys, the other night," he stopped and shook his head. "The other night, I was a jackass. I acted like an idiot. I was so far out of line ..." he stopped and shook his head.

"It's okay, Dad," Randy said.

It annoyed Brett that Randy kept breaking in. He thought the others were too, but he wasn't sure.

Jeremy smiled, looked at each of the boys and at Vicky and said, "No, it isn't okay, and it wasn't okay."

He turned to Two and Brian and said, "I was disrespectful to you both. I am so sorry. I want to assure you there is nothing wrong with your relationship. You two have a beautiful friendship. You guys are brothers. There is nothing wrong with the way you act towards one another, and nothing wrong with how you treat each other. I need you to believe that."

Two stared at the table and wiped tears from his eyes. He never acknowledged what Jeremy said.

Brian wanted to put an arm around Two's shoulders, or at the least, take hold of his hand, but he dared not. What flashed through his mind was the conversation he had overheard in the study between Jeremy, Michael, and Brett. It occurred more than a month before, but it was still fresh in Brian's mind. Jeremy had asked Two if there had been anything sexual between him and Brian. Of course, there hadn't, and Two was quick to set that straight. Brett jumped in, got angry, and said the same thing, plus other things Brian wished he had not said. But Brett was Brett and if there was anyone in the family who was going to speak what was on his mind, it was him.

"Brian, Jeff spoke with both your mom and me. And after he left, I had a long conversation with your mom."

He turned to Bobby and said, "Bobby, this applies to you, too."

Bobby's mouth was so dry, it felt like he swallowed sand. He had a feeling he knew what was coming, and he didn't dare look at Brian or anyone else.

It hadn't happened in months, but Brian's right hand shook like he had palsy. Fortunately, his hands were on his lap where no one could see it.

Episodes like this popped up when he returned from Arizona. The therapist stated the shootout on top of the mesa might have been the cause. Sometimes his left hand shook, but mostly it was his right.

He and the therapist worked on it, and he had learned how to recognize its onset and how to control it. He hadn't been to the therapist since late September. Brian had also been on medication, but he had stopped it around the same time he stopped seeing the therapist. This episode was a setback. He knew it, and he didn't want anyone else to see it.

"Your mom and I, mostly me, treated the two of you unfairly. I disrespected who you are. Who you both are."

He stopped and waited for a reply from either boy. When nothing came, he said, "I know being gay is not something you can control. It's like being left- or right-handed. It's like having blue eyes or brown eyes. I could understand it and I could accept it with kids on my caseload. But I had trouble accepting it with two of my sons."

"We both had trouble accepting it," Vicky said. "Deep down, I knew Bobby might have been gay as far back as late elementary. I thought he'd outgrow it or something. When you, George, and Brett were in Arizona, Bobby and I had a long talk. That's when he came out to me."

She smiled sadly and said, "Even then, I hoped it wasn't true. I knew he was involved with you, Bri, and I think that angered me. Maybe not angered me. Mostly frustrated me. I was worried about how the two of you would be accepted by others. I worried about whether you'd be picked on and made fun of."

She shook her head and said, "Watching the two of you, knowing the two of you were involved with each other," she shook her head again, and said, "it's just difficult for a mom or a dad to accept. Especially because the two of you lived in the same family. I can't help but think that part is wrong. Not being gay, but being involved as the two of you were while you lived in the same household."

Brian had enough. It wasn't anger. It wasn't even frustration. It was sadness rooted in the fact that nothing he could or would say would matter.

Before he or Bobby could say anything, however, Randy did.

CHAPTER FORTY-FOUR

"Our family has changed in the last couple of years." He said this looking down at the table, at his hands. "I mean, Billy and I started our family with dad. Just the three of us. Then George. Then Brett and Bobby. Then Brian, and now Two."

Brett squinted at him, wishing he would shut the hell up, and wondering where he was headed with this. Worried, George remained stone-faced. Billy shifted in his seat and frowned at his twin.

"It mostly changed when Brian got involved with Bobby. That's when I noticed how Bri got along with dad. Or maybe, didn't get along with dad."

Bobby leaned forward, glared at Randy, and said, "I've told you over and over. I was the one who came onto Brian. It wasn't Brian coming on to me. If anyone is to blame, I am. I caused this mess."

Jeremy leaned forward and said, "Bobby, it isn't a mess. Having the feelings the two of you had ... or have, is," he shook his head, searching for something, anything. He settled on, "It's as normal as George loving Rebecca. It's just that the two of you are brothers. At least, that's how your mom and I are raising you."

Brian sighed, slouched in defeat, and placed both hands on the table. He didn't care who saw his right hand. It shook like it would fall off. Brett tried to take hold of it, but Brian waved him off.

"Look, I need to say something." He sighed again, thought about what he wanted to say, and decided to just plunge on.

He looked at Jeremy and said, "When my mom and dad died, I asked you if you really wanted me to live with you. *Really* wanted me to live with you. You said you did."

"And we still do," Vicky said. Jeremy nodded.

"Randy's right. A lot has happened, and a lot has changed. Some of us are closer to each other than others. I guess that's normal, I don't know. In my other family, it was just Brad and me. I've never been a part of a family like this. No one has." The boys signaled their agreement by nodding or shaking their head.

"Bobby and I fell in love. Describing it like that might gross you out, but I have no regrets. I told Bobby this last night, but I want all of you to hear it. I love Bobby and I always will."

He paused and, looking directly at Bobby, he said, "It doesn't matter to me who started it or, as you said, who came onto who. It doesn't matter. What matters is that I love you more than anyone. I know I won't love anyone else like I love you, and I don't regret anything we did. I don't regret anything I felt. It was love and there's nothing wrong with love. I'm not ashamed of who I am. I'm not ready to announce it over the PA or take out a billboard or anything. But I would like to live my life the way I want to. I don't care what others might think of me except you guys."

Randy leaned forward and said, "I ..."

That's as far as he got before Brett snapped, "Randy, be quiet. Let Brian finish what he needs to say."

Randy blushed and sat back and tried to disappear in his chair.

Brian turned to Jeremy and said, "You don't have to worry about Bobby and me anymore. I ended our relationship. At least, that part of our relationship. Bobby and I talked about it, and I think he agrees with me.

Bobby nodded and wiped tears out of his eyes.

"You and I have never been the same since Bobby's and my relationship began. That's the only thing I can think of that caused it."

He sighed. He didn't know how what he said next might land, but he said, "Honestly, I don't think you like me, and I don't think you love me. I don't know if it's because I'm gay or because of Bobby's and my relationship or what. But that's how I feel."

Jeremy leaned forward and objected when Brian said, "Please, let me finish. Please."

Remembering Jeff's caution to him, Jeremy nodded, his eyes downcast.

"My relationship with Bobby hurt this family. I never meant for that to happen, and neither did Bobby. As hard as it is, he and I needed to end it. Mostly me, I guess."

Jeremy leaned forward again, but Brian held out his hand to stop him from speaking.

"I love this family. I love living here. Or at least I did. Honestly, I'm not so sure anymore." He made eye contact with each of the boys, except for Randy, and said, "But you guys are my friends."

His right hand shook even more, so he held onto it with his left. He took a deep breath.

"I gave a lot to this family. That guy in the woods. I kept thinking, 'I can't let him get to the house. I have to stop him.' I kept thinking that. I didn't want anyone hurt or killed. He had to be stopped."

"We know, Brian," Billy said.

"Please, let me finish," Brian said.

Billy nodded. Vicky took a tissue and dabbed at her eyes. Randy stared at his folded hands on the table. George looked down at his lap. Two glanced around the table at everyone, mostly at Jeremy.

"When we were in Arizona, I had to protect Brett and George." Brian turned to Vicky and said, "I know you blame yourself for what happened, but I would have done the same thing even if I didn't make that promise to you. I love Brett and George."

"He turned to Jeremy and said, "I know how important George is to you." He turned to Vicky and said, "And I know how important Brett and Michael are to you."

Brian paused as he chose his words carefully and deliberately. He finally said, "I know how important Randy, and Billy, and George are to dad, and I know how important Brett, and Bobby, and Michael are to you." What he didn't say, but felt, was that he didn't know if he was important to either of them.

He felt a lump growing in his chest, and a tear dribbled down his cheek, followed by others.

"I did what I did in Arizona because I love this family. I didn't want our family ruined. If something would have happened to either Brett or George or Michael, our family would have been a mess, and I think I would have been blamed."

Both Vicky and Jeremy objected. "No, Brian, that's not right." "You did more than you should have. You put your life on the line."

Brian heard it, but it didn't matter. Brett reached out and tried to take hold of Brian's shaking hand, but Brian snatched it away from him.

"I look at everything that has happened since then." He held up his shaking hand and said, "This. My nightmares, even though I haven't had them in a long time. The scars around my right eye." He grabbed at the white hair on his head and said, "This shit." He took off his glasses, and smashed them on the table and said, "I have to wear these stupid things."

The boys blinked and sat back like a grenade had been tossed on the table. Vicky jumped in her seat. Jeremy felt like he needed to say something, anything. But Brian plowed on.

He chuckled without mirth, and said, "And you know what? I'd do it all again to make sure you guys were safe. All of you. Even you, Randy."

He shook his head, wiped tears off his face with his hands and said, "I think about the night before you went to the hospital and all the stuff you said. I know you were upset about the letters, but I think there was more to it than that. Like I said, I don't think you like me, and I don't think you love me. I think you regret adopting me and you regret letting me move in."

Brian sighed, stood up, and said, "Sorry if it upsets you, but that's how I feel. No matter what I do or what I've done to help this family, it's not good enough. I've screwed it up. For all of you."

He pushed his chair in and said, "The one thing I regret the most is when we were in Arizona, when I walked up the hill above George's ranch and I was alone. What I regret the most is that I didn't pull the trigger."

Brian walked out of the kitchen despite Jeremy urging him to stay. He left the broken glasses on the table and walked up the stairs to his bedroom. He shut and locked the door behind him. He didn't even allow Papa or Jasper in the room with him.

CHAPTER FORTY-FIVE

"I'll go talk with him," Randy suggested. "I think I need to apologize."

"Just leave him the hell alone," Brett barked. "Everyone! Leave him alone, especially you, Randy! He isn't ready to talk, and he isn't ready to listen." He calmed down, but only a little, and said, "Everyone, leave him alone. Before we go to bed, George, Billy, Two, and I will talk to him. If he lets us. Either Two or I will sleep with him. He'll need to be with someone."

"What did he mean when he said he regretted not pulling the trigger?" Bobby said.

"Exactly how it sounded," Brett said, wiping tears from his eyes.

"That was when he called me," Jeremy whispered, eyes distant, picturing the moment.

He was in the study. The phone rang. The caller ID said it was Brian, but Brian never spoke to him. It sounded like Brian was crying. No, not crying. Sobbing.

Brett nodded and said, "He told me he had called you. After what Rebecca said to him, he felt George had betrayed him. He and George have worked it out since then. But he was afraid you had the same thoughts as George did. That all of us had the same thoughts George did." He wanted to add to Jeremy, *I guess he was right*, but he didn't.

"I did not know," George said as he shook his head as he wiped tears off his face.

"He told me that night we camped out before we left Arizona. We had shared a blanket. I woke up, and he was gone. I went to look for him and found him sitting on a boulder looking out over the valley. We talked, and he told me what happened." He shrugged and said, "What he almost did."

"He wouldn't do that, would he?" Two asked.

Brett shook his head and said, "I don't think so." He shrugged, thought about it, and said, "No. He's tougher than that. He's tougher than anyone sitting here. It hurt him to break up with Bobby, but like he said, he did it to help our family. The crap that happened the night before dad went into the hospital, and the stuff that happened at the hospital. All that shit hurt him. But Brian is Brian. He wouldn't do that. He knows it would hurt the family even more if he did."

CHAPTER FORTY-SIX

For what it seemed to be the longest time, Brian sat on the floor, leaning against his bed and weeping. In actuality, it wasn't long at all. He pulled out his phone, dialed up Tony, and face-timed him. Tony picked up right away, though Brian wasn't looking at his phone.

Alarmed, Tony said, "Brian, what's wrong?"

Brian held his phone with his left hand, while his right was in his hair. His face was down and eyes shut.

Tony waited patiently, though he was worried, fearing something had happened to Brian's dad.

"I'm sorry," Brian whispered.

"For what?"

Brian shook his head. He took a deep breath and whispered, "Did you ever tell the truth, even though the truth hurt others?"

Tony cocked his head, wondering if the question was rhetorical.

"I mean, the truth shouldn't hurt anyone, right?"

Tony didn't know how to answer, so he remained quiet.

"I said what was in my heart. I said what I meant to say. Exactly what I wanted to say. But it hurt too many people. People I love and care about. Truth shouldn't do that. Lies do that, but not the truth."

"Brian," Tony started, stopped, and tried again. "Brian, I'm not sure I know what to say."

For the first time, Brian looked at his phone and saw the concern on Tony's face. He shook his head, wiped his eyes on his sleeve, took a deep breath, and said, "I'm sorry. I just didn't know who else to call."

Tony said, "You don't have to apologize. I just ... I'm not sure how I can help you. I want to, but I don't know how."

Brian took another deep breath, wiped his eyes with his right hand, smiled weakly and said, "I'm not sure if anyone can."

"Did something happen to your dad?"

Brian shook his head. It was a loaded question. But he said, "No. He's home now."

The two boys sat on either end of the call, letting the silence drag on. Brian heard a knock on his door, and then the handle jiggled.

"Brian, are you okay?"

He recognized Brett's voice and the worry in it.

To Tony, he said, "I better go. A couple of my brothers want to speak to me."

"Okay, but will you call me before you go to bed? Please?"

Brian nodded and said, "Yeah, I will. Thanks, and sorry again."

Tony shook his head and said, "Nothing to be sorry about."

The call ended, and Brian took a last swipe at his eyes with his sleeve, took a deep breath, and opened the door.

The dogs, Papa, Momma, and Jasper, raced in. They wanted their pets and to give Brian doggie kisses. Right behind them, and just as he suspected, Billy, George, and Two were with Brett. He sat down on the side of the bed and waited.

Brett sat down next to him. George pulled up the chair under the desk to face him. Billy and Two sat on the bed behind Brian and Brett.

"Who was on the phone? Jeff, Sean, Gavin, or Tony?" Brett asked.

"Tony. I told him I'd call him back before I go to bed."

Brett nodded. He didn't know what to say, only that he should say something. For the millionth time, he wished he had Randy's or Bobby's ability with words.

It was George who spoke. He and Brian were the quietest of the brothers.

Speaking formally as he did when a serious moment called for it, he said, "We are worried about you, Brian."

Eyes glued to the floor, Brian said, "I'm fine."

Brett slipped his arm around Brian's shoulders and gave him a squeeze.

"I'm fine," Brian repeated, though some tears fell.

George leaned forward and said, "Brian, I am sorry for what happened on Navajoland. I ruined the trip for you. I ruined our friendship."

Brian shook his head, sighed, and said, "George, we're fine. I'm fine with all of you guys. It's over and done."

"Brian," Two said. He never finished.

Brian turned around and said, "Michael, all is good between us."

Two shook his head and wept.

The five boys sat in silence. None of them knew what to say, though each knew something needed to be said.

Eventually, Brian broke the silence by saying, "Guys, I have to get some homework done."

He stood up and stretched.

And there was a knock on the door.

"Brian, do you mind if I come in?"

Brian's shoulders sagged. His right hand shook as if someone had flipped a switch. He tried to hide it by holding onto it with his left hand, but his brothers saw it.

He said, "Sure."

Jeremy opened the door, took a step in and said, "Am I interrupting anything?"

Silently, the boys stood up and trooped out of the room single-file. Brett was the last to leave. He said, looking from Brian to Jeremy and then back to Brian, "Do either of you want me to stay?"

Jeremy shrugged and said, "It's up to Brian. Either way is okay with me."

Brian shook his head and said, "No. It's okay," though, but from his tone of voice, shaking right hand, and body language, both Jeremy and Brett knew Brian was clearly not okay with being alone with Jeremy.

Brett gave one last long look at Brian and said, "I'll catch up with you before you go to bed. Either Two or I will sleep with you." He left the room and shut the door behind him.

Jeremy looked pale and thin. His eyes had a sunken look to them. Normally bright blue, they almost looked gray.

"Do you mind if I sit down?"

The two of them sat side by side on the bed, but not close. Papa took up what looked to be a defensive position facing Jeremy, and it was not lost on the man. Jasper lay on Brian's feet, his head facing Jeremy. Momma lay near the door, but faced Jeremy and Brian.

Jeremy thought he should address Brian's shaking hand, but didn't. Other than that, it appeared neither knew what to say or how. Jeremy thought, *I'm a counselor and I do not know what to say? Not even to my own son. What the hell kind of counselor or father am I?*

"Dad, I'm sorry for what I said. I didn't mean to hurt you or anyone. I'm sorry."

Brian wiped tears off his face with his sleeve.

Jeremy mulled it over, and finally said, "Did you mean everything you said?"

Brian frowned. How could he answer? If he said yes, then Jeremy would be hurt even more than he was. If he said no, then what he said was a lie, and everyone knew Brian didn't lie. He didn't respond.

"Everything you said, did it come from your heart?"

That, Brian could answer. He whispered, "Yes."

"And, because it came from your heart, it was the truth as you believe it to be?"

Jeremy caught him, and Brian didn't see it coming. More into his chest than to Jeremy, he whispered, "Yes."

Jeremy moved closer to Brian and put his arm around him. The two sat there and wept. Jeremy wiped his eyes and cleared his throat and said, "Then it seems I have a lot of work to do to repair our relationship."

"Dad ..."

Jeremy gave Brian's shoulders a squeeze and said, "You never have to apologize for your feelings, Brian. They're yours and yours alone."

"But I didn't mean to hurt you or mom or anyone."

"I know that, Brian. Everyone knows that. I also know you don't lie. You never have. So, if what you said was your truth, I have work to do."

Brian shook his head, and Jeremy said, "Please hear me out, okay? Please?"

Brian nodded, his chin landing on his chest, his shoulders sagging.

"Once upon a time, our relationship was rock solid. You felt safe, and you knew you could depend on me. Somehow, our relationship fell apart. I don't think it was because of your and Bobby's relationship, but it could be. I have some soul-searching to do. But I know our relationship isn't what it once was, and I miss that."

"Me, too."

"I don't know how long it will take, but I want you to know I will do everything I can to fix our relationship. I know it will take time for you to believe in me again. I know it will take time for you to trust me again. But I'm willing to do everything I can to prove to you how much I love you."

"Me, too," Brian repeated.

"You are my son. You carry my last name. That means something to me. I love you as much as I do anyone else in our family. But I know you don't believe that right now. I know it will take a long time to prove it to you. But I want you to know I'm going to do all I can to repair our relationship. I promise."

Brian nodded.

"There are two things I'm going to ask of you. One is a favor, and the other is important to me, to your mom, and to your brothers."

Brian glanced at him, but failed to maintain eye contact.

"The first is I hope you give me a chance. Keep an open mind. Please."

Brian nodded and said, "I will."

"Like you often say, I know we can't start over. But we can start where we are and go from there."

Brian sighed and nodded.

"Good. The other thing is important. I ask that you don't hurt yourself. Please. If you ever have those thoughts again, please speak to someone. It doesn't have to be me if you aren't comfortable with me. It could be mom or one of your brothers. Maybe Father Donahue. You're pretty close to him. It doesn't matter who you talk to, as long as you talk to someone."

Brian blushed deep crimson, shook his head, and said, "Dad, I don't feel like that anymore. Honestly. You don't have to worry about me. Or that."

"In case you ever do. Please reach out to someone."

"I will."

"Those are the only two things I ask. The rest is up to me. I'm going to work hard to repair our relationship. You mean that much to me."

"I will work on it too."

Wanting and needing to change the topic to something neutral, Jeremy said, "Try to get some sleep. The first game is tomorrow night."

"I will." Brian sighed again and said, "We look good."

Jeremy said, "You read my mind. I was just going to ask."

Brian wiped his eyes on his sleeve and said, "Big Gav is a monster. Bobby could start. He's that good. He and Mikey add depth. We're going to be tough."

"Good to hear. I don't know if I'm going to go yet. Your mom and the doctor and I are discussing it. I still have time to work on them."

Brian smiled, and then Jeremy leaned over and kissed the side of Brian's head. "Goodnight, Brian. I love you."

"I know. I love you, too."

Jeremy stood up, stretched, and left. Brett came back into the room, leaving Jeremy to wonder if he had been standing with his ear pressed to the door. Jeremy smiled to himself and thought Brett was just being a protective brother.

"Goodnight, Brett. Love you. Get some sleep. Game tomorrow night."

"Goodnight. Love you, too. I will."

He shut the door after Jeremy left and said, "How are you doing?"

"I'm fine. Tired. I want to go to bed."

"Let me see your hand."

Brian held it out, but the shakes had stopped. He hadn't noticed it until Brett asked to see it.

Brett nodded and said, "Bri, you know if you need anything, you can come to me, right?"

"I know, Brett."

"I mean, I love you. More than anyone. I mean it. We love you. Our family wouldn't be the same without you."

Brian shut his eyes and sighed. He said, "You don't have to worry. I'm fine."

Brett nodded and said, "You might want to reassure Two and Bobby. They're kinda freaked out."

"I will. Is he sleeping in here tonight?"

Brett smiled and said, "Yes. I lost. Rock, paper, scissors."

Bri smiled and said, "I love you, Brett."

The two boys embraced, and Brett kissed Brian's cheek. "Always."

"Always."

Before he got himself ready for bed, Brian called Tony, who picked up right away.

"Hey, Tony. I'm sorry about, you know, before. There was a lot going on and I was kind of messed up."

Tony nodded and said, "With your dad?"

"No, actually. Well, maybe, I guess. But he's okay. But I'm sorry about," he shrugged, made a face and said, "you know."

The truth was, Tony didn't know, other than Brian was hurting. He said, "No problem."

"Um, you're still sleeping over this weekend, right?" For clarity, Brian added, "Both Friday and Saturday?"

"You sure you want me to? I mean, I'm not sure what's happening and all."

Barely able to keep his emotions in check, Brian said, "I really want you to. Please." He calmed down and said, "Besides, I'm okay. Please?"

Tony smiled and said, "Yeah, I'll sleep over. My aunt and uncle already said I could. I just wanted to make sure you were still okay with that."

Brian smiled back at him and said, "I'm happy we're friends."

"Me, too."

"I'll pick you up in the morning."

"See you then."

They signed off, leaving Brian feeling lighter than he had since the family conference.

CHAPTER FORTY-SEVEN

Two lay in bed on his back. He was not in his normal spoon position with Brian. That was how they slept each night. Not on this night, however. At least not yet. He flipped to his side, facing away from Brian, and then onto his stomach. Finally, he ended up on his side, facing Brian.

"What?" Brian asked softly.

"Did you mean what you said about pulling the trigger?"

"Yes," Brian whispered. "But I don't feel that way now."

"Why?"

Brian sighed. As much as he dredged up the past, he didn't want to stir it up any further.

The initial stink was enough.

"I don't want to talk about it, but it's important for you to know I don't feel like that anymore. I'm okay. I'll work it out."

Two regarded him silently, unable to sleep and unable to turn off his own thoughts. He was tired, but not so much that he needed to sleep right away.

"I felt like that once," Two whispered.

Brian rolled to his side to face Two. "When?"

"After the first couple of nights I was with Lou. All he wanted to do was touch me. Do stuff. At first, I thought he'd get over it. But all he wanted was more. Every night. Most mornings. He never stopped."

"Why didn't you just leave?"

A tear dribbled down the side of Two's nose. "'cause I had no place to go."

"Now you're safe. No one will do that to you anymore."

"Do you remember when we were up north and you were putting gauze and stuff, you know, down there? I told you that sometimes, I miss doing stuff."

Brian nodded.

"Does that make me gay?"

"No, that doesn't make you gay. It means you miss the physical intimacy, that's all."

Two wasn't convinced, and Brian could see it on his face.

"You like girls, right? I mean, more than as just friends, right?"

Two nodded.

"Have you ever been attracted to a guy? You see someone in the shower or at school and think, 'Man, he's hot.'"

Horrified, Two whispered, "No, never!"

"And when you see a girl in one of your classes or in the hallway or in the cafeteria, do you think to yourself, 'I would like to get to know her better.' Or maybe you think, 'I wonder what she feels like under that shirt.'"

"Yes, sometimes."

"There's your answer." Brian reached out and pushed Two's hair out of his face and behind his ear. "That's the difference between you and everyone else in our family, except for Bobby and me. Bobby and I look at guys and we think, 'He's cute.' And we wonder if he might be gay or if he'd be willing to do stuff. Bobby doesn't look at girls like that. The thing that makes me different is that I look at guys like Bobby does, and I look like girls like you and the others do. I can go both ways."

Brian watched Two's expression change, and he brushed the tears off Two's face.

"Did that help?"

Two nodded.

Brian had another thought. "One more thing. If you are gay like Bobby and me, it's okay. I have your back and so does Bobby. Brett, Billy and George would tear apart anyone who makes fun of you. I mean that. You don't have to worry about who you are. You love who you love. No one can change that. No one should change that. Love is love, and love is always good."

Two smiled. "I love you, Brian."

Brian smiled at him, caressed his cheek with the palm of his hand and said, "I love you too, Michael. You are the best little brother anyone could ever have."

They embraced. "We need to get to sleep."

Two smiled at him, and then flipped over into his normal spoon position, with Brian draping an arm over him.

CHAPTER FORTY-EIGHT

"Does this tie go with this shirt?"

Brian did a double-take. Two wore a pale blue button-down shirt with khaki slacks with short white athletic socks and white Jordans. Two had chosen a blue-striped tie. The only difference in what Brian wore was a white shirt with a purple and blue striped tie, with dress socks and brown penny-loafers.

He said, "Yes, but why are you dressing up?"

"Everyone else is, so I thought I would, too."

"I don't think George is," Brian said.

"That's okay. But you have to help me with the tie."

Any residue from the night before had vanished. That was fine with Brian. Nothing said or remembered was best in his mind, as long as the truth in what he said to Two sunk in.

"Come on in the bathroom and I'll help you."

The two boys walked across the hall, and Brian stood behind Two. As he tied it, he talked about what he was doing. "It might take you a couple of tries, but you'll get it eventually."

"How did you learn?"

"My dad." Then he added, "Before I moved in here. My first dad."

Brian finished with Two's tie, and the two of them stood admiring themselves in the mirror.

"The girls will like it."

Two smiled and said, "You think?"

"Yup. It will set you apart from the other guys."

"I'm going to ask Meghan to go to the game with me. Trevor is asking Carmen."

Brian smiled. This was the second or third girl Two had been interested in. Brian said, "How will you get there?"

Stumped, Two said, "We'll figure that part out later."

"Do you have money to pay for her and your ticket?"

Worried, Two asked, "Will ten cover it?"

Brian pulled out his wallet and handed Two a ten and a five. "Better to be safe. This should also get you both a drink or something."

"I'll pay you back," Two said brightly.

Brian smiled and said, "No worries."

Brett walked into the bathroom holding a yellow tie with black dots just as Brian and Two were leaving. He wore a white shirt and khaki slacks with tan deck shoes.

"My turn. I can't get it right this morning."

"You're a dork. You tied your own tie all football season," Brian said as Two laughed.

"Well, I can't get it right this morning for some dumb reason."

Brian chuckled and said, "Operator error," which made Two laugh harder. Both Brian and Brett laughed along with him.

It was a little more difficult tying Brett's tie than it was Two's tie. Brett was bigger and an inch taller. Done, the three boys assessed themselves in the mirror.

"I like dressing up," Brett said. "I didn't use to," he added with a shrug.

"Me, too," Two said.

To Brett, Brian asked, "You nervous?"

Brett wagged his head from side to side and said, "No, not really. We just don't know much about them. That's all."

"But we know what we have. Gav gives us an aircraft carrier underneath. A big guy with guard skills and who can hit from the outside. Bobby gives us an outside shot and tough defense." He paused and said, "The only one I'm nervous about is Mikey. If he comes in, he can't be too ..."

"Excited," Brett finished for him.

"I'll talk to him before the game during warm-ups," Brian said. "Gav, too. He won't need it, but reminding him is good. And I'll talk to Bobby. I think he might be reluctant to shoot, and he can't be. We need him scoring from the outside."

Brett smiled at him.

"What?"

"You just said all the things dad might say before the game."

Brian shrugged and said, "It's true, though."

"Oh, I know," Brett said. "Let's go eat."

CHAPTER FORTY-NINE

Security escorted Nada Sherry to the conference room just as the first block began. She sat at the large table by herself. The security guard, Nancy Hilton, stood by the door. Nada asked questions that were met by silence, and she eventually gave up.

"I want to scare the shit out of her," Graff said to Farner, Tobin, and O'Connor. "We won't charge her with anything. Instead, we'll let the school decide on the punishment.

"What would you like me to do?" Cathie Tobin asked.

"We need video footage of Nada bringing the cookies to Billy Schroeder yesterday morning, before school. They were in the cafeteria where Billy and the guys normally sit."

Tobin took notes on her hand. O'Connor didn't understand why. There were sticky notes on Farner's desk.

"We'll go in and question her. When you get the footage, please record it on this thumb drive," he handed her one, "and bring it into the conference room. I want to make her as uncomfortable as possible."

"Got it. I'll do it now," and she walked out of Farner's office, shutting the door behind her.

Tobin had confidence, as well as intelligence. A former softball coach, she moved and acted like a jock. She had a presence. O'Connor thought she must have been quite the player in her day. She'd make a good cop. The last was just a hunch, but his hunches were dead on.

She left and Pat asked Farner, "Is she married?"

Farner smiled and said, "Yes. Three kids."

"Oh."

"You're not too subtle, are you?" Graff asked with a grin.

"I was just curious," O'Connor said, not making eye contact with either man.

Graff checked his watch. "She's been in there about ten minutes." He nodded to no one and said, "Let's get it done."

Graff took the lead in questioning her and jotting notes, with O'Connor taking mental notes and watching for any tells and giveaways. Farner brought a notepad and pen and would take notes because the school needed documentation. He would observe until they gave him the go ahead to do the school side of things. Though she would have no role in the interrogation, Hilton would remain in the room because she was female, and they didn't want the girl in the room alone with three males.

Graff knocked on the door, and Hilton opened it. Graff and Farner sat down side by side across from Nada. O'Connor leaned against the wall near the door and facing Nada.

Nada sat with her hands folded in her lap. Her shoulders were hunched, and her eyes darted from one man to the other randomly. There was no expression on her face. Neutral, at best.

"Nada, I am Chief of Detectives Jamie Graff of the Waukesha Police Department. This is Detective Pat O'Connor, and of course, you know Mr. Farner."

She blinked, but there was no other response. Her hands appeared on the table in front of her, but the sleeves of her sweater swallowed them.

She was slight, unassuming, and unattractive. The word that came to Graff's mind was waif. Her hair was stringy and oily. Graff wondered when it was last washed.

Graff made a show of taking out the plastic evidence bag containing the cookies and placed it on the table in front of him, in plain sight of Nada. She glanced at them and smiled.

"You gave these to Billy Schroeder yesterday morning, before school in the cafeteria." Graff purposely made it a statement and not a question. "Do you remember that?"

She smiled. Her teeth, small, had a yellow-brown tint to them, and her smile was sickening, sly. Her face resembled that of a snake. Other than the smile, she didn't answer.

"I asked a question. Do you remember giving him these cookies?"

"So what? Two are missing." She smiled again and said, "I hope he ate them both."

"And why is that?"

Her smile, if Graff could call it that, was a snarl. She leaned forward, and her eyes narrowed and turned dark. Stunned, Graff inadvertently glanced at Farner, who hid his expression behind his hand.

"Because he's a pig. He gets what he deserves."

"And what exactly does he deserve?"

Nada didn't answer. She wiped her nose on the sleeve of her sweater, then cocked her head at Graff.

Graff waited patiently. Nada refused to add any other comment. A standoff between a skilled veteran cop and a kid.

Cathie Tobin knocked once on the door and entered the room. Without making eye contact with Nada, she handed him the thumb drive.

"Everything we need?"

Tobin smiled and said, "Exactly like you said it would be. Game, set, match."

O'Connor smiled and once again considered that Tobin would be a formidable cop.

"You're welcome to stay if you like," Graff said.

"Thank you." To Hilton, the security guard, she said, "Thanks for your help, Nancy. I'll take it from here."

Hilton nodded and left silently.

"Why are you here?" Nada snarled, eyes open to only slits.

"Because I invited her," Graff said.

Nada glared at him, then at Tobin, and then her expression changed all together, as if nothing had happened at all. The sudden shift in expression caught Graff off guard. He heard O'Connor grunt behind him and knew O'Connor had caught it, too.

After a minute or two, Graff said, "We had the FBI analyze these, and they found an inordinate amount of a laxative in them. Anyone eating one of these could get terribly sick."

Nada shrugged dismissively. She said, "My mom uses it and she doesn't get sick."

"So, you admit to putting a laxative in these cookies."

Nada shrugged again and shifted in her seat. She placed both elbows on the table, and the sleeves of her sweater covered both hands and her mouth, as if she was hiding.

Graff held up the thumb drive Tobin had brought in and said, "We have you on video handing these to Billy Schroeder yesterday morning."

"So?"

Trying a new track to throw her off guard, Graff said, "What can you tell us about the letters you've been sending to Randy Evans, Bobby McGovern, and Danny Limbach?"

Her eyes darted around the room like pinballs in a machine. She said, "I don't know nothing about any letters."

As if she hadn't responded, Graff said, "Nineteen letters so far."

Nada kept her eyes downcast.

"The most recent letter to Danny Limbach had a substance in the envelope. Can you tell me what was in it?"

No answer. Eyes glued to the table.

"Do you have a crush on Danny?"

She looked up and said, "It's not a crime. Almost everyone does."

"If that's the case, why would you threaten to hurt him?"

Without looking up from the table, she said, "I don't know nothing about any letters."

Graff leaned forward and said, "The letters need to stop. None of the boys want them. Danny, especially, doesn't want them. If you have a crush on him, it needs to end. He isn't interested in you. He wants nothing to do with you. Do you understand me?"

Nada shrugged and said, "It's a free country."

"What's that supposed to mean?"

"I know my rights," she said smugly. So smugly, Graff wanted to reach across the table and smack it off her face.

"And Danny, Randy, and Bobby have rights, too. Any letter threatening them in any way is against the law. Do you understand me?"

She leaned forward and snarled, "I already told you, Mister Big Policeman, I know nothing about any letters."

"And none of us sitting or standing here, believe you. And I'm warning you for the last time, the letters and the threats end. Do I make myself clear?"

She stared at him. Eyes narrow and dark. Her mouth was a straight line. Small wrinkles on her forehead. She said nothing, but her expression said it all.

"I asked you a question, and I want an answer."

"I heard you, but you didn't hear me. I don't know nothing about any fucking letters."

As if Graff didn't hear her, he said, "If the letters don't stop, and if the cookies and cake or anything else you bring to Danny, to Billy, to Randy, to Bobby or to any of their friends don't stop, the next time you and I talk, I'll bring my handcuffs and arrest you. Do you understand me?"

Nada sat there, arms folded across her chest. She didn't even blink at him.

"I asked you a question and I want an answer. I want you to know beyond any doubt what will happen if I have to come back here and talk to you again. Do you understand?"

Nada leaned forward and saluted him.

"That's not an answer. I want to hear from you that you understand."

"Yes, I understand. I also told you I don't know nothing about any letters."

"The letters will stop. The gifts to Danny or to anyone else will stop. Is that clear?"

"How many times are you going to ask me those fucking questions?"

"I will keep asking these questions until I get a simple and clear response from you. Will you stop bringing any presents or baked goods or notes to Danny or any of his friends?"

"Yes," she snarled.

"And the letters will stop immediately."

She rose out of her chair, leaned over the table and said, "I don't know nothing about any fucking letters!"

Tobin and Farner stood up as if joined by a rope and pulled out of their chairs.

Tobin said quietly, almost daringly, "Sit down in that chair and don't you move a muscle. Don't even flinch. Don't you ever raise your voice or use that language to anyone in this school, especially an adult or police officer again. Do you understand me?"

Nada shrunk back and looked to be on the verge of tears.

Tobin barked, "I asked you a question and I want an answer right now!"

In a voice barely above a whisper, Nada said, "I understand."

Graff blinked at the girl's reaction to Tobin. *Shit, if I would have only known ...*

CHAPTER FIFTY

The two cops stepped out of the conference room, looked around the guidance area lobby, and eyed Jeremy's empty office. Graff walked up to Kristi Johnson.

"Could we use Jeremy's office for a minute or two?"

"Yes. It's unlocked," she answered with a smile.

"And when Bob and Cathie are done with the kid, can you let them know where we are?"

She smiled and said, "Sure, no problem." She jotted a note for herself on a sticky note and placed it on the fringe of her computer screen.

The two cops entered Jeremy's office and shut the door. Graff sat at Jeremy's desk, and O'Connor sat in one of the visitor's chairs. Both men stared at each other before Graff said, "She might be the scariest kid I've spoken to in a helluva long time."

"She reminds me of Nelson Alamorode or Alan Nelson, the psycho Brian shot in the ass. I'm no shrink, but did you see the change in her?"

"I think I saw three changes, at least. Had I known Tobin would have had an effect on the kid, I would have tag-teamed the interview with her."

O'Connor nodded and said, "Tobin could be a helluva cop. Hell, when she got in the kid's face, I almost pissed my pants."

Graff laughed and said, "I've never seen Farner move so fast. Damn. For a big guy, he can move."

The two men sat quietly with their thoughts. Graff jotted some additional notes on his pad of paper, sighed, and put his pencil down.

"Besides the fact this girl is a whack-job wannabe, what do you think?"

"No wannabe about it." O'Connor thought for a minute and said, "She knows about the letters. I don't think she sent them. I don't even think she wrote them. But I think she knows about the letters and I think she knows who is responsible."

"My thought exactly." Graff thought for a minute and said, "If what we think is true, is she smart enough to get the message to the person or persons involved with the letters to stop sending them?"

"She might, but then again, will that other kid give a shit what she says? I mean, would you take that sick fuck seriously?"

"Or would the person care what might happen to her if they don't stop sending letters?" Graff added with a shrug and a shake of his head. "I think if Nada is involved in this, and I think she is, she was duped and used only as a convenience. She was a pawn."

O'Connor looked off into space and shrugged. "Honestly, and this is sad, but I don't think anyone cares about her."

Graff sighed, ran a hand over his face, and shook his head.

They heard a bustle of activity in the lobby area, and both men looked out the window in the door. They saw Kristi point a pencil at Jeremy's office and Farner look in their direction. He walked towards the office, and both O'Connor and Graff stood up.

"Let's go to my office. It's more private."

They followed him down the hallway, past the conference room, to Farner's office. He opened the door and sat down behind his desk. Graff shut the door behind him and then sat down next to O'Connor in the visitor's chair.

"Anyone else feel like they need a shower?" Farner said. "Jesus! How can a kid get so fucked up?"

Graff chuckled dryly and said, "You deal with more kids than we do, and you're asking us?" He chuckled again.

"Can I ask, what kind of punishment did you give her?" O'Connor asked.

"Cathie suggested a three-day suspension, depending upon her letters of apology."

"Letters of apology?" Graff asked. "To who?"

Farner smiled. "One to Billy Schroeder for the loaded cookies, and one to you for her behavior and language."

O'Connor and Graff exchanged a look, but before either of them could say anything, Farner added, "You talked about letters sent to Danny, Bobby, and Randy. I thought you would want to compare her writing and word choice- to quote Tobin- with the letters the boys received."

He leaned back in his chair, folded his hands on his belly, beamed, and said, "Yes, I know. We're brilliant."

"Damn, you're good." To O'Connor, Graff said, "I told you they were good. And you doubted them."

Feigning indignation, Farner said, "You doubted moi?" He laughed, got serious and said, "Unless it is need to know, can you tell me about the letters?"

Graff nodded and said, "They began as fan mail. You know, things like 'You're awesome! You're the best!' to 'You don't need Randy and Bobby, so kick them out of the band!'. Then they progressed to 'You're not listening to me! Maybe I need to show you, I mean business.' Those types of letters. Gradually becoming more threatening."

Farner frowned. "Whoever wrote them doesn't know music. The three of them are perfect together. I might be showing my age, but they remind me of the Eagles and Poco." He wagged his head from side to side and said, "With heavier guitar and more country."

"You know your music," O'Connor said.

Farner shrugged and said, "I like to listen. I enjoy going to concerts. I can't play a thing and dogs howl when I sing. But I've learned a lot from Danny and Bobby. Even Garrett, though he is kind of a screwball."

Graff laughed and said, "I like that kid."

"So do I." Farner laughed and added, "Don't tell him, though."

Tobin rapped a knuckle on the door, stuck her head in, and said, "Can I come in?"

Both O'Connor and Graff stood up, though O'Connor was quicker.

She made a wry face, pushed hair out of her face and said, "I have her apology letters. If you call them letters of apology. Or for that matter, letters."

She handed them to Graff, and O'Connor leaned over to look.

Billy,
I am sory for th cookys. I wuz rong to do that.
Nada

Graff blinked at Tobin, who was unsuccessful in stifling a grin, which turned into a laugh, doubling her over. She held up her hands and said, "I'm sorry, but God!"

Both cops laughed with her, and Graff said, "This is sad," as he shook his head and handed the letter to Farner.

"And she's not special ed? If she's not, I don't know who is," O'Connor said. He chuckled, and said, "She writes better than Eiselmann, though."

All four laughed at O'Connor's joke.

Graff looked over the apology to him, but couldn't get past the opening without laughing.

Offisur Gruf,
I am sory for swaring at you and for being lowd. I wil not do that agan.
Nada

"Offisur Gruf! I like that!" O'Connor said, smacking Graff on the back. "I can't wait to get back to the office."

Through laughter, Tobin said, "I'm pretty sure she isn't the author of your letters." She gathered herself and said, "God, I'm so unprofessional," and then she broke into laughter again.

Farner put his head on his desk and belly laughed.

O'Connor and Graff joined them.

Graff and O'Connor thanked them for their help and left shortly thereafter.

Once in the car, Graff ran a hand over his face and said, "If she isn't the author, then who is?"

"I was having a pretty good day," O'Connor said. "Fuck me."

CHAPTER FIFTY-ONE

The day flew by, mostly. When PE came around, it slowed, almost like slogging through a swamp of waist high mud. Brian wasn't interested in swimming with the game that evening. But working on the breaststroke wasn't taxing. In fact, Brian found it relaxing.

He watched George and Tony two lanes over. George struggled at first, but like most things George did, he got it down and looked smooth. Tony got it down right away. So much so, Coach Harrison pulled him aside and spoke to him. Brian smiled, knowing Coach was asking him about his potential interest in the swim team.

Coach blew his whistle. The shrill sound bounced all over the concrete walls, hurting ears and making everyone cover them and wince.

"Everyone out of the water, dry yourselves off, grab your gear, and head to the locker room. Hope to see all of you at the game tonight."

"What game?" Brian yelled back.

Everyone laughed, and Harrison smiled. He said, "Evans, you don't have to show up. We have your position covered."

Almost everyone in the class said, "Oooo!"

"You would miss me!" Brian laughed.

"Not even for a minute," Harrison said with a straight face.

The class repeated, "Oooo!"

"Now get to the locker room, Evans, before I kick your butt! George and Tony, drag him if you have to."

Both boys laughed, as did Brian.

Brian slung his arms around George and Tony and said, "You guys going to drag me or what?"

"No, I'll just kick your butt," George said with a straight face.

"Tony, George pretends to be tough, but he's a softy."

George said with a smile, "I might be a softy, but I can still kick your butt."

"Yeah, yeah, yeah."

Tony found the exchange amusing.

As Tony and Brian changed into their clothes at their lockers, Brian said, "I'm going to work on a story in the library while you and George, and Michael run. Text me when you get done, and I'll come down to the locker room. We'll go get something to eat, and then we'll run to your house and pick up whatever you need for the weekend. Then we will pick up Big Gav and Mickey for the game."

"That's a lot of running around for you."

Brian laughed and said, "Not nearly as much as you, George, and Michael will do."

Tony made a face and said, "I know. We're running hills."

"Hills suck. For that matter, running sucks," and both boys laughed.

As they walked out of the locker room, Brian leaned over to Tony and said, "Tonight's going to be a good night."

Brian smiled and gave Tony's arm a squeeze. "See you in a while." To George, he said, "Don't kill him too badly."

George laughed, causing Tony to wonder just what he was in for.

The three of them rounded a corner, and Brian literally walked into Coach Harrison. Harrison grabbed Brian and put him in a headlock and rubbed the top of Brian's head, causing him to swat at his hand.

"How do you two put up with him?" Harrison asked.

"I do just what you're doing. Tony doesn't know him well enough yet. Eventually, he'll catch on."

"Aren't either of you going to help?" Brian asked from somewhere under Harrison's armpit.

"No," both answered in unison.

"Thanks a lot!" Brian said as Harrison finally let go.

"Bri, do you have a second?" Harrison asked.

"Sure."

He followed him back into the locker room and into Harrison's office, and sat down in front of Harrison's desk. Harrison shut the door and sat down on the other side of his desk.

"You ready for tonight?"

Brian smiled, nodded and said, "You bet. I think we're all ready."

Harrison was a former baseball player in the day. Pitched Triple A for the Braves organization. Bounced between the big leagues when a starter in the rotation was injured, then came back to Triple A. He still had friends in the organization and golfed with several during the summer. Now, besides running basketball camps, he put on hitting and pitching clinics.

Pictures dotted the wall behind him. A couple showed Harrison on the mound for the Braves. A framed copy of a program listing him as a starter. A frame of his baseball card in a Braves uniform alongside his baseball card in a Gwinnett Stripers uniform, the Triple A team in Lawrenceville, Georgia.

"Why don't you coach baseball?" Brian asked as he looked at the pictures for the millionth time.

"I like basketball. More action. Faster game."

"You'd be a good baseball coach."

Harrison cocked his head and said, "Are you saying I'm not good as a basketball coach?"

Brian laughed and said, "Of course not." He shook his head and said, "You're a dork."

Harrison smiled. He liked the guys on his team. They were his boys. Even though he tried not to show it, he had his favorites. Brian, being one of them. Brett and Billy being the other two.

"You've had quite a couple of months," Harrison said as he nodded at Brian.

Brian knew Harrison meant the scar around his right eye.

"Then your dad with his heart thingy," using the term the boys used. "How are you doing, Brian? Really doing?"

He didn't want to go into the shitty week he had, which was topped off by last night, which was shittier than the week. He didn't want to go into the scar around his eye or the other scars. Brian didn't know how much Harrison knew, but he suspected Brian or Billy or even his dad had filled him in on some of it.

Brian said, "I'm okay. Not great, but okay."

Harrison marveled at Brian's honesty, and his ability to compartmentalize his life. There was Brian's school life, separate from sports, and each sport separate from each other. There was life at home, and there was his social life. Tony seemed to be a part of Brian's life now.

"Anything I can do?"

Brian smiled and said, "No, I'm okay."

Harrison nodded and said, "Yes, that's what you said. If you ever need anything, I'm here."

"Thanks, Coach."

Changed subjects, Harrison asked, "Is your dad going to be at the game tonight?"

Brian shrugged and said, "We don't know yet. I think we'll find out at game time."

"Your dad has a pregame ritual with you guys."

Brian nodded and said, "I've got it covered. I'll talk to each of my brothers, along with Mikey and Gavin."

Harrison smiled and said, "I figured as much."

Brian smiled and felt himself blushing.

"You would have made a helluva captain. Last year, you and Brett were Co-Conference Players of the Year. You earned the respect, not only of your teammates but also the coaches in the conference."

Brian shifted uncomfortably in his seat and said, "Thank you, but honestly, being a captain means more to Brett and Billy. Brett, because he is the point guard and the coach on the floor. He's our leader in a lot of ways, besides basketball. Billy, because he's a leader and he works so hard. The guys see it."

"Just so long as you don't shrink from leadership if it comes to you."

"I'd never do that."

Harrison nodded, thought for a minute and said, "Seems like you and Tony have hit it off."

Brian blushed and said, "He's a good guy. All the guys like him."

"I think he's as good for you as you are for him."

"Meaning?" Brian asked.

"This is philosophical, but I believe people come into other's lives for a reason, just like people leave other's lives for a reason. I know you, and I know your heart, and I know you've struggled in ..." he wagged his head and said, "relationships. I think Tony is good for you."

Brian felt a chill run up his back. He felt sweaty. He suspected Harrison was talking about him being gay, but he wasn't sure. He didn't know who knew he was gay, and he didn't want many people to know. He particularly didn't want his coaches or teachers to know. If that was what Harrison was talking about.

"I'm not sure," Brian said, but stopped.

"I believe everyone needs to live their own life. Unless we're talking about an axe murderer or some psycho. But when it comes to living your own life, there is no wrong or right. We are given a life. We are given moments. We have to make the most of those moments in our lives." He paused, smiled, and said, "That's all I'm saying." He leaned forward and said, "I want you to make the most of your moments. In whatever you do, and with whoever is in your life. After all, it's your life."

Brian tilted his head, and he was pretty sure Harrison was tip-toeing around the issue. Brian's issue. He didn't know how he should respond or even if he should respond.

"Kids follow you. They look up to you. That's an enormous responsibility. What you do and what you say can have a great impact on others."

Puzzled, Brian shook his head.

"I had a college teammate. Another pitcher. He was above average, but he knew he wasn't going anywhere beyond college. He was a good guy, and everyone liked him. I was dating this girl, and I tried to set him up with her friend. They went out once or twice, but it didn't go anywhere. Another teammate did the same thing. The guy went out a few times with this other girl, but it didn't go anywhere. It was his choice. He didn't say anything, and he never explained anything. This guy was content to live his life the way he wanted. And I think he lived his life the way he needed to. Later on, much later on after college, I ran into him and saw how happy he was. I was proud of him."

He leaned forward and said, "I watch kids in the hallways, or the cafeteria or in my class. Some are shy. I get it. Some are struggling with who they are. I feel sorry for them. They are wasting their lives and their moments. Hiding who they are. I know our society and maybe our school isn't ready for them, and it makes me sad.

"I am divorced and I have a daughter. At some point, I'm getting married to a wonderful lady named Kerri. She has two sons who I like a great deal. We'll end up being a family, including my daughter. That's my life right now, and my moment, with more of my life and more moments to come. Just like the pitcher I knew in college, he has his life and he's living it. Last I heard, he's happy."

Brian shook his head, unable, and perhaps unwilling, to say anything.

"I want you happy. I want you to live your life and live your moments. If along the way you can help others do the same," he smiled, letting the statement hang there.

"How did you?" Brian asked, unwilling to finish the question.

"How did I know?" He chuckled and said, "Brian, you are one of the most transparent guys I've ever been around. Your honesty is my favorite quality. That, and your toughness. Keep living your life like that."

George, Two, and Tony walked into the locker room. Brian felt relieved. Maybe rescued was a better word.

George stuck his head in the office, smiled, and said, "We're back."

All three were dripping with sweat. George looked like he had run a routine workout. Nothing strenuous. Two smiled at Brian and Coach Harrison, and didn't seem the worse for wear.

Tony, however, dragged himself forward. He hung onto the doorframe with both hands and said, "You told George not to kill me, right?"

Brian laughed. "Yeah."

"He didn't listen."

George, Two, and Brian laughed, and Harrison smiled.

George said, "You kept up. You're in better shape than you think you are."

"Shoot me or yank my legs off, and I'll feel better than I do right now."

Everyone left and Tony followed George and Two to the locker area to get cleaned up.

Brian turned around and faced Harrison. He glanced once over his shoulder to make sure no one was around and then he said, "Coach, this conversation is between you and me, and no one else, right?"

Harrison's eyebrows lifted, and he tried to look innocent when he said, "We talked about basketball, the game tonight, and my old baseball days. What's wrong with that?"

CHAPTER FIFTY-TWO

They were on a Zoom call, Graff and Pasquale. Graff had made it to the office, and his butt barely touched the chair when Pasquale phoned him and asked for a Zoom meet.

"Flour?" Graff asked. "You mean the stuff you bake with?"

Pasquale laughed and said, "The same."

"Huh."

"The letter was, shall I say, obnoxious. I'm going to post it up on the screen for you."

"Yes, please."

Pasquale hit a few buttons, and up popped the note.

Now that I have your attention, are you going to listen to me?

Puzzled, Graff said, "That's it?"

Off camera, Pasquale said, *"Yeah, that's it. No salutation. No ending. If there wasn't an address, you'd never know who the letter was for."*

Graff thought for a minute. This letter not only amped up the threat level, but it was clearly different from the others. In some respects, it was more personal than the others. The powder was clearly a threat. But no *Danny-* or *Dear Danny-* which made it less personal. It would need to be sent to Skip Dahlke at Quantico to get his take on it.

"Are you still there?"

"Yeah, sorry. I was just thinking."

"It's a puzzler."

Graff laughed and said, "I thought you were good at puzzles."

"I said I liked puzzles. I didn't say I was good at them. Though, I am better than some are. Still, this one is a puzzler."

"Can you do me a favor? Bag and tag it and send it to James Dahlke at Quantico?"

"Sure. How is Skip?"

"He's good. I don't think he'll ever look older than fifteen-years-old."

Pasquale laughed and said, *"Ain't that the truth? Some of us get older, and he's drinking from the fountain of youth."*

Graff thought for a minute and asked Pasquale, "Did you work on the three cars that blew up in the stadium parking lot last month?"

"Not initially, but it ended up on my desk. Why?"

"One of the detectives I'm working with wondered why a bomb was constructed, when a simple long fuse shoved down the gas tank would have sufficed. It would have even worked better than the bomb. And he wondered why the sedan and not just the Escalade."

Pasquale took the letter down from the screen and frowned. Pasquale thought for a moment, and Graff let him. He was about to interrupt his thoughts, and Pasquale put his hand up to prevent him from doing so. Graff waited longer.

Frowning at Graff, Pasquale said, *"The thinking was the sedan was the target vehicle. The other two vehicles were collateral to make a bigger boom."* Pasquale shook his head and said, *"What you're suggesting is that the Escalade, the vehicle in the middle, was the target. That makes things more complicated. It changes the investigation."*

Marveling at his mind and memory, Graff nodded and said, "Yes, we know. We didn't consider it until recently."

"And you're thinking the letters might have something to do with the car bomb?"

Surprised Pasquale made the connection, Graff said, "It's a possibility, yes. And we think a kid made and set the pipe bomb."

"That explains why the bomb was constructed the way it was. A pretty shitty design. This changes things. Shit! When I was a kid, I built stuff with my erector set, and played on the computer. The only things I blew up were little green army men with firecrackers to simulate war."

Pasquale leaned forward, eyes dark. His thick bushy eyebrows gave him an Einstein look, even though Pasquale's were black. *"How can I help?"*

CHAPTER FIFTY-THREE

Graff, Eiselmann, and O'Connor had phoned ahead and raced to the Evan's home to meet with Jeremy and Vicky before the boys got home. Jeff Limbach was going to meet them there. The three cops also wanted to get something to eat before the game.

Jamie said, "Since the last time we spoke, we made some headway into the case." He took a deep breath and said, "There is a girl, a freshman, who bring cookies and cake and stuff to Danny. Nada Sherry. Does that name ring a bell?"

Jeremy frowned at Graff and said, "I don't know her, but I know of her. She's in Lloyd's caseload. Kind of small. Odd."

Graff wanted to say that odd didn't even come close to describing her, but he didn't. What he said was, "Pat and I met with her yesterday. Bob Farner and Cathie Tobin were with us. It turns out Danny seldom, if ever, ate anything she brought him, but would give it away. Billy ate some of it. Others did too."

He told them about the chocolate chip cookies, and then took a deep breath, not knowing how Jeremy or Vicky would take the rest of it.

"Yesterday, she brought a plate of cookies for Billy. She said she wanted to teach him a lesson, so one ingredient was a laxative like Ex-Lax. A large amount. Fortunately, no one ate any. George bagged them and texted me, and Paul and I took them to the FBI office in Milwaukee for analysis. We got the results back earlier this afternoon."

"I always knew Billy was full of shit. The cookies might have taken care of that," Jeff said with a straight face.

Jeremy and Vicky laughed at Jeff's joke.

Jeremy said, "Ex-Lax?"

Graff nodded and said, "Yes. Quite a lot from what the FBI lab said."

Jeremy and Vicky exchanged a look, and it seemed to Graff they were relieved.

"When Pat and I interviewed her, we pressed her on two things. First, the letters."

Jeremy chuckled and shook his head. "I don't buy it."

"What?" Vicky said.

"She's not capable," Jeremy said.

Graff nodded and said, "That's exactly what we thought. Tobin made her write an apology to Billy for the cookies and to me for cursing and yelling at me, and there is no way she wrote the letters."

"But we believe she knows who did," O'Connor said.

"I don't have any doubt about that," Graff said. "I believe we scared the shit out of her and the message will get to the right person to stop. Pat, Paul and I will follow up and grill her to get her to tell us who the letter writer is."

"Sounds great," Vicky said with a smile. She caught the expression on Graff's, Eiselmann's and O'Connor's face, and said, "What am I missing?"

Graff took a deep breath, puffed out his cheeks, and said, "Only Jeff and Danny know. The other boys don't. But Danny received a letter addressed to him. Jeff intercepted it. The letter contained a white powder, and it turned out to be flour, the kind you cook with. The letter itself was one line: *Now that I have your attention, are you going to listen to me?* This raises the level of threat, at least to Danny."

"This is why we are going to press hard on Nada to find out who the letter writer is," O'Connor said. "For her to know and not tell us, makes her an accessory to a felony. That alone should scare her enough to give up the letter writer."

Jeremy and Vicky sat and thought for a minute and Jeremy said, "Randy or Bobby didn't receive a letter like that?"

"No, not to our knowledge. We're going to stop by your mailbox on the way out, and we'll see if anything arrived today. But so far, no," Eiselmann said.

Vicky shook her head and said, "I already picked it up. Nothing."

Graff, Eiselmann, and O'Connor glanced at each other, and Graff said, "We'll see if anything shows up tomorrow, but we think Danny is now the focus of attention for the letter writer."

"On one hand, I'm relieved. On the other, Danny is as important to us as our boys are," Jeremy said.

"As long as you three have a handle on this, and as long as you put the screws on cookie girl, I'm okay. Danny will be too," Jeff said.

Graff wanted to see how this conversation went before he divulged the other not so small tidbit.

"With the FBI, we are reopening the car bombing that took place last month in the stadium parking lot. We want to investigate whether the letters and the car bomb were related."

Eiselmann leaned forward and said, "It will be a two-prong approach. Jamie pulled in Greg Gonnering and Carlos Lorenzo to reexamine the evidence, alongside the FBI."

It didn't take long before the question reared its ugly head.

Vicky said, "I'm puzzled. Concerned, too, but mostly puzzled. Early on, you said the evidence showed they placed the bomb on TJ's uncle's car. Or did I get that wrong?"

"You're right," Graff said. "We want to make sure that is the case."

"What makes you think the two are related to each other? The letters and the car bombing?" Jeremy asked.

"Honestly, we don't know if they are," Jamie said. "That's why we're reexamining the evidence with the FBI."

"One of the investigative avenues is to press cookie girl on who the letter writer is," Eiselmann added. "If she gives us a name, we can press both of them on the car bombing."

"If the two are related," Graff said.

Jeremy stared at Vicky, and the two of them held hands. O'Connor noticed their grip tightened.

"We've got this," O'Connor said. "We won't let anything happen to the boys."

Jeff said, "Anything else?"

Graff glanced at Eiselmann and O'Connor and said, "No, that about covers it."

"Well, thank you," Jeremy said. "For everything."

"Absolutely," Graff said. "Jeremy, how are you feeling? Are you doing okay?"

"Yes, I'm okay. I have work to do. Get in better shape. Eat better."

"Good to hear," Jamie said. O'Connor and Eiselmann nodded their approval.

"Are you guys going to the game tonight?" Vicky asked.

"Absolutely," Graff said as he stood up. "We have to hustle. Grab something to eat and get to the game."

"The team will have a fresh look," Jeremy said. "We finally have a big guy underneath."

"They'll be fun to watch for sure," Eiselmann added.

The three cops said goodbye and left Jeff, Jeremy, and Vicky in the kitchen. Jeremy was a little tired, but he wasn't going to say anything. He wanted to go to the game to watch his boys. Vicky had noticed, but didn't mention it, because she thought he'd be fine. Tired, but fine.

Jeff said, "Are you ready for all the questions?"

Jeremy knew what Jeff meant. He had thought about it, and it was one part of the evening he wasn't looking forward to. On the plus side, with whatever was going to be said or asked this evening, perhaps less would be said or done at school on Monday. That was his hope, anyway.

CHAPTER FIFTY-FOUR

The Vittoria house was large and modern with a tan vinyl siding, in one of the newer subdivisions in Waukesha. The two-story home had a hedgerow and white picket fence running along the front and both sides. A two-and a half car garage and walkway sat to the right. The house itself was almost as large as Brian's house. Brian's home had to fit nine people and four dogs. Tony's family only comprised a family of five. Brian didn't know about any animals.

"Mom, you remember Brian? He showed me around the school on my first day," Tony said.

"Of course I do," she said as she stood up and shook Brian's hand. "I'm Giana, Tony's aunt." She smiled at Tony and said, "I like it when you call me mom." She said, "Why don't you show Brian around the house and show him your work?"

Tony smiled, blushed, and said, "Sure." To Brian, Tony said with a laugh, "This is the kitchen."

"Really? I wouldn't have guessed," Brian said, feigning amazement.

"I see you are a smart ass, too," Giana said, causing Tony and Brian to laugh.

Tony showed Brian around, pointing out his drawings and paintings at his aunt's urging. They were beautiful. Spectacular, even. Almost like photographs. Some were large and covered most of a wall. Others were portrait size.

The three of them walked into a formal living room. It looked so new Brian didn't think they used it. On the wall were several large pieces of art. Two were drawings, and one was something else. Brian didn't know what it was. Abstract, maybe?

Tony's aunt saw him looking at it, and she said, "This drawing won blue ribbons at the county and state fair." Tony blushed. Giana, who had trailed behind them, added, "It also earned Tony a best of show at the state fair."

She left them and Tony said, "My aunt and uncle are pretty proud of them."

"They ought to be. You too, Tony. These are fantastic," Brian said, staring at the drawing of his cousins, Benny and Sophia, watching TV. It reminded him of the photo Brett took of him and Bobby watching TV.

"This picture of your aunt and uncle. What did you use?"

"Pastel. I wanted to balance the black and white drawing of Benny and Sophia with color."

"Damn, Tony. You're fantastic."

Tony gave him an 'aw shucks' shrug and said, "Thanks."

"Let's go up to my room. I need to change and pack up some stuff," Tony said. He caught Brian checking his watch and said, "It won't take long. I promise!"

The two boys climbed the staircase to the second floor. At the top, it opened up to a balcony overlooking the front entry and the chandelier hanging from the ceiling. Along the wall up the stairs were pictures of the family at various ages. Tony didn't appear in any until more recent times.

"When did you move in with your aunt and uncle?" Brian asked.

"About two years ago. During the summer."

He didn't elaborate, and Brian didn't push him. It was up to Tony how much he wanted to share and when he wanted to share it.

Tony's room was the first room at the top of the stairs on the right. It was about as big as Brian's and Michael's room. A queen-sized bed with a blue and gray striped comforter, a desk and lamp, two nightstands with lights. The nightstand on the left had a clock, so Brian figured Tony slept on that side.

On the wall above the headboard was a large drawing. Brian was stunned to silence.

The drawing in pencil was Tony. Only this Tony had a crewcut and was younger. Tony had his knees drawn up to his chest, and he hugged them with both arms. His head was down, and he looked to be crying. He wore a t-shirt and jeans, and had nothing on his feet except socks.

"Tony, come here," Brian whispered.

Tony had begun to change clothes, and had on only his boxers, socks, and his shell necklace. He stood next to Brian.

"This is so sad," Brian whispered, not able to take his eyes from the drawing. "It looks like you were hurting. Damn, this is sad."

"It was a dark time."

Brian turned to Tony and said, "What were you thinking?"

Without taking his eyes off the drawing, Tony said, "I had a shitty life, and I was tired of it."

Brian gazed at Tony, reached out, and put his left hand on Tony's side just above his boxers, and his right hand on Tony's upper arm.

"Tony, look at me."

Tony did so, but couldn't sustain eye contact.

"Look at me," Brian said, as he wrapped both arms around Tony's waist.

Tony couldn't help but look at him. There were tears in his eyes.

Brian said, "You have to promise me. If you ever feel like that, I don't care when, how late it is, or where you are, you need to call me."

Tony said nothing.

As he did to any of his brothers, Brian put his forehead on Tony's and said, "Tony, I know it's only been a few days, but you mean a lot to me." Brian pulled Tony against him, and repeated, "You mean a lot to me. Promise me you will call me if you ever feel this way again. If you can't get a hold of me, call Brett, or Billy, or George. But call one of us. Please."

Brian and Tony rubbed noses, and Brian loosened his hold on Tony only a little. A single tear ran down Tony's cheek. Brian thumbed it away.

Neither said a word, but both felt the heat, like an electric current between them.

Brian put his forehead on Tony's and, as close to kissing Tony without actually kissing him, Brian whispered, "You mean a lot to me. I know I'm not the best-looking guy in the world. I hope you can look past this ugly scar around my right eye and the stupid white patch in my hair. I really want to be your friend. You mean a lot to me."

Tony never moved, but he smiled. He whispered, "I don't see the scar when I look at you. I see your eyes. They change color and they sparkle. I see the little freckles under your eyes and across your nose. You are special to me, too."

Brian rubbed Tony's nose with his and said, "I'm happy we're friends." He wanted to do more, and he thought Tony did too. He didn't know for sure, so he didn't push it.

Tony smiled and said, "Me, too."

Neither wanted to break contact with the other, but Brian said, "I wish we had more time for," he shrugged and said, "whatever, but we have to get going."

Tony took a deep breath and said, "I want you to get to know me, but that's scary."

"Why is it scary?"

"Because you might not like what you find out."

CHAPTER FIFTY-FIVE

During the shoot-around portion of warm-ups, Brian made his way to each of the players and gave them a technical pep talk or sometimes an inspirational message. In Mikey's, Bobby's, and Gavin's cases, he spoke to them about what to expect, as well as what the team expected of them. All three were nervous, though it seemed to Brian that of the three, Gavin was the least nervous. Purposely, he saved Randy for last after speaking to all of his other teammates.

He walked up to Randy, who was shooting threes from the corner. Brian took a shot himself and said, "You ready?"

"I think so."

"If you have the shot, take it. Mostly, we'll need you for defense and rebounding."

Randy nodded.

"I don't know who will get what minutes, and I'm not sure coach knows. I think he'll play it by ear. But whatever minutes you get, make the most of them. Leave it on the court."

As Brian turned to leave, Randy said, "I thought Brett and Billy were captains."

"They are. And, good luck with the anthem."

Brian walked away to the far side, unwilling to engage with him further. It wasn't worth it. No matter what he said or did these days, it wasn't good enough. He even thought it might never be good enough.

The ref blew the whistle and called for the captains at center court in front of the scorer's table. The rest of the team came over to the bench, got water, and got ready for the start.

"Bri, come here a minute," Coach Harrison said.

Brian jogged over.

Harrison spoke quietly, but he made sure Randy, who stood next to him, heard what he said. "Thanks for speaking with each of the players. I appreciate it."

"No problem."

"Are you set?"

"Yup. Like I said to them, we don't know what to expect, so we play our game. That should take care of most of it."

"I'll need you and Bobby to shoot, because it will take pressure off the guys underneath."

Brian smiled and said, "That's what I told Bobby."

Harrison gave Brian a knuckle bump and said, "Get ready for introductions."

Brian walked to the end of the bench, grabbed a bottle of water, took a long squirt, and took off his warm-ups. He sat between Brett and Billy. Gavin and Troy rounded out the starting five.

Randy and Bobby joined up with Danny, Chris, and Sean for the anthem at center court. Troy would join them after introducing starting line-ups.

The introductions for the Lasers of Kettle Moraine High School had a variety of handshakes for their walkout. One player stood at the end of the double line and would chest bump or give a specific handshake to each starter. They had choreographed the routine ahead of time.

In contrast, the NorthStar starters gave low fives to the double line, and ran to the opposing bench and shook the hands of the head coach and each assistant. Clean and simple. The way Harrison preferred it.

After the introductions, each team lined up single-file in front of their team bench and faced the large flag on the wall at the near end of the field house.

"Welcome to Waukesha North High School, home of the NorthStars!" the public address announcer, Chuck Malone, said. The partisan crowd cheered. "Tonight's game features our NorthStars hosting the visiting Lasers of Kettle Moraine High School. Will everyone please stand and remove your hats, as our own, Bits and Pieces, sing their rendition of the National Anthem."

They began with the chorus of *America the Beautiful* in four-part harmony, and transitioned into the National Anthem. Randy and Bobby alternated on the melody, with the others singing the harmony. Danny sang high harmony with Sean, and finger-picked the song on his acoustic electric. They ended to a raucous ovation from both visitors and the home team fans.

Brett whispered to Billy and Brian, "Nailed it!"

"Damn, they're good!" Billy said.

Both teams lined up for the opening tip. Gavin stood three inches taller than the Laser center. Brett took the backcourt defensive position, with Billy and Troy on either wing. Brian took the offensive position. It was something they had worked on.

Gav won the tip easily, tapped it to Billy who broke to the NorthStar basket. He spotted Brian and hit him with a pass. Brian had his man beat and without thinking and with no hesitation, dunked it with both hands, something he had never done before. Brian was as shocked as everyone else. Perhaps more so.

The crowd went nuts! Chants of "Bri-an! Bri-an!" rose from the student section, reminiscent of the past basketball season. The NorthStar bench whooped and hollered!

Stunned, Harrison looked back at Jeremy and shrugged. Jeremy shook his head in answer, but cheered along with everyone else.

Brett stole the inbound pass, kicked it to Brian for a quick three-point shot. He swished it, nothing but net.

Brian stole the next inbound pass, drove to the basket, and made it look like he was going for a layup. Instead, he reached for the basket with his left hand, but passed it behind him to Billy, who caught it and slammed one home for his own dunk.

7 to 0, NorthStars leading in less than one minute.

The crowd went nuts again. Billy's dunk wasn't unexpected. He did it at practice. Still, it was thunderous, and it resulted in a quick timeout by the Laser coach.

By the half, North was on top 34 to 17. Harrison used every player available in the first half, with multiple combinations. One grouping, the Evans boys, didn't allow a basket. Jeremy and Vicky enjoyed watching their sons play together.

North led 82 to 48 at the final buzzer. Kettle Moraine was not a bad team, but North was a terrific team with deep talent.

Almost every player on the North team scored. The team celebrated Mikey's first five points of the season. Gavin finished with 15, second only to Brian, who had 17. Bobby finished with 14, and Billy had 13.

In the end of game huddle, Harrison said, "Nice balanced scoring. We dominated on defense and on the boards. You guys were unselfish, you hustled, and put in the effort." He paused and added, "Don't let this game go to your heads. It's one game. We have more to play and some will be tougher. Much tougher."

He let it sink in. Then he smiled and said, "For a first game, I'm pleased with the result. You should be too. Enjoy it. But Monday, we're back at it. Don't do anything stupid over the weekend. Make good decisions and great choices."

Brett finished with, "All hands in," as he held his hand to the center. Everyone put their hand on his or at least his arm or shoulder. "One team, united, on three."

He counted down, and they yelled, "One Team, United!" After, they walked off to meet up with parents, girlfriends, and friends.

CHAPTER FIFTY-SIX

Tired and sweaty, the jubilant players mingled with interested spectators. Students hashed out plans for the evening and weekend. There were a couple of parties planned at houses parents may or may not know about. The fieldhouse floor was so crowded, players had trouble hooking up with their friends or family. The hum and buzz of the crowd was a deep undercurrent constant before, during, and after any game or contest. Most got used to it. Others ignored it. Most annoying was the crush of bodies making the fieldhouse floor claustrophobic. Whoever it bothered would eventually leave.

Troy left the bench area to join up with Sean and Chris. Big Gav, a sudden celebrity, and Bobby and Mikey, hooked up with Garrett, Andrew Westlake, Danny, and members of the JV team, victorious in their game before the varsity match. Brian, Brett, and Billy sought their parents. Randy trailed behind them after joining up briefly with Troy, Sean, and Chris. Bobby joined the family group soon after.

"I didn't know you could jump like that!" Jeremy laughed.

Brian laughed and said, "I didn't either!"

"Seriously, dude, what would have happened if you missed?" Billy laughed.

"Probably fell on my butt and died from embarrassment," Brian laughed again. He said, "You had a nice one. Two, I think?"

"Yeah, but, dude, I work on them in practice. I don't just wing it in a game."

Everyone laughed.

"It was a great game, fun to watch," Vicky said. "I thought everyone played well."

"We're tough," Brett said. "Bobby, you were smoking from the outside."

"And you had a nice drive and dish to Gav," Brian added.

"I was nervous when I first went it," Bobby said.

Brett said, "I could tell. But after you warmed up, you played really well."

Bobby blushed and smiled and said, "Thanks."

To include Randy in the discussion, Billy said, "Randy, you played well. You had some rebounds and a couple of loose balls."

"And you scored," Brett added.

Randy shrugged dismissively. Clearly, he wasn't pleased. It was either his performance, which wasn't bad at all, his playing time, or something else unrelated to the game. Jeremy couldn't tell. He would have to have a conversation with him.

Randy was as fierce a competitor as Billy. It was just that Billy was raised from little on in a jockstrap and had the support of his original adoptive parents. Randy, on the other hand, had a tough go of it with his adoptive parents. Not much support for anything. Still, Randy had the natural ability Billy had. While Billy was golden at anything he touched, Randy had to work for it.

"Who is George talking to?" Vicky asked as she glanced over her shoulder.

"Oh, that's Tony and his family. His aunt and uncle and his cousins. I want you to meet them. All of you."

"I'm going to go shower," Randy said, and headed off to the locker room before anyone could prevent him from doing so.

The small group walked over to George, Tony, and Tony's family.

Brian put his arm around Tony's shoulder and said, "Mom, Dad, I want you to meet Tony Vittoria. He's spending the weekend with us. Tony, this is my mom and dad, Jeremy and Vicky Evans."

"I'm Matteo, Tony's uncle. Please call me Matt," he said as he shook Jeremy's hand.

"And I'm Giana," Tony's aunt said as she reached for Vicky's hand.

"Mr. and Mrs. Vittoria, these are my brothers. You already met George. This is Brett, Bobby, and Billy. Randy was here, but he went to the locker room to shower and change."

"Tony is helping with my drafting project for school," Billy said.

"Yes, that's what Tony said," Matt said.

"Thank God you're helping him!" Brett said to Tony. "He can't draw to save his life!" he added with a laugh.

"I'm not that bad," Billy protested.

"Probably worse," Bobby said, making everyone laugh.

"Our brother, Michael, is around here somewhere," Brian said as he searched the crowd. "But you might have met him already with George."

Billy turned to Tony's little cousins and said, "You're Ferdinand and Cleopatra, right?"

Both laughed and Benny said, "I'm Benny and I'm five, and this is Sophia. She's three."

Billy gave both a fist bump.

Two walked up and took hold of Brian's arm. Brian turned around and said, "Mr. and Mrs. Vittoria, this is our brother, Michael."

He shook hands with them and said, "Everyone calls me Two, except for Brian, Tony, and Mom. I met you when George and I brought Tony home for his running stuff."

To Brian, Two said, "I'm going to get something to eat with Meghan, Trevor, and Carmen."

"How are you getting there?"

"Trevor's mom."

"Did you get mom's or dad's permission?"

Two blushed and said, "Oh, shoot. Sorry." To Vicky, he asked, "Would it be okay if I went to get something to eat with Trevor, Meghan, and Carmen? Trevor's mom is taking us."

Vicky smiled and said, "Yes, that's fine. How will you get home?"

Two turned to Brian and said, "Can you and Tony pick me up?"

Brian smiled and said, "Yup, no problem."

Two smiled and said, "I want you, and Tony, and George to meet her. I mean, them."

"Why can't we meet her? I mean, them?" Billy protested with a laugh.

"It's too many. Besides, you'd say something to embarrass me."

Feigning indignation, Billy said, "Who, me?"

"Especially you!" To Brian, George and Tony, Two said, "Come on, let's go."

Brian and George said goodbye to the Vittoria family and to Jeremy and Vicky.

"I'll text where we are and when we leave for home after I pick up Michael. I think we're meeting up with Troy, Chris, Sean, and a bunch of others."

"You don't mind the extra running around?" Jeremy asked.

"No, it's all good."

As they walked away, Brian said, "Michael, how much money do you have?"

"Fifteen. Trevor's mom paid for our tickets to get in the game."

"Fifteen won't be enough if you pay for Meghan's and your meal. You at least offer to pay for her. You know where my locker is and what the combination is?"

"Yes."

"After you introduce us, excuse yourself and go get a twenty and a five from my wallet. But make sure you lock my locker back up, okay?"

"Okay, thanks."

"Text me when you want to be picked up and where you'll be. And listen, I want you to be safe and smart. Stay together."

Two smiled and said, "Yes, dad."

Brian put him in a headlock and said, "Don't be a smartass."

From somewhere under Brian's arm, Two answered, "Better than being a dumbass."

Two introduced Brian, Tony, and George to Trevor's mom, and to Meghan, Carmen and Trevor. They shook hands. Two excused himself and said he'd be right back. Brian and George visited with them, while Tony hung in the background.

After a little while, Brian looked around for Michael, but didn't see him. He said, "Michael will be back in a second or two. We have to go shower and change. It was nice to meet you."

They waved and left. Brian put his arm around Tony's shoulder and said, "This is going to be a great weekend!"

Tony smiled as best he could. The fact was, he had never been this nervous. Almost to the point of throwing up.

CHAPTER FIFTY-SEVEN

The night air at the end of November was typical for Wisconsin. Daytime temps could reach low sixties, but usually stayed in the high forties to low fifties. Nighttime temps would dip into the low forties, and sometimes the thirties or twenties, the closer it got to December. It was not altogether uncommon for flurries to fill the sky and fall, resulting in a frosty white blanket covering the ground. Nose hair would freeze, as would cheeks, fingers, and toes.

On this evening, however, the air was chilly, but not freezing. Danny huddled with Chris and Sean, and with friends from band and chorus in the parking lot waiting for rides. He, and they, rocked back and forth or stomped their feet, working to keep feet warm. Most had their hands shoved into coat or sweatshirt pockets. Some had them up around their mouths and blew on them.

He didn't mind the wait for Troy, Bobby, and Randy. Still, he was hungry. He checked his watch for the second time. Any minute now, they'd walk out of the locker room door to the parking lot, laughing and shoving each other, he thought.

Maryanne Sturgis walked towards him. Danny turned away, hoping she'd get the hint to leave him alone, but she didn't.

"Danny," she breathed. "The anthem was really beautiful. I loved your guitar part."

"Thank you."

"I wish you would sing it as a solo. I think it would sound even better."

Danny sighed and said, "No, it wouldn't. I like the sound we have together."

Maryanne shook her head and said, "You have a magnificent voice. You sound better ..."

She didn't get to finish. Danny said, "You know what? I think you need to just stop. I need you to stop bagging on my friends. You need to stop cutting them down. It's annoying, and you need to stop."

She sputtered, started to speak several times, but nothing came out.

Danny continued. "Leave my friends and me alone."

He turned his back on her, walked back to his friends, and joined their huddle, leaving her standing by herself.

No one noticed her tears or her clenched fists. She hunched her shoulders, stormed off, got into her car, and drove away by herself.

CHAPTER FIFTY-EIGHT

Jimmy's Grotto was one of the favorite haunts for high school and college kids, especially on Friday or Saturday nights. Troy, Chris, Sean, and Danny commandeered enough tables to accommodate the large group. The Evans boys and Tony showed up, and more friends gathered with them. By the time everyone settled in for pizza, garlic bread, and pitchers of soda and water, the Grotto was rocking.

Nervous, Tony sat with Brian on his left and Brett on his right. Shannon Pritchert showed up with a couple of her friends, and Brett made room for her to sit on his other side. He wasn't subtle about it either. Of course not. Brett was seldom subtle about anything.

While they were eating, Brian would casually touch Tony's thigh or his hand, once giving Tony's hand a squeeze. No one noticed, since it was under the table. At least Brian didn't think so.

Tony was unsure of the message Brian sent him, if it was a message. Ever since the first day, Tony noticed Brian talked with his hands, and when he spoke, he often touched the hand or arm or shoulder of whomever he spoke to. The first sign of potential intimacy was in the art room after Tony gave him the thank you note, and then after school in his bedroom before the game.

Tony wasn't used to Brian or anyone else touching him. Not for the last three years, since the spring of eighth grade. He did nothing to encourage it, but also nothing to discourage it. He didn't want to offend Brian or make him uncomfortable. Brian kept the touches under the table and out of sight, and Tony appreciated that.

Only a few stray pieces of pizza remained, along with three pieces of garlic bread. Billy eyed them hungrily, and Brian wondered when Billy would break down and snag a piece or two.

"You eat like horses!" Shannon said with a laugh. "I was afraid to reach for anything because I didn't want my hand chewed."

"We're not that bad," Billy protested.

Shannon cocked her head and stared at him.

"Well, I'm not!" Brett said.

"Yeah, uh huh," Shannon responded with a playful eye roll. She patted Brett's shoulder and said, "Believe that if you want to."

"Tony, you have the whitest hair," Bobby said. "It's not blond, it's white!" he said with a laugh.

"Like a polar bear," Billy said.

Troy asked, "Were you always good at art?"

Troy stood a solid six-three. His arms, chest, back and shoulders were sculpted by weightlifting. He looked impressive in a basketball jersey. He was a better baseball player than he was a basketball player, but he was good at basketball. Chris, his best friend, was built like Troy, though he only stood five-ten. Troy had dark, short-cut hair like the Evans twins and Brett, and had light brown skin like other Latinos. Chris was blond, wearing his hair much like Brian and Bobby. The joke among the boys was that no one knew who would burn faster if Brian and Chris laid out in the sun to tan.

Sean had golden blond hair and bright blue eyes. He wore a perpetual smile, even with braces on his teeth. He was slender and normally quiet in group settings. Sean and Brian had been friends since elementary school. They could talk about anything with each other and usually did. A while back, Brian even dated his cousin, Caitlyn, or Cat for short. They had been friends for about as long as he and Sean were, and their friendship blossomed into an intimate, if not torrid, relationship lasting months. Now, Cat was currently dating Billy. Billy insisted he and Cat hadn't done nearly what she and Brian had done, and Brian believed him.

Tony shrugged and said, "I don't know. When I was six or seven, I started drawing cartoon characters. It kinda grew from there. Kinda like Danny and his music, I guess."

Randy shook his head and muttered, "Danny's a genius. A musical savant. There is no one like Danny."

Tony blushed and explained, "I didn't mean I'm a genius or anything. I just like to draw and paint. That's all."

Brett flashed a look at Randy. The message was simple but clear. *Back off.*

"Do you have some of your work on your phone?" Chris asked.

"He has some hanging up in his house. There is one in his room above his bed that's powerful. Sad and lonely," Brian said. "They almost look like photographs."

Tony dug his cell out of his hoodie's front pocket, opened up an app, and found what he was looking for. He handed it to Chris and said, "Scroll left to right."

Troy, Chris, Danny, and Billy crowded around it. Randy leaned away. He took sips of water from his glass.

"When you're done, let me see them," Bobby said.

"Me, too," Shannon said.

Shannon Pritchert had long, blondish-brown hair and blue eyes. She stood five-seven, and Brian considered her to be the toughest girl in school. For certain, Shannon was the best defensive player on the girls' soccer team. Brian thought she would start on most boys' teams.

"It's cool how everything is black and white, but you color in the eyes," Chris said.

Tony blushed again. "It's something I picked up from somewhere. I've been doing it for a couple of years now. I think it sets me apart from other," he was about to say artists, glanced at Randy, and said, "people."

"And you sign them, *Tony V.* That's cool!" Troy said.

"Well, that's his name," Randy muttered.

Troy, Danny, Sean, and Chris stared at him, but said nothing. Randy saw everyone else at the tables staring at him, too.

"I mean, how else is he supposed to sign them?" Randy said.

"It's the *way* he signs them. His graphic is distinct. I like it," Danny said.

Chris said, "If I give you a picture of my mom and dad, could you draw them? It would be a cool Christmas present. I'd pay you for it."

"I can do that," Tony smiled. "I would need more information from you, though. I want to make it personal. Things they like to do together, types of clothes they wear, things like that. The season you want them in. And I would need their eye color."

"Sure, okay," Chris smiled. He handed the phone to Shannon, and she and her friends huddled around it. "Both of my parents have blue eyes like me."

"I would like one of my dad," Danny said. "You know, hunched over his laptop. Or looking out the window in front of his laptop. Something like that."

Tony laughed and said, "Sure."

"How much do you charge for a drawing?" Bobby asked.

Tony squirmed. "Mrs. Arney said I need to charge for them, otherwise, I'd just do them for free. She suggested I charge $30 for an eight by ten, and $50 for an eleven by fifteen. I feel funny charging, though."

"You shouldn't," Danny said. "It's your time and talent."

"What happens if it turns out crappy?" Randy asked. "Do you still charge them?"

Shannon held up Tony's phone and said, "Have you even looked at these? There's nothing crappy in here."

"Besides, he still took the time to draw it. Plus, he uses his supplies. They would have to be paid for," Danny said.

Tony squirmed and blushed, uncomfortable at being at the center of the conversation. His eyes darted from Danny and Chris to Randy and back. He said, "I think if you or Chris don't like what I drew, I'd work on it until I get it right."

"I just sent you a couple of pictures," Chris said. "I'll bring you the money on Monday."

"Shouldn't you wait until he's done with it before you pay him?" Randy asked.

"Why don't you keep your nose out of their business?" Brett asked hotly.

"No, Randy's right," Tony said, glancing at Randy and at Brett, and then at the others. "You would pay after I'm done and after you like it."

By the time the group broke up and walked out of the parking lot, Tony agreed to do drawings for Troy, Chris, Danny, and Shannon. They sent him texts with pictures and eye colors, promising to send a text or an email later about hobbies, habits, and clothes.

Other than Randy, Tony thought the evening was a good one. He'd have to see, though.

CHAPTER FIFTY-NINE

Billy sprawled out on the couch and Brett commandeered the Lazy-Boy. George took one pillow and laid down on the floor. Brian and Tony sat side by side on the floor, leaning against the couch and each other. The TV was tuned to a Mission Impossible movie, but Brett set the volume low.

Brian wrestled with Papa, who liked his belly rubbed, and of course, Momma and Jasper had to have their pets, too. Jazmine watched it all from George's side.

To Tony, Brett said, "Brian is the dog whisperer."

"Horses, too," George quipped.

"Not as good as you are," Brian said.

Two tiptoed into the family room and jumped on Billy, an almost nightly routine. The two of them wrestled, and everyone knew what the outcome would be, including Two. Eventually, Billy shoved Two on top of Brian and Tony, and it was Brian's turn to torment Two. He pinned him on the floor and poked him in the ribs. Two laughed, swatted at Brian's hands, and lost the battle. Eventually, Brian let him up, and Two sat down between Brian's legs with his head against Brian's chest. Like most nights.

Brian reached back and asked Billy, "Can you hand me the blanket, please? It's chilly on the floor."

Billy handed Brian a blue crocheted blanket, and he covered Two and himself, along with Tony, who moved closer to Brian. Brian hugged Two with his right hand, and squeezed Tony's hand under the blanket with his left, resting it on Tony's upper thigh.

"How did all of you end up getting adopted?" Tony asked.

"Long story," Brett said with a laugh. "We should probably start at the beginning."

Billy told Tony about Randy's life in his previous home, getting abused and running away to find Billy. "He knew he was adopted and a twin, and he knew he came from Milwaukee. I didn't know I was adopted, or that I was a twin. It was only after a picture of Randy and dad appeared in the paper when I found out. My mom never wanted me to know, so we fought. My dad and mom fought, and they divorced and my mom moved away. We don't have contact with her and I don't want to. I think I caused their divorce." Billy shrugged, thought for a minute and said, "I have dad and mom and Randy and these misfits for brothers now. I'm happy with that."

"What happened to your dad?" Tony asked. "The first one, I mean?"

Billy sighed. "I came home from school one day and found him. He died from a heart attack. I think that's why when our dad had his heart ... thingy, I freaked."

"I'm sorry," Tony said.

Billy patted Tony's shoulder and said, "It's all good. Dad's fine, mostly."

In part to rescue Billy, Brett said, "I think George is up next, but Bobby, Brian and I are all tied together with George."

George lifted himself up and sat cross-legged, facing Tony. As he petted Jazmine, he said, "When I was twelve or thirteen, I took turns with my brother, William, and my grandfather, watching our sheep. We had a hogan and a small ranch on *Diné Bikéyah*. It's Navajo for Navajoland."

Tony smiled and said, "Say that again. It sounded cool."

George smiled and said, "*Diné Bikéyah*."

"Cool."

"It is common for rustlers to steal sheep, sometimes cattle, on the land. There is seldom anyone around, and the space is wide open. From my position on the side of the hill, I can see a great distance. I saw a van stop at the edge of our land, and I thought it was rustlers. But it wasn't. Two men pushed a boy forward, made him kneel, and they shot him from behind. A third man stood by the van."

"The kid was naked, and they handcuffed his hands behind his back," Brett said. "That happened to each kid they wanted to get rid of."

Tony didn't know whether to believe him, but it sounded too awful to not be true. He said nothing.

"I contacted my cousin, who worked for the Navajo Nation police, and he reported it to the FBI. After they came out and did an investigation, they flew me to Wisconsin because Agent Kelliher wanted me to identify the two men who shot another boy."

"They were found dead in Northern Wisconsin, along with another kid," Brett said. "The kid who was killed in Wisconsin was found the same way as the kid George found."

"Wait!" Tony said. "It was on the news. It was a sex ring or something."

"Exactly like that," Brett said, who looked at George to continue.

"While I was in Wisconsin, the men behind the sex ring took revenge on my family. My younger brother, William, was watching the sheep. They thought he was me because we looked alike. They shot him and my whole family, and burned our hogan to the ground."

"Jesus! Your whole family?" Tony said.

George nodded. His eyes were downcast, and Tony and the others knew it still shook George.

"His mother, his two brothers, his sister, his grandmother, and his grandfather," Billy said.

"George, I'm sorry," Tony said.

George nodded, but said nothing.

"Agent Kelliher placed George with dad, Randy and me in order to keep him safe. Kind of like protective custody. Eventually, dad adopted George," Billy said.

Tony tilted his head, wanting to question him further. Brett could almost see the question marks dancing in Tony's mind. *Why Jeremy and why Wisconsin? Didn't he have anyone else in Arizona he could have lived with?* Most of those questions were for George to answer, so instead, Brett said,

"George kept his last name, Tokay, out of respect for his grandfather and family."

"I kept my last name, Schroeder, because I loved my first dad," Billy said. "Nothing against Jeremy. He understands and is cool with it."

"He is," Brett said. "And that brings the story to me, I guess." Brett took a deep breath before he continued. "You said you know the story about the sex ring?"

Tony nodded.

"You know Mikey and Stephen? I introduced you to them in the cafeteria on the first day. Mikey plays basketball with us, and Stephen is on the JV team," Brian said. He stopped to let Brett finish his story.

"One night, Mikey and Stephen were abducted off the street and ended up in Chicago. There was thirteen of us there. They locked us in rooms and perverts used us for sex. Stephen was the one they wanted, but because Mikey was with him, he was taken, too. If the FBI and Detective Graff hadn't showed up that night, Mikey would have been dead the next morning."

"You were there?" Tony asked in a whisper. "You had to ..." Tony dared not finish the question.

In a partial answer, Brett said, "For a little over twenty-two months." He looked off at nothing, as if he relived the entire nightmare again.

Brian said, "Brett saved those thirteen kids. He saved Kelliher's life, too."

Brett shrugged dismissively.

"How?" Tony asked.

"It's not important, really," Brett said. "I'm not a hero. I did what I needed to do to get us all out safely. My souvenir is the scar from the bullet wound in my shoulder."

"I wondered about that. I noticed it in the locker room and at the game."

There was silence. No one knew what to say next. Brett shrugged.

"The same time I was in Chicago, Bobby was being molested by my uncle. My uncle set me up to be taken. For Bobby, it lasted six months. My uncle blackmailed him into doing whatever he told him to do. He told

Bobby if he refused or said anything to anyone, he would make one phone call, and I would be dead. It would have happened."

Brett paused before plunging on.

"After they rescued us, my mom and dad divorced, and Bobby, mom, and I moved to Waukesha. Mom and Jeremy dated and got married, and here we are."

"But at first, your dad, Thomas, wouldn't let you," Billy said. "What made him change his mind?"

Brett looked down at his hands in his lap, deciding if he wanted to tell the secret only Brian knew. He sighed and decided enough time had passed.

"This goes nowhere. I mean it. This stays right in this room. Got it?"

Heads nodded.

CHAPTER SIXTY

"I told Brian, but I didn't tell anyone else," Brett said, as he stared at his hands.

As an explanation, Brian said, "Brett asked me not to say anything."

Brett sighed. His chin quivered, he blinked back tears, and he swallowed once.

"Do you remember when Tim was shot by the pervert doctor? The one who worked for the sex ring and who did shit to Mikey during his physical?"

Two cocked his head, and Brian explained, "It was a couple of years ago, before you came to live with us."

Brian tightened his grip on Tony's thigh and tightened his arm around Two's waist. Tony responded by placing his hand on Brian's, entwining their fingers. Two held onto Brian's arm with both hands.

"Mom called Tom and let him know she and Bobby and me wanted to move to Waukesha. You know, for a clean start."

He looked up at the circle of boys, brushed a couple of tears out of his eyes, and said, "We needed to. All of us. After I got home, Bobby and some friends had a pickup basketball game. He got a black eye from his best friend. That asshole made fun of him. He said shit like, 'How many blowjobs did you give your uncle? How did it feel when he fucked you up your ass?' Shit like that. Bobby smacked him, but got a black eye in return. They never did anything else together after that. None of his friends called or came over. It was just Bobby, mom, and me. And that was Bobby's best friend. My best friend never stopped over after I got out of that shit hole. He never called me. Bobby asked me if that was how it was going to be from then on."

Brian felt Tony squirm. Tony gripped Brian's hand tightly.

"My *dad* cheated on my mom so many times. She didn't deserve it. By cheating on mom, he cheated on Bobby and me, too. We didn't deserve it, either."

His voice rose, and there was as much vitriol as the boys ever heard from him. "When my pervert uncle showed up to kill my mom, Bobby, and me, my *dad* was at the university. He claimed he was grading papers, but my *dad* was screwing some underclass bitch like he did hundreds of times, and an FBI guy walked in and caught him." He stopped and took a deep breath.

"Meanwhile, our pervert uncle came to our house to kill us. He shot MJ, and he took a shot at my mom. I got MJ's gun, and when he shot at my mom, he took his eyes off me. I said, 'Hey fuckhead!' or something, and I shot the gun out of his hand. Then I shot his other hand and his arm. I shot him in both knees, and then," he looked up at the boys and whispered, "I walked over, stood over him and shot his dick and balls off. He's in prison and he's in a wheelchair and pisses through a tube into a bag."

Brett clenched and unclenched his fists, and wiped tears out of his eyes with his knuckle.

"Anyway, Tim was in the hospital, and I knew mom had talked to him about moving, and I knew it didn't go anywhere. So, I went outside, and I called him. No one knew except O'Connor. He followed me out of the hospital. Protection. The conversation was supposed to be private, but O'Connor heard all of it."

He paused and wept. George scooted over next to him, but Brett waved him off.

Directly to Tony and Two, Brett said, "When we were rescued from that shit hole, CNN and Good Morning America and other shows wanted to interview us. All of us, Mikey and Stephen included, agreed we wouldn't say anything to them. There were offers for book deals and a movie and a TV movie of the week, but we turned that shit down, too. We didn't want to relive that shit. No one wanted to relive that shit."

The tears slowed to a trickle, but never completely stopped. He shrugged and sighed and said, "I told my *dad* if he didn't let us move here, I was going to go on CNN and tell them about that night with good ol' Uncle Tony and why my *dad* wasn't at our house like he should have been. I told him I figured the university had a rule against professors screwing their students. But I told him if he let us move to Waukesha, I wouldn't say anything."

Brett stared out through the sliding glass door to the little garden George, Billy, and Vicky had planted. Brett exhaled, relieved he didn't have to carry that burden any longer.

"Tom said he would give mom permission to move, but in return, he wanted nothing to do with me. He said I was dead to him." Brett shrugged, and said, "I didn't think it would matter much, because I thought he wouldn't follow through with it. But he did."

Brett stared at his hands and said, "I didn't think it would bother me, but he was ... he was my dad."

"That's why you never went with Bobby to visit him," Billy said in a whisper.

Brett nodded with his face awash in tears.

CHAPTER SIXTY-ONE

"That was a hard secret to keep," Two said as he wiped tears from his eyes. "For both of you."

"I'm good at keeping secrets," Brian said.

"I couldn't tell mom, because we might never have moved. But I had to tell someone." Brett smiled weakly and said, "That's how Bobby, mom, and me came to this family. Mom and dad dated, and they got married."

"Which means I'm next," Brian said.

To Tony, he said, "You already know about the sex ring. And Brett said he and Bobby and George and I were all tied together. We are."

Brian took a deep breath, smiled at Brett and George. He felt Billy's hand on his shoulder. Brian let go of Tony's hand, pulled it out of from the blanket and rested it on his lap.

He said, "I don't know if I told you I was a twin. *Am* a twin."

Tony shook his head.

"His name is Brad. We did everything together. We had the same friends, but I would rather be with Brad than with anyone. Same with him." He shrugged and said, "He was way better than me at everything. Basketball. Soccer. Name it. We played on the same travel soccer team together. Sean was on it. Mario, Cem. You met them."

Brian sighed and then took a deep breath. He said, "One night, we had a game. You probably heard about a shooting at a soccer field. Men, women, kids, soccer players all died."

Tony nodded.

"Then I don't have to go into much detail. It was in all the papers and on local news. Probably national news. You could probably Google it. Some bitch wanted to create a diversion, so she set up a machine gun with a remote switch so she could set it off with a cell phone. We saw two FBI guys and Graff searching the trees and bushes on the edge of the field. The game stopped as we watched them. Then, the gun went off and kept firing. It was so loud. The bullets ripped through everything. People. Cars. Buildings."

He stopped and shook his head. His eyes were far away, as if the entire night played on a tape in his head. It did, often. When awake. When asleep. The tape never turned off.

Brian continued. "It hit One FBI guy with the first bullets. Sean got hit in the arm. Bobby ran onto the field and tackled Mario and Cem or they would have died. Shit, Bobby could have gotten killed." He shrugged and said, "My brother, Brad, got hit in the stomach, and he died in Big Gav's arms."

"I'm sorry, Brian," Tony said. "I'm sorry for you, too, Brett."

"I miss Brad every single day," Brian whispered.

Tony asked, "Did they ever catch the women who set it up?"

Billy answered, "Brett caught her."

Incredulous, Tony said, "How?"

"They paid her to kill Tim and me because we escaped from the ring. Revenge, I guess. Some cops who got away paid her to kill us," he explained. "She showed up at the hospital."

Brett stared at George and then at Brian, hesitating to go further. First, George nodded, and then Brian did the same.

Brett nodded and said to Tony, "What I'm going to tell you sounds unbelievable, but it's the truth. Please don't repeat it to anyone else outside of this room, okay?"

Tony nodded and said, "I'm a good secret keeper." He shrugged and said, "For a long time."

He said it with conviction. Enough conviction that Brett and George blinked at him. A knowing smile broke across Brett's face, and he nodded.

Brett said, "What I'm going to tell you is the truth. Believe it or not. Up to you." He took a deep breath and said, "George's grandfather, the one who died, appeared to me. He told me to get ready because she was coming."

Brett waited to see what Tony's reaction was, but Tony's face was blank. It looked to Brett as if Tony had accepted it. He went on.

"I peeked out in the hallway and saw the cop who was in charge was gone, and the cop outside our door was asleep in his chair. I went back inside Tim's room and made sure Tim's bathroom door was locked, or maybe I blocked it off. I can't remember exactly. I made Tim hide in the corner and I put pillows and blankets in Tim's bed to make it look like he was still in it. To make it harder to see, I turned the lights down. You know, like Tim was sleeping. There was a small step-stool by the door and a small fire extinguisher hung on the wall. One of those handheld ones people have in the kitchen."

Brett shook his head and said, "My left arm was still in a sling from being shot in Chicago, but I'm right-handed. I stood on the stool and waited. George's grandfather told me to get ready, because she was almost there. God, I was scared, but Tim was my best friend from the Chicago shit hole, and I didn't want either of us to die by some bitch asshole."

He shook his head. "She tiptoed into the room, pulled out a gun with a suppressor on it, and put a couple of bullets into Tim's bed. I swung the extinguisher down and smashed her wrist, surprising her. She dropped the gun. Then I smashed her in the face, and I kept swinging. I shattered her jaw, and it shifted to one side. It was gross, but I kept swinging at her head. She fell against the door and slid down.

"My arm was tired, so I put the rubber hose in her mouth and emptied the extinguisher down her throat. Then I threw it at her head and grabbed her gun. I think I emptied it into her. Maybe not emptied it, but pretty damn close."

"You killed her?" Tony whispered.

"Yeah. It was that, or you'd be talking to a ghost right now."

Brian took his arm out from under the blanket, put his arm around Tony's shoulder, and hugged him. "You'd be surprised at how many people the four of us killed." He said this last in a quiet voice, and Tony turned to face him more squarely.

CHAPTER SIXTY-TWO

"Every person we killed or shot at was in self-defense," Brett said. "But it was never easy, and it makes us feel dirty."

"Ashamed," Brian said. "It's not something we *wanted* to do. It was something we *had* to do. That or die. None of us wanted to. None of us enjoyed killing people. I think all of us feel guilty and ashamed."

"You killed people, too?" Tony whispered.

"He saved our butts more than once," Brett said.

"You never said how you got adopted," Tony said to Brian with a gentle elbow to Brian's ribs.

"Yeah, well, that," Brian said with a shrug, relieved he didn't have to talk about killing people.

"After Brad died, my parents changed. I know death is something you never get over. You live with it as best you can. The hole is still there." He touched his heart with the palm of his hand. "But my mom and dad were like zombies. It's like they stopped living."

Tony didn't know if he wanted to hear any more. Part of him did. Part of him didn't.

"I spent a lot of time at Big Gav's house," he shrugged, "Sean's house, but mostly, I stayed here. These were my friends, especially Randy and Billy, but the more time I spent with George and Brett and Bobby, the more I liked it here. Jeremy and I would talk about stuff. Like Brad and I did with our parents. This felt like home. It felt like family."

He shook his head, wondering just how it all turned to shit. Of course, he knew. The only one who didn't know was Tony.

"My parents stopped coming to watch me in anything. Or if they came, they left early. Last year, after my first game on varsity, my parents didn't bother to show up." He shrugged and said, "Sometimes you get used to it and it doesn't hurt as much." He was lying to himself. Brian knew it, and so did everyone else.

"After the game, Jeremy," he turned to Tony and explained, "He wasn't dad yet."

Tony nodded.

"Jeremy and I were going to ask my parents if I could spend the night. It was a school night. Jeremy and I were about to walk into the house, but George stopped us."

"Why?" Tony asked.

"I had a feeling. It didn't feel right. And my grandfather warned me."

"George went in and found my mom and dad in Brad's room, dead. Mom shot my dad and then shot herself. Jeremy asked me what I wanted to do. I could have lived with a couple of uncles and aunts, but none of them lived here. Here is where my friends are. Jeremy offered to let me live here, so I did."

This last, Brian said with a shrug. While Brett, George and Billy understood it, Tony didn't. It left him puzzled.

CHAPTER SIXTY-THREE

Two fidgeted. He felt all eyes on him. Two knew the expectation was for him to be as honest as the others were, and that was the hard part.

He couldn't bring himself to look at anyone. He kept his eyes on his hands, and his hands on his lap.

In a voice barely above a whisper, he said, "My mom died from a drug overdose. She was always strung out, so I wasn't surprised. Crack, mostly. Heroin. She had tracks up and down her arms. She wanted me to try it, but I said no. I didn't want to be a fuckin' zombie."

He took a deep breath and sighed. "I never knew my dad. George and I had the same dad, but I never met him, and I didn't know George until this past summer. Neither one of us knew we were step-brothers. I mean, yeah, we look and act alike, I guess, but that didn't mean anything. I could say the same thing about a lot of guys. I had no place to go, and I didn't think anyone would give a shit about me."

The boys struggled to make eye contact. Billy and Brian were fortunate to be behind him. Tony sat next to Brian, and Two sat between Brian's legs, making eye contact difficult. Brett and George weren't as lucky.

"I knew the guy my mom got her drugs from. Lou, who owned the diner. I went to him and told him what had happened. He offered me a place to stay and a job where I could make money."

Tears fell, and Two remained quiet. One hand attempted to wipe away tears, but no matter how hard he tried, more appeared.

"It's okay, Two," Brett whispered.

"The way he looked at me, I knew what Lou wanted. There was only one bedroom and one bed. The first couple of nights, It's all he wanted. I had to let him or he would have thrown me out." His voice broke, and more tears dribbled down his face, but he had to make them understand. He sobbed. "I had nowhere else to go. Nowhere."

"It's okay, Two," Billy said. "We understand."

Tony turned around and blinked at Billy. Both of them had tears in their eyes. All of them, except for Brett.

"I smoked grass. I did pills, but only sometimes. Lou told me I could make money if I sold to people who came into the bar. He said I could make even more money if I did stuff with them."

Two balled up his left hand, and his right covered his face. "I feel so dirty. I'm sorry."

Brian hugged him and leaned his forehead on Two's shoulder. "It's okay, Michael. We've all done things that made us feel dirty and ashamed. You aren't alone."

Two turned around and faced Brian, sobbing. Almost shouting, he said, "I never wanted you to know. I told Brett, because he guessed I had been doing stuff with Lou the night we stayed there after those men chased us. He saw the stuff on the nightstand and the one bed. He saw the one dresser with his and my clothes in it. I didn't want you to know because I didn't want you ashamed of me. None of you, but especially you!"

Brian reached out to hold Michael, but Two pushed him away. Brian was stronger, and eventually, Two gave up and melted in Brian's arms. He sobbed into Brian's chest, "I'm sorry, Brian. I'm sorry. I don't want you to hate me."

Brian held and rocked him. "Shhhh. It's okay, Michael. I don't hate you. I could never hate you."

"I'm sorry, Brian."

"Hey, aren't you listening to me? Huh? You did what you did to survive. Look at all Brett and Bobby did."

"But they were forced to. They had no choice. Yeah, they did a lot of shit, but they were made to. I wasn't. I just did that shit and I feel so dirty. I don't want you to hate me or be ashamed of me," he sobbed.

"Michael, look at me."

Two shook his head.

"Please, Michael, look at me."

"I can't."

Gently, Brian placed his hands on Michael's cheeks and leaned his forehead on Michael's forehead. "Michael, I need you to listen to me. Please. Okay?"

Two nodded, but shut his eyes so he didn't make eye contact.

"Michael, do you do any of that stuff now?"

"No, but,"

"Shhhh, just answer my question. Do you do any of that stuff now?"

"No."

"No drugs, no pills, no weed?"

Two shook his head and said, "No."

"I am going to tell you two things, and I need you to listen to me without interrupting, okay?"

Two nodded.

"First, I love you. You are the best little brother anyone could ever have. Nothing will change that. Nothing. Second, just like Brett and Bobby, all that stuff is in the past. You don't do any of that stuff anymore. But I want you to know something, and this is important. So listen to me. Every word, okay?"

Two nodded.

"What Lou did to you was wrong. He was the adult, not you. That's important for you to understand. You did what you did to survive, and Lou took advantage of that. That's why he's in jail, and he'll stay there for a long time. None of it is your fault. Okay?"

At first, Two merely looked up at Brian. His face registered unbelief.

"Okay?" Brian repeated.

Two hesitated, but eventually nodded.

"Okay. Now here's the most important part, so listen closely."

Two nodded and wiped tears out of his eyes.

"There will come a time when you decide you love someone. *Really* love someone. Only you can decide if that someone will be a girl or a guy. It doesn't matter, because sometimes, most of the time, love doesn't care. You love who you love. No one, and I mean no one, can tell you who to love. Not me. Not George. Not mom. Not dad. George told me a long time ago that if two hearts are meant to be together, they will find each other. I'm going to add that those two hearts will find a way to be with each other. Do you understand what I'm saying?"

"Yes, but,"

Brian jumped in and said, "No buts, Michael. You are going to love who you love, and no one can or should make that decision for you. Only you can do that. Let your heart be your guide."

Two nodded.

"Can you do that?"

"Yes," Two whispered.

"You will know, when you know. Your heart will know." Brian tapped Two's chest. "Listen to it."

Two nodded again. His tears ran out. He took a deep breath and tried on a smile.

"Are we good?"

"Yes."

Brian hugged him fiercely, and Two hugged him back. After, Brian rested his forehead on Two's and said, "Never, ever think I don't love you or that I'm ashamed of you, okay?"

"Okay."

"Promise?"

"Promise."

CHAPTER SIXTY-FOUR

Jeremy and Vicky had never left the kitchen after working out a diet and training program that had begun in the hospital. It was Vicky who had urged him to remain.

She bit the inside of her cheek and said, "We're not really eavesdropping. We're working out a plan for you. It's easier here in the kitchen than anywhere else in the house."

Jeremy was reluctant to stay, but he said, "I can't help but think that each of those boys suffered so much. More than they let on. The doctors want me to work on my stress, but damn, Vicky, those boys lived through stress, too. Most of them had it worse than I ever will."

"But you are dad to them, and you are a natural protector. You naturally suffer from stress to keep them safe."

"But those letters seem so insignificant compared to what those boys have been through. I feel foolish."

One story after another. Billy. George. Brett. Brian. Two. Almost numbing.

They sat in stunned silence. Just when Vicky thought she had run out of tears, fresh ones rolled down her cheeks. A box of tissue sat between them, and a pile of used tissues sat next to the box.

They held hands, fingers alternating between tight and loose, firm and limp in rhythm with their thoughts.

"How could we have missed it?" Vicky asked. She shook her head.

"Two seemed so happy, so easygoing. It never dawned on me he felt that way," Jeremy said.

"Mostly, I assumed he grew up like George. I know what Graff and O'Connor shared with us about Michael when they brought him to us this summer, but never in a million years did it occur to me he had that rough a life."

Jeremy hung his head and said, "The bond between Two and Brian." He stopped and shook his head. "To think I could have damaged it." He shook his head again.

"But you didn't," Vicky said. "For all Brian has been through, especially this week," she stopped and shook her head. "The way he handled Michael."

"Amazing. And the secrets those boys held onto. The weight of them would crush anyone else."

"We have strong kids. We're lucky."

Jeremy said, "I wish I could have seen the physical interaction between them. The only word that comes to mind is moving."

"And astonishing."

"Our boys are and have been resilient. We have to guard against them reaching a breaking point, though."

Vicky's face clouded over. Yes, everyone had a breaking point. The problem is, no one knew what the breaking point is until it is reached. When that happens, it's often too late.

CHAPTER SIXTY-FIVE

Pushing 11:30 PM, all was quiet. No words. No one moved. The only sounds were normal house sounds. A pipe thumping quietly, or the refrigerator turning on and off, or whatever it was refrigerators do. The furnace turned on, ran, and then turned off.

Beyond the sliding glass door, the world outside was dark and quiet.

Even Momma and the two pups had their heads down, resting on their paws. In Papa's case, his head rested on Tony's shin. But his eyes were wide open.

As tired and as spent as the boys were, both physically and emotionally, they were awake. Still, they were at peace.

Brett said, "Tony, how did you end up living with your aunt and uncle?"

The million dollar question. Tony knew it was coming. He was the only one whose life story wasn't shared. It was only fitting, since he was the one who opened up the gas can. Brett merely struck the match and handed it to Tony to do with it what he wanted.

As nervous as he was, Tony felt a flickering flame of hope. The brothers admitted to killing people. He didn't know the circumstances other than they defended themselves. Still, he couldn't think of anyone he knew who had killed someone. That was a big deal. Might be bigger than his story, though he wasn't sure. Brett said their records were sealed by the FBI and the courts, and even though they said they were defending themselves, he didn't know the circumstances or situations they had been placed in.

And then there was what Brett and Bobby went through and how the boys rallied around them. And what Michael went through, and how he was accepted by his brothers, especially by Brian. If anyone was going to understand his story, they would.

What was more important to Tony was what Brian said to Michael. Tony listened to every word, listened to every nuance and inflection. He watched the reactions of George and Brett. They were more than sympathetic. They were empathetic, like Brian.

The biggest difference, however, was that Tony wasn't a member of the family. He was new to the school and with only three days, still an unknown.

Tony stared at his hands, gathering up his courage as much as his thoughts on how he wanted to express himself, and how much to tell them. It was now or never, he decided. He started at the beginning.

He felt Brian's hand on his thigh, giving him a squeeze, perhaps in encouragement.

Tony stared at his hands, fidgeting in his lap. He couldn't help it. His shoulders sagged. In a shaking voice, almost in a whisper, he said, "There was this guy. Marshall. He was good at everything. Like you guys. Sports. School. Popular. Everyone wanted to be his friend. Me, too, even though I didn't have anything in common with him. We were in eighth grade, and it was the Friday before Easter vacation." He shrugged.

He looked up, searching for understanding, first at George, then at Brett, and lastly at Brian and Two. There were tears in his eyes, and his chin quivered.

"We never hung out. Like I said, we didn't have much in common. Marshall asked if he could come over to see some of my art. I was surprised, but excited at the same time. I tried to act nonchalant, but I probably acted like a dork. There was a problem, though. I wasn't supposed to have anyone over when my parents weren't home. My dad worked construction and my mom was a receptionist at a dental office. But I knew they wouldn't be home right away, and I wanted to be friends with him, so I took a chance and both of us walked to my house."

Tony's right hand covered his eyes while he wept silently. Brian tilted his head at Tony, then looked at George, who remained impassive, and then at Brett, who nodded at him. Brian wasn't sure of Brett's meaning.

"Tony, you don't have to tell us anything," Brian said. "It's okay."

Tony shook his head, waved a hand, and said, "Just give me a minute."

Brian slipped his arm around Tony's shoulders and the boys waited.

"The thing is, I don't want anyone else to know. No one, especially Randy. I don't think he likes me, and I don't know what he would do or what he might say to anyone."

Brett said, "Tony, if you haven't figured it out already, we're pretty good at keeping secrets. Nothing anyone said tonight will leave this room."

Almost as if Tony didn't hear Brett, he said, "People don't know me yet. You guys don't know me yet. I want people to know me because of my art. As a guy who runs cross country and track." He paused, and said, "I want people to know me as a regular guy who sits in class and plays the saxophone in the band. Not for anything else."

"We get it," Billy said.

It was hard for Tony to judge Billy's reaction because Billy was behind him. But his words sounded sincere.

Tony nodded. He said, "I showed him some art my mom had hanging up in the house, and then we went to my bedroom. I had stuff on the walls and some pieces on my desk that weren't finished yet. Eventually, we sat on my bed and we were just talking."

He looked up, and with his voice shaking, he said, "I promise. That's all we were doing. I wasn't expecting anything else."

"Hey, it's okay," Brett said. "I think we get the picture."

Tony shook his head and said, "No, you don't. There is more. Way more."

"You don't have to go any further, Tony," Billy said. "It's okay."

"I need you to understand. But I don't want anyone else to know. It has to stay here. No one else. Especially Randy."

"You're safe, Tony," Brian said. "Honest."

Tony looked over at him. Tears were in his eyes, and he blinked to clear them.

"Is this why you were afraid to spend the night?" Brian asked.

"Partly."

Brian nodded, and said, "It's okay. Whatever you have to say, we will understand."

Tony hoped they would, but would they really?

CHAPTER SIXTY-SIX

"We were talking, and then he leaned over and kissed me. I wasn't expecting it, and I didn't know what to do." Flustered, turning red, he said, "I let him."

"You kissed him back." Brett said it as a statement, not as a question.

Tony nodded.

He glanced at Brett and George to see if they were going to make fun of him. But George's eyes were sad. Brett's too. He glanced at Brian, but because he felt Brian give him a hug, he knew he was okay with him. At least so far.

"He leaned into me, and I ended up on my back. I had never kissed anyone before, I mean, besides my mom and dad and grandparents. And no one ever kissed me like that. He French kissed me, and I kissed him back the same way. I didn't know what I was doing. We did that for a while. I think both of us liked it. And then, he put his hand, you know, down there. Not in my shorts, but on it. He was kind of rubbing it. No one ever did that to me. I didn't know what to do."

"Did you do anything to him?" Billy asked.

Tony shook his head and said, "No. I was too nervous. Like I couldn't think. I knew he shouldn't have done it, and I knew I shouldn't have let him, but ..."

"But you liked it, and you kind of liked him," Brett said.

"Yes." Tony's answer was barely audible, like he couldn't actually bring himself to say it out loud.

"He kissed you, and then he felt you, kind of," Billy said, this last as he wagged his head from side to side. "Tony, it isn't a big deal. It's nothing to be ashamed of. It happens."

Tony said, "My shirt was up, and his hand was on, you know ... My dad must have gotten off early from work, and that's when he walked into my room."

"Oh, shit!" Billy said.

"My dad grabbed Marshall by the hair and threw him on the floor. Marshall ran out. My dad slapped me and punched me. He yelled, 'You faggot! You dirty goddamn faggot! How many times have you done this?' I tried to explain, but he kept slapping me. I ended up with a bloody nose and a bloody lip, but he kept hitting me."

"Jesus!" Two said.

"No offense, but your dad's an asshole," Brett said.

"He said, 'You might be a faggot, but you're not going to act like one and you're not going to look like one.' My dad tore down any artwork I had up on my walls. He said, 'Art is for sissies and faggots!' He destroyed everything and took my medals and ribbons and the whole pile of stuff to the backyard and burned it in the barrel behind the garage. My dad even took the stuff I was working on and burned that, too. He left my room and went through the house, tearing down anything mom had hanging on the walls. All of it. Every piece."

"Your dad's a piece of shit," Billy said.

"While he was outside, I hid my two sketch books. He came in and told me to hand them over, but I lied and said they were at school. He slapped me around some more, calling me a dirty goddamn faggot. Then he grabbed me by the hair and pulled me out of my room and down the stairs, and threw me in the car."

"Why?" Brian asked.

"My hair was as long as it is now. He said, 'You're not going to look like a faggot. Clean yourself up. You're going to get a haircut.' I grabbed some napkins from the glove box and wiped the blood off my face, but some of was already dry. My lip was swollen, and I had a shiner."

"What did they do to your hair?" Two asked.

"A crew cut. Almost bald."

"Didn't the barber or anyone ask about your lip or your bloody nose?" Brian asked.

Tony shook his head.

"Your dad's worse than an asshole," Brett said.

Tony shook his head and said, "It was worse after we got back from Easter vacation. None of my friends would talk to me. I found notes and signs on my locker calling me Gay Boy or Faggot. Guys would ask me how many dicks I sucked, or they'd ask what it felt like when someone sticks it up my ass."

"That's what I was afraid was going to happen to Bobby and me if we hadn't moved here. That same shit."

Tony wiped tears from his eyes, but they continued to flow freely. "Marshall lied and told everyone I kissed him and stuck my hand down his pants and felt him up. I'd go to the restroom and guys would shove me around. One time, two guys held me over a toilet while another guy pissed on my head. I hated going to PE. The locker room was the worst. One time, three guys pinned me down on the floor while Marshall and a couple of guys snapped towels at my balls."

Tony covered his face with both hands and sobbed.

"Where in the hell was the teacher?" Brian asked.

"I don't know. It didn't last long, but it was long enough."

"Did you tell anyone? A teacher or a counselor or someone?" Two asked.

Tony shook his head. "I was too embarrassed. Besides, if I told my parents, my dad would say it was my fault and slap me around. If I told a teacher or a counselor, my parents would find out and the same thing would happen. My dad would blame me. There wasn't anyone I could talk to. No one. I thought eventually they'd quit. I *hoped* they would eventually quit. But they didn't."

"How did you end up living with your aunt and uncle?" Brian asked.

"That June, we were at my grandparents' for my grandfather's birthday. My cousins, Benny and Sophia, were there, and I was showing them some art things. Simple stuff. They were coloring, and I was helping them. My aunt and uncle took some pictures and thanked me. But my dad saw what we were doing, and he came over, grabbed the drawing I was working on and ripped it up. He called me a faggot in front of everyone and slapped me twice. He caught my nose and lip just right, and I bled all over my shirt. I pushed him away, and he punched me.

"I must have blacked out, because when I came too, my aunt and grandmother were cleaning me up. Benny and Sophia were crying, and my dad was arguing with my uncle. My uncle came over to me, took a couple of pictures of my face, and told me I was going home with them. My dad said, 'Fine, the little faggot can live with you. I sure as hell don't want a faggot in my house.'"

"You never went back home?"

Tony shook his head and said, "My uncle is a lawyer. He drew up paperwork giving him and my aunt legal guardianship and custody rights. He threatened my dad and my mom that if they wouldn't sign the documents, he'd go to court and have both of them locked up. He used the pictures from that day, including my black eye and some bruises on my ribs and upper arm my dad gave me. Two cops escorted my uncle and me to my house to pick up my clothes and stuff, and I've never been back since. I changed schools in the fall, and everything's been okay."

"What about that asshole, Marshall?" Two asked. "What happened to him?"

Tony made a face and said, "Just before I moved in with my aunt and uncle, two guys came to my house. They used to be friends. I thought they had come to do shit to me, and I almost shut the door on them. They said they came to apologize. Marshall tried to do the same thing to them as he did to me. They apologized because they knew Marshall lied and did it all, not me."

Brian shook his head and said, "Way too late for an apology."

Tony's panic was almost gone. But he leaned forward and gestured wildly. His eyes were saucers, even through the tears. "But please, don't tell anyone. I can't go through it again. Please don't say anything to anyone. Please don't. Especially Randy."

Brett scooted over in front of him, took hold of Tony's hand with both of his and said, "Tony, no one is going to say anything to anybody. You're safe."

Billy added, "We will not let anything happen to you."

Tony shook his head and said, "I never told this to anyone else. This is the first time I told anyone. This is the first time since all that stuff happened that I went to someone's house."

"Didn't you have friends at your new school?" Billy asked.

"Yeah, but I never spent the night at anyone's house. I always made up excuses, and eventually, they stopped asking me."

"I'm going to ask you a question. You don't have to answer it if you don't want to," Brett said, still holding Tony's hand.

Tony hung his head, knowing what Brett was going to ask.

"Are you gay?"

Tony looked up. Fresh tears fell. He said, "For the longest time, I denied it. But, yeah, I think so."

"You aren't sure?" Billy asked.

He sighed and said, "Yeah, I'm pretty sure. I'm gay."

Tony looked around the room as he tried to gauge the reaction of Brett, George, Brian and Two. He turned around to look at Billy, who shrugged, then smiled. He put a hand on Tony's shoulder and gave it a squeeze.

Tony said, "If you don't want me to spend the night, I understand. You can drive me home and I'll tell my aunt and uncle I wasn't feeling well. Or I can sleep on the couch."

Brian reached out and hugged him. He whispered, "I want you to stay."

"Do your aunt and uncle know?" George asked. It was the first thing George had said, which wasn't surprising. He had always been a listener and someone who preferred to observe.

"I came out to my aunt last year. She said she thought I might be. Then she and I told my uncle. He said he thought it would be a good idea for us to learn more about what being gay is, so we went online and found a book on Amazon."

"Is it a good book? I mean, did you find it helpful?" Brian asked.

Tony nodded and said, "Yeah. We would read a chapter and then talk about it. We finished the book in about a month."

Brett let go of Tony's hand, took out his cell, and said, "What's the name of the book?"

"*On The Outside*. It's pretty good."

"I'm ordering a copy," Brett said.

"Get one for me," Billy said. "I'll pay you back."

"I'm getting one for all of us," Brett said, eyes down, fingers tapping. "I think it can help our family."

"Mom and dad, too?" Brian asked.

"All of us."

"What do you mean?" Tony asked suspiciously.

Brian turned and smiled at him. "I'm bisexual. Probably mostly gay. I've been in three relationships. Long-term relationships. One girl and two guys." Purposely, he never mentioned with whom he had been in a relationship.

"Oh," Tony said. From his expression, he was surprised.

"I don't know if that makes you uncomfortable, so if you don't want to sleep with me, I'm cool with that. But if you do, I promise not to attack you too much or anything." This last, he said with a laugh.

"Do your parents know you're gay?"

"Yes. Everyone in our family knows. I don't wear a sign or anything. I'm not announcing it in the middle of the cafeteria or anything, but friends know. Or at least, suspect."

"Who knows you're gay?" Tony asked. He sounded amazed anyone would know and not give Brian any crap like he had gone through. Brian smiled.

"Well, my family. Big Gav was the first I told. Sean was probably the second. Garrett- you know, we call him G Man. Mikey, Stephen, Danny and his dad. Shannon Pritchert, Cat. Coach Harrison. Three cops who are friends of ours." He turned to his brothers and asked, "Am I missing anyone?"

"I think Chris and Troy suspect," Billy said. "Maybe Mario, Cem, and TJ."

Brian nodded and said, "TJ knows. But it's not like I care or anything. I'm going to be me. If people find out, fine. If they don't, fine. I'm okay either way."

"So, are you good?" Brett asked Tony, smiling at him.

Tony nodded and wiped his eyes with his t-shirt sleeve. "Sorry about all the tears. You guys must think I'm a big baby."

"No, Tony. I think we all cried tonight," Brian said. "We understand better than anyone how pain feels. And just like the rest of us, you're tougher than you think you are."

"It's late and if we're still going running tomorrow morning, we better get to bed," Brett said.

"Can I have a glass of water?" Tony asked.

The boys trooped into the kitchen and found Jeremy and Vicky sitting at the table. Besides their glasses of water and the sheets of paper with Jeremy's plan, there was a pile of used tissue on the table between them.

Jeremy and Vicky looked to be as surprised as the boys were.

CHAPTER SIXTY-SEVEN

"I thought you had gone to bed?" Brett asked as he glanced at his brothers and Tony.

"We were working on me getting healthier," Jeremy said with a smile as he held up his plan.

"Did you ..." Brian asked.

Jeremy took a deep breath and finished his sentence for him. "Hear everything? Yes, most of it anyway."

There was an awkward pause and everyone knew what everyone else was thinking. No one wanted to bridge that chasm. Finally, Jeremy spoke up.

"Guys, I know it's late, but could all of you sit down for a minute? Please?"

The boys took seats around the table. Tony sat between Brett and Brian. Brian placed his hand on Tony's thigh and kept it there. Two leaned his head on Brian's shoulder. All of them were ready to listen.

"Do you remember what I told each of you along the way, that if we can't be honest with each other, we can't have a relationship? Remember me discussing that with you?"

Heads nodded. Nervous, Tony sat there, dumbstruck and uncomfortable. He reached under the table and held onto Brian's hand. His grip was firm but sweaty.

"What your mom and I overheard, I understand why you felt the need to keep your secrets. Two, mom and I had suspected what you had gone through. Like Brian said, you did what you had to do to survive. We're proud of you, not ashamed of you. You made some hard choices, and no one has the right to judge you. Brett, you are one of the strongest people I know. What you did for Bobby, your mom and yourself, was courageous and selfless. Brian, I continue to be amazed by your strength and your character. What you said to Two was dead on. I couldn't have said it any better. In fact, you probably said it better than I would have."

Jeremy sighed, smiled at Tony, and said, "Tony, I know I just met you this evening. But I want to say something and I ask that you listen closely."

Tony blinked and shifted in his seat. He didn't let go of Brian's hand.

"We're sorry about what you had to go through." Jeremy shook his head and said, "I'm sorry your dad treated you the way he did, and I'm sorry your mom didn't defend you. I'm thankful your aunt and uncle rescued you. You are you, whoever you choose to be. I think you heard the support you have from our sons, and I want to assure you Vicky and I support you, too, just like we support Brian and Bobby."

Tony nodded, struggling to keep his composure.

Brett cleared his throat and said to Tony, "Our brother, Bobby, is gay, too."

Jeremy blushed and pulled on his ear. He misspoke by mentioning Bobby. He sighed, knowing he had screwed up.

He said, "Just like Brian and Bobby, you may share your story or not. It is up to you. But it's important for you to know it will be your choice, just as it is Brian's and Bobby's choice. Please know we support you."

Tony nodded again. His eyes were downcast.

Vicky smiled and said, "You picked an excellent group of friends, Tony. And I think, they picked a good friend in you. I want you to know you are always welcome here. Anytime. Our house is open to you."

"I know it's late, and I know you guys are getting up early to run," Jeremy said as he stretched and yawned. "I'm tired, and I'm going to bed."

The boys stood with him, said their goodnights with hugs and kisses on Jeremy's and Vicky's cheek. Tony stood, but didn't move. It was Vicky who came to him, hugged him and kissed his cheek. Jeremy hugged him, and they left.

The boys got their water or juice or whatever it was they wanted and trooped up the stairs to bed.

CHAPTER SIXTY-EIGHT

Brian walked into his bedroom after giving Momma some pets. As usual, her perch was just outside his door, facing the stairs. He hesitated just inside his room, deciding whether to shut the door completely or keep it open a couple of inches. He shut it completely.

Tony stood in front of the dresser Brian and Michael shared. He wore red, loosely fit cotton pajama pants with Coke written in white script down his right leg, and a white t-shirt. Brian wore his normal loose fitting gym shorts and a t-shirt. Both boys were barefoot.

Brian walked up next to Tony and slipped his arm around Tony's waist.

"Brett took these," Tony said. "I recognize them from my first day when he showed me some of his work."

"Sometimes, I stand where you are and stare at them. Some great memories. Some not so great."

"This picture of you and Bobby." Tony glanced at him and then back at the picture. "Did you, you know, have a relationship with him?"

Brian blushed, but said, "Yes. For a long time, off and on. I broke it off because it was hurting our family. Mom and dad were against it because even though we aren't related, we're living in the same house as brothers." He shrugged and removed his arm from Tony's waist.

"Do you still love him? I mean, in that way?"

"Yes. I will always love Bobby, but Bobby and I know we can't have that kind of relationship. He and I are okay with that."

Tony glanced at him, and Brian smiled and said, "Honest."

Tony nodded.

"Tell me really, what were you thinking in this picture? You said you were thinking the trip sucked, and you wanted to be back home. Why?"

Brian sighed. He didn't want to go into detail, but he owed Tony an explanation. He gave him a partial answer. It was the truth, but only the partial truth.

"The trip was supposed to be a hunting trip. Brett and I hunt, but we never hunted elk before. We went with George, because his friend, Charles, was missing. George's girlfriend is Charles' sister. The trip was tense. We ended up fighting this wealthy landowner who wanted to take George's and other ranchers' land. These men went after Brett and me. Michael was with us. There were two shootouts. Just like the old west."

Brian shook his head. "Honestly, we didn't know if we were going to make it. We almost didn't. I almost didn't." He pointed to his face and said, "It's how I got this scar. I almost lost my eye."

Tony nodded. It didn't appear to Brian that he questioned it, and it didn't appear Tony was passing judgment.

"You ready for bed?" Brian asked.

Tony nodded and faced Brian.

Wanting to make him comfortable, Brian placed one hand on Tony's wrist and said, "Listen, I won't attack you. I think you know I'm attracted to you. From the first day. I could be wrong, because I'm not very good at this stuff, but I think you're attracted to me, too. But I don't think we should do anything or much of anything until you're ready. Until both of us are ready. I'm happy we're friends. I mean that. Our friendship has to come first. And whatever kind of relationship we end up having or not having, I want our friendship to last."

Tony swallowed. His blue eyes searching Brian's face. He said, "That first day just before I went into art."

Brian cocked his head.

"That was when I was attracted to you. And before the game this afternoon, when we were up in my room, I thought you were going to kiss me."

Brian felt hot and sweaty. The electricity he felt in Tony's bedroom came back as a bolt of lightning racing up and down his spine. His legs felt weak. His armpits were damp with sweat. So was his chest.

He wiped his mouth because he didn't know what to do with his free hand.

He had never felt this way with Bobby. He had never felt this way with Mikey or Cat. This was a new experience for him. An exciting experience.

His mouth went dry, and he was tongue-tied. He had no words and didn't respond.

Tony smiled, his eyes downcast. He said, "I wouldn't have minded."

Brian couldn't help but smile. He said, "I wanted to. I just didn't know if you wanted me to. And if we did, I thought we might be late for the game."

Tony smiled and shrugged, turning red.

Brian put his arms around Tony's waist, gently pulling Tony into him. Tony went willingly. He rested his forehead on Tony's. Tony put his arms first around Brian's shoulders, but one hand moved to the back of Brian's neck, his fingers down the collar.

Cautiously testing the waters, Brian kissed Tony, and Tony held it, parting his lips to allow for a deeper kiss. Brian did the same, their bodies pressed together. There was no disguising each other's arousal, and neither wanted to. Almost as a reflex, Brian shifted his hands. One hand slid up Tony's shirt on his mid-back, and the other slid down his pants, gently caressing his butt cheek. Tony felt smooth and soft and warm. What made Brian the happiest was that Tony made no move to prevent it.

Tony pulled back slightly and whispered, "Your dad or mom won't walk in here, will they?"

Brian smiled at him and said, "They would knock first. But they went to bed."

"Your brothers?"

"Michael would just walk in, but not until morning. Brett, George and Billy won't come in. They already said their goodnights."

Tony kissed Brian again, pulled back, and smiled.

Brian couldn't help but smile back. He said, "What?"

"I might be ready to go to bed now."

Brian kissed Tony, unwilling to end the moment, unwilling to move his hands, and afraid it might be his last kiss until some point in the future. The great mysterious unknown. Eventually, he pulled back a little and whispered, "Okay, now we can go to bed."

They separated, but held hands. They stared at one another, eyes roaming downward. Both smiled. Brian led him to the bed. Tony climbed in, and Brian crawled over him to his side of the bed.

They faced one another, noses almost touching. Brian's hand on Tony's hip, and Tony's hand on Brian's chest.

It was Tony who kissed Brian, his hand sliding down into his shorts. Brian arched his back in return, and he did the same to Tony. Shortly thereafter, shorts and pajama pants and t-shirts ended up on the floor. It was much longer until they fell asleep, wrapped in each other's arms, wearing nothing but smiles.

CHAPTER SIXTY-NINE

Tony couldn't stop yawning. Even though the project he and Billy worked on at the kitchen table was interesting, and working with Billy was fun, he wanted a nap. He marveled at Billy's prowess with the CAD program and at the design of the lake house. Billy began by explaining Brian's dream, and how it took shape with each of the brothers contributing to it. He explained the financing, but not in great detail.

Brian and Michael were asleep on the couch in a spoon position, with Brian's arm over Michael's chest. Brett dozed off and on in the Lazy Boy. The TV was tuned to a Badger game with the volume down low. George was with Jeremy in the study. Randy and Bobby were with the band practicing or writing.

Vicky moved quietly around the kitchen and humming a familiar tune. She was preparing an apple and cranberry crumb cake she needed both Billy and Tony to taste before she popped it into the oven. They were happy to lend their tastebuds to her, and Tony couldn't wait to sample the finished product.

The early morning run was easy by George's, Two's and Tony's standards. No hills, a chilly breeze, and stars twinkling overhead. Three miles out, and three miles back. Brian, Brett and Billy kept up, probably more out of not wanting to look out of shape in front of one another.

The best part was right after they got back. George, Two, and Billy practiced what George called knife exercises. It was something his grandfather taught him, and Two and Billy adopted. It looked like martial arts or yoga. As the sun rose, Billy sat down on the back stoop with Tony and Brett, and watched and listened as George and Two did their morning prayers, welcoming Father Sun.

The songs and hand gestures were simple and beautiful. Not so much the singing voice either had, but the ceremony itself.

Brian had excused himself and wandered off by himself to the side of the house near the hot tub.

"Where's he going?" Tony whispered.

"To pray," Brett answered. No further explanation was given, mostly because Brett didn't think there needed to be.

"Every morning, but usually in his room," Billy explained. "In church tomorrow before mass, too."

When Tony cocked his head, Brett said, "You'll see."

Riding horses was fun, something Tony hadn't done before, other than at the fair as a toddler. And then, it was on a pony chained to a pole and only in a circle. Not worth remembering.

Brian, George, and Michael rode bareback because the saddles were needed by Jeremy, Jeff, Billy, Tony, and Brett. The four dogs trotted along with the horses.

After and as Brian suggested, Tony felt soreness on the inside of each leg, especially on the inside of each ankle. The light-blue cross trainers he wore didn't offer the protection like the boots worn by others. Two had given Tony his cowboy hat to wear. Two wore his camo bucket hat he wore hunting. Jeff, George, and Brian wore cowboy hats, and Brett and Jeremy wore baseball caps.

After the ride, the boys took turns showering. Brian coated the hotspots on the insides of Brett's thighs near his knees with Neosporin and did the same for Tony on the insides of his ankles. Smelling much better than horses and stable, they dressed comfortably and casually. Before leaving the bedroom, Brian and Tony shared kisses, but stopped well short of anything more.

It was nearly noon when Randy, Bobby, and Danny laughed their way into the kitchen from the backdoor.

"I thought you guys would still be practicing," Vicky said.

"No, we were writing. G-Man and Andrew worked on the lights and sound system," Danny said. "We're hungry. Garrett and Andrew might come over in a little while."

"Who is Andrew?" Vicky asked.

"Andrew Westlake. He moved here six weeks ago, and he's a freshman and into music," Danny said.

"He doesn't play an instrument, but he's a good guy. He picked up the lights quickly. Garrett likes him and they work well together," Bobby added.

Randy said nothing. He frowned, mostly at Tony. Tony hadn't noticed, or if he did, he ignored him.

"What smells so good?" Brian asked through a yawn. He hunched down, peering into the oven window. Two followed him in and did the same.

"Apple and cranberry crumb cake," Vicky said proudly. "It's a Weight Watchers recipe."

"We sampled it," Billy said with a smile.

"It's good!" Tony said.

"If you guys are hungry, make yourself a sandwich or something. There's plenty to eat in the refrigerator," Vicky said as she cleaned up her dirty dishes in the sink.

"You guys want me to make you something?" Brian asked Tony and Billy.

"A sandwich and chips for me," Billy answered.

"Same, thanks," Tony said.

Danny and Bobby went about making their lunches alongside Brian and Two.

"What are you two doing?" Randy asked Billy.

It wasn't the question that made everyone stop and face him. It was the way he asked it.

"Tony's my partner for a project," Billy answered.

"He's not in drafting," Randy said.

"Nope, he's in art. Mr. Jett said we can partner with anyone we wanted, and Mrs. Arney gave him permission as long as Tony adds some art to it."

"What's the project?"

"The lake house. We're adding landscaping. Bushes, flowers, and stuff like that. Tony has a cool idea for a patio between the back of the house and the beach."

"The lake house is supposed to be our project. A family project."

"It's a school project. What we come up with might or might not be used by us. It's up to mom and dad and Jeff," Billy said rather testily.

"That reminds me," Danny said. "My dad was wondering if it would be too late to add a deck to the apartment above the garage. He thought you could add it to the stairs from the outside."

"It's definitely doable," Billy said.

"Something like this?" Tony said as he sketched it on a piece of paper.

"Wait! We don't have any say in what gets put around the house?" Randy asked.

"No, we don't," Brian said, glaring at Randy. "The landscaping has always been up to mom and dad and Jeff. If Jeff wants a deck on the apartment, that's his call, because he made it clear he's paying for the garage and the apartment." To Danny, he added, "The deck might be a change order thingy, and I think it will cost $100 plus supplies."

"Not a problem," Danny said. To Tony, he said, "You drew it so quickly. How do you do that?"

"Something I learned to do." He turned the drawing around so Danny could see it better. "There are a couple of ways it can be done, but it's up to Billy and your dad. I think the easiest way is to extend the deck from the slider, run it to the stairs, and then go around to the back of the garage. The balcony might end just outside the slider to his bedroom. But it's up to him and Billy." He continued to sketch it upside down so Danny could see it right side up. "Like this."

Vicky walked to the other side of the table, looked over Danny's shoulder and said, "It nearly mirrors the balcony on either side of the house facing the lake. I'm sure he's going to like it."

"That's why I drew it this way," Tony explained to Vicky. "You want both structures, the house and the garage, similar to each other, so they don't compete with each other."

Brett walked in from the family room and looked over Danny's other shoulder, and stood next to Randy.

Jeremy and George walked in from the hallway and joined everyone in the kitchen.

"What's everyone doing?" Jeremy asked, smiling. "And whatever is baking smells terrific."

Vicky kissed Jeremy and said, "It's dessert, and this is Tony's and Billy's idea for a deck for Jeff."

"That's really nice! I'm assuming this is Tony's work, and not Billy's. Billy, I've seen you draw."

Everyone laughed. Tony smiled and said thank you while Billy playfully protested.

"I think Billy and Tony are going to show us what they have for landscaping the lake house." To Billy and Tony, she said, "Are you guys ready?"

Tony and Billy looked at one another and nodded. "I think so," Billy said.

"This is where the art lesson Mrs. Arney wants me to do comes in."

"Why does Arney want you to do an art lesson? This is Billy's project, and it's a drafting class, not art," Randy asked.

Tony blinked, opened his mouth, but shut it.

Billy said, "It's Tony's and my project, not just mine. She wants to use this as a grade for him." He stared at his twin and said, "That's why." He paused, stared at Randy, and said, "Go ahead, Tony."

Tony flipped his MacBook Pro around so everyone on the other side of the table could view it.

"I'm going to pop up a painting and I want you to look at it but don't say anything. Here we go." He clicked his mouse and said, "Okay, look at it."

It was a picture of a pretty young woman sitting at the base of an oak tree, surrounded by animals and bushes. It was reminiscent of a drawing of Snow White in the forest.

After three or four seconds, he asked, "What was the first thing you saw?"

"The lady, but only part of her. A lot of deer and birds and stuff," Danny said.

"The first thing I saw was the large tree," Vicky said.

Brett said, "The first thing I saw were the animals and bushes. Then I saw the lady."

"What were we supposed to see?" Brian asked.

Tony smiled and said, "There is no right or wrong answer. It's a matter of personal perspective. Now, I'm going to show you another picture, and the same thing. Don't say anything, just look at it."

He clicked his mouse, and at first, there was no reaction. Then, either everyone stifled a laugh or laughed out loud. The picture was of the lake house, but in the foreground was a fountain with four naked chubby babies spitting water into the base.

"Oh my God!" Bobby said. "No way!"

Vicky and Jeremy laughed with everyone else. Jeremy shook his head and said, "You're kidding, right?"

Tony and Billy burst out laughing, and Tony said, "Yes, but to prove a point." He clicked his mouse and Billy's rendering of the lake house appeared on the screen. There was no landscaping of any kind.

He said, "Billy did a great job on the house. It looks fantastic, and because of that, it has to be the focal point. You don't want something ambiguous like the lady in the woods," he clicked his mouse, and the lady appeared, "And you don't want something to distract from the beauty of the house, right?"

Vicky said, "Right, thank God! Though the chubby babies are cute, if not over the top." She ended up laughing with everyone else.

"Right. I'm happy you thought my chubby babies were cute. They were Billy's idea. Our idea is to enhance the house, but not distract from it."

He clicked the mouse again, and green bushes appeared along the back of the house. A stone paver pathway led to a small patio. The patio had stone benches, but enough room for a grill and lawn chairs. At the corners of the back of the house were lilac bushes. Surrounding the patio were other purple bushes, and in front of the green bushes was a small fuzzy whitish plant.

"That's pretty!" Vicky said. "What is the small ground cover in front of yellow and green bushes?"

"The larger yellow and green bushes are golden euonymus. I think I'm saying it right. They're durable and don't require much care. They contrast nicely with the brown and tan of the house. The ground cover in front of those is diamond frost euphorbia. They contrast nicely. Pretty durable. You can always cut it back if it gets unruly, as my aunt would say."

"What are the purple bushes around the patio?" Jeremy asked.

"Those are butterfly bushes. They smell pretty and they actually attract butterflies," Billy said.

"What's it going to cost?" Randy said.

Vicky ignored him, Jeremy squinted at him, and the rest turned their heads to stare at him.

"What? I'm not allowed to know what the cost is? I'm helping to pay for it."

"You know, I've about had it with you, Randy," Vicky said rather pointedly.

"Jeff, dad and I have a budget of $25,000 for landscaping. We also have a contingency budget in case there are overruns. According to Billy and Mr. Jett, there almost always are," Brian said.

"Tony and I did the math, and we won't even come close to $25,000, and that includes the landscaping around the garage," Billy said.

"We can add some Knockout Roses spaced out between the green bushes if you like," Tony said. "That would make things pop, without distracting from the house."

"You sound like the guy from Queer Eye," Randy muttered.

"Why? Because he's an artist? What the hell is wrong with you?" Bobby asked.

"It was meant as a joke," Randy said, turning his head away from everyone.

"The hell it was! It wasn't funny. It was disrespectful and rude. You could have said Flip or Flop, Fixer Upper, Property Brothers, or even Maine Cabin Masters. But you went with Queer Eye. That's offensive," Bobby said.

Billy was fuming. "Last night at the restaurant, you were all over Tony's ass, butting in when it had nothing to do with you."

Tony's face was beat red. He put an elbow on the table and his hand over his eyes. "Look, I don't want to step on anyone's toes. I'm sorry." He turned to Billy and said, "Maybe you can do this presentation without me." He looked up at Brian and said, "Maybe I should go home."

"No, Tony! Please don't," Vicky said as she came around the table to hug him from behind. "I know Brian would be disappointed if you did, and I think the others would be, too." To Randy, she said, "You owe him an apology and I don't want to hear anything else coming out of your mouth! Is that understood?"

Randy shrugged and said, "I'm sorry."

"That was dripping in sincerity," Brett said. "I'm sure Tony feels welcome now."

"Randy, leave the room," Jeremy said. "You will not treat a guest in our house like that. He's not only Brian's friend, he's everyone's friend."

Brian and Billy were seething. Both stood with their hands clenched into fists.

"Randy, I've been thinking for a while now. Remember, a couple of years ago when the guys and I were in the hospital in Chicago after we were freed from that shit hole? You would go from room to room and talk to us, listen to us, and encourage us?" Brett asked. "I miss *that* Randy. I don't know where he went, but he's been AWOL for a while."

"Screw you!"

"Yeah?"

"Oh? What? What are you going to do?" Randy spat.

Brett slammed Randy into the wall with a forearm and grabbed the scruff of his shirt around his neck. A picture fell to the floor. In a small, but menacing voice, he said, "Dad told you to leave the room. If you don't, I'll help you leave, but you might not be in one piece. Tony is our friend. All of ours. You will not treat him disrespectfully or rudely. You will treat him as you treat Bobby or Danny."

"Or what?"

"You really want to go there? Because I'm ready if you are."

George and Jeremy quickly pulled them apart. Bobby, Danny, and Two stood in front of Brian, who was more than ready to come to Brett's and Tony's aid.

Jeremy grabbed Randy by the arm and pulled him outside. George held Brett only as long as Jeremy needed to get Randy out the door.

The silence in the kitchen was deafening, except for the timer on the oven notifying Vicky her dessert was done. She opened the oven, inspected her cake, and decided a few more minutes wouldn't hurt.

She didn't realize how angry she was. She gulped air in deep breaths, chest heaving in and out. Hot tears sprung from her eyes. She threw the hot pad across the kitchen.

She pulled out the chair and sat down next to Tony, and took both of his hands in hers.

"Tony, I hope you can find it in your heart to forgive us. Please don't judge Brian or his brothers or Jeremy or me by the words and actions of one individual who has a burr up his ass about something. Please don't." As she said this, she squeezed his hand and shook them, emphasizing each word.

"You heard the boys last night say they weren't going to let anything happen to you. I think what you saw is proof of that," she said as she wiped tears off her face. "If they're willing to take on their brother, just imagine what they would do to someone who isn't family."

His ice-blue eyes were blurry from tears, but he blinked them back. He was red in the face, hot and sweaty, and his shoulders sagged. He felt defeated and frightened that all he had tried to avoid would start up again. Yet he managed a smile and a nod, stealing a glance at Brian and Brett before and after. Both smiled and nodded their encouragement.

Billy tapped him on the shoulder, smiled, and said, "You want to finish up or take a break?"

CHAPTER SEVENTY

The three cops decided on a bad cop and badder cop routine, with Graff, or Gruff as Eiselmann and O'Connor insisted on calling him, as the bad cop. O'Connor was the badder cop. They had been hammering away for almost a half an hour, but Nada Sherry stuck to her story. In his notes, Eiselmann titled it, *Didn't See and Didn't Know*. He suspected it had been rehearsed.

Her mother, Kristine, sat with her arms hugging herself, hunched forward and on the edge of the kitchen chair. Her right knee bounced rapid-fire.

Nada slouched with her arms crossed over her chest and with a sullen look on her face. Her legs were stretched out in front of her, one foot over the other. Though it was mid-afternoon, it didn't look like she had bathed or showered that morning. Her greasy hair and oily skin gave her an unappealing countenance. Her clothes were as unwashed as she was. Either the girl or her clothes had an unpleasant odor causing all three cops to lean or back away from her.

"Mrs. Sherry, we are certain Nada knows who wrote the letters and who set off the car bomb," Jamie said. "If she does not cooperate and give us the name or names of who else is involved, if anything further happens, she will be charged with a felony and obstruction, and she's looking at jail time."

"Sure," Nada mumbled.

O'Connor leaned forward, and then moved his chair so his knee touched her leg. He pointed at her and said, "Do you think this is a game?"

She stared at him with a smirk he wanted to smack off her face.

O'Connor reached around and pulled his handcuffs tucked into his belt at his back.

"Detective Graff, I've had enough. I'm going to read her rights, and then I'm arresting her for obstruction."

He took the Miranda card from his pocket and began reciting it, just as regulations called for.

Nada sat up straighter and her eyes grew wide. Her chapped lips formed a perfect O.

Graff shrugged and said, "Nada, I warned you. You aren't cooperating, so we have no choice." He turned to Eiselmann and said, "Detective Eiselmann, call juvenile detention and tell them we have an underage female we will process at the police station and then transport to their facility. We should have her there by four or four-thirty."

"Yessir!" he said, standing up with his cell and walking to the doorway between the kitchen and the family room. He didn't plan on speaking to anyone, and hadn't dialed any number. But into the phone loud enough for both Nada and her mother to hear, he said exactly what Graff had asked him to say. Eiselmann even smiled and nodded and gesticulated, all part of the show.

Graff said, "Nada, it looks as though you have something to say."

"Too late," O'Connor said. "Nada, stand up."

Nada looked up at him with big pleading eyes behind her glasses that kept slipping down her nose.

O'Connor barked, "I said, *STAND UP!*"

She shrunk away from him, tears welling in her eyes, and said, "I don't know her name. I don't know what grade she's in. All I know is that she has a class with Danny. That's all."

"Oh, really," O'Connor said. "You don't know her name or her grade, but you know she has a class with Danny." He shook his head and said, "You expect us to believe you?"

"It's the truth!" Little raindrops of spit flew from her mouth. Her breath, disgusting.

"Which class?" Graff asked.

"I don't know," she answered, ringing her hands.

"Okay, that's it," O'Connor said.

As he moved towards her, Nada sprung from her chair and backed away behind her mother, using her as a shield.

"It's band or choir. Something like that," she said, hiding behind her mother.

Mrs. Sherry seemed oblivious to what was happening in the kitchen. Her eyes were clamped shut, and she hugged herself and rocked back and forth. Eiselmann wondered absently if they needed to do a welfare check on her.

"Pat, wait. I think Nada wants to cooperate with us. Nada, please sit down and let's talk," Graff said.

"Make him go away," Nada said, pointing a shaking finger at O'Connor.

"Pat, could you wait in the other room, please?"

"I will, but if I think she is lying or withholding any information, I'm coming back in with the handcuffs."

Pat made a big show of hanging his handcuffs out of his front pocket. He took one glance back at her, said, "Sit your ass back in that chair and tell Detective Graff everything you know. If I think you're holding anything back or lying, I'll be back in here faster than you can blink."

CHAPTER SEVENTY-ONE

"I should have arrested her for smelling like shit and not bathing since she was born, and for bad breath, and for spitting when she talked. I think she got some on me," O'Connor said with a shiver. "I want to go home and scrub myself with steel wool and heavy duty disinfectant. If we ever have to go into that home again, I want a hazmat suit."

"I can't imagine living like that," Eiselmann said. "I've been in crack houses that looked and smelled better."

He stuck his head between the front seats and said, "Do we need a welfare check on the mother? I don't think she's all there."

"About ten cars missing from an eleven car train," O'Connor mumbled.

"Like she was having a breakdown or psychotic break."

Graff took his time driving to the station, satisfied the end of the case was in sight.

Dismissing the talk about her mother, he said, "Let's go over what we have." It was almost as if he said it to himself.

Eiselmann said from memory, "The mystery girl planned everything. Especially the letters mystery girl mailed. Nada helped with the wording."

Graff chuckled. "God, I don't know how that's possible." He shook his head and said, "Paul, if you would have seen what she wrote for Tobin and Farner," he shook his head.

"The author obviously cleaned up the language and wrote the letters, Detective Gruff," O'Connor said.

"Oh, and thanks for the sign above my door." Graff shook his head and laughed. "I'm assuming everyone knows. Does the Cap?"

O'Connor laughed and said, "The sign was his idea."

"Bullshit!"

"Truth!"

Jamie had walked into the station the day after the visit with Farner and Tobin at North High School to snickers and surreptitious glances. He found a sign above his door: *Offisur Jamie Gruff, Esquire, Chief of Detectives.*

"We thought you'd like that," O'Connor said with a chuckle.

"You were in on this, too?" Graff said, glancing in the rearview.

"Maybe a little." Eiselmann shook his head. He thought for a minute, wanting to keep the discussion focused on the case. He said, "Nada said she knew nothing about the car bombs."

Graff said, "Do either of you believe her? About the car bomb, I mean?"

"Fifty-fifty," O'Connor said. "Nada might know. But she might have been brought in after the bomb."

"Or the bomb was done without her knowledge, and the mystery girl wanted it that way," Paul suggested. "Or the car bomb is separate from the letters."

Graff nodded. "I think we contact Farner and see if we can get a class list with pictures of the band and chorus section Danny's in. If it's chorus, chances are Randy and Bobby are in the same section."

"Would he be willing to come in tomorrow and run us a list?" Eiselmann said.

"I can call and ask, but I'd rather not intrude on his weekend if we don't have to. I think if we get there on Monday before school begins, we can tie everything up before noon. Especially if Nada is still on suspension until Tuesday."

"Sounds like a plan," Eiselmann said.

"I think you ought to buy us dinner, since Paul and I played our parts so well," O'Connor said.

"Kelly and I are going out to dinner, but I can pop for ice cream."

"Deal!" O'Connor said.

CHAPTER SEVENTY-TWO

Brian drove to the city slower than George, who always drove five under the posted limit. He didn't want the weekend to end. Both boys were tired, and both seemed content to listen to the radio and look out the window. The only concession was holding hands, fingers laced.

"You seem quiet. Is everything alright?" Tony asked.

"Yes," Brian said with a smile. "Except that I'm driving you home and I won't see you until tomorrow." He glanced at Tony and added, "That part sucks."

Tony smiled back at him, his hand tightening on Brian's and said, "We were together all weekend."

Brian shrugged, and said, "It sucks it has to end."

"I have to go home sometime, right?"

Brian smiled at him and shrugged. Tony laughed.

Brian thought for a minute, took a deep breath and said, "Um, I know it's only been a couple of days, but do you, you know, *like me*, like me, or are we just friends?"

Tony chuckled and said, "You're speed talking."

"Because I'm nervous. I'm never nervous. I don't like being nervous."

Tony chuckled again and said, "To answer your question, though I think it's pretty obvious, yes, I *like you*, like you."

"So we're friends, then?"

Tony laughed and said, "Again, I risk stating the obvious. Yes, we're friends."

"Do you think we can be more than just friends? Or maybe you and I are already more than friends?"

Tony shifted in his seat as much as he could, tucked his leg under him and said, "Given all you and I did together, I thought we already are more than just friends. Unless you don't want to be."

"No, no, no, that's not what I meant."

Brian let go of Tony's hand and placed his hand on Tony's thigh. "I want to be more than friends. I liked everything we did and I can't wait until we're together again, you know ... but I want us to be really *us*. More than friends, and more than just ... the sex stuff. Don't get me wrong. I liked everything we did. I mean, just thinking about it drives me crazy."

Tony laughed and said, "You're speed talking again."

"I can't help it. I'm nervous, and I don't know how to explain myself."

Tony took Brian's hand in both of his. He said, "Are you asking me to go with you, you know, steady?"

"Yes, that's what I'm trying to say. I want you to be mine and me to be yours. For a long time. Maybe forever. Hopefully, forever." He quieted down and said, "If you want to, that is."

"Yes, as long as no one knows I'm gay," Tony said. "Not yet, anyway."

Brian shrugged and said, "I'm okay with that. People might find out, though, but I'm okay with that, too. You know, both. People knowing and people not knowing. I'm okay with it."

"Why are you so nervous?" Tony laughed.

He had never seen this side of Brian, and didn't think he even had this side. He always acted confident and together. In school. Playing basketball. On the horse. When they were alone in his room. This was a whole new side to Brian, and Tony found it fascinating.

"I don't know. I've never felt this way about anyone before. Not Cat. Not Mikey. And not Bobby, and I really love Bobby. But I've never felt this way before. Ever."

"Is it okay with you? Feeling like that about me?"

"Oh my God, yes! Seriously!"

Brian thought for a minute and said, "If It's okay with you, I mean. For me to feel like this about you."

Tony laughed and said, "I feel the same way about you. So yes, I'm okay with you feeling like that about me."

"Really? You feel the same way about me as I feel about you?"

Tony said, "I don't know how else to tell you. Yes, I feel the same way about you. Maybe I'll have to show you when we get to my house."

Brian sped up.

CHAPTER SEVENTY-THREE

Butts dragged on Mondays. The cool sprinkle pretending to be a steady shower didn't help. Jeremy's opinion was that if it was going to rain, then rain. Not this spitting and sputtering nature has a way of doing sometimes. But nature didn't care about Jeremy's opinion.

He had arrived at school early, before many of the teachers and kids. Busses wouldn't be rolling in for another five or ten minutes, and the parking lot was only semi-full. Jeremy checked his mailbox, ran into a few faculty members and Bob Farner, and then made a beeline to his office. He knew it was inevitable word would spread about him being back.

No sooner did he sit down in his chair when a steady line of staff lined up to find out how he was doing. Ironically, he used the same line the boys had used while he was in the hospital, but added that he needed to watch his diet and get more exercise. That set them at ease, and Jeremy relaxed.

As much as Brian speed-talked and was nervous as he drove Tony home the day before, Tony found Brian quiet, almost on edge. As soon as Tony buckled up his seatbelt, Brian touched his hand tentatively, then linked pinky fingers with him.

Tony glanced over at him, but Brian kept his eyes on the road. He shrugged, okay with the almost non-touch, since it was only Brett and Billy in the truck with them, and Tony assumed Brian had told them about their status. About half-way to school, Brian laced his fingers with Tony, and Tony let him.

Both Tony and Billy had worn dress shirts, ties, dress slacks, and dress shoes. They looked the part they needed to portray for their presentation.

"I'm nervous," Billy said.

"We'll be okay," Tony answered. "I'll follow your lead and come in on my part. It will be fine."

"You're going to bring your computer?"

Tony nodded. "I have an HDMI cord for it, but I can go wireless if we need to."

They arrived at school and Brian parked close to where they normally parked. George's truck was two cars over, and George sat in it alone and behind the wheel. Randy, Bobby, and Danny had already walked into the building. When George saw Brian pull in, he got out and waited.

"Billy, I'll meet you in drafting. I'm going to drop my stuff off in art first," Tony said.

"But don't be late," Billy said. "Mr. Jett has a thing about arriving early."

"If you're not early, you're late," Brett said with a laugh.

"Just like dad," Billy said.

They walked on, but Brett tugged on Brian's and George's arms and said, "Guys, hold up a minute."

The five of them stopped and faced Brett. Brett looked around and saw they were relatively alone.

He said, "What's wrong?"

Billy shook his head and Tony shrugged, but both looked at Brian and George as if they had the answer.

"What?" Brett said.

George shook his head and said, "Something." He shook his head again.

"You, too?" Brett asked Brian.

"Yeah, something."

"Did I do something wrong?" Tony asked cautiously.

Brian smiled, and said, "No, nothing with you, us. We're good."

"Do either of you know what's wrong?" Brett asked.

Brian and George stared at each other, and then back at Brett. Brian said, "I can't explain it. Just, something."

"Yes," George said.

"What's going on?" Tony whispered. He didn't know why he whispered. It just felt like he should.

Without taking his eyes off Brian and George, Brett said, "Sometimes George and Brian have feelings. We're learned to take them seriously. You know, out of precaution."

"Most of the time," Billy added, "the feeling becomes something."

"Oh," Tony said, not sure what was going on. But he trusted them, especially Brian.

"So, we need to be cautious. You two need to let all of us know if something happens, preferably before it happens. If you can," Brett said. "Agreed?"

Heads nodded.

"Okay, let's roll."

They made it into the building just before the skies opened up.

"I'm heading to art to work on my story," Brian said.

"I'm going to the cafeteria," Brett said.

"Same," George said.

"I'm going to the cafeteria, then drafting," Billy said. "Tony, I'll meet you there."

Tony smiled and said, "I'll be there, and I'll be there early. Don't worry, we're going to do great."

Billy took a deep breath and said, "Okay, I'm outta here." He turned and left.

Tony shook his head and said, "I never thought he would worry so much."

"He usually doesn't," Brett said. "But this presentation means a lot to him."

"We'll do fine," Tony said with a smile.

Brett put his arms around the shoulders of both Brian and Tony and whispered, "You two are great together. I'm happy for both of you."

He turned and walked off with George.

Tony looked quizzically at Brian.

"Brett guessed. I didn't tell him anything. Honest."

Tony shrugged and said, "I guess we're official, then. At least between us and your family, anyway."

Side by side, they walked silently to art, though both were smiling. For the moment, whatever troubled Brian had disappeared.

CHAPTER SEVENTY-FOUR

Eiselmann jogged to Graff's car, carrying his laptop in one hand and a piece of raspberry Danish in the other. The motor was running, Graff was behind the wheel, and O'Connor sat shotgun.

"Sorry I'm late," Eiselmann said. "I had to run Alex's lunch to school for her. She forgot it and didn't have money to pay for the school lunch."

"Not to worry," Graff responded. "All is good."

"I think you should dock his pay," O'Connor said. "Serve him right using his daughter as an excuse."

"And for not bringing us a piece of the coffee cake."

Eiselmann slid into the backseat, threw his laptop next to him, and buckled up. "I'll be happy to give you a bite-by-bite report on its merits. So far, it's delicious."

"Of course, we could always stop at Speedway, pick up coffee and a couple of donuts," O'Connor suggested. "Farner and Tobin might like one."

Graff tried not to smile, but failed. "You realize Tobin is married, right? With three kids."

"Hey, I'm just being polite for all the help they're providing us today."

"Uh, huh. Sure."

CHAPTER SEVENTY-FIVE

Mrs. Arney moved around the room, hanging art up on three wires stretched and secured from wall to wall. Tony assumed the art was from a beginning class, judging from the assignments. They weren't sophisticated or all that difficult or interesting.

Tony and Brian, sitting side by side, were the only two students in the room. Tony sketched while Brian sat in front of his laptop. He had turned his computer on, had opened the saved file containing his book, and the cursor blinked on and off where he had left off the day before. His hands were in his lap and he hadn't touched his keys.

Tony whispered, "Everything okay?"

Brian frowned, thought for a minute that seemed like an hour to Tony, and whispered, "I need you to be safe."

Tony's face clouded over. He shut his sketchbook and stared at him.

"Would it freak you out if I said I think I love you?" Brian whispered.

Tony's face softened. His eyes lit up, and he couldn't contain his smile.

"Because I think I do."

Tony had no words. Speechless. But he couldn't stop smiling.

Mrs. Arney had her back to them, hung her last project up, and turned around. She saw them, tilted her head and said, "Boys, is everything alright?"

Tony and Brian beamed at her. It was Brian who answered.

"Yes," Brian said.

"Fantastic!" Tony said, as he blushed. He still couldn't lose his smile.

"Oooo-kaaay."

"I have to leave for a minute or two," Brian said. "Would you watch my stuff for me until I get back, please?"

"Sure, but I don't think I can write you a pass to your next class."

"That's okay. Mrs. Rios will understand." To Tony, he said, "I have to run." He mouthed, *"Be safe,"* and then, *"I love you."*

Without waiting for Tony's response, Brian quick-walked out the door, leaving both Tony and Mrs. Arney staring after him.

CHAPTER SEVENTY-SIX

Brian stepped into the hallway and almost ran into George. Other than him, the hallway was fairly empty. The mass of students held in the cafeteria hadn't been released, and wouldn't be for another twenty minutes. There were only a few stragglers in the hallways on a pass or allowed by administration. Some teachers, like Arney, allowed students in their rooms.

"What?" Brian asked.

George shook his head and ran a hand through his long black hair. "I am not sure. Yet."

Brian nodded. "Where are the others?"

"Brett and Billy are in the cafeteria. Billy is going to drafting to get ready for his presentation. Brett has my backpack and duffle, and is getting ready to go to class."

"Where are Bobby, Randy, and Danny?"

George squinted at Brian and said, "I thought you might know."

Brian pulled out his cell, located the finder application Brett had talked them into using, opened it, and found three colored dots with initials showing where the three of them were. "In the chorus room."

Without waiting for George, Brian headed towards the room.

The two of them walked further down the fine arts hallway. Mrs. Arney's room was the first room in the wing, next to another art room and a storage closet custodians used. Next came the band room and storage closets for uniforms and instruments, followed by the orchestra room and more storage closets. On the opposite wall was the auditorium and doors leading to auditorium seating.

At the end of the hallway was the chorus room. However, neither Brian nor George heard any singing.

Brian slowed his pace and held a hand out to slow George down. Brian felt a tingling sensation run up and down his back. The little hairs on the back of his neck stood at attention, and goosebumps broke out on his arms.

Out of habit, George reached down and patted his hip where he normally wore his big knife. However, it wasn't there. George never wore it at school.

Brian stepped to the side of the door and peeked into the window.

His two brothers and Danny stood side by side near the outside door with their hands up, like victims of a robbery. Facing them were two girls. One, Nada Sherry, held a handgun. A .38. Brian didn't know who the other girl was.

There was no time. He and George had to act.

Brian carefully and quietly backed away from the door, pulling George with him.

"Nada Sherry has a gun pointed at them. Some other girl is with her. I don't know who it is."

He looked around the hallway, saw a fire alarm, and had an idea.

"George, pull the fire alarm," Brian pointed at it. "The alarm will get everyone out of the building, and it might stop Nada from doing something stupid. I'm going to go in the room and try to get the guys out the door. I'm leaving it up to you to get the gun away from Nada without getting yourself shot."

George hesitated. He placed a hand on Brian's shoulder and said, "What is to stop her from shooting you and them?"

The calmness Brian displayed in Arizona was clear in his eyes and in his posture. George knew there was nothing he could say that would stop him from acting, even it if it meant danger to himself.

CHAPTER SEVENTY-SEVEN

Tony packed Brian's computer and mouse into Brian's backpack. He picked up both the backpack and Brian's duffle bag and said, "Mrs. Arney, where would you like me to put these?"

"How about in the corner behind my desk?" She thought for a minute and said, "Any idea where he went or when he will be back?"

"No, not really. He didn't say anything to me."

"Hmmm, okay. You're off to Mr. Jett?"

Tony smiled and said, "Yes. Billy wanted me to get there early. He's nervous."

Mrs. Arney laughed. "I don't know him like some others in the family, but he always struck me as confident."

Tony laughed just as the fire alarm went off.

"That's weird," Mrs. Arney said.

Tony stood with Brian's bags in each hand, unmoving.

"Well, set those behind my desk and let's go out this door."

Tony did as he was told. They stepped out into the morning mist, and Tony blinked, not believing what he saw.

CHAPTER SEVENTY-EIGHT

Brian burst into the room, ignoring the gun in Nada's hand. He didn't know if that was the correct play, but he chose it. George had yet to appear.

"Guys, we need to get out of the building!" he said, running to Danny and his two brothers. Deliberately, he placed himself between the gun and the three of them, his back to the two girls.

He shoved them towards the door. Randy was the first through it and ran from the building as quickly as he could. Brian could hear him yelling for help. Bobby was at the open door, but he hesitated. He reached for Danny, missed on his first attempt, but latched onto his arm with his second attempt. He grabbed his arm and yanked.

"Stop! Don't you fucking leave!" Maryanne Sturgis yelled. "I swear, if this bitch won't shoot, I'll take the fucking gun and shoot you myself!"

That stopped him. Bobby knew they needed to run, but his feet felt like cement blocks. As light as Danny was, Bobby couldn't budge him.

"Shoot those fuckers, you bitch! Shoot them!" Sturgis yelled.

While the two girls focused on Brian, Bobby, and Danny, George had crept in and made it to within six yards of the two girls. His intent was to get to Nada before she could pull the trigger.

Nada held the .38 with both hands. Her hands shook like a case of palsy, and so did the gun. She sobbed uncontrollably.

"Stop yelling at me! Stop yelling!" Nada screamed, trying to make her voice as loud as the fire alarm.

"You stupid cunt! Shoot them before they get away!" Sturgis yelled.

"Guys, get out! Now!" Brian yelled.

He shoved Danny into Bobby, and then both out of the door. He knew he should have followed, but he also knew he couldn't leave George to face them alone.

"Shoot, you stupid fucking bitch! Shoot, you cunt!" Sturgis screamed.

George didn't move fast enough. He had almost reached Nada as the gun went off.

CHAPTER SEVENTY-NINE

"*Báháchi'ii', your brother needs you.*"

Brett knew the voice, but didn't know the word he said. He knew it was Navajo, though, and he understood the urgency.

In his mind, knowing it was the correct way to communicate with him, Brett thought, *"Where is he, Grandfather?"*

"*Nida'ałkáá'i' is in the room where they sing. Shadow is with him.*"

Brett heard a gunshot and took off.

CHAPTER EIGHTY

Graff, O'Connor, and Eiselmann were in the parking lot, halfway between the car and the building, when the fire alarm rang. Graff had always hated the noise. As effective as it was as an alert system, it sounded like thousands of angry cicadas.

"Couldn't they just use a bell or a buzzer instead of that?" Eiselmann said as he squinted at the building. He should have known squinting did nothing to protect his ears.

"Always hated that sound," Graff said as he shook his head. "Odd time of day for a fire drill."

"Might not be a drill," O'Connor said. "Could be a faulty something or other, or some smartass pulled a switch for grins and giggles."

Then the three of them heard it.

"Gunshot," Eiselmann said.

"Light for a .45," Graff said.

"Heavy for a .22," O'Connor responded.

"Which direction?" Eiselmann asked as all three took off running towards the building.

CHAPTER EIGHTY-ONE

"Where am I going?" Tony yelled out loud as he ran to the door he just exited.

"Tony, what the hell?" Mrs. Arney said. "Get back here."

Tony didn't listen, but hit the door, threw it open, and charged through.

"Grandfather told me to get, Dibé yázhí bi ghaa' naha lin goh bi tsii' dishoh dóó dits'oz. That's you."

Tony had no clue what the boy said or called him. He said, "Where am I going?"

He heard it and knew instinctively it was a gunshot.

The boy wept. He said, *"Chorus room. Hurry! He needs you!"*

Tony ran faster, panicking now, afraid he would be too late.

CHAPTER EIGHTY-TWO

George wrenched the gun from Nada. He felt and heard the sickening snap of at least one finger, maybe two, as he yanked the gun away. In anger, he shoved her backwards. Her back hit the first step of the risers, and her head hit the second step. She howled. Blood dripped as she lifted her head. She held her mangled hand to her stomach and cried out in pain.

Maryanne Sturgis, whom neither George nor Brian knew, lunged at George with fingers and nails like claws. Her mouth contorted in anger.

He tossed the gun on the floor away from them, ready for her.

"You fucking cocksucker! You cocksucker!"

George swung a right hook, feeling her nose crunch on his fist. Blood and snot poured out of her nose, flattened against her skull. His punch only caused her to pause her attack. She kept coming at him. Using her momentum, he picked her up and flung her headlong into a pile of chairs and music stands. She hit head first and lay still in the tangle of metal.

Tony ran into the room, took one glance at the girl amidst the chairs and music stands, and then at the other girl sobbing and moaning in a heap on the risers. He saw George in a rage, taking great gulps of air, hands clenching and unclenching. Tony thought he saw blood on one of his hands.

He gasped when he saw Brian on his back near the door.

Tony ran to him and couldn't take his eyes away from the blood pouring out of his chest near his right shoulder.

"George, call 9-1-1. Gunshot to a chest. Need an ambulance fast!" Tony yelled as he tore off his white shirt, buttons popping. With the tie still around his neck, he looked like a Chippendale Dancer.

Trying unsuccessfully not to panic, he pressed his white shirt down on the bleeding hole in Brian's chest. Brian reached up with a bloody hand and held Tony's face. Then it slipped to Tony's chest, and then to Tony's arm. The shirt Tony used to stop the bleeding was soaked through, leaving his hands wet with blood.

"Hurts. Can't breathe." He sucked in shallow gulps of air. Tiny red bubbles rose from his mouth with each exhale. "Hurts," he breathed.

Brett ran into the room, surveyed what was going on, and saw Tony kneeling down over Brian. He darted to Tony's side.

"Can't breathe. Hurts."

"Shhh, don't talk, Brian. Lie still," Tony said.

"Hurts," Brian moaned.

Brian's hand fell away, and he stopped breathing.

"No!" Tony yelled. "No!"

"Chest compressions, Tony!" Brett yelled. "Now! George, call 9-1-1. Gunshot wound upper right chest. Small caliber."

"Did. It's a .38."

In Tony's head, he repeated the lyrics to the Bee Gees song, *Stayin' Alive*, to keep the rhythm for the chest compressions. Brett stripped off his shirt, threw Tony's soggy shirt to the side, and did what Tony had done moments before with his shirt.

"Air now!" Brett said. "Give him air!"

Tony gave Brian mouth to mouth, but he didn't know how effective it was. One puff. Two puffs. Then back to chest compressions.

"Nida'ałkáá'i', it is not your time."

It was clear, as if he stood in the room. Tony stopped with the compressions, looked around, but didn't see anyone.

"But grandfather, I miss Brad. I want to be with you and him."

"Brian," said the voice Tony recognized when the alarm first sounded. *"There will be time for us. Just not now."*

Tears appeared on Brian's cheeks. His lips didn't move, hadn't moved, yet Tony heard Brian's voice. Was he losing his mind? Tony didn't know for sure.

"Brian, please listen to them. Please. Don't go."

It was Brett's voice, but Tony never saw his lips move. Nothing came out of his mouth. How was this possible? Tony didn't know how, but he heard it all.

"Dibé yázhí bi ghaa' naha lin goh bi tsii' díshoh dóó dits'oz loves you, and you love him. Nida'ałkáá'i', your time is not now." That seemed to end the discussion, but then George's grandfather added, *"However, it is a choice."*

"Please, no. Brian, please no," Tony whispered, unaware he was crying.

Brian's eyes fluttered and then opened fully. Tony could feel Brian's heart beating, slow and unsteady at first. Then it beat regularly, but weakly. Tony stopped with the compressions.

"It fucking hurts," Brian whispered.

Neither Tony nor Brett knew if Brian meant the wound in his chest or the turmoil he felt.

Tony bent low, kissed Brian's forehead, and whispered, "Please don't go."

Brian reached his bloody hand, first to Tony's face, and then grasped Tony's hand, though it was weak.

Sirens, faint at first, grew steadily louder. Graff, Eiselmann, and O'Connor burst into the choir room with guns drawn, but only at the ready, fingers on first positive and not on the trigger. They cleared the room of any danger, saw George standing midway between the two girls, and then saw Tony and Brett in the corner, bent over Brian.

"Ah, fuck no!" O'Connor said as he ran to see what aid he could provide.

"Come in quickly," Graff called.

The school nurses, Sharon King and Flippa Unger, charged into the room, followed by the principal, Chuck Gobel and assistant principal, Bob Farner. King carried the oxygen, gauze and bandages, while Unger carried other medical gear, a laptop, and paperwork.

The room was suddenly filled with radio chatter. Graff yelling orders into his. School traffic coming through on Gobel's, Farner's, and King's.

King quickly assessed the situation. She was a veteran nurse who did a couple of tours in Iraq, and kids and staff loved her, as they did Unger.

"Did the bullet go through?" she asked.

"Shit, I didn't think of that," Brett said. "Sorry."

"Brian, can you hear me?" King asked as she patted Brian's hand.

"Yes," he whispered, his face in a grimace. "Hurts. Can't breathe."

"He's been in and out," Tony said. "His heart stopped, but I did chest compressions and mouth to mouth. It's going again, but it's weak."

"Good thinking. What's your name?"

"Tony Vittoria."

"Tony is a friend of ours," Brett explained. "We heard the gunshot and ran here." He didn't want to go into detail about the voices they heard or the ongoing conversation that took place.

"Chest compressions helped. Fluid from the wound is entering the lung and chest."

"What's the ETA on the ambulance?" Unger asked O'Connor. Her eyes said much more to O'Connor than her question.

O'Connor opened the door and pulled out his cell. The ambulance was behind the firetruck.

He stuck his head back in the door and said, "They're here." He waved at the trucks and made sure they had spotted him.

King hooked up the oxygen and slipped the mask over Brian's face. She said, "Boys, you'll have to step back to let these men work when they come through the door."

Brian waved a frantic hand and stared at Tony.

"I'm right here, Brian."

The firemen and paramedics burst through the door and took charge. Even King and Unger stepped back. King filled them in on what Tony had told her and what she suspected. One, a young lady, hooked Brian up to a monitor. One other started an IV of clear liquid. Brett knew from experience it was saline. Another with a stethoscope put a blood pressure cuff on Brian's arm and a finger clamp for heart beats. She listened, frowned, and shook her head.

"Shallow. I can hear fluid. Lung is not clear, BP is weak."

One man, Brett wasn't sure if it was a fireman or EMT, cut Brian's shirt off. Two of the men rolled him to one side and inspected his back. Brian screamed in agony.

One said, "Not a through and through. Might be lodged in the scapula. Scapula might be broken."

The other said, "We don't have much time. The fluid will build up and compress the lung and the heart."

"I could hear it," the lady said to them.

The first man looked at the woman, then at the other man, and said, "Needle decompression."

Both Brett and Tony looked away as they stuck a needle into Brian's chest.

King explained, "It will ease the pressure in Brian's chest and help him breathe."

O'Connor said, "Here comes his dad."

Jeremy ran through the door and stopped dead in his tracks. Randy, Bobby, and Danny were on his heels. Graff took Jeremy by the elbow and guided him away and more to the middle of the room. Randy and the others stood next to Brett and Tony, but out of the way.

One paramedic walked over to Graff and Jeremy. He said, "We're calling Air Med. We can't get him to the hospital fast enough. He coded twice already. The blond boy saved him the first time. We caught him the second time. Do you have a hospital preference?"

Jeremy's head was swimming. Overwhelmed, he ran a hand over his face and then through his hair.

Graff said, "Froedtert. It's where his mom works. Take him there."

"Yes, Froedtert," Jeremy said.

The paramedic walked the short distance to Goebel and Farner. Goebel was on his cell with someone, and the paramedic assumed it was a supervisor, probably the superintendent.

"We're calling in Air Med. We'll need a place to land."

Farner said, "Football stadium parking lot. Or the field itself. Once we get him there, we'll determine which."

Unger gave the female paramedic a copy of Brian's information sheet the school clinic had on file. She nodded and said, "Do we know his blood type?"

Brett said, "A-positive. Same as me, mom, and dad."

"And me," Tony said.

O'Connor gathered the boys together with Eiselmann, Graff, and Jeremy.

Graff said, "Here's what's happening. I have Gonnering and Lorenzo coming to run the crime scene. George, you, Tony, and Brett will need to give statements, but that can wait until you get to the hospital. Same with Randy, Bobby, and Danny. I have two cops coming to take the two girls to the station."

"Wait! Where's Billy?" Brett asked.

Head shakes and shrugs.

"Shit. He might not even know."

Brett pulled out his cell and texted Billy to meet them in the parking lot immediately.

Eiselmann said, "Jamie is going to drive Jeremy's truck straight to the hospital. I'm going to remain here until Gonnering and Carlos get here, and supervise the transfer of the two girls to the cops. Pat is going to take Tony, Brett, and George to Butler to get Two. One of you will need to tell him what happened. I would prepare for that now. Pat is going to drive George's truck."

"I've arranged for police escorts with lights and sirens from here to the hospital," Graff said. "We'll leave from the stadium parking lot after Brian is airlifted to the hospital."

"No lights or sirens for us until we leave Butler. I don't want any more of a circus than there might be," O'Connor said.

Graff looked at Tony and Brett. "Your quick thinking saved Brian's life. Tony, do you realize you're still wearing your tie without your shirt?"

He blushed, shrugged, and took it off.

"You and Danny need to get ahold of your parents and let them know you're okay and that you're going to the hospital."

Jeremy embraced Tony, then Brett, slinging his arms around the two of them. "Thank you for what you did." There were tears in his eyes. "George, you too. Thank you."

Brett broke free, ran to Brian, and grabbed his cell from his back pocket. "Tony, where are his keys?"

Tony shrugged and said, "In his backpack in Mrs. Arney's room."

The paramedics had already loaded Brian on a gurney and were about to leave. One paramedic said, "He's asking for the blond boy, but I think his dad should ride with him."

Jeremy and Tony moved to Brian's side. Tony said, "Brian, I'll meet you at the hospital. Your dad is riding with you." He kissed Brian's forehead, gave his hand a squeeze, and walked away.

"Tony, let's go!" Brett said.

CHAPTER EIGHTY-THREE

They waited in Wegner's conference room, just as they had done when Jeremy was in the hospital. Déjà vu hit George and his head swam from it.

The principal, Mark Wegner, threw open the door and ushered a bewildered Two into the room. Two gasped at Tony's and Brett's blood-stained hands, and in Tony's case, his arm, face and hair. At least Brett wore Brian's sweatshirt and Tony wore his own workout t-shirt, otherwise they'd be shirtless with bloodstained torsos.

"What the?" he couldn't complete the question. Then shock and fear set in. He said, "Dad?"

Brett stepped forward, put his hands on Two's shoulders, and said, "We don't have much time. There was a shooting at the school. Brian was hit. We don't know how bad. Just that it's bad. He's being flown to mom's hospital. O'Connor is driving us, but we have to go now."

They jogged out of the room. Brett turned around and said, "Mr. Wegner, I'll text you."

They left the school running and jumped into George's truck.

The sirens, front and back, wailed with blue lights flashing. They had to be pushing eighty, Brett thought. Riding shotgun, he leaned over and read the speedometer. He was right.

Tony, Two, and George sat in the backseat. Two wept quietly, his eyes staring at his hands. Tony wept as he stared out the side window. George, even as stoic as he normally was, had trouble keeping it together.

Brett couldn't sit still. He turned around and said, "Guys, we don't know anything yet. Brian's tough." He didn't know what else to say, so he shut up. Brian had always been better at that stuff.

He read texts from their group of friends, but didn't answer them. He advised his brothers not to answer any, either.

News had gotten out about Brian. School was dismissed, though most of the students hadn't left the school hallways or parking lot. Many students were in classrooms being consoled by teachers or staff. Television and news crews showed up and hovered in the parking lot. Few students were willing to engage with them. Gobel read a bland statement in front of cameras, followed by an equally bland statement from Detective Greg Gonnering, promising to have more details later in the day.

Brett was happy he wasn't there, though the trip to the hospital was no joy ride. He also knew the hospital would suck, too.

CHAPTER EIGHTY-FOUR

Vicky was allowed in surgery, but not to assist. She understood, though it was tough for her to not step forward and hand equipment or direct traffic like she did four or five times a day, five days a week.

On any other surgery, she was caring and concerned, but impartial. After all, she was a seasoned pro. This surgery, however, made her stomach turn, and she fought back waves of nausea.

Brian was her son. To see him opened up and defenseless, with clamps inside of him, with bloody gauze and various tubes hanging in and out of him, and an endotracheal tube down his throat was too much.

Vicky had faith in Ben Cavenaugh as a surgeon and knew the team assembled around Brian was as good as it can get. Brian was in excellent hands. Still, Brian was her son.

Brian had been hooked to an IV in his right arm and had blood running into his left arm. Chest x-rays had shown a broken rib, caused by the bullet lodged in Brian's scapula. It passed through his lung, causing blood and fluid to enter his chest and lung, making it difficult for Brian to breathe, and the fluid buildup interfered with his heart. That caused him to code in the choir room twice. At the hospital, after they inserted the chest tube and intubated him, his numbers improved, and he had been stable since.

The bullet had been removed, and the team was currently mending his lung and his broken rib, and closing off any bleeders.

"Vicky, you have one tough kiddo," Cavenaugh said without taking his eyes off his patient. "He's going to be sore as hell, but I think he should be able to leave in three or four days, depending upon how he responds to the surgery and aftercare.

"Besides the rib and a crack in his scapula, nothing else is broken. You can read his numbers for yourself, but his heart and breathing are functioning well, and I think he's out of the woods. Time will tell if he springs a leak, which can happen, but from my vantage point, all looks good."

Vicky hadn't realized she had been holding her breath during Cavenaugh's discourse. She shut her eyes and breathed deeply, relieved that so far Brian had come through it as well as can be.

"After I'm done here, I'll get myself cleaned up and then come out and speak to your family. I want to meet the two boys who saved his life. They deserve a medal. I'm guessing I should be another twenty or thirty minutes in here."

CHAPTER EIGHTY-FIVE

It was a long morning with no word on Brian. It was the unknown that had everyone's nerves frayed.

George, Brett, and Tony spent time in the bathroom cleaning blood off of them, helping each other. Tony had the most on him, and he didn't remember how. His hair, face, arm, hands, and chest. He even had some on his back. George had the least. All he needed to do was wash his hands. He remained in the bathroom until Brett and Tony were cleaned off.

"What happened?" Tony asked. "I mean, who was the kid I saw? The voices I heard? Who were they? And how was that possible?"

For longer than Tony expected, George and Brett said nothing but stared at each other. It was Brett who answered.

"Remember this morning when I said sometimes Brian and George had feelings and we learned to listen to them? When you spent the weekend, we mentioned we've seen and heard Brad, Brian's twin, and George's grandfather. You heard them talking with Brian."

"I don't understand how." Tony didn't doubt it. He just didn't understand it.

George said, "We do not understand it, either. We just know it happens. They have guided us in the past when we faced danger."

"What was the name your grandfather called me? He had a name for Brett and Brian, too."

George nodded. "He calls me Shadow. There is no word-for-word translation between Navajo and English. We have to look at the situation and the individual my grandfather is talking about. For Brian, my grandfather calls him *Nida'ałkáá'i'*. The name means, 'one who thinks', or 'Thinker'. He calls Brett, *Báháchi'ii'*. The name means, 'intense one'. Your name is long, because grandfather described you as well as named you. *Dibé yázhí bi ghaa' naha lin goh bi tsii' díshoh dóó dits'oz*. It means this. *Dibé yázhí*, means Lamb, *bi ghaa'* means wool, *naha lin goh*, means similar to or like, *bi tsii'*, means hair, *díshoh*, means soft, *dóó*, means and, and *dits'oz*, means curly. You put it together and get, *Dibé yázhí bi ghaa' naha lin goh bi tsii' díshoh dóó dits'oz*, or the boy with soft white, curly hair like a lamb."

Tony didn't know what to say.

"The thing that's freaky," Brett said, "is that we hear them talking. Each of us at the same time. We speak to them not with voices, but with thoughts."

Tony nodded. Now he understood why he heard Brian and Brett speak, but didn't see their lips move.

"One last thing," Brett said. He smiled and said, "You heard grandfather say you loved him and that Brian loves you."

Tears sprang to Tony's eyes, and he shook his head.

"It was supposed to cheer you up," Brett said, glancing at George.

"Just before Brian left the art room, he whispered he loved me. I was happy. But I never told Brian I loved him. I need to tell him before anything happens."

Brett put a hand on Tony's shoulder and said, "He knows. Grandfather wouldn't have said it if Brian didn't already know."

"I need to tell him."

Brett smiled, embraced him, and said, "You will."

Tony dried his eyes, and the three of them left the restroom. The waiting area was somber and quiet. Everyone seemed eager to hear something, hopefully good news.

Jeremy paced with one hand in his hair, the other in his front pocket. Randy, Bobby and Danny sat in three chairs by themselves. Billy sat with Graff and O'Connor, and looked up as the three boys came out of the restroom. O'Connor stood up and walked over to them, and guided them to a corner.

He sighed, opened his mouth, shut it, and began again. It was O'Connor's thing, and the boys, except for Tony, were used to it.

"Guys," he began again. He looked over his shoulder to make sure no one was listening. "I know sometimes Brad and George's grandfather speak to you." He stopped and waited.

George nodded. Tony glanced quickly at Brett and then at George.

"I'm assuming that happened this morning." He held up a hand and shook his head. "I don't need to know the details. But Gonnering and Lorenzo are on their way to get your statements. Be as honest about what happened as I know you guys to be."

Graff stood up and joined them. He said, "I'm proud of the three of you. You saved Brian's life. It could have been much worse, but your quick thinking saved Brian."

"It was Tony, really," Brett said. "All I did was try to stop the bleeding."

"And all I did was get the gun from Nada," George said. "It was Tony." He thought for a minute and said loudly so all of his brothers and Jeremy could hear, "It was Brian who saved Randy, Danny, and Bobby. He stood between them and Nada and shoved them out the door. Brian saved their lives."

"And took a bullet for his trouble," Brett added. "Kind of like what happened in Arizona."

"We know." Graff said.

"And we don't know if Brian is going to make it," Brett said.

The collective sigh was audible. Jeremy even stopped pacing. He stared at Graff and O'Connor, two of his friends, and then at his sons and Tony.

He said, "Guys, we have to hope. And pray. It's all we can do at this point. Only positive thoughts."

Heads nodded. Brett jammed his hands into his pockets. Randy leaned forward, head down, his elbows on his knees. Bobby stared off into space, but slipped an arm around Danny, who wept quietly.

Danny had wondered out loud if his outburst at Maryanne Sturgis after the game on Friday night triggered it all. Tony hung his head, wondering if he had done enough. Only George remained stoic, his face granite, though he wondered if he could have moved faster to prevent the shooting from taking place.

Billy got up and joined them. "I thought Two was with you in the restroom."

George shook his head and said, "I've not seen him since we went into the restroom. I thought he was out here with you guys."

Graff and O'Connor looked around the waiting room. It wasn't large, so clearly, Two wasn't in the room.

"Do you guys know where Two went?" Graff asked Randy, Danny, and Bobby?

They shook their heads.

Jeremy said, "Where is he?"

"Father, I will go look for him," George said.

"I will come with you," Jeremy said. "The rest of you stay here with Jamie and Pat. Text me if your mom or the doctor come out to talk to us."

CHAPTER EIGHTY-SIX

The little chapel, darkened except for dim lighting and votive candles, was empty except for Two, who sat in the second pew on the left. Head down, shoulders hunched, weeping quietly.

Jeremy and George sat down on either side of him.

"I thought I'd feel Brian here."

Neither Jeremy nor George responded.

"I prayed just like Brian taught me. I came with thanks and praise. Then I asked God to protect Brian."

Jeremy sat back, shocked. What else did Brian teach him?

"I think I prayed correctly," Two said as he wiped tears from his eyes.

"I'm sure you did," Jeremy said as he slipped an arm around the boy's narrow shoulders.

"But why couldn't I feel him?"

It came out as a sob, and Jeremy hugged him and kissed the side of his head.

"Because Brian is alive," Jeremy whispered, hoping he was correct.

Two shook his head. "Brian can't die yet."

"We don't know anything yet, Two."

"No, you don't understand. It's cold and rainy outside. Brian wants to die on a sunny day with a bright blue sky and fluffy white clouds. But not until sunset. That's his favorite time of day. Sunset is when he talks to God about his day. He talks about how he screwed up and he apologizes and promises to do better. He can't die yet. It's raining, and it's cold, and it's not sunny. It's not sunset. He can't die yet."

How could Jeremy argue with that? He knew there was nothing he could say that would make sense to Two. It wasn't the time or place to talk to his youngest about weighty thoughts.

"I want to be with Brian. He shouldn't be alone," Two whispered as he wiped away tears.

Jeremy gave Two a hug, kissed the side of his head, and said, "Let's go back to the waiting room. The doctor or your mom should be out soon, and they'll give us an update."

Two sighed, nodded, and the three of them stood and left the chapel together to be with the rest of the family. And wait.

CHAPTER EIGHTY-SEVEN

Matt Vittoria showed up and spoke first with Tony, who recounted the morning, and then with Jeremy, offering his help. Jeremy shook his hand and said thanks.

Jeff showed up almost at the same time as Matt. Jeff went first to Danny, who told him what had taken place. Face ashen, shaking, he spoke with Jeremy, who, like Matt, offered his help. Then he spoke with Graff and O'Connor. He wanted to hear their version.

Dr. Cavenaugh stepped into the waiting room, smiling. Jeremy took that as good news. Vicky hadn't shown up yet, so Jeremy assumed she was with Brian.

The boys jumped to their feet and gathered around Jeremy. Tony stood a little behind until Brett took him by the arm and had Tony stand next to him. The other adults stood behind the boys.

"One of the first things I was told this morning was two of you boys saved Brian's life."

Brett shrugged, and Tony looked down at his feet.

"Which two boys?" Cavenaugh asked.

The boys turned and looked at Tony and Brett, who said nothing. Jeremy said, "This is my son Brett and Brian's friend Tony."

"Boys, what you did this morning saved his life. If you hadn't acted when you did, as quickly and as correctly as you did, we'd be having a much different conversation right now."

Tony's face felt red hot, but he dared not look up from his shoes. Brett shrugged again.

"To answer the question on everyone's mind, Brian should be okay. He's a tough young man. He has a broken rib and a crack in his scapula. There was damage to his lung, which has been repaired. His scapula will heal on its own. In the next twenty-four hours, we'll monitor him for any bleeders. I think we caught them all, but you never know. With the amount of damage he sustained, it isn't uncommon."

"What happens if there are any? Bleeders, I mean?" Billy asked.

"We'll have to go in and close them up." He purposely made it seem routine, though he knew it wasn't. Any number of unforeseen things could happen.

"When can we see him?" Two asked.

Cavenaugh smiled and said, "Maybe later this afternoon, but we'll have to see. More than likely, tomorrow. Your mother is with him now in recovery. I'll take your dad back in a minute or two. Before I do, are there questions?"

"Um," Billy said. "Brian plays basketball and soccer. Will he be able to play again?"

Cavenaugh nodded, "Yes, in time. Recovery time will be six to eight weeks. He's going to be sore and in a great deal of pain. The broken rib and the scapula will take time to heal, and so will the lung. All three will cause his breathing to be short and shallow for a while. The scapula is a major support for his back and his shoulder. Your mom said he is right-handed. He will have trouble doing things you and I take for granted. Feeding himself. Cleaning himself."

"But he'll be able to play basketball and soccer again, right?" Brett asked.

He smiled and said, "Yes."

"When can Brian come home?" Two asked.

"A lot will depend on the next twenty-four hours. If everything goes like I think it will, and depending upon how he does in PT, maybe Wednesday afternoon or Thursday. A lot of it will depend on his pain management, his discomfort, and if he springs a leak."

The boys smiled and nodded.

Patiently, he said, "If there aren't any other questions, I'll take your father back to see Brian."

Jeremy smiled at his boys and said, "Good news, right?"

The boys smiled back at him.

"Listen, it's past lunch and I'm guessing you're hungry. Why don't you get something to eat from the cafeteria?" Jeremy suggested. "If you want to go somewhere else, please let me know where you are and with whom, okay? Do you guys need money?"

"It's on me," Jeff said.

"You don't have to, Jeff."

"I want to. Brian saved my son's life and the lives of Bobby and Randy. Tony and Brett saved Brian's life. It's on me. Cops and Tony's dad, included."

"What about the two detectives who are coming for our statements?" Bobby asked.

"We're talking about food," Graff joked. "They can wait."

"I've been thinking about this," Brett said. "How did the bullet not exit?"

Jeremy and Dr. Cavenaugh stopped to listen in.

Cavenaugh said, "The bullet was lodged in the scapula. A big bone."

Graff nodded and said, "We've seen this before with gunshot wounds and victims. The bullet was a 128 grain, unjacketed hollow point. Several things worked in Brian's favor. The distance from the shooter. The further away, there is less force on impact. Brian has bulked up in the last year, just like all of you have. He has quite a bit of muscle in his chest. His muscle and the rib, plus the scapula, stopped the bullet."

He turned to Cavenaugh and asked, "Do I have that about right?"

Cavenaugh nodded, smiled, and said, "Just about perfect. You forgot pure dumb luck."

CHAPTER EIGHTY-EIGHT

The rain had stopped, but it was damp and wet, and the wind made the late afternoon raw. The boys, emotionally drained, napped with heads on each other's shoulders. Tony, Brett, and Two did not sleep. George looked to be napping, but as he did often, just rested his eyes.

Graff, O'Connor, and Eiselmann left after Gonnering and Lorenzo gathered the statements from the boys. The four cops huddled briefly with Jeremy and Jeff, though neither spoke nor asked questions. Gonnering and Lorenzo tag-teamed the initial report from their investigation.

"The investigation was a slam dunk," Gonnering said. "I mean, there wasn't much to investigate. The statements corroborate our initial thoughts."

"The Sturgis girl brought the gun from home. She took it without her mother knowing it, which makes her mother not culpable in the crime," Lorenzo added. "Sturgis arranged with the Sherry girl to pick her up before school, and take her to school, even though the Sherry girl was on suspension. According to the Sherry girl, the idea was to do the shooting and then leave right away before they got caught."

"We laid it all out for the DA, and what he's thinking is that Sherry will get charged with four counts of attempted first degree homicide, reckless endangerment with the use of a firearm, and possession of a firearm in a school zone," Gonnering said. "Sturgis will probably get charged with party to the crime of attempted homicide, party to the crime of reckless endangerment with the use of a firearm and party to the crime of possession of a firearm in a school zone."

Lorenzo added, "Because of the seriousness of the crime, the girls will have a hearing to determine whether they get charged as juveniles or adults. Greg and I gathered from the DA that he is going to seek a waiver to get them tried as adults."

Graff, O'Connor and Eiselmann mulled that over. Graff said, "Any movement on the car bombing?"

Lorenzo shook his head, and Gonnering said, "Neither one admits it. We're getting a warrant for the Sturgis girls' and family's electronics. Maybe we'll find a search history or something. We're also getting a warrant to search the Sturgis house."

"The girl is smart, kind of clever, but she's a kid. Like Greg said, maybe we'll find something to tie it to her. That would add more charges, according to the DA," Lorenzo said.

Jeremy left the waiting area to sit with Brian and Vicky. Tony's dad left after spending a great deal of time speaking with Tony, and after Tony said he wanted to stay at the hospital. Brett arranged for Troy and Chris to stop at the house to let Papa, Momma, Jasper, and Jasmine outside and give them fresh water and some food.

Troy sent Brett and the guys pictures of Brian's truck, still in the school parking lot. Students used it as a memorial. Teddy Bears and other stuffed animals, cards, posters, letters, and some candles filled the truck bed. Chris blew out the candles because they didn't want Brian's truck to blow up.

Students and parents kept coming. Some said prayers. Some just wanted to be near. All wanted assurance Brian would be okay. So far, so good, was the response given to them.

Sean was currently supervising the truck with Big Gav and Coach Harrison. It was their intention that at least two people would be present overnight. The boys decided not tell Jeremy, Vicky, or Brian, wanting to surprise them.

Brett watched Jeff. He couldn't tell what was on Jeff's mind. His face had worry lines, and it was clouded over. Jeff would stare at a spot on the floor, or walk to a window, or take a short walk up and down the hallway outside of the waiting area. He never spoke and seemed oblivious to anyone else in the room, including his son, Danny, who napped fitfully against Bobby's shoulder.

It was the middle of the afternoon when Jeremy came through the door, ran a hand over his face, and sighed. His face was ashen, and his shoulders sagged.

Brett was the first to see him. He shook Billy awake, got Tony's and Two's attention, and then he said, "Dad? What's wrong?"

The question woke up Randy, Danny, and Bobby. They didn't stand, but sat at attention. Brett, Tony, George and Two sat on the edge of their chairs.

"There's been a setback," Jeremy said. "Brian had to go back into surgery."

Billy stood and asked, "Why?"

Jeremy shrugged and shook his head. He seemed to be on the verge of tears.

"Brian was awake briefly, and he acted like himself, but tired. He fell asleep, and we noticed his breathing change. Shallower. There was a grimace on his face, like he was having a bad dream. Mom noticed Brian's numbers dropping. An alarm went off, and nurses and a doctor ran into the room, did some tests, and they moved him to surgery."

Shock and concern were written all over the boys' faces.

"I don't have any other information. Mom is with him. I don't know how long he'll be in there."

"This morning, the doctor said something about bleeding. Is that what happened?" Bobby asked.

Jeremy shook his head and lifted his hands in defeat. "I don't have any other information."

Other than a page for doctor so and so or a page for a nurse, it was silent in the waiting room. No one said anything. No conversation. No movement. Nothing.

CHAPTER EIGHTY-NINE

The sun had set, leaving the world outside the windows as dark as the atmosphere in the waiting room. Brett checked his watch. It had been almost an hour and forty-five minutes since Jeremy came through the door.

Though everyone was awake, no one spoke, except in one or two word whispers. Most just sat waiting. A few scrolled through their phones, texting friends, or checking Instagram or Twitter. Jeff and Jeremy had a brief conversation away from the boys, and because it was low and hushed, the boys didn't know what was talked about.

Vicky pushed through the door, looking not much better than Jeremy. She did, however, manage a smile. The boys, and Jeremy and Jeff, gathered around her.

She said, "First, Brian is okay. Dr. Cavenaugh mentioned to you Brian would be monitored closely for twenty-four hours. He also mentioned there is a possibility of Brian springing a leak, because of the amount of damage the bullet caused. That's what happened this afternoon. Two leaks, actually. Dr. Cavenaugh repaired the damage, and now Brian is on the mend. Obviously, he can't have any visitors until sometime in the morning. He's heavily sedated anyway, and he's hooked back up to machines, and the nurses and doctors will monitor his progress through the night."

"What you're saying is, Brian isn't in any danger. At least right now," Brett said.

"That's a good way of putting it, yes."

"But we don't know if something could go wrong tonight," Billy said.

"Honestly, there are no guarantees," Vicky said. "But I will say Brian's chances are a hundred percent better because we caught these bleeders quickly, and before they could cause any further damage."

"So, Brian is okay. So far," Randy said.

"Yes, that's correct."

"What do we do then?" Billy asked.

Vicky smiled and said, "Unfortunately, there isn't much for you to do here. Your dad and I will stay here with Brian. But I think you will be more comfortable at home."

"But what if, you know, something happens to Brian?" Two asked.

"Honey, I promise if there is even a hint of anything happening, we'll let you know. In fact, I'll contact Jamie Graff and Pat O'Connor and let them know where you guys are, so if anything happens, they'll get you guys here safely and quickly," Vicky said with a smile. "Sound like a plan?"

The boys were noncommittal. Feet shuffled. Hands were stuffed in pockets. Heads were hung.

"Really, guys. You will be more comfortable at home," Jeremy said. "Just stay together and be safe."

Reluctantly, the boys agreed.

"Tony, are you spending the night with us or at home?" Billy asked.

"I'll ask my aunt and uncle."

"George, just in case, why don't you leave your truck here for mom and me?"

George nodded.

"Brett, can you drive my Expedition?" Jeremy asked.

"Sure," Brett said.

"Some of you can ride with me," Jeff said. "Brett, be careful, okay?"

"I will."

"You'll give us updates, right?" Bobby asked.

"I promise," Vicky said with a smile.

The boys gave Vicky and Jeremy hugs and kisses goodbye. Tony felt awkward, but Vicky and Jeremy treated him just as they did their own boys.

Jeff embraced Jeremy, then Vicky, and said, "I'll keep my eye on them."

Out of earshot of the boys, Jeff walked Jeremy and Vicky to the door and said, "I can't help thinking that if Brian hadn't stood between Danny, Randy, and Bobby, one or more would have gotten shot. Maybe died. Brian took the bullet. Again," referring to Arizona and the gunfight on the mesa.

"It's been weighing on my mind, too," Jeremy said. "More than either of you know."

Vicky gripped Jeremy's hand and said, "We have to make sure this stops."

CHAPTER NINETY

That evening, there wasn't much meaningful conversation. Brett spent most of his time with Two and Tony, as did Billy, George, and Bobby.

When everyone had gathered in the family room, Randy walked in. His eyes were red and puffy. He had tried to compose himself, but failed.

At first, he stood in the doorway with his hands in his pockets and his chin on his chest. Then he cleared his throat and said, "I want to apologize to everyone. I've been an ass." He shrugged and said, "There's no excuse."

He looked directly at Tony and said, "I treated you like shit ever since your first day. I was angry at Brian's and Bobby's situation and what our parents made them do." Bobby was about to object when Randy said, "Mom and dad never told them to break it off, but the message was pretty clear. I felt bad for both of them, but I took it out on Brian because it was his idea. It was wrong of me. And then I took it out on you. Like I said, I was an ass. I had no right."

No one objected. What ran through their minds was the fact they had heard these apologies before, only to have Randy do and say stupid shit again.

Almost as if he read their minds, he said, "I know I've apologized before. You have every right not to forgive me. I can accept that. Tony, I just want to say, I'm sorry. You didn't deserve any of the shit I said or did. I don't blame you if you never want to speak to me again."

He sighed, and said, "I'll have to wait to apologize to Brian. If he'll even speak to me again. I wouldn't blame him if he didn't."

He turned and left the room, leaving the guys to stare at the doorway.

Brett called out to him. "Randy, we're getting ready to watch a movie. Why don't you stay and watch it with us?"

There was no answer, and Brett didn't expect one.

CHAPTER NINETY-ONE

The boys waited impatiently for their opportunity to see Brian. Each time the door opened, they looked up hopefully. When they saw it wasn't for them, they sat back in their chairs, disappointed.

It was after ten when Vicky came through the door smiling. She looked tired, with dark circles under her eyes, and lines deepened on her face. Her hair, normally styled simply, looked wild.

The boys stood around her expectantly.

"Brian is awake. The pain meds he's on make him groggy, but they seem to be working. Unfortunately, when he moves a certain way, he experiences pain. His breathing is improved and almost normal, even with the broken rib and the mended lung."

"He must be in real pain if he's taking pain medication willingly," Brett said.

"I didn't say he was taking them willingly," Vicky laughed. "Dr. Cavenaugh told him if he didn't, it would take longer to recover."

"Can we see him?" Two asked. "Please?"

"Yes," Vicky said, nodding her head. "We don't normally let this large a group in at one time, but we're making an exception for you. Please be respectful of the nurses and doctors, and especially the other patients. No unnecessary noise. Keep your voices low. Okay?"

The boys and Jeff followed Vicky through the door, down the hall, and past the nurses' station. Brian's room was a single unit and other than a bed and a couple of chairs and monitors, nothing else was in the room. A TV, on but muted, hung on the wall facing Brian's bed. A tray with a cup with water and ice sat on a tray over his bed.

Brian was propped up with his right arm in a sling. Jeremy sat in one chair at his side. A monitor was on Brian's left index finger, and wires ran from electrodes on his chest to a monitor behind the bed. A blood pressure cuff on his left arm cycled on and off at timed intervals. A cannula for oxygen was in his nose.

Brett had brought clean clothes for Jeremy and Vicky, and clean underwear and shorts, and a t-shirt for Brian. The boys also brought the normal hygiene things for Brian and the things Vicky and Jeremy requested.

After the small talk of *'How are you feeling?'* and *'How much pain are you in?'* the boys got into the real conversation.

"I was so scared," Danny said. "I thought she was going to shoot us."

"I thought we might have a chance when Brian and George showed up," Bobby said.

Randy stood at the back of the group next to George. Tony stood next to George and felt he didn't belong. He would have preferred going in by himself or with Brett, Billy, or Michael.

Danny said, "Brian, weren't you scared?"

Brian cleared his throat. It was still sore from having been on a ventilator. He took a sip of water before answering.

"I needed to get you guys out of the room before Nada did something stupid. I was worried about George getting the gun away from her."

"I did not move fast enough, Brian. I am sorry," George said.

"All is good, George."

"She was pointing the gun at you," Bobby said.

"And you deliberately stood between her and us," Randy said.

Brian took another sip of water, gathered his thoughts, and said, "Jeff only has Danny. I needed to make sure nothing happened to him." To Randy, he said, "I know how important you are to dad." To Bobby he said, "I know how important you are to mom. I had to get the three of you out of the room."

"You could have run out of the room with us," Randy said.

Brian shook his head and said, "I couldn't leave George by himself."

The silence in the room was thick. Thoughts swirled in heads, begging to be set free, but no one was willing to release the shackles.

Brian broke it. "I knew Tony and Brett were on their way."

"How?" Jeff said.

Brian cleared his throat and said, "I heard Brad and Grandfather Tokay. I knew grandfather spoke to Brett, because I remembered Brett's name. I don't know how I knew Brad was talking to Tony. I just knew."

"The freaky thing was when we heard them talking to you," Brett said."

Bewildered, Bobby said, "We didn't hear anything."

Brett said nothing, only shrugged.

George said, "The first time it happened was after we got home from up north when the hired killer tried to kill Detective Pat."

"Really?" Jeremy said. "You never mentioned it to us."

George did not answer him.

"What is the name George's grandfather calls you?" Vicky asked.

Brian and Brett looked at George. He said, "Brian is *Nida'ałkáá'í'*, which means 'thinker' or 'one who thinks'. Brett is *Báháchi'ii'*, which means 'intense' one. Tony's name is much longer. It is *Dibé yázhí bi ghaa' naha lin goh bi tsii' díshoh dóó dits'oz,* which means 'the boy with white, soft, curly hair like a lamb'."

Brian nodded.

"And the three of you heard Brad and Grandfather Tokay talking?" Jeff asked.

"And Brian," Brett said. "It happens in our head. That's how we talk to them."

"What were you talking about?" Bobby asked.

The four boys, George, Brett, Tony, and Brian, looked at each other. None of them seemed willing to answer the question. Brian sighed. Tony stared down at his shoes. George remained impassive.

Brett said, "Brian wanted to be with Brad. Brad and grandfather convinced Brian it wasn't his time. Grandfather told him it was a choice Brian had to make. Tony and I told Brian not to leave."

Brian's eyes were downcast.

"When Tony gave Brian mouth to mouth and the chest compressions, Brian's eyes fluttered and he regained consciousness. That's when we knew Brian was going to live. At least, we hoped so."

The room became uncomfortably quiet. There were many other questions not answered. Brian felt all eyes on him.

Two reached out and held Brian's hand. Brian looked up and smiled at him with tears in his eyes.

CHAPTER NINETY-TWO

"Dad, Brian is freaking out," Billy said with a smile.

"How so?"

"He's afraid people are going to make a big deal about him getting shot. Lots of questions and crap."

"He doesn't know, does he?" Jeremy said with a smile.

Billy grinned back at him. "Not a clue."

"It's going to be cool," Brett said with a laugh.

Brian shuffled his way into the kitchen and said, "What's cool?"

"The game tonight," Brett lied. "Coach is going to start us out in a full court man-to-man press. Pressure everywhere." That part was the truth.

Brian frowned and said, "That isn't much different from the way we played the first game."

"It's the way we're pressing," Billy said. "That's the cool part."

Brian made a face. To him, a press was a press, and with a man-to-man press, there were only so many changes that could be made.

It was Friday morning, the day after Brian was discharged from the hospital. He had slept fitfully in the Lazy-Boy in the family room. Michael had slept on the couch to keep him company, and Papa, Momma, and Jasper joined them.

Brian tried hiding his pain, but he grit his teeth when he stood up or sat down. He also had to stop every so often to catch his breath. The doctor wanted him to wait until Monday before he attempted school, but there was a game, and Brian insisted he went to school so he could go to it.

Jeremy and Vicky pretended to compromise with Brian. Vicky would drive him to school by 10:00 AM. Class would be in session at that time. She didn't want to drop him off at the start of school when there would be people in the hallways and cafeteria who would swarm him with questions, or possibly bump and jostle him. To Brian, that worked because he didn't want all the questions and pity. The crap, as he called it.

The time was set up by Jeremy after a conference call with Chuck Gobel, Bob Farner, Tommy Harrison, and Jamie Graff, who represented Police Chief Jack O'Brien. That way, there would be enough time to set everything up.

Brian had no clue what was going to take place. Of course, Jeremy, Vicky, and his brothers knew. Even Tony played along, since he had been brought in the loop.

"Whoever is getting a ride with dad, let's get going," Brett yelled. In response, there were footsteps and thumps down the stairs.

"George, you're going to take Michael to school and pick up Tony, right?" Brian asked.

George smiled and said, "We have it worked out."

To anyone who would listen, he said, "I don't understand why you didn't bring my truck home. I don't think it was safe sitting in the student parking lot."

Brett smiled, and careful of his rib and shoulder, gave Brian a hug, and said, "We made sure it was going to be safe."

"I don't see how," Brian countered.

"Trust me, okay?"

"Whatever."

"And text me when you get to school. I'll come out to meet you."

Brian sighed. "You don't have to. I'm just going to school. It's not a big deal."

"You're right. It's not a big deal. I already got permission from Farner to meet you at the front door."

"Whatever."

Brett put his forehead on Brian's, rubbed his nose, and said, "It's going to be fine. You're going to be fine."

Brian tried glaring at him, but ended up smiling.

"You know I love you, right?" Brett said.

"Love you, too."

"All right, let's roll!"

CHAPTER NINETY-THREE

Just as Vicky drove up the road approaching North High School, Brian texted Brett. As expected, Brett stood outside the school, waiting for him. Unexpected was the entire basketball team, both JV and varsity, along with members of the soccer team, were outside with him, along with other friends.

"Ah, shit, mom! This is what I was afraid of," he said in disgust. "Why didn't he listen to me?"

Vicky smiled and said, "I'm betting he listened to you, but there are so many people wanting to see how you're doing and happy to see you, they joined in. Think of it as a compliment."

Brian made a face at her making Vicky smile.

"Do you need help with your backpack?"

"Noooo, I've got it," he said as he got out of the car, shut the door, and slung the backpack on his left shoulder. He struggled to find a comfortable spot for it.

He trudged towards the school. He had trouble catching his breath, and the pain in his shoulder and chest barked at him, despite the meds he had taken. The discomfort was visible on his face and in the way he walked.

"Are you sure you're okay with this, Brian?"

Brian nodded as stoically as he could, gritting his teeth all the while.

He reached his friends, and Brett and the others must have recognized the pain he was in. Other than a few "Good to see you!" and "Are you in much pain?" statements and questions, worry was on their faces.

"Here, give it to me," Brett said, as he reached for Brian's backpack.

"It's okay," Brian protested.

"Quit being stubborn, Bri," Brett said, softly. "I've got it."

Brett slipped it off Brian's shoulder, much to Brian's relief.

Big Gav and the others gave him knuckle bumps. They left and headed to the field house. That puzzled Brian. Vicky, Brett, and Brian were left to enter the school alone.

Just inside the entry-way, Brian stopped in his tracks. He couldn't miss the display of stuffed animals, signs, and unlit candles in the hallway between the front office and the field house. His mouth hung open as he leaned over to touch one or two, reading the signs and a few of the letters and cards.

"Did you?" Brian asked.

Vicky shook her head and dabbed at her eyes. Brett smiled and nodded.

"Hey, Little Man, you'll have plenty of time to check those out," Coach Harrison said from behind him.

"Got to go, Bri. I'll see you soon," Brett said as he walked to the field house, taking Brian's backpack with him.

"I'm going to leave you with Coach. Are you sure you're up for this?" Vicky asked.

Brian nodded, though he didn't feel up to anything. She followed Brett to the field house.

The hallways were eerily quiet. Unsettling. No one was around. From one end of the hallway to the end of a different hallway, there was no one. All was quiet.

He cocked his head at Coach Harrison, the question written on his face.

Harrison smiled and said, "Remember when you and I had a conversation about moments? About not walking away from a call to leadership?"

Brian nodded warily.

"You're about to have one of those moments, Bri. I think you know that."

Brian blinked at him. He didn't understand. Yet, deep down, he did. And he knew it was going to happen and there was nothing he could do to prevent it. As uncomfortable as he was, he also understood he couldn't walk away from it.

"Did Brett know?"

Harrison smiled and nodded.

"My other brothers and my parents?"

Harrison smiled.

Brian stared at his shoes.

"It's needed, Brian. The school needs this. The students need this. They need a happy ending."

Brian shook his head and said, "I don't know if I can."

"Remember the forty-seven-yard field goal you kicked to win the regionals? Remember last year when you sunk the last-second shot against South? Remember the goal you scored with about a minute left to beat South in soccer?"

Head down, Brian nodded.

"This means more than those accomplishments ever will." He pointed to the memorial of stuffed animals and cards and signs and candles. "This was in the back of your truck and in the neighboring two parking spots. Kids and parents and teachers and staff needed to let you know how they felt about you. Now, they need to know you are okay. That you're going to live. This is their opportunity to see for that themselves. That you survived."

Brian wiped tears from his eyes, but he nodded.

"You have an opportunity to give the entire school a moment. More importantly, you have an opportunity to give yourself and those who love you a moment. Don't shrink from it, Brian. Embrace it. Like you do on the court, take the last-second shot. Just like you did in the regional game, win it from forty-seven-yards out."

Brian looked up at coach with tears in his eyes and said, "I don't know what to say."

"The words will come. Just listen to your heart."

"Will you be there?"

"Of course I will, Little Man. I wouldn't miss this for anything. And so will your parents, Jeff, your brothers, Tony, Tony's parents, and your other friends. We'll all be there. We've got your back, Bri."

Brian took as deep a breath as his ribs and his sore lung and chest would allow. He nodded.

"You ready?" Harrison asked with a hand on Brian's good shoulder.

"I guess."

Harrison pulled out his cell, said, "We're coming in now. Let us get into the field house first." Then he shut it off, smiled at Brian, and said, "Okay, let's go."

CHAPTER NINETY-FOUR

Harrison held the door open for Brian and then led him into the fieldhouse.

At first appearance, it was quiet and looked empty, only because Brian couldn't see around the bleachers. There was no sound, other than creaking bleachers.

As he neared the edge of the court, he saw students, teachers, and staff packed into the bleachers on the far side. When he stepped fully into the fieldhouse, the band struck up the North School Song, and the gym erupted in applause and shouts and everyone took up the chant, "Bri-an! Bri-an! Bri-an!" as if he had sunk the last-second shot in a tough game.

Brian lowered his head, and with his good hand- his left- he covered his eyes, and wept, his feet rooted to the floor. He was not the only one weeping, however, but he didn't know that.

Even Harrison had tears in his eyes as he gently placed his arm around Brian's shoulders and led him to the far side of the court near the free throw line, where a podium and microphone had been set up, along with chairs. Two were not filled, and Harrison ushered Brian to one of them. Brian dared not look up. He couldn't. If he did, he would have seen both sides filled. He sat between Tony and Brett, and Brett took hold of his good hand.

Along with Brett and Tony, were the two school nurses, Sharon King and Filippa Unger, and George, and Police Chief Jack O'Brien. There was also an older lady Brian didn't know.

Brett, George, and Tony looked uncomfortable, but not as uncomfortable as Brian.

It took time for the students and staff to quiet down and sit.

Gobel stood at the podium and greeted everyone. He said, "We're here to honor some very special individuals. Five of them did all they could to make sure Brian would live. Brian nearly sacrificed his own life so two of his brothers and a friend would live. What these individuals did surpasses heroism. What they did was courageous and selfless."

He introduced the school district superintendent, Dr. Andrea Bengier, who waved politely to the crowd, but declined to speak, and then Police Chief Jack O'Brien, took the podium.

A newspaper reporter and photographer recorded the assembly, as did several school photographers. One television crew with a reporter and cameraman was present, and a separate microphone had been placed on the podium alongside the microphone for the field house.

"I am honored to be here this morning." He gave a definition of heroism and courage, describing what each individual did. Then, one by one, he brought King, Unger, George, Brett, and Tony to the podium to receive certificates. Tumultuous applause and cheers accompanied each name.

He turned and smiled at Brian, who looked up briefly, afraid he'd lose it if he looked too long.

"Brian, I don't want to keep you any longer than we need to because I know you are in a great deal of pain, but could you stand for me, please?"

As Brett and Tony helped him to his feel, the students started up the Bri-an! Bri-an! chant again. Brian could feel his face on fire and he knew he was blushing profusely. Nothing he could do about it. He kept his chin pinned to his chest.

"You okay, Bri?" Brett asked.

Brian nodded.

"Brian, I read the police reports, the reports from those who were in the room that day, and the reports of those seated beside you. Those reports stated you rushed in, thought nothing of your own life, but only thought of getting Danny Limbach, and your brothers, Randy Evans and Bobby McGovern, out of harm's way. You had George pull the fire alarm to get everyone out of the building to safety, and it was you who placed yourself between the shooter and your brothers. The courage and bravery you displayed can only be described as above and beyond what very few individuals had done during my twenty-six years serving this community as a police officer."

Brian only half-listened to the positive things O'Brien said next. He knew his time to speak was coming up, and he had no clue what to say. Nothing.

O'Brien handed Brian his certificate, shook his good hand, and said, "I was told you might want to say something."

Brian heard the voice clearly, as if he stood next to him. From the looks on Brett's George's and Tony's faces, they heard it too.

"You have this, Bri. Speak from your heart. Don't think. Just speak."

"Nida'ałkáá'i', control your breathing. Focus. These people, these Biligaana, *need to know the strong heart of one of the Dine'. My grandson."*

'My Grandson'? Brian thought.

Shocked, Brian stared at George, who wiped a tear from his eye and smiled back. Tony and Brett were of no help. Both stared at him with tear-filled eyes.

Brian took as deep a breath as his aching chest would allow. He hung onto the podium as if it were his life float. He searched for Harrison, and spotted him standing against the far wall with his arms folded. Harrison smiled at him and nodded. Brian nodded back.

"I want to thank all of you for your cards and letters, and for the signs and stuffed animals. I also want to thank George for getting the gun away before anyone else got shot."

"I want to thank Mrs. King and Mrs. Unger for performing first aid on me until the paramedics showed up."

Brian lowered his head, wiped tears from his eyes, took another breath as deeply as his pain allowed, and said, "I want to thank Brett for trying to stop the bleeding, and I want to thank Tony for performing CPR on me. Without doing what you did, I would have died. Thank you."

He looked up and gazed at both sides of the field house stands. Students stood. Most wept, along with the teachers and staff in the stands and those standing on the opposite side of the court.

"If you don't mind, I just have a couple more things to say. They're important, so I hope you listen. Please sit down."

Harrison nodded at him.

Brian didn't know where it came from. Obviously, he had rehearsed nothing, but it was as if his mind cleared and his heart burst with all the things he needed and wanted to say.

"Coach Harrison and I talk about a lot of things. Not just sports, but about life. One thing he said to me was that life is made up of moments. And these moments give us choices. He said many of us, you and I, aren't taking advantage of the moments given to us. We live lives that aren't ours. We hide behind the way we dress, the way we act, the words we choose. And then we wonder why we aren't happier, why we're sad."

Brian sighed and said, "I want you to know I don't hate Nada or Maryanne. I don't," he said, shaking his head. "People treated them unkindly. They tried to get attention, anyone's attention, but no one listened. No one cared enough to talk to them.

"They made a choice. It was a poor choice. Their choice almost took my life and almost took the lives of Danny and two of my brothers."

He shook his head, turned to Chief O'Brien and Mr. Gobel and said, "I'm really not a hero. Tony and Brett are the heroes because they saved my life. The paramedics and the doctors and the nurses, Mrs. King and Mrs. Unger, are the heroes for what they do every day with no one noticing and sometimes without anyone thanking them. They're the real heroes. Not me."

The stands erupted in cheers and applause.

Brian waited a moment and said, "I just have a couple more things to say. I promise."

Everyone sat down, and it got quiet. Almost scary quiet.

Brian caught Harrison's eye again, and he smiled and nodded. Brian nodded back.

"I mentioned before we are given moments. Each day. Every day. When I was in the hospital, I thought about what would have happened if Tony and Brett wouldn't have come in the room when they did, and if Tony and Brett wouldn't have done what they did. I died twice. Tony saved me once, and the paramedics saved me the second time.

"I thought about not being in Mrs. Rios' English class and how much I would have missed that. I thought about not spending time before school in Mrs. Arney's art room. We don't do much. I watch Tony draw or paint. Mrs. Arney would hang stuff up or grade work at her desk. But I thought about how safe it is in her room. How she accepts everyone.

"I thought about missing Mr. Cooper's geometry class. Not that I like it." Everyone laughed, and Brian smiled. "I actually hate it." Some students cheered and most everyone laughed. "But Mr. Cooper, you care. You care more about us than you do math. You take the time to help us understand that math helps us think. It gives us discipline.

"I thought about not being with the guys on the basketball court, or the soccer field, or the football field. I thought about not having conversations with Coach Harrison. I thought about not being with my brothers and my mom and dad. I love my family more than anything. The thought of not being with Tony, probably one of my best friends," he stopped, looked over at him, and shook his head.

"The thought of," his voice caught, and Brian wiped tears from his eyes before continuing, and said, "the thought of not being with them, or not seeing another sunset," he stopped and shook his head, "or not hearing Randy or Bobby or Danny sing, or not wrestling with Michael, or listening to Billy's jokes. That made me sad.

"But it also helped me realize how important moments are. It helped me realize I cannot, and you cannot, take these moments for granted."

He took a deep breath and plunged on.

"I'm going to live *my* life. From now on, I'm going to love who *I* want to love. Some of you might not like it, but I'm going to love who *I* want to love. I'm going to spend my time, my moments being nicer and kinder. I'm going to listen better."

And then he thought of one more thing to say to bring it to a close.

"And Mr. Cooper, I suck at math, but I'm going to try to do better. I promise."

Everyone laughed and cheered. Tears forgotten. Pain lifted.

And standing at mid-court were Brad and Grandfather Tokay. They smiled at him. Brad clapped and cheered along with everyone else. And Grandfather Tokay smiled and nodded his head.

Brian smiled, wiped his eyes, and nodded back.

ABOUT THE AUTHOR

After having been in education for forty-six years as a teacher, coach, counselor and administrator, Joseph Lewis has semi-retired and now works part-time as an online learning facilitator. He uses his psychology and counseling background to craft thriller/crime/detective mysteries.

Lewis has previously published eight books, each to excellent reviews and multiple awards earned.

Born and raised in Wisconsin, Lewis has been happily married to his wife, Kim. Together they have three wonderful children: Wil (deceased July 2014), Hannah, and Emily. He and his wife now reside in Virginia.

NOTE FROM THE AUTHOR

Word-of-mouth is crucial for any author to succeed. If you enjoyed *Fan Mail*, please leave a review online—anywhere you are able. Even if it's just a sentence or two. It would make all the difference and would be very much appreciated.

Thanks!
Joseph Lewis

We hope you enjoyed reading this title from:

www.blackrosewriting.com

Subscribe to our mailing list – *The Rosevine* – and receive **FREE** books, daily deals, and stay current with news about upcoming releases and our hottest authors.
Scan the QR code below to sign up.

Already a subscriber? Please accept a sincere thank you for being a fan of Black Rose Writing authors.

View other Black Rose Writing titles at
www.blackrosewriting.com/books and use promo code
PRINT to receive a **20% discount** when purchasing.